ALSO BY SCARLETT ST. CLAIR

When Stars Come Out

HADES X PERSEPHONE
A Touch of Darkness
A Game of Fate
A Touch of Ruin
A Game of Retribution
A Touch of Malice
A Game of Gods
A Touch of Chaos

ADRIAN X ISOLDE
King of Battle and Blood
Queen of Myth and Monsters

FAIRY TALE RETELLINGS
Mountains Made of Glass
Apples Dipped in Gold

TERROR AT THE GATES

SCARLETT ST. CLAIR

Bloom books

Published by Bloom Books, an imprint of Sourcebooks
1935 Brookdale RD, Naperville, IL 60563-2773
(630) 961-3900
sourcebooks.com

Cataloging-in-Publication data is on file with the Library of Congress.

The authorized representative in the EEA is Dorling Kindersley
Verlag GmbH. Arnulfstr. 124, 80636 Munich, Germany

Manufactured in the UK by Clays and distributed by
Dorling Kindersley Limited, London
001-351410-Jul/25
10 9 8 7 6 5 4 3 2 1

*To the women who were told they must
submit to the dominance of man.*

TRIGGER WARNINGS

Religious trauma, sexual assault specifically by an authority figure in the church (NO on-page sexual assault, but referenced on pages 51–52, 138–139, 351, and 459–460), child abuse and emotional abuse by a parent and authority figure in the church.

Are you a survivor? Need assistance or support? Call the National Sexual Assault Hotline at 1-800-656-HOPE (4673) or go online to hotline.rainn.org.

PRONUNCIATION GUIDE

Elohim—EL-o-heem
Elohai—EL-o-hi
Lilith—LIL-ith
Zahariev—ZA-har-reev
Lucius—LOO-shuhs
Analisia—ANA-leese
Cassius Zareth—KAS-seeus ZA-reth
Gabriel De Santis—GAY-bree-l De SAN-tis
Esther Pomeroy—EST-er POM-a-roy
Colette "Coco" D'Arsay—CALL-let "COCO" DAR-say
Macarius Caiaphas—ma-KAR-e-us KAI-uh-fuhs
Eryx—EAR-ix
Ashur—AH-shur

FAMILIES

Zareth—ZAR-eth
Leviathan—La-VI-a-thin
Viridian—ver-ID-de-un
Sanctius—SANK-tus
Asahel—AH-sha-el

PLACES

Nineveh—NIN-a-vah
Akkadia—a-CAID-dia
Galant—GAL-ant
Hiram—HI-rim
Gomorrah—ga-MORE-uh
Sumer—SUE-mur
Kurari (Sea, Canal, Islands)—qu-RAR-ee
Nara-Sin Desert—NA-ra-sin Des-ert
Mount Seine—Mount Sin

ARCHANGELS

Zerachiel—zer-AK-e-el
Raziel—RAZ-e-el
Uriel—UR-e-el
Menadel—MEN-a-del
Arakiel—ARA-key-el
Sariel—SAR-e-el
Metatron—MED-a-tron

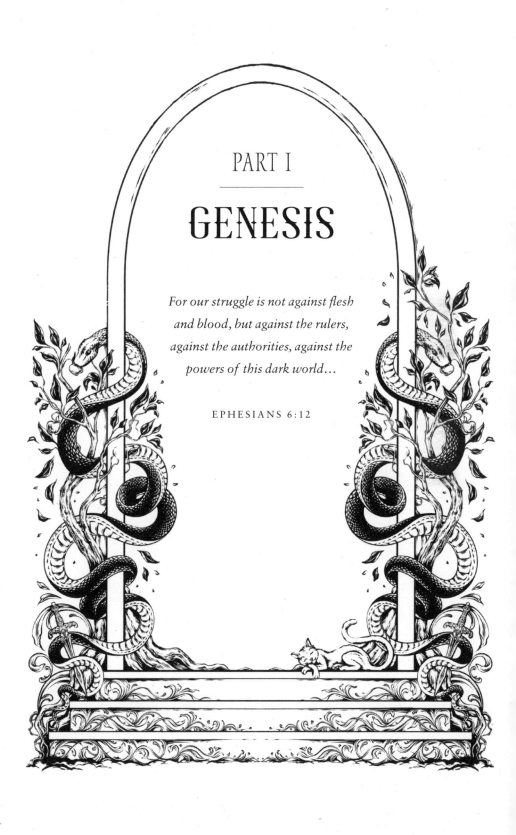

PART I

GENESIS

*For our struggle is not against flesh
and blood, but against the rulers,
against the authorities, against the
powers of this dark world…*

EPHESIANS 6:12

CHAPTER
ONE

R itual was teeming. Glossy tables and velvet couches were already overcrowded, leaving people standing shoulder to shoulder beneath pulsing blue and purple light as they waited for the entertainment to begin.

They would come from above, the aerialists, their red silks unfurling in the dark like ribbons of flame, hypnotizing the audience with their strength and grace as they soared, suspended in the smoky air. It was a popular attraction in Nineveh. Those who came down from the other four districts would have the church believe it was this tame performance they'd come to see, but we all knew otherwise.

Their descent began like clockwork. On Friday at three, Procession Street, the only road in Eden that connected all five districts, would fill with bumper-to-bumper traffic. The onslaught started with the financiers from Hiram, then the industrialists from Temple City, the merchants from Galant, and the artists from Akkadia. Though once they crossed the border into Nineveh, where they were from didn't matter. They were all just hypocrites.

Crits, the locals called them.

Most spent the weekend roaming from club to club on Sinners' Row, returning to their respective districts to worship at temple early Sunday morning. By Monday, they would be cleansed and forgiven, ready to live piously until the weekend.

Forgiveness is an invitation to sin. It will be our ruin.

I ground my teeth as my mother's words came unbidden, roaring to life in my mind. Her doctrine was etched into my memory, conditioned to surface anytime I came into contact with anything that contradicted her teachings, though this was one of few I actually agreed with.

Forgiveness *was* an invitation to sin. I witnessed it every week, which was why I'd decided a long time ago that I did not care to be forgiven.

I'd rather be a sinner than a hypocrite.

I wove my way through the flock dressed in red, as vibrant as the aerialists' silks, but unlike them, I went unnoticed. It was a choice. I could draw attention if I wished, but among those present, I had yet to spy anything of worth.

And tonight, I needed something expensive.

Rent was due, and my landlord had just hiked the price again.

My roommate, Coco, short for Colette, had gone into work down the street where she danced at Praise. She'd asked me to stay home, but only because she didn't like the way I managed to make ends meet.

I was a procurer of goods, usually of the religious variety, but I wasn't picky. I'd sell anything if I could get a good price. The issue was, my job was technically illegal since the church prohibited the sale of holy items.

4

Coco called my methods stealing, but I called it using my resources, which just so happened to be *magic*.

Honestly, I wouldn't need to if Zahariev, the head of the Zareth family and the district of Nineveh, would let me dance at one of his many clubs, but he refused.

You would start a war, Lilith, he had said.

I rolled my eyes. *You are dramatic, Zahariev. No one has to know who I am.*

You are the daughter of House Leviathan, he said, as if that explained everything. *Besides, I like my balls, and your father would cut them off and feed them to me if he found out I let you dance.*

Let me.

Zahariev.

Zahariev.

Zahariev.

He was a beautiful, frustrating man. I had known him my entire life. He was eight years older than me and had ascended to the head of his family after his father died five years ago. He had always been quiet and controlled, mostly unemotional, as were all Elohai. That was the name of the bloodline that gave each family magic and, with it, the right to rule.

Except that was all really bullshit, because the blood of the Elohai—the blood of God—only gave magic to *women*. It made *us* powerful, a power we could not even utilize because we were subservient to men.

It is what we deserve for tempting the First Man, my mother would say.

She liked to quote the *Book of Splendor*. It was the religious doctrine that ruled our society, that said men should be wary of women.

It also meant that unlike Zahariev, who had been trained to ascend to the head of his family, I had been trained to be a wife, and since I was the only child of my house, my father would choose my husband, the next head of House Leviathan.

I fucking hated it, but that was why I'd run away.

And while Zahariev might not let me dance, he did let me take refuge in his territory.

A hand snaked around my waist, and I was pulled against an older man. I put my hands out, flat against his soft chest. He wore a buttoned shirt, open at the collar and sweat stained. His forehead was shiny, his hair thinning. He chuckled as he drew me closer.

"Where are you going, pretty girl?" he asked.

I narrowed my eyes and glanced at his person. His suit jacket hung off the back of his chair. It was cashmere, evenly stitched, and accented with genuine animal horn buttons. The man was obviously from Hiram, the financial district. I was more than familiar with the area. I was born and raised there.

It was also where my father, Lucius, governed as head of the Leviathan family.

The man looked me up and down before his gaze settled on my breasts. They weren't really that big, but in this dress, a sheath with thin straps, they swelled over the neckline.

"They don't make them like you anymore," he said.

I raised a brow. "Say that again," I said. "*To my face.*"

The man lifted his gaze. I had felt his lust from the moment he drew me near, rampant and dark, but now I could see it. His pupils were blown, swallowing the color of his irises, his skin was flushed, and his cock was hard, straining against the fabric of his dark trousers.

"Defiance," he said, a thin smirk curling his mouth. "I like it, but you'll never find a husband with it."

I kept my hands planted on his chest, both to maintain distance between us even as he tried to pull me closer and to give me more control over his arousal.

"Let me tame you, sugar," he said. "I'll be real good."

A violent shudder went through me, and I suspected few women ever left this man's clutches alive.

I let one of my hands drop to his thigh, the other remaining at the center of his chest. His lips pulled back from his teeth as he chuckled in triumph, but I was reaching into his energy, seeking the parts of him that fueled his sex drive. I knew his by feel—a dizzying, nauseating force. I pulled it into the space between us. Outside his body, it no longer had purpose or intention—it was just fuel I could use to kill his sex drive.

"Let go," I said, imbuing my command with magic.

He dropped his hand, and at the same time, his cock deflated as if pricked by a needle. His slimy smile fell, and his pupils constricted so that I could see the color of his eyes, a dull gray. Now pale, he looked far older than before, almost frail.

It felt like a just punishment.

I slipped back into the fold without a word, wanting to put distance between us before he recovered from the effects of my magic. They varied among men depending on their emotional state, stamina, and age—and those were just ones I'd observed. Either way, some recovered faster than others. I suspected this man would have difficulty achieving equilibrium, and the thought filled me with rapturous joy.

I smiled despite shivering, recalling the feel of his hands on my body, clammy and rough. I'm sure he thought he was entitled to me. *She was asking for it*, he would argue, as evidenced by my exposed skin. I wondered if Zahariev or his brother, Cassius, had caught the exchange. If so, my magic wasn't the worst thing that would happen to him tonight.

As much as I despised men like him, I should have been more aware. There was always one whose desire was so raw and uncontrolled, it broke through my shield. I hadn't figured out how to fix that flaw yet. I assumed I just wasn't powerful enough, and if that was the case, then I was fucked.

I pushed those thoughts away and instead focused on the clientele.

While there were quite a few women, most were men. I could tell where they were from by the way they dressed. People from Hiram were white-collar and wore wool suits; people from Temple City wore polyester. Those from Akkadia dressed more casually, in cotton, linen, or blended fabrics, while those from Galant were more blue-collar and wore durable and dark fabrics. Visually, it was easy to see where we all fit in the hierarchy, but here, in the City of Sin, we were equal in one thing—*desire*.

And right now, I desired something valuable I could sell on Smugglers' Row that would pay my rent...and I might have glimpsed just the thing.

It was a dagger. I noticed it because the gems inlaid on its hilt and sheath glimmered, catching the scattered light at the slightest bit of movement from its owner. It was not unusual for people to carry blades if they worked in the temples or guarded the gates, but those were most often plain. This one looked expensive, looped on the belt of a middle-aged man from Hiram.

With my target chosen, I studied him from afar.

He was handsome and sported short, graying hair and

a well-manicured beard. He looked fit and relaxed, almost reclining at the bar, one elbow on the tabletop, another perched on the back of his chair, a glass of amber-colored liquid clutched between the tips of his fingers. He didn't wear a ring, which meant he wasn't married or he'd taken it off.

The problem was he wasn't alone. Two men, likely his colleagues, sat beside him. I couldn't hear what they were talking about, but the story must have been amusing, because now and then, their laughs erupted, rising over the roar of the crowd. I wondered if my target's friends would get in the way of my work. I could attempt to charm them all, but that would take a lot of magic, and a lot of magic made a lot of energy, which would alert security to my presence, and I didn't want to get dragged away before I got my hands on that blade.

As if he sensed my gaze, the man's eyes slid to mine and then down my body. I took that as an invitation to approach and wandered up to the bar, slipping between him and his two companions. I didn't look at him immediately and instead hailed the bartender. There was a downside to coming to places where I was familiar, and that was being recognized.

The bartender, Eli, raised a thick, disapproving brow at me as his gaze flicked to the man beside me.

"Hey, Lils," he said. "What can I get for ya?"

"My usual," I said.

My usual was a strawberry daiquiri. I don't know why it was my usual; I just liked that it was sweet and Eli always added a whole strawberry to the rim.

"You got it," he said.

"Thank you, Eli," I sang.

9

He tried not to smile, head down, focused on his task.

I took a moment to glance at my target's two colleagues.

"Here, beautiful." The one nearest me said, giving up his chair. "Take my seat."

I didn't protest and instead smiled. "What a sweetheart," I said. "Thank you."

There were no other empty seats at the bar, leaving the man standing. His colleague winked at me before slipping from his chair. Together, they wandered into the crowd, leaving me alone with their friend.

I turned to face him. His eyes matched those of the man from earlier, so blown out I couldn't tell their color. I didn't need the physical cues to know he was aroused though. I could feel it flare in the air between us.

He smiled, showing his teeth, a row of straight pearl-white veneers.

"Hello," he said. I thought he sounded like someone who had to put in effort to deepen their voice.

"Hello," I said in the most sultry tone I could muster, rising onto the tips of my heeled feet so I could slide onto the barstool.

His eyes dipped down again, bouncing over the contours of my body, launching his lust into overdrive.

My claws were in him deep.

Eli slid my drink toward me. The sound of glass grating against granite set my teeth on edge.

"Put it on my tab," said the man.

"Oh, you don't—"

"I insist," he said.

I smiled again and offered my hand. "Lilith."

"Ephraim," he said.

"It's nice to meet you, Ephraim," I said, holding his gaze as I sipped from the straw in my drink.

"What brings you out tonight?" he asked.

"Oh, I just wanted to have a little fun," I said. "You?"

"I can be fun," he said.

His desire rose, each wave stronger than the last. I could feel the ebb and flow, my magic anchored to his energy. It made me dizzy, but not sick like the last man.

When my powers first developed at eighteen, the whole experience made me violently ill. It still did if they had an appetite for violence.

My magic was the downfall of my obedience. It wasn't until then I realized everything the church had tried to say about women was a lie. We were not responsible for lust in men. We existed, and they desired.

Sometimes that desire was mutual. Sometimes it wasn't, but men had a hard time wrapping their dicks around the word *no*, and since our world valued them more, we were the ones who suffered.

"That is a beautiful necklace," said Ephraim.

"Thank you," I said, taking the pendant between my fingers. It was a gold cross with a pointed end that made it look more like a dagger. My father had gifted it to me on my sixteenth birthday. He called it an amulet, said that it had been forged from gold found in the Nara-Sin Desert and imbued with some kind of protection properties.

I didn't know if any of that was true, and I didn't care. The necklace mattered because it had been a gift from my father. I hadn't taken it off since.

Men always commented on it, though I didn't know if they actually appreciated the beauty or if it was just a universal excuse to look at my boobs.

"You are from Hiram," I said, still clutching the pendant. It kept me focused. "What do you do there?"

"Investments," he said.

I tilted my head to the side, frowning a little.

"What does that mean exactly?" I asked, pretending not to know. I didn't get far with many men from Hiram if I didn't let them feel important.

"I make money for people," he said.

"A lot of money?" I asked.

He chuckled. "More than you could imagine."

I ignored his slight. I had nothing to prove to this man who presumed to know me, but the truth was he only thought he knew wealth.

"You must be *very* skilled at your job," I said, inching closer, letting my eyes drop to his belt. I let out a quiet gasp. "What a beautiful dagger."

The man's gaze dropped too, as if he'd forgotten it.

"Oh yes." He cleared his throat. "Isn't it?"

"Can I touch it?" I asked, lifting my gaze to his, trying not to cringe at my behavior. I didn't like what I had to do to make money any more than Coco did, but it kept us sheltered and put food on the table.

"Darlin'," he drawled. "You can touch anything that belongs to me."

A slow grin curled over my mouth, though what I really wanted to do was roll my eyes. Still, I would not pass on the chance to see that dagger up close.

The man took the blade off his belt and handed it to me. It was heavier than I expected, and as I pulled it from its gilded sheath, I tasted something metallic on the back of my tongue.

Strange, I thought, but chalked it up to the alcohol.

12

"It is beautiful," I said, looking into his eyes again. "Where did you get it?"

"I made a trade," he said.

I narrowed my eyes slightly, smiling, imbuing my voice with a sultry charm I reserved only for situations where I wanted more information.

"Are you lying, Ephraim?"

"Yes," he said, blinking, obviously startled that he'd told me the truth.

"Tell me, Ephraim," I said. "Where did you get the knife?"

I wanted the information for a lot of reasons, including leverage.

"I stole it from a man on the street," he said, speaking almost robotically, but that was because he couldn't stop my magic from sifting through his tangled thoughts, unraveling his bitter truths.

"Oh, Ephraim," I said in mock disappointment. "Who was the man?"

"I don't know him," he said, frowning. The look in his eyes was distant, as if recalling the evening he found the blade. "I think he worked for the church. He was not a bishop or priest. His robes were too simple."

"Where is the man now, Ephraim?"

"He is dead," he confessed in a whisper. "I killed him."

A trickle of fear shook my spine. I had not expected a murder confession. Still, I continued with my questioning. So long as he maintained this level of lust, I could keep myself safe.

"Tell me more, Ephraim."

"The dagger did not belong to him. Look at it. It is too lovely for a man of the church," he said. "So I followed him.

I didn't mean to kill him, but he fought back. I was protecting myself."

"Killing a member of the church is a capital crime, Ephraim."

"Please don't tell," he whispered, his eyes full of fear.

I twisted the pointed end of the sheath into the tip of my finger as if considering.

"What will you give me to keep this secret?" I asked.

"Anything," he said.

"The dagger?"

"Whatever you want," he promised.

He was so thoroughly under my spell, drool dripped from the corner of his mouth.

I leaned forward and kissed him on the cheek. "Thank you, Ephraim."

I left the bar and my drink behind, tucking the blade between my breasts as I merged with the crowd. I had a limited amount of time before my magic wore off and Ephraim came out of his trance. I didn't know if he would remember what he'd confessed, but I was certain he would remember me and accuse me of stealing his dagger.

Escaping wasn't about getting in trouble. It was about having to give the dagger back, which Zahariev would likely demand.

I kept my gaze on the neon exit sign, growing more and more relieved the closer it came, but then I broke through the crowd and found my way blocked by a man in a suit. When I saw him, I turned, intending to vanish into the crowd, but found I'd been caged by two other men in black shirts and cargo pants.

Fuck.

"This way," the man in the suit said. I turned to look at him as he gestured for me to walk in front of him.

14

I didn't argue and made my way down a dim hallway to an elevator.

Inside, the two men in dark shirts flanked me. I looked at each of them. They reminded me of every man in my father's employ, wannabe made men who played at being tough, their thick, muscled arms crossed tightly over their chests.

I called them *hopefuls*. They preferred *associate*, but that sounded far more official than it was. These men were desperate for a permanent position within the ranks of the five families and they'd do just about anything to get it, even things that ruined them.

I didn't envy their work. Next to my father, Zahariev was probably the most feared among the five bosses, a feat considering he had no wife, which meant he had no direct access to magic. He ruled through fear because his currency was information. He had enough dirt to ruin every man in power, even my father.

Sometimes I wondered how he was still alive.

The elevator came to a hard stop, turning my stomach. When the doors opened, the man in the suit stepped off, and I followed, the hopefuls trailing behind me. They herded me into a room at the end of the hall with nothing inside but a metal table. I turned when I heard the door shut, finding I was alone with the man in the suit.

"You must be new," I said.

I'd never seen him or the two other men before. It made me wonder where their predecessors had gone. Though it was usually one of two things: They'd either moved up in rank or were dead.

"Why is that?" he asked.

"The man who had your job before, he always let me go," I said.

"Maybe that's why he is no longer employed."

"I don't think so."

The man tilted his head to the side, studying me. "Does that mean you are going to be difficult?"

"Define difficult," I said.

"Are you going to hand over what you have stolen? Or will I have to search you?"

"If you are accusing me of stealing, then you will have to search me," I said.

"We watched you obtain a knife from a patron," he said, as if that might convince me to cooperate, but I wasn't in the mood.

I shrugged. "He said I could have it."

"We read the signatures. You used magic."

I suspected as much. They'd literally been waiting for me at the exit. I wasn't really surprised. Nearly every business across Eden used technology to target the heat signatures of magic. What I'd done tonight was illegal. I was not allowed to use my magic without some kind of male oversight. Since I was unmarried, my father dictated when and how I used my power, though even when I'd lived at home, he'd ignored my magic.

I didn't really blame him though. I imagined it was very uncomfortable for my father to know his daughter had developed sex magic at the age of eighteen.

"You refuse to comply?" the man asked.

"I rarely change my mind," I said.

"So be it," he said and took a step toward me while withdrawing a knife. "Strip or I'll help you."

I raised my brows. I couldn't help feeling amused. This was the problem with hopefuls. They wanted to show off, prove themselves in stupid ways. This was likely the last night he'd work for Zahariev.

16

I looked at the blade and then met his gaze.

"I am afraid you will have to help."

I wasn't even flirting. I just wanted him closer.

I waited until he touched me to strike, slamming one hand into his elbow and the other into his face. He staggered, dropping the knife as he held both hands to his bleeding nose.

Then I kicked him in the balls, and he collapsed to the floor.

There were some perks to being the daughter of one of the five families. My father always wanted me to be able to protect myself. Despite his participation in this indoctrinated world, he knew religion bred hostility, especially toward women.

I swiped the blade from the ground and straddled the man. Grabbing a handful of his dark hair, I placed the knife to his throat.

He whimpered.

"I told you to let me go," I said.

The door opened.

I expected the guards, but a heavy sigh told me someone else had joined this meeting.

I looked up to see a man. He was the kind of handsome that pissed me off, probably because I knew him well and didn't want to find him attractive, but it was impossible. To me, he had a perfect face—a beautiful jawline, pillowy lips, blue eyes, and thick, dark hair that was shaved low on the sides. He had a habit of running his fingers through it when he was frustrated, and around me, that was all the time.

He was dressed for business in a tailored black suit. My eyes traveled from his face to his neck, where a set of waning

moons were tattooed. They merged with clouds that bil-
lowed across his chest, cut through with beams of light.
Though they were only partially visible beneath the unbuttoned collar of his red shirt, I had seen the entire thing and
knew that angels battled along his sternum and stomach. It
was a scene from Armageddon, the end of the world.

"Lilith," he said, his voice a deep baritone. He sounded
bored and a little annoyed, like I was an inconvenience.

Which wasn't unfair. I was an inconvenience.

"Zahariev," I said, straightening before dropping the
knife. "Took you long enough."

His gaze swallowed me. I wanted to shiver beneath it
but refused, grinding my teeth to keep still. I wondered if
he knew the power of his stare. I suspected he did. I felt
pinned by it, hating that I questioned if it meant he was
disappointed in me.

The man at my feet groaned, and Zahariev's attention
turned to him. Relief washed through me, but I refused to
let my shoulders fall.

"Isiah," he said, and the man staggered to his feet, holding his nose. Blood seeped from between his fingers. "Tell
me why you are locked in a room with the daughter of
House Leviathan?"

The man looked at me, wide-eyed. I almost grinned at
his shocked expression.

"She was stealing!" he sputtered.

"Prove it," I hissed.

"I was *trying*!"

"By removing my clothes?" I asked.

Zahariev rarely showed emotion, but his eyes narrowed
slightly upon hearing that.

"I gave you a *choice*!"

18

"You threatened," I said.

"Enough!" Zahariev's command was like a slap to the face.

We both shut up and looked at him.

"My office, Isiah," he said.

"Sir—"

Zahariev didn't have to do anything but stare, and Isiah went silent, his mouth tight. He nodded once and then left the room.

"What makes you think he will actually obey you?" I asked. "If I were him, I'd run."

"Because some people, despite their stupidity, have a sense of loyalty," said Zahariev.

"Was that supposed to hurt my feelings?" I asked.

"You have feelings?"

"Fuck off."

Zahariev smiled and approached, his shining shoes clicking as he came close. His energy was like lightning. It moved through my body, straightening my spine and prickling my flesh. It wasn't the energy I usually felt from men. There wasn't a drop of desire, just raw power.

As much as I resented it, I was a little intimidated by it.

He stopped only a few inches from me, holding my gaze. He smelled good, like vanilla and sandalwood.

"Give it," he said.

"Take it," I challenged.

He just stared at me. I knew he wouldn't. I had goaded Zahariev for years, and he had never given in, never touched me.

It disturbed me, which was why I pushed so hard.

I rolled my eyes and sighed. "I hate you."

I pulled the small blade from the bodice of my dress,

disappointed that Zahariev's eyes didn't even dart to my breasts.

This fucking man, I thought.

Just once, I'd like to feel as if I had power over him.

I held the knife between us, and he took it, raising his brows.

"It's not like you to seduce a man for pretty, useless things," he said.

I thought it was odd he called the knife useless. It was heavy with gemstones. Those were obviously worth something, but then it occurred to me that maybe we had different ideas about what made something valuable. I hoped that meant he'd let me keep it.

"You should know I like the thrill," I said.

While there was a practical element to my work, for lack of a better word, it was true I liked a challenge.

"There are other ways to get your kicks, Lilith."

"Any suggestions?" I asked, rolling my shoulders. "I'm getting restless."

"Perhaps I should give you a list," he said. "It isn't as though you listen to me. Maybe it would keep you out of trouble."

"I'm not in trouble," I said, gazing at him through my lashes. "Am I, Zahariev?"

I wanted that mouth to do something other than frown at me, but he remained firm.

"All it takes is once, Lilith. The wrong target, the wrong territory."

I rolled my eyes. His words just ignited my anger, and I pushed past him.

"God, would you just *stop*? I'm not a child."

"This has nothing to do with your age. This is about your magic."

"For the love of all that is fucking holy," I said, turning to face him. "Have you been talking to my mother too? Has she shared how disappointed she is in my magic or how she hopes to marry me off in the next year to keep it contained?"

He stood there, quiet, his hands in his pockets. My rage wasn't different from my body. It did not affect him.

"I don't care how you use your magic, but people talk. The commission talks."

The commission was made up of the heads of each family. There was Zahariev, of course, then my father, Lucius; Victor Viridian, who oversaw Temple City; Serafin Sanctius over Galant; and Absalom Asahel over Akkadia. Their goal was to keep peace between families and address disputes before they escalated on the ground. They also enforced social law, which usually only applied to women as dictated by the *Book of Splendor*.

I knew what the commission said about me. My mother made sure of it. I was silly and rash—an embarrassment. I had been told so often, I decided to just embrace it, even knowing one day my decision would have consequences.

"Since when do you care about what the commission has to say?"

I heard him approach but refused to look, surprised when his fingers touched my chin.

Reluctantly, I met his gaze.

It was hard to explain, but I felt like he had the deepest eyes I had ever seen, yet they held absolutely nothing.

"I care because they are wrong about you," he said.

"How are they wrong, Zahariev?"

I only asked because I wanted to know what he was thinking, not because I cared about the commission.

21

He stared, the bright blue of his eyes on full display. It was unnerving, the way he read my face. I wondered what he saw, or worse, what I hadn't concealed.

"Their judgment is fear, Lilith," he said. "And fear is power."

I swallowed, and my eyes fell to his lips. Zahariev seemed to take that as a sign to stop touching me, because he dropped his hand.

"Go home, Lilith. Or I'll make you."

Make me, I wanted to say, because there was a part of me that wanted to see what he would do, but then I knew—he'd shove me in one of his SUVs and order Felix, his driver, to take me home and walk me right to my door.

So I didn't challenge him.

"The man who had the knife said he killed a priest for it," I said.

Zahariev paused at the door. He did not look at me, but he turned his head, listening.

"You should probably detain him."

He nodded once and then left.

I waited for a few minutes before letting my hands drop from behind my back. In one, I held the dagger I'd slipped from Zahariev's pocket. I should feel triumphant, but I knew better.

Zahariev had let me take it.

ZAHARIEV

"She treats your territory like she owns it," Cassius said when I stepped outside the holding room.

"That is how Lilith treats the world," I replied.

CHAPTER

TWO

I went home like Zahariev ordered but only to change into dark jeans and a tank top. I needed something that wouldn't draw attention as I made my way down Smugglers' Row, a street in what was probably the most dangerous part of Nineveh, known as Gomorrah. I also needed my gun, which I kept holstered under my jacket.

The streets were crowded tonight, but that was because there was just as much garbage as there were people. The ground was sticky, and I had to peel my boots up with every step, but there was no way I'd venture into this part of town without at least two inches of rubber between me and these piss-filled streets.

It was a stark contrast to Hiram where I'd grown up. It was a district full of tall white buildings and mirrored sky-scrapers. There, the sidewalks were quartz and scrubbed clean every night, though it was easy to do since a strict curfew was enforced. No one was allowed out past ten, and anyone caught was arrested and fined, though that wasn't even what kept people obedient.

It was the threat of having your name and face splashed across every billboard in the city at rush hour the next morning.

In Hiram, there was nothing more powerful than shame.

Nineveh might not be as beautiful, and life here might be harder, but I would take it over the simulated perfection of Hiram.

The blare of a horn caught my attention, and my gaze shifted to the street, which was lined with sleek sports cars and roaring vintage trucks. A man with shorn hair yelled out the window of a shiny red convertible. "Hey, beautiful, want a ride?"

My lips quirked, though I wasn't amused.

"You're going the wrong way," I said, continuing down the sidewalk.

"I can change," he said, and to my great annoyance, he exited the car and jogged up to me, falling into step beside me.

"I'm afraid you're wasting your time," I said, not only because I wasn't interested but he wasn't either. I couldn't sense a single drop of lust in this man.

"Why?" he asked. "You married?"

"No," I said.

"Then I don't see a problem," he said, cutting me off. I tried to step around him, but he stuck out his arm to stop me. I let my gaze slide to his, and still there was nothing, no sign he was the least bit aroused by me. I suspected he'd pegged me as an easy target, some young woman he could snatch from the streets and sell into the sex trade, a market Zahariev didn't condone in Nineveh, though I couldn't say the same for the other families.

I studied his face. I wanted to remember it so I could give Zahariev a good description.

I tilted my head to the side. "You think you can change my mind?"

"Just one ride, baby," he said with a grin. "That's all it takes."

I dropped my gaze and laughed. "You know the problem," I said slowly, so he could keep up. "It takes over two inches to satisfy me."

"Bitch," he said, his lip curling.

I drew my gun and pointed it at his crotch. "Fuck. Off."

He jumped back, holding up his hands. No one so much as batted an eye at our exchange. It was usual for the area, especially on this street.

"You know what? Fine," he said, stepping off the sidewalk. "Not even that fucking hot."

"Whatever makes you feel better," I muttered. "Bastard."

I holstered my weapon and continued down the sidewalk, passing bars, clubs, restaurants, and antique shops. Though some were exactly what they preached, others were fronts for very different kinds of businesses, the kind that Zahariev didn't want the commission to know about. Take Sons of Adam. It was a bar that happened to serve some of the best mozzarella sticks in Eden. I tried to eat there at least once a week. Their owner, a man named Samuel, sold weapons out of the warehouse in the back. I know because it was where I got mine.

The problem was guns were illegal in Eden but essential to protecting yourself in Nineveh.

Zoar was a dance club known for their raves. It was also where Zahariev had stored a recent shipment of jade, a street drug he'd stolen from my father before moving it to the port of Nineveh. I hadn't told Zahariev I knew he'd taken it. I was saving that little piece of information for a rainy day.

26

Don't give away your secrets, Lilith, Zahariev had advised me long ago, so I didn't, even when they involved him.

But I wondered what he was going to do with it. It wasn't for the profit. For as long as I'd known him, he prohibited the sale and distribution of drugs in his territory, and anyone caught doing so was punished severely. I guessed time would tell.

Next to Zoar was Raphael's Relics.

The guy who owned it wasn't actually named Raphael. He went by Abram. When I asked him who Raphael was, he said no one. When I asked him why his business was named after him if he was no one, he said it was because nothing rhymed with Abram.

I pointed out he could have called it Abram's Antiques. He told me *no one likes a smart-ass.*

The shop name was displayed in a gilded arc across a large window, but windows were risky in Nineveh, so it was barred and blacked out from the inside. His door was rotting, the green paint peeling, and when I opened it, a bell dinged over my head.

Abram was standing behind a polished wooden counter that looked a lot like a bar, especially because a mirror served as his backdrop, but I knew he used it to keep an eye on his shop when his back was turned. Abram was an older man with white hair and a matching beard. He had a round face and a stout body. When I entered, he looked up at me over his half-moon glasses and grimaced.

"You again?"

"Don't pretend you aren't happy to see me," I said.

He slipped his glasses to the top of his head. "All you do is clutter my shop with junk."

"You pay for it."

Abram huffed and returned the coin he'd been inspecting to a tray before moving the entire thing to the counter behind him.

"What useless thing have you brought today?"

"What have I brought you that you haven't been able to resell?" I asked.

He paused and then bent, heaving a large, wooden crate full of random shit I'd sold him over the last two years.

"Hey, those are really nice sunglasses," I said, reaching for them.

Abram moved the crate out of my reach.

I met his sour gaze. "You have to admit, I've gotten better."

Arriving in Nineveh was a lesson in survival, and it had taken me a few months to get my feet under me. In that time, I'd had tons of my own stuff stolen. Apparently everything I had screamed Hiram, and it made me a target for a while, until Zahariev threw his credit card at me and told me to buy new clothes, which seemed counterintuitive, but in Eden, fabrics equaled status.

The clothes had helped me blend in, but nothing acclimated me like time.

I rose onto the tips of my toes for a closer look at the box.

"I don't see that relic I brought you two weeks ago," I said. "Or the cross from the week before."

The relic was a necklace with a plait of hair encapsulated in glass. It was said to belong to Saint Sebastian, a man whose life I knew nothing about, save that the church had canonized him. I doubted the hair actually belonged to him, but who really knew. In any case, people paid good money for a piece of a saint, no matter how small. I'd taken the cross from a priest. It was solid gold, set with rubies, and had dangled from his belt—a belt he'd been willing to remove without any encouragement from my magic.

Though other than creation, celibate priests were probably the biggest myth in Eden.

"Lying is a sin, Abram," I said.

"Sin is our currency, girl," he said, shoving the box under the counter. "Well?"

"Don't call me *girl*," I said, drawing the blade Ephraim had given me from my pocket. I refused to say steal. I set it on the counter. Beneath the light of Abram's antique shop, it looked a little less stunning, but I thought that was intentional. He wanted everything to present poorly so he could lowball his customers.

His expression changed, bushy brows rising as surprise flashed in his eyes, though he managed to put a cap on his interest when he spoke, not a hint of wonder in his voice.

"Where did you find this?" he asked, picking it up to examine it closely.

"Around," I said. Usually, I would get straight to the point and demand a sum of money, a few hundred dollars more than I wanted in hopes that Abram would negotiate down to what I needed, but this time, I was actually curious about the blade. Plus, if he gave me details, perhaps I could get more than just a few months' rent out of him. "So? What is it?"

"A dagger," he replied.

I rolled my eyes. "I know that, asshole. It's special, isn't it?"

He didn't answer me but paused to open a drawer. He pulled out a jeweler's eyepiece, using it to scan the stones.

I didn't like his silence and crossed my arms over my chest as I waited, tapping my foot. After a few seconds, he tossed his eyepiece into the drawer and closed it before resting the blade on the counter.

"Two hundred," he said.

I couldn't tell what I felt more keenly: anger or shock at his offer.

"Fuck you. That blade is worth at least three thousand, and you know it!"

Abram chuckled. "Might be what it's worth, but I have to make a profit."

I glared at the old man. "Fine," I said. "I'll just pay my rent with the fucking dagger."

I went to snatch it back, but Abram grabbed it first.

I reached for my gun, furious. I had done business with this man since I'd moved to Nineveh, and this was how he treated me? Fucking blade must be worth a small fortune, but when I met the old man's gaze, I froze.

The whites of his eyes were red.

The color drained from my face, and for a moment, I ceased to breathe.

"Abram?"

He blinked, and a trail of blood raced down his cheek.

He lifted his hand, touching his face. When he pulled it away, he rubbed his fingers together, brows furrowing, as if he did not understand what was happening.

I didn't understand what was happening.

The old man lifted his bloody gaze to mine. His face had turned a garish color. A low, strange whine came from his mouth, like he was a balloon leaking air, and as he made that sound, he seemed to fall in slow motion, hitting the ground with a hollow thud.

For a few seconds, I stood stunned, unable to process what the fuck had just happened.

30

"Abram?" I called and then jumped, resting my stomach on the counter as I peered down at the floor. He lay on his back, eyes pools of blood.

He was definitely dead.

"What the *fuck*," I muttered under my breath.

I dropped down from the counter. My body felt weird, like my bones were shaking, but then I realized I really was shaking as I drew my phone out of my pocket to call the only person I could think of—my emergency contact, Coco.

The phone rang and rang.

"Come on, come on, come on," I murmured under my breath. When she didn't answer, I hung up and called again. Then the bell rang, signaling someone was entering the shop. I bolted for the door, shoving my weight against it. Whoever was on the other side shoved back.

"We're closed!" I shouted, fumbling for the lock. I clicked it into place despite my trembling fingers and put the phone back to my ear.

"Lilith?"

"Coco, thank fuck!" I said. Relief descended through my body like a cooling wave, though it did nothing to ease my racing heart.

Someone punched the door.

"Fuck off!" I yelled.

"Lilith, what is going on?"

"Coco, something bad has happened."

"Where are you?"

"Raphael's Relics," I said. "Look, Abram is dead."

"Dead?"

"Yes! I don't know what to do!"

I couldn't think. It felt wrong to leave him, but he also had cameras everywhere. I realized I wasn't exactly responsible, but I also didn't trust the enforcers to believe me, even with video. They worked for the church, and I was a woman. It was likely, being the daughter of Lucius Leviathan, I wouldn't have to serve time, but they would definitely use any excuse to send me back to my father, and I'd do just about anything to avoid that.

"Hold on," Coco said.

There was a sound like static and the distant echo of music. I waited, my throat feeling tighter and tighter.

"It's Lilith," I heard Coco say. "She's in trouble."

There was a pause, and then I heard Zahariev's voice.

I almost groaned. Of course she would go to *him*.

"Lilith." He said my name and nothing else.

"Abram is dead, and I don't know what to do," I said.

There was silence on the other side. I wondered what he was thinking, what he looked like. Was he clenching his jaw or pursing his lips? He did both when he was frustrated.

"I'm coming," he said and then hung up.

Slowly, I let my hand drop to my side, clutching my phone. It was the first time I realized how loud silence could be. I looked around, feeling crowded by everything in the cluttered shop. After a few seconds, I crept around the counter. Abram lay still, and despite the lack of movement, I called his name. I don't even know why. I didn't expect him to answer.

There was silence.

My eyes shifted to the blade. He'd been holding it when he collapsed, and now it lay beside his body. The way it shimmered beneath the dull light made me think it was taunting him. I inched forward until I was close enough to reach for the knife, using the tips of my fingers to pull it toward me. I wasn't sure why I was so afraid of this dead man, maybe because I did not know why he had died so suddenly, but the reality was, once I was out of here, I still had rent to pay.

I shoved the blade into my pocket, skin crawling as I retreated to the front of the store. I was alone, but I still felt like someone was watching. Maybe it was because of the cameras.

Eventually, I chose a spot on the floor and sat, pulling my knees to my chest. The sounds outside kept my spine straight. I waited for someone to break down the door or shatter the glass window, fueled by drunken revelry or a wild high. Antique shops were a frequent target for robberies for those seeking gold, relics, and weapons to move through the black market. Based on my luck, if anyone was going to break into Raphael's, it would be tonight.

Maybe I was just more paranoid because I was keeping vigil with a dead body.

Where the *fuck* was Zahariev?

Just then, I heard a sound, like the slamming of a door. While I hoped it was Zahariev, I couldn't be sure, so I shifted closer to the counter and drew my gun, heart racing as I waited for whoever had joined me and Abram to appear.

"Lilith?"

Relief washed over me when I heard Zahariev's voice, something I did not feel too often.

I holstered my weapon and popped out from behind the counter. I was surprised by how quickly he came toward me, stopping when he was near, eyes raking down my body. It wasn't a sensual look. It was an assessment.

"Are you okay?"

"I'm fine," I said, slightly annoyed, though I didn't know why. Maybe it was because I knew his concern was for his balls, since he'd promised my father he'd take care of me while I *went through this phase*—my father's words, not mine.

"Where's Coco?" I asked, looking around him like she might be trailing behind, but no one was there.

"Why would I bring your friend to a crime scene?" he asked.

"Don't call it a crime scene! I didn't murder anyone."

The corner of his mouth lifted.

"I'm so glad you find this amusing," I said, crossing my arms over my chest.

"I don't find this amusing," he said. "I find *you* amusing." He stepped past me, and I turned to follow. "Where is he?" he asked.

"Behind the counter," I said, nodding toward it.

Zahariev approached, silent as he leaned over to look at Abram. I watched him, swallowing around the thickness in my throat. After a few seconds, he straightened.

"What happened?" he asked, eyes meeting mine.

"I don't know," I said. "I was trying to sell the fucking knife I stole."

"I thought you didn't steal," he said.

"God, I cannot *stand* you."

His lips twitched. "So what? He looked at the knife and died?"

He said it like it was a joke, but it wasn't.

"Yes," I said. "Exactly."

He frowned, eyes narrowing slightly. "Let me see the knife."

I wasn't sure why I hesitated to give it to him, maybe because I was still hoping it might solve some of my problems, even though it had obviously caused me more.

34

"Lilith," Zahariev said.

"I know, okay," I said, frustrated as I handed it over. I knew I wasn't getting it back when he didn't even look at it as he slid it into his pocket.

We stared at each other for a few seconds before he spoke.

"I thought I told you to go home," he said.

"Can you not scold me right now? I told you rent was due, and that fucker, Paul, keeps raising it."

Zahariev paused before asking, "Did Abram say anything about the blade?"

"No," I said, but that was his tactic. The more information he offered, the more it was likely worth. "How is he supposed to lowball me if he tells me how valuable it is?"

"What did he offer?"

"Two hundred," I said.

Fucker, I thought, because it felt wrong to speak ill of the dead, at least aloud, but he'd definitely tried to cheat me.

"Hmm," he said but added no other commentary. Instead, he just left, walking past me into the back of the store.

"Where are you going?" I called after him.

He said nothing. I let out a frustrated sigh as I followed him through the back room, which was crowded with junk.

"So what do you think happened to him?" I called after him.

Zahariev pushed the back door open, propping a crumbling brick against it. As he bent over, his necklace dropped, a gleaming silver cross swinging on the end. The pendant had nothing to do with his religion. Similar to mine, it had been a gift from his father.

"Maybe a heart attack," he suggested as he straightened.

"His eyes were fucking bleeding, Zahariev," I said.

"You asked what I thought," he said. "I'm telling you what I think."

"You're lying," I said, shaking my head. "You're such a terrible liar."

"You're the only one who would say so, little love," he replied.

I was used to Zahariev's nickname for me, but it still made me blush.

He dropped his hand from the door and moved out of sight. I followed, finding a line of black vehicles waiting in the alleyway. Two were SUVs and two were vans, the kind that looked like they were made for kidnapping and murdering people, no matter how nice and shiny they were. Men dressed in dark clothing stood beside them like soldiers, though I supposed that was what they were—men who did Zahariev's bidding.

Once we were outside, they entered the building carrying a variety of cleaning supplies.

A man dressed in a long coat slammed the doors of a van closed. He turned, a cigarette dangling from his mouth.

"Gabriel!"

He grinned as I raced to him, hugging him around the middle.

"Hey, baby girl," he said, squeezing me tight. He was warm, and his embrace was comforting. It was nice compared to the cold distance Zahariev always put between us.

"Where have you been?" I asked.

"Oh, you know me. Just doing the Lord's work," he said.

I rolled my eyes as I pulled away from him, tipping my head to meet his gaze.

"Well, while you were doing the Lord's work, I was almost strip-searched."

His blond brows rose high, and he glanced at Zahariev.

"Who?"

36

"Isiah," said Zahariev. "Don't let her fool you. She broke his nose within seconds."

Gabriel let out a breathy laugh.

"He deserved it," I said. "I warned him not to touch me."

"I'm not blaming you," said Gabriel. "What I want to know is what Z did to him when you left."

I looked at Zahariev as he was lighting his own cigarette. He took a long drag from it, holding it between his thumb and forefinger before expelling a plume of smoke into the night. He gave no answer.

Sometimes he looked so menacing, I hardly recognized him. A shiver ran down my spine.

"You cold, baby girl?" Gabriel asked, already slipping out of his jacket before I could answer. I let him drape it around my shoulders.

"You always take care of me," I said, smiling up at him.

"You know it," he said, then he looked at Zahariev. "You taking her home?"

He nodded once.

"I love you, baby girl," Gabriel said, patting my shoulders.

"Tell Esther I said hi," I said.

Esther was his girlfriend, and I loved her. Ironically, I thought my mother would have loved her too. She was everything I wasn't—nurturing, compassionate, domestic.

If only she hadn't been born in Nineveh.

"Tell her yourself," he said. "You know you're always welcome."

"I know," I said. "Thank you."

He nodded and then vanished into the dark of the antique shop.

My gaze shifted to Zahariev. He dropped the cigarette to the wet ground and crushed it beneath his boot.

"You ready?" he asked, approaching. He put out his arm to herd me toward the SUV at the front of the line but didn't touch me. His energy was all around me, heavier than Gabriel's jacket.

Zahariev opened the door, and I slid into the back seat.

"Miss Leviathan," the driver said with a glance in the rearview mirror.

"Felix," I said. "It's been a while."

"You think two weeks is a while, Miss Leviathan?"

It was, considering Felix had been tasked with taking me home every other day, mostly because Zahariev got sick of my antics.

"Aww," I said. "You counted."

He snorted.

I thought for a moment that Zahariev wasn't going to join me for the ride home. I didn't like the small twinge of disappointment blossoming in my chest. I told myself it was because he still had my knife, but honestly, I wasn't exactly sure where the feeling came from.

It vanished the moment he opened the other door and slid into the back. His energy was suffocating. Why was everything about him so electric? It was like he had magic.

If I hadn't been looking out the windows, I wouldn't have known Felix had put the car in drive. His acceleration was smooth. I glanced at Zahariev, his profile illuminated periodically by the glow of the streetlights and neon signs.

"Are you mad at me?" I asked.

He was quiet for a moment before speaking, which was usual. I never asked him why it took him so long to answer, because I knew he was thinking through his response.

"Would it do any good?"

"Probably not," I admitted.

"Then no."

"Are you going to let me have that knife back?"

"No."

"Zahariev," I said, turning toward him. "I need—"

"I'll take care of it," he said, cutting me off.

"I don't want your help," I said. "I want to do this myself."

I needed to, for reasons he wouldn't understand.

"I know you want to," he said, meeting my gaze. "But right now, you can't, so let me take care of it."

I appreciated his offer, truly. There was comfort in knowing that he would help me if things got bad, but I was capable, and I wanted to earn my living.

"If you would just let me work—"

"Lilith, we have been through this."

"No one has to know," I said. "Isiah didn't know me!"

"And look where that got him," Zahariev countered.

"Where did it get him, Zahariev?"

"In the fucking ground," he said.

"You didn't." A twinge of guilt turned my stomach.

"We have rules in Nineveh, Lilith. You know them well. He threatened you. He touched you. He gave up his life. Imagine the bodies that would pile up if you danced for me."

"Those rules don't apply when I work for you."

"That's the problem, isn't it?"

"Fuck you," I said. I'd come here to escape one prison, and he wanted to put me in another. "You might not pay me, but that doesn't mean other men won't."

I tried to open the door, despite the fact that the SUV was still moving.

"Child locks, Miss Leviathan," said Felix.

I released the handle and let out a frustrated growl as I sat back in my seat. This was not the first time we'd had this conversation, and it had gone as well as it had all the other times.

We were quiet after that. I thought about how I was going to make money, and not just something that got me by for the month. Real money. An income. The issue in Nineveh was, outside the clubs, people weren't looking for women to run their shops.

Finally, Felix came to a stop outside my ruined apartment complex. I was never so relieved to be home. I started to open the door but remembered I was basically locked inside.

Felix exited the driver's seat and let Zahariev out first, which irritated me. I didn't need him to walk me to the door, though he would.

He always did.

I didn't look at Zahariev as I left the SUV, heading straight for my second-story apartment. A few residents who gathered to smoke occupied the stairs. I didn't know them by name, but I knew their apartment numbers. Usually, when I came home, they didn't move, so I had to play hopscotch just to get to my apartment.

Tonight, with Zahariev looming behind me, they fled.

I took the stairs two at a time, thinking if I got far enough ahead, I might be able to shut myself inside my apartment before Zahariev caught up, but when I arrived at my door, I couldn't slide my key into the lock. It was a little bent, so it always took some maneuvering to get it to work. On top of that, I was so frustrated, my eyes were blurry with tears.

I didn't want to cry in front of Zahariev, which only made me more desperate to get inside before he noticed, but then his arms came around me, and his hand closed over mine as he guided the key into the lock like some fucking magician. For the briefest moment, his warmth surrounded me, easing into my bones.

Then he let me go, and I shivered, even with Gabriel's jacket on.

"Lilith," Zahariev said, his voice quiet.

I didn't want to look at him. I turned the knob and entered my apartment, but Zahariev jammed his foot in the doorway.

"Fuck off, Zahariev," I snapped, but he didn't move. He waited until I met his gaze. His eyes seemed brighter, maybe because he stood in the semidarkness, only part of his face illuminated by my pallid porch light.

"Praise, two p.m.," he said, removing his foot from the door.

My eyes widened, and a flush of adrenaline raced from the pit of my stomach to my chest.

"You mean it?" I asked.

"I never say things I don't mean," he said and started to walk away but paused to look back at me. "Let me know if you lose your nerve. I hate wasting my time."

I glared. "Why would I lose my nerve?"

"Because," he said. "You're going to dance for me."

ZAHARIEV

"That girl's gonna be the death of you," said Felix.

I didn't need to be told something I already knew.

"The owner of this apartment complex," I said. "Find out where he lives. We're going for a visit."

CHAPTER
THREE

I was cold, shivering so deeply, I couldn't stay upright. The wind sliced through me, carrying bits of sand. They struck me like fine shards of glass. I kept my head turned, my eyes gritty. All around, dunes rose like cresting waves, dark against the star-filled sky. I could only guess that I was outside Eden, somewhere beyond the gates in the Nara-Sin Desert.

I didn't know what kept me going, but I knew I had no choice.

The sand moved like serpents at my feet. I followed as if they were my guides. Ahead, in the indigo night, something gleamed. It caught and held my attention. Mesmerized, I continued toward it. The wind slowly ceased until the night was still and quiet. The silence pressed against my ears like physical hands gripping either side of my head.

The pressure built, like my brain was swelling, pushing against my skull. My temple throbbed. The pain was so intense, my eyes watered, and as the first few tears spilled down my cheeks, I reached the glimmering treasure at my feet.

A gold dagger, set with radiant gems. I dragged my tongue over my dry lips. The metallic taste of blood turned my stomach.

I took the blade in hand. It was heavy, already a burden. At my touch, the wind picked up again, roaring around me, carrying words of warning.

Beware she who bleeds, bound in chains.

Beware the exile, the young winged beast, who dances unafraid before fire.

Beware the woman with many names, the maiden, the whore, the scarlet serpent. Beware the temptress who whispers in the dark.

She is the beginning and the end.

She is peace and chaos.

She is terror knocking at the gates.

My head pounded, pounded, *pounded* with each strike as I stared down at the blade, unable to look away. Tears trailed down my face and spattered the knife with blood.

The wind screamed, and my head exploded.

———

I woke up coughing, my throat so dry I couldn't swallow. At the same time, I was aware of an incessant knocking at my door. I reached for the water I usually kept on my nightstand but only found my phone.

I could barely breathe as I scrambled from bed, eyes watering. Frantic, I swiped at my face and inspected my fingers, only to find normal tears, not the blood in my nightmare.

Now my heart was racing too.

This is how I die, I thought, stumbling into the kitchen, past the front door, which shook with each hard knock. Whoever was on the other side wasn't going away.

I retrieved a glass from the cabinet and filled it with water from the faucet before downing it like I'd never had it in my life. I gulped a second glass before slamming it on the counter.

Now certain of my survival, I stalked to the door.

"What?" I roared as I tore it open, only to have a piece of paper flung in my face. I flinched and flailed as I struggled to catch it against my chest, only to find my landlord standing in front of me.

"There's your goddamn receipt," he snapped back, but I was too distracted by his face to really hear him. His eye was nearly swollen shut, and his lip was split.

"What happened to your face?"

"What do you mean what happened?" he seethed. At first, I didn't understand why he was so angry with me. I didn't punch him, but then he continued. "Zahariev Zareth happened. You could have warned me you were fucking him."

"I'm not fucking him," I said.

The last thing I needed was that kind of rumor reaching my father's ears.

"Well, maybe you should. He paid your fucking rent. Three goddamn months."

He pointed at the piece of paper I clutched to my chest. Finally, I looked at it, realizing it was a receipt showing exactly what he said.

Our rent was paid up to November.

Zahariev, I thought. *You motherfucker.*

I was torn, feeling grateful but also frustrated. I hadn't told Zahariev about my rent because I wanted his money. Now I just felt like a greater burden and wondered if he would rescind his offer to let me dance at one of his clubs.

"Next time you're gonna be late, just *don't...fuckin'... tell him*," said Paul. "I'll fucking work with you."

You'll work with me?

I never thought I'd hear Paul say those words, though I doubted he wanted Zahariev to bash his face in a second time.

I didn't want that either.

I'd just wanted a fucking job.

Paul stormed away, disappearing into the dark morning.

Slowly, I closed the door, locked the dead bolt, and slid the security chain in place. When I turned, Coco stood at the front of the hallway looking very sleepy, her face smeared with last night's makeup. Still, she was beautiful—tall and blond, her hair dark at the roots. She probably could have been a model if she'd been born in Temple City or Hiram.

"Did you hear that?" I asked.

"Zahariev paid our rent," she said.

"Yeah." I handed her the receipt.

She took it and read it over. "Lilith...did you ask?"

"No," I said. "I asked for a job."

One I hoped was still on the table.

"I don't think Zahariev is ever going to let you on one of his stages, babes."

"Actually," I hedged. "He told me to meet him at Praise at two today."

Coco's eyes widened, just as surprised as I was when Zahariev had said it. Then she gave an excited scream and threw her arms around me. I hugged her tight around the waist.

"Wait," she said, holding me at arm's length. "What else did he say?"

I shrugged. I didn't want to tell her I would have to dance for him. I was pretty sure that wasn't usual. Most

46

of the women I knew, including Coco, had to audition for Hassenaah, the manager and choreographer. If Zahariev actually let me onstage, Hassenaah wouldn't be happy.

"He just said not to be late," I said.

Coco's eyes narrowed the tiniest bit. I wasn't any better at lying than Zahariev. She knew me too well, but she also didn't press.

"I need your help," I said, taking the conversation in a different direction. "I don't know what to expect or what to wear."

"You know what to expect," she said. "You already know all the routines."

I knew them because Coco had taught me. That was back when I thought I could audition without Zahariev noticing, except that after I'd spent hours in front of stone-cold Hassenaah, she'd told me I'd never make it to her stage. Zahariev was partly responsible, but I also knew that Hassenaah didn't like me. She saw me as a spoiled brat, a rich girl who didn't appreciate the life I'd been given, which wasn't unfair.

I was a spoiled brat.

I was a rich girl.

I didn't appreciate that life.

But people down here in Nineveh only saw a fraction of the truth.

They saw the beauty, the glamor, the money, but they didn't know the cost.

Hassenaah was like many who lived in the City of Sin. They didn't believe people in the other districts had problems; they only knew their own suffering. Which was fine. I wouldn't try to convince her of mine. I knew why I'd left my family, and so did Zahariev.

I thought that was one reason he let me stay, even facing the disapproval of the commission.

"What if I'm not good enough?"

I wasn't even talking about my ability to dance.

"Babes, you're good enough," Coco said. "Trust me."

I moved to the couch, sinking onto the cushion.

"I trust you," I said. "But you're forgetting that Hassenaah doesn't like me."

"It doesn't matter what Hassenaah thinks so long as Zahariev wants you onstage," said Coco.

"I don't think Zahariev wants me onstage," I said. "After last night, I think he believes he has no other choice."

"What happened last night?"

I took a breath as everything that had transpired came rushing back, including that awful nightmare. My skin pebbled, and for a moment, I was back in the desert at the center of a cyclone of sand and wind. I shivered and wrapped my arms around myself.

It had all felt so real.

"I...still don't know," I said.

I told Coco everything, about meeting Ephraim, getting the knife, and my visit to Raphael's Relics. An image of Abram lying on the ground with bleeding eyes flashed in my mind. Had he taken something before I'd entered his shop? Had the blade been laced with some kind of poison and he'd gotten too close? If that were the case, why had Ephraim lived? Why had *I* lived?

"Now I understand why Zahariev decided to let you dance," Coco said when I was finished.

I lowered my brows. "Why?"

"To keep you out of trouble," she said.

"I wasn't *trying* to get into trouble," I said.

48

Coco raised a challenging brow. I already knew what she was thinking before she said anything.

"You steal for a living, Lilith," she said.

"Not anymore," I said, so long as Zahariev kept his word. "But I will remind you that all this could have been avoided if Zahariev had just let me dance in the first place."

"Maybe he doesn't like the idea of other men looking at you," said Coco.

My laugh sounded more like a scoff; that was ludicrous. "If that were true, Zahariev wouldn't have let me parade around his clubs and use my magic to prey on male lust for the last two years," I said. "He's worried about what the commission will say when they find out a daughter of House Leviathan is dancing in a club on Sinners' Row."

Not to mention the war he would start with my dad.

"He doesn't seem like the type to care about authority," said Coco, moving into the kitchen, which was open to the living room. There was a set of alphabet magnets on the yellowed fridge that I'd used to spell the word *slut*. Coco used the *s* to hang Paul's receipt.

"You only think that because you see one side of him," I said.

He might be the king of sin, but he still quoted the fucking commission every chance he got, just like he'd done last night after Isiah had brought me into the holding room.

They are wrong about you, he'd said, but really, they were right. I was everything they said. I was silly and rash. I was an embarrassment. I had no intention of behaving the way they wished, and every time Zahariev reminded me they were watching, I was reminded of his loyalty.

"What's the other side?" Coco asked.

I shook my head. I didn't know how to explain it, but

watching him was an experience. There was an entire world of opulence beyond the borders of Nineveh, and Zahariev could transition into it effortlessly. He knew how to act among the religious and the rich despite building his throne on a bed of heresy.

Sometimes I thought he was a sheep, and sometimes I thought he was the wolf.

Most of the time, though, I felt like I didn't know him at all.

"It doesn't matter," I said. I had gotten what I wanted, and now I just had to make sure I kept it.

I sat up, shifting onto my knees. I let my hands rest on the arm of the couch.

"Are you ready to help me choose an outfit?" I asked.

Coco smiled. "I already have something in mind."

———

It felt really fucking weird to go to lunch with my dad, knowing I was going to dance half-naked in front of Zahariev in less than two hours, but whatever. It wasn't like he would ever find out, and I would not miss a chance to see my dad.

Since I'd left home, he made it a point to clear his schedule for me every other Saturday so we could have lunch. Despite my desire to be independent and my hatred of the church's rules, I loved my dad. When I left, it had hurt him deeply. Every time I thought about it, my chest tightened. But every time I thought about the alternative—being married off and used as a siphon—I knew I'd made the right decision.

I took a taxi to the border of Nineveh, which was marked by a statue of Zerachiel, the archangel of judgment. He towered over all, his eyes cast down, disapproving of everyone who entered our district. He was supposed to be a deterrent—a reminder that the church was watching, except he was easy to ignore in the dark when the crits made their way into our part of town.

There were six other statues across Eden: Raziel, Uriel, Menadel, Arakiel, Sariel, and Metatron. *A watcher for each Gate*, said the *Book of Splendor*, which never made sense to me. Once, during service, I'd asked how it was possible for statues to protect anything, which apparently meant I was questioning not only my faith but the power of the archangels. As punishment, I'd had to meet with Archbishop Lisk alone.

I was nine.

There was no one I hated more than Archbishop Lisk. He was the figurehead of the church but led worship at First Temple in Hiram. It was a prestigious role, granted to him by the commission. Even at a young age, he had frightened me, though there was nothing unusual about him. He was an average older man with a hooked nose, wild eyebrows, and horn-rimmed glasses.

For two hours straight, he made me write one sentence over and over: *I will not question the authority of the church*. When I started to grow tired and my penmanship became messy, he would hit the table with a ruler to startle me, but it wasn't long before he hit me.

When I finished, he led me out of the room to my waiting mother, who apologized profusely for my behavior, ignoring the red welts on my hands and my tear-stained face.

"It is not your doing, Analisia. I know your devotion," Archbishop Lisk had assured her. "Some children are born with demons in their hearts."

He'd gone on to suggest that I would benefit from a few

more private sessions with him. I'd begged my mom not to make me go, but my pleas were dismissed in favor of appearances.

You must, she said. *One day, you will be the face of House Leviathan.*

Father is the face, I said.

Your father is a puppet, she said. I still remember the wild look in her eyes as she snapped at me. It was a look I'd grown to fear and one that haunted me to this day. *I have built our reputation, and you will carry my legacy.*

It was a legacy I never wanted, but it was one I might not have run away from if it wasn't for Archbishop Lisk. He was the man who had turned me against the church. It might have begun as an institution for good, an organization that provided order and a sense of morality for people, but that all hinged on who ran it, and if the leadership was corrupt, everything else must be too.

While I waited for my ride, I texted Zahariev.

I still wasn't over that awful nightmare. Even now, my throat felt raw, still parched from the desert sand.

Do you still have the knife? I asked.

He would probably think it was a silly question, but truthfully, I didn't know what he planned to do with it. When I woke up from my dream, I half expected it to be in bed beside me, as real as my parched mouth.

I do, he texted back.

Are you sure? I wanted to know if he actually knew. Had he gone to wherever he'd stored it and checked?

I wouldn't lie, he said.

I'm not accusing you of lying, I said. I just want to know if you saw it with your own eyes.

I realized I sounded a little ridiculous.

What's this about? he texted back.

Zahariev. Please check.

I could practically hear his annoyed sigh, but when he didn't message back immediately, I knew he was doing what I asked. Minutes passed, and then he texted.

Safe and sound.

Thank you, I replied, pausing before I sent the next text forming in my head. You aren't going to take back your offer, are you?

I waited, staring at the screen.

There was no indication Zahariev was typing. My heart sank, so I continued.

I didn't tell you about the rent so you would pay it, I said. I'll pay you back, I promise.

There was no word from him.

I tried not to think about what the silence meant. He was a busy man. Maybe he'd been interrupted by a call.

My worry distracted me. I didn't notice a black SUV had stopped in front of me until my father's chauffeur exited the driver's side, intending to open my door. I reached for the handle anyway.

"Miss Leviathan," he said, catching the door as I climbed inside. I met his gaze and offered a small smile as he tipped his cap and closed me in, suddenly surrounded by the scent of new leather. I wondered how recently my dad had purchased this vehicle. He never held on to one long and sent more than a few to his own scrapyard.

I didn't have to be a genius to know why. My father

enforced the law the same way Zahariev did, through fear and violence.

The chauffeur entered the driver's seat and adjusted his mirror.

"Let me know if I can change anything for you, Miss Leviathan," he said.

"Thank you," I replied.

While I'd have liked to take a taxi from Nineveh to Temple City and not involve anyone in my dad's employ, it was impossible. No one born within Nineveh was allowed into the other districts, except for Zahariev and any member of his family. Among the five, we called it the Eden Rule, and it meant that districts closest to the Garden of Eden had more freedom. For example, those born in Hiram could enter Temple City, but those born in Temple City had to have special permission from the commission to enter Hiram. Those born in Akkadia and Galant could go between their districts and down to Nineveh but not up to Temple City or Hiram.

Nineveh was open to all, but that hospitality was not reciprocated.

It was a quiet ride north up Procession Street to the city. I looked out the window as we passed the barred entrance to Akkadia and Galant. Akkadia was more colorful than Galant, whose buildings were a dusty brown, once white. They made up for it with greenery, their terraces adorned with lush trees and flourishing bright flowers.

I'd always thought both districts were beautiful, but truthfully, they did not compare to Temple City, which was divided by Procession Street, with one side dedicated to family homes and the other to business. The architecture was mostly made up of rotundas, round buildings of various sizes with domed roofs. Some were copper and varying hues, from russet to bluish green, while others were gleaming gold.

The chauffeur turned into the border entrance, which was manned by uniformed officers. The guardhouse matched the district, a round stone building with a dome-shaped gold roof. Ahead, the road was blocked by a gate, but as soon as my driver inched forward, it opened. All my father's vehicles were equipped with passes. It was the same for the other families.

We crossed the bridge over the Johra River and into the district center.

I felt small here, where the buildings towered so high, they were always in the clouds, but my father liked Temple City. I wasn't sure if it was because he favored this particular restaurant, Fig and Dove, or he just wanted to minimize the risk of someone from Hiram seeing us together and telling my mom. I suspected my mother knew Dad made time to see me and that she vehemently disapproved, but he had always chosen me despite the judgment of others, even when the church suggested excommunication.

This is just a phase, I'd overheard him say when Archbishop Lisk and his ministers came to visit. *She thinks the world has opportunity. Let her discover otherwise, and she'll come back, more disciplined and grateful than ever.*

Of course, Archbishop Lisk had argued. *What sort of example are we setting for young women then? That it is okay to disobey their parents, the rules of the church?*

She will be an asset to you, Archbishop Lisk, my father assured. *When she returns, she will share her testimony about how she was led astray. She will serve as an inspiration to all women to remain pious because she knows true evil. I know my daughter's heart, Alarich.*

She has one year, Lucius, the bishop had warned. *One year, and I will insist the commission make a decision.*

I was more than a year into my so-called phase, yet my father had managed to keep the archbishop at bay, though I had a feeling that would not last much longer. Sometimes I wondered if my father kept up our biweekly lunches just so he could shame me into returning to Hiram. I knew he cared, but I also knew he cared about his image and the legacy of the Leviathan family.

I breathed through the guilt squeezing my ribs, but I'd decided long ago that I wouldn't make decisions about my life based on this feeling.

There were worse things than guilt; there were worse things than shame.

The chauffeur came to a stop in front of the glass-fronted Fig and Dove, which was on the ground floor of a high-rise. I didn't open the door on my own. With my dad watching, I preferred to follow at least a few of his rules.

"Miss Leviathan," the chauffeur said and offered his white-gloved hand.

I took it and let him help me out of the vehicle and onto the curb.

"Thank you," I said.

A porter welcomed me as I approached and opened the door. I gave him a nod as I strolled into the restaurant.

Every table was empty, save one in the far corner where my father always sat. I couldn't help smiling when I saw him. He looked too large for the booth he had chosen. He was dressed sharply, in a navy three-piece suit. The color suited him well, warming his skin, which was a few shades

56

darker than mine. His hair was longer and graying, but he wore it slicked back and gathered into a small ponytail at the nape of his neck. Sometimes, he grew a mustache and beard, other times, like today, he was clean-shaven. When he smiled, his eyes crinkled, and the scar on his face deepened. I liked to think of it as a dimple, but I knew better. Many years ago, he'd been attacked on the street with a knife. He'd come away with other wounds but alive.

"Lily," my father said as I approached. He placed his hands on the table as he rose to his feet, the signet ring on his pinkie gleaming. The image etched on its surface was a dragon-like serpent, our family crest.

We embraced, and I squeezed him tight.

"I missed you," I said, taking a deep breath, filling my lungs with his comforting scent. My father would always come to my rescue when my mother was being impossible— berating me for frizzy hair or a too-short skirt—arguing that I was just fine.

That was a word I couldn't hear without cringing—*just fine* but never *enough*, or at least that was what it felt like he was saying. Still, I was grateful to be defended at all, especially against my mother.

He kissed the top of my head. "I missed you too, pumpkin," he said.

We drew apart, and as soon as we were seated, a waiter approached.

"Mr. Leviathan, Miss Leviathan," he said as he placed a colorful salad in front of each of us.

"Thank you, Demetrius," my father said.

"Of course," he replied, folding his hands together. "Please, let me know if you need anything. I'll return soon with your entrées."

My father was a creature of habit. Since he'd started coming to this restaurant, he ordered the same thing every time—a salad to start and then a rare steak with truffle potatoes. For me, he ordered baked chicken with vegetables. Among the families, women did not order their food; we ate what our husband or father chose for us. It was something I despised, but I couldn't bring myself to take the choice away from him, because even though I knew I'd never go home again, I couldn't handle the thought of him losing hope.

So I ate chicken and vegetables every fucking time, and tonight, I'd order pizza and devour the entire thing.

My father waited until I took a few bites of the salad to speak.

"You look well," he said, as if he were relieved.

I wondered what he had expected when I arrived today and immediately became suspicious. I thought about everything I'd done over the last two weeks, but the only thing that came to mind was Abram and the blade. Had Zahariev told my father?

Even as the thought crossed my mind, I felt it wasn't true, mostly because Zahariev would have to admit to my father that he'd lost track of me, which happened a lot because Zahariev actually gave me freedom, far more than my father realized.

"I am well," I said, offering him a small smile.

"Your mother will be pleased to know," he added.

My body instantly reacted, muscles locking up. Just hearing about her made me feel on edge, ready to fight at any moment.

"You don't have to lie," I said.

I just wanted to get through one meal—*through one fucking meal*—without him bringing her up.

58

"I don't lie, Lilith."

His voice was cold and firm.

I averted my gaze and ground my teeth. I didn't want to argue with him about whether Mom cared. In the end, he would side with her anyway, even when he defended me.

After a few moments of tense silence, my father sighed.

"Lily," he said, reaching across the table. He placed his hand over mine. The band of his ring was cold against my skin. I winced, but he didn't seem to notice. "I know you and your mother haven't always seen eye to eye, but she cares about you. She loves you. She only wants what's best."

He was right. She did only want what was best—for herself.

If I fell in line, it made her look good.

I didn't say any of that aloud, because I knew my father's wishes were aligned with hers. They wanted me home, devoted to the church, and ready to marry whoever they chose.

I wondered if they were scouting despite my absence, but then again, I didn't really want to know.

My phone lit up, and a message flashed across the screen. Zahariev had finally replied to my earlier text. I was glad for the distraction, because I wasn't sure how I was going to extricate myself from a conversation around my mother without a fight.

I'm not asking you to pay me back, he said. I'll see you at 2, little love.

My face grew hot. I wasn't sure which part of his message I was reacting to: the reminder that I was going to dance for him in an hour or the nickname he insisted on using.

"Who is it?" he asked.

I looked at my father, and I knew by his expression he

59

noticed the change in my demeanor. His gaze felt heavy, a weight analyzing every part of my reaction to Zahariev's message. His mouth tightened, and I suspected he didn't like what he saw.

"It's just Zahariev," I said, slipping my phone off the table.

My father pulled his hand away and wiped his mouth with his napkin. His eyes didn't leave my face.

"How is Zahariev?" he asked.

"I guess he's fine," I said. This line of questioning made me uncomfortable.

"You aren't seeing him, are you?"

"What?" I laughed, not because what he said was funny but because it was ridiculous. "Dad, no."

I thought I hated the direction of our last conversation, but I hated this more. My relationship with Zahariev had boundaries, even when I teased. We'd never touched each other in a sexual way, never kissed. I wasn't sure what kept that line so solid, but neither of us crossed it. Maybe it was because we were both, in some ways, indoctrinated—the families wouldn't allow an heir to be with another heir, so there was no reason to give in to the temptation...not that there was any.

My father stared at me, and I knew he was trying to decide if I was telling the truth. Eventually, he relaxed and picked up his fork again.

I guessed he believed me.

"Do you have something against Zahariev?" I asked.

"No," he replied. "Unless he touches you. Then I'll kill him."

His threat sent a chill down my spine, even though it was unnecessary. My father might have asked Zahariev to watch

60

over me, but he did so because he had no choice. He didn't trust the head of the Zareth family with me, his only child and heiress of the Leviathan family.

That was what he was really trying to protect: his empire.

"You can stop planning his murder, Dad," I said. "Zahariev isn't ever going to touch me."

ZAHARIEV

"You think he got drunk and fell in?"
Cassius asked.

I stood opposite my brother, a few feet
away from the steep embankment of the
Kurari Sea Canal, staring down at the bloated
body of a man. The skin was a grayish blue,
and his tongue protruded from his mouth.
Blood had dried in watery rivulets on his face.

This was Ephraim, the man Lilith had
told me about last night.

"I'm not sure he's that kind of victim,
Cassius," I said.

"Suicide?" he suggested.

It was what I would have assumed if it
wasn't for the blood.

"Only if he remembered confessing his
sins to Lilith," I said.

"You know something I don't?" Cassius asked.

I didn't reply. The answer was no.

I tensed, feeling someone nearing, and shifted slightly to see a man approach. His name was Histori. I knew him well and wasn't surprised to see him. I suspected he'd been the one to drag Ephraim out of the canal. It wouldn't be the first time he'd pulled corpses from the water.

"Just great," I heard Cassius mutter under his breath.

I cast him a disapproving look.

"Tori," I said.

"H-hey, Mr. Zareth, sir," he said.

There were times when Tori sounded like an adult and times when he sounded like a twelve-year-old kid. Right now, he sounded like a kid.

"Did you pull ole Ephraim here out of the canal?" I asked.

"Y-yes, sir," he said.

"Did you see him fall in?"

He shook his head.

That was a little disappointing.

After a breath of silence.

"Are you trying to figure out how he died?"

"We know how he died," said Cassius. "Look at him. He drowned."

Tori shook his head hard and fast. "He was dead before that. He was dead the moment his eyes bled."

I frowned, watching Tori, but he was staring at the dead man.

"It's a warning," he said, his voice hushed.

"Here we go," said Cassius with a hint of annoyance.

I ignored him. "A warning from who, Tori?"

When he looked at me again, the kid was gone. A different person stared back at me, a man who was seeing something beyond this world.

"The gods," he said, his voice firm and unwavering. "Can't you hear them? They are knocking at the gates."

CHAPTER
FOUR

We avoided the topics of my mother and Zahariev for the rest of lunch. When we were finished, my father walked me outside. This was the part I dreaded, not because I had to say goodbye but because I always wondered if this was the day Lucius Leviathan got sick of my shit, tossed me in his car, and took me home.

I wasn't sure why he hadn't yet. I thought he still hoped I would return on my own so he didn't have to be the bad guy.

The thing about my dad was that he knew me pretty well. If he forced me to go home, I'd never forgive him. That word wasn't part of my vocabulary any more than it was part of his. Still, I knew there was an expiration date on my time in Nineveh, even if I didn't want to admit it.

"Lilith," my father said, his steps slowing as we neared the SUV. I didn't like the way he said my name. There was an edge to it, like he was trying hard not to sound commanding.

This is it, I thought. *My time is up.*

I thought through my options, though I didn't have many

in the face of my hulking father and his men, two of whom lingered nearby, alert and on guard. I felt the hair lift on the back of my neck and on my arms as I tensed. I wouldn't go down without a fight.

"I want to ask a favor."

I blinked, surprised. My father rarely asked for favors. He didn't want to feel like he owed anyone anything.

"What is it?" I asked. I didn't bother hiding the suspicion in my voice.

"Your mother is hosting her annual gala…"

"Dad—" I started to say, knowing where this was going. He wanted me to attend. He wanted to present some semblance of a united family, not only for the church but also for the the commission.

"Lilith. *Please*."

My father never said please, and I could tell it had taken him a lot of practice, because part of his plea sounded like an order.

"Attend for me."

I stared at him, refusing to hide my irritation.

"Does Mom know you are asking?"

"I'm not asking for her permission," he said. "I want you there."

Why? I wanted to ask. *So you can pretend we are one happy family?*

Except that wouldn't go over well, and I was also running out of time. I had thirty minutes to get to Praise, and it took about that long just to get back to Nineveh, and that was if traffic was good. Zahariev wasn't joking about being late either. He was a man of his word to a fault.

"I'll think about it," I said, already in motion toward the waiting SUV.

My father followed, taking hold of the door. He filled the entire opening, blocking the sun and its searing heat. I'd hoped I could just say goodbye and that would be it, but I should have known better.

He frowned at me, his lips tight and eyes slightly narrowed. I'd pushed my luck a little too hard. I was no longer face-to-face with my dad. I was face-to-face with Lucius, and I felt every ounce of his disapproval.

"Do more than think," he said and shut the door.

I waited until the SUV was moving to let myself breathe, shuddering as the tension left my body.

I used to be better at navigating conversations with my father, able to deflect his attempts to pull me back into his world with a few carefully worded replies, but it was getting harder and harder to pretend I was someone I wasn't. I thought my father could see that, and he wanted to remind me who I was supposed to be—quiet and compliant, a proper daughter.

Except that I'd never been those things, even when they'd tried to fit me into that box, even when my father had begged me to pretend.

"Would you like me to take you home, Miss Leviathan?"

Every driver who came to pick me up asked. I suspected they had been instructed to do so by my father, but I always said no. I was sure he knew where I lived, so it wasn't about trying to hide; it was about maintaining my anonymity. The last thing I needed was one of my neighbors watching me arrive home in a vehicle that clearly belonged to the Leviathan household.

It was one thing to be associated with Zahariev, another to be associated with the House of the Sea Serpent.

"No, thank you," I said. "You may drop me off at the border."

The chauffeur did not argue, a lesson they'd all learned the first time I'd journeyed between districts. A man my father had hired refused to let me out unless it was on my doorstep. I sent a single text to my father, which had resulted in a call to the driver. The moment he answered, he paled and unlocked the door without a word.

I never saw him again, and after that, no one argued with me.

I left my father's car and watched as the driver made his way around the traffic circle, heading north on Procession Street and back to Hiram before I hailed a taxi.

This car was very different from my father's. The blue leather on the seat was worn to the point that the yellow cushion peeked through. The windows were down, likely because the air conditioner didn't work. The driver was an older man with long hair and a matching beard. He wore small, round sunglasses, and his arms bore faded greenish tattoos.

"Where to, darlin'?" he asked, flicking the ashes of his cigarette into a Styrofoam cup.

"Praise," I said. "If you can get me there in seven minutes, I'll pay you double."

For someone who couldn't afford her rent, it probably wasn't the best move, but with Zahariev's contribution and a job on the horizon, I was feeling hopeful that the extra cash in my wallet would only grow.

"You got it, darlin'," he said and stepped on the gas.

———

I arrived at Praise a minute past two.

The club itself didn't stand out from any other on Sinners' Row. The brick was painted black, and a red neon sign spelled out the name in cursive. There were no windows on the first floor, but the ones on the second were back-lit in red at night. Sometimes performers danced in front of them to entice customers inside. That wasn't unique to Praise though. A lot of the clubs showcased their talent in windows along the street, just in different shades of neon.

Despite the demure exterior, inside, the club was arranged for entertainment. The stage was low and large so that the entire audience would feel immersed in the experience. There was also a catwalk where the girls could saunter, suspended over the floor, to another stage. This one was round and sat atop the bar. Though there was seating—plush red sofas, chairs, and barstools—the floor was always packed beyond capacity, with standing room only. The exception was VIPs, who sat on the opposite side of the club, their balcony level with the bar stage.

When I entered the club, the floor lights were on, and the red tones of the carpet and furniture were almost garish. This was when Praise lost a bit of its luster. It needed the dark to come alive and hide the cracks in its facade—the stained floor, the peeling paint, the worn furniture—but that was true of the entirety of Nineveh.

Zahariev was waiting.

He stood, looking deep in thought, with a cigarette pinched between his fingers. His brows were furrowed, his mouth tight, a sign he was displeased with something—usually me.

His gaze shifted to mine when he heard the door close. He rarely let it trail my body, but today, he gave me a cold once-over.

"Is that outfit part of your routine?" he asked.

"Fuck off," I said, smoothing my pencil skirt. "You know I had lunch with my dad."

He smiled and took a drag from his cigarette.

"How is he?" Zahariev asked.

"More desperate than ever to have me home," I said. I let my eyes narrow. "Do you know something I don't?"

"I'm sure Lisk is putting pressure on him," said Zahariev, smoke drifting from his mouth as he spoke. "They want you married."

"No one's going to marry me," I said. "I've ruined my reputation."

"You underestimate man's desire for power," said Zahariev.

"Is the church pressuring *you* to marry?"

"No, though the commission likes to suggest potential brides every time we meet."

"Like who?" I asked. I didn't like the jealousy that roared to life inside me at the thought of Zahariev getting married. I told myself it was because there was no chance the woman chosen for him would approve of me. His selection was limited to the second and third daughters of the other three families, and none of those women liked me. "I bet Victor put Violet forward. Don't marry her. She's a bitch."

Zahariev raised a brow and took another drag from his cigarette. "Are you ready?"

"I just don't want you to make the wrong decision when it comes to your future bride."

"There is no bride, Lilith," he said. "I won't marry."

"Never?" I asked. I disliked how much I wanted him to answer that question and how disappointed I was when he didn't.

"Don't you want a siphon?" I continued to poke. "It's all the rage. Think about how powerful you could be."

I didn't know a single Elohai who didn't leech magic from their wives, sometimes even their daughters. Officially, the families were only supposed to use their magic to support the church, who pretended they only used it to perform miracles —calming storms, healing the sick, resurrecting the dead. Though the latter had only happened once as far as I was aware. Of course, not everyone was a receiver of such gifts. Sometimes, a Elohai's magic was used to punish. Sometimes, they were the reason for the storms, the sickness, the death.

Our role in this world is to reinforce the power of faith, my mother would say.

Faith in what? I asked. *It's our magic, not God's.*

My mother had jerked me by the wrist. It wasn't painful, but I still remembered the fear that had unfurled inside me as I met her severe gaze. When my mother was angry with me, she became a different person, a monster.

You are Elohai, she had said between her teeth. *The blood of God is in your veins. It is* God's *magic. It has always been* God's *magic.* Never *forget.*

I hadn't forgotten her words, but I also didn't understand why my mother, who was strong, determined, and more independent than any of the other family matriarchs, gave her power to this institution that had done nothing but harm me.

I still didn't understand, but that was why I had run and why I was begging Zahariev for a job.

"I don't need magic to be powerful, Lilith," Zahariev said. "Stop stalling."

"I'm not stalling," I said, glaring at him. He was the one who asked about my father and the one who mentioned marriage. I glanced around the room before meeting his gaze. "Where do you want me?"

Zahariev's quiet laugh made my stomach flip. I wanted to know what he was thinking, what made his eyes gleam as he beckoned me.

"Come on, little love."

He turned, and I followed as he led me down a hall, past the public restrooms, and around a corner where there were several private suites. Each included a leather couch and a curtain for privacy. The thought of dancing for Zahariev in one of these rooms with no lock between us and the outside world made me anxious. Anyone could walk in on us, and they were bound to get the wrong idea, but I didn't say any of that aloud, because I didn't want to be accused of stalling again.

He chose a room on the left, closing the curtain after I slipped inside ahead of him. He turned and looked at me, and it felt like he had sucked all the air out of this tiny room.

I couldn't breathe, and for a moment, my confidence faltered. Maybe it was the room, but the way Zahariev was looking at me felt different. There was a serious edge to his expression that had nothing to do with his usual irritation. Maybe the closeness made him realize just how far he'd let this go.

I thought he'd expected to call my bluff, but I was serious about working, even if it meant having to dance for him to land the job.

I let myself relax and smiled at him.

"You look a little tense, Zahariev. Why don't you make yourself comfortable?"

I didn't think he liked my suggestion by the way his

eyes narrowed, but he took a seat as I busied myself in the corner. I set my bag down and started to undress. Hooking my fingers into the fabric of my skirt, I shimmied out of it to reveal a cute pair of cheeky black underwear. They were lacy in the back and had a bow and a little more frill on the front. I didn't think about the fact that I was basically giving Zahariev a full view of my bare ass until he spoke.

"What are you doing?"

I straightened and started unbuttoning my shirt.

"Getting dressed," I said.

He had one leg crossed over his knee and an arm on the back of the couch, the last of his cigarette pinched between his fingers. I met his gaze as my final button came free. I didn't slip out of my shirt though. I planned to use it as a prop during my dance. Beneath it, I wore a matching bra. It was accented with silk bows, one on each of the straps and one between my breasts. I liked this one because it actually made me look like I had boobs.

I adjusted the straps and let my hands fall to my hips.

"Do you like it?" I asked.

I'd meant to tease, but then he smiled, and the sight made my heart skip a beat. Zahariev was so fucking beautiful. It was sometimes hard to remember, because so often I felt like I was under his guardianship.

He sat forward, taking a final pull from his cigarette. He looked up at me through his lashes as he expelled a plume of smoke.

"Praise isn't a strip club," he said. "It's the only reason I'm considering letting you dance here."

"I'm not stupid, Zahariev," I said. The brief attraction I'd felt toward him vanished. I reached into my bag for a pair of thigh-high stockings. I balanced on one foot as I rolled one up my leg and then the other.

"I'm not calling you stupid," he said, putting out his cigarette.

"What do you call telling me something I already know?" I asked.

"A warning," he said.

"What makes you think I'd strip for anyone?"

"Let's not pretend you wouldn't do just about anything to fuck with me," he said.

"You do realize I make decisions all the time without thinking about how you will react," I said, retrieving my heels from my bag, the final piece of my outfit. I slipped my foot inside one, using the table in front of Zahariev to buckle them.

"I do," he said. "Which is why I am telling you now, before we do this, there is no bend to these rules, Lilith. You do what I say, or you don't work at all."

I could feel myself coiling up inside like a snake. The reaction was automatic. I didn't like being told what to do, but that was why Zahariev was warning me. He knew my rebellious streak wasn't a streak. It was just part of my personality.

"Yes, daddy,," I said, my voice thick with sarcasm.

Zahariev's jaw ticked, but the corner of his mouth lifted, eyes gleaming darkly.

"Good girl," he praised, his voice low and rough. He sat back, crossing one leg over the other. "Now dance for me."

I ground my teeth, glaring at him, but I knew by the way he stared back that this was part of his test. He knew I didn't like authority, especially when he tried to enforce it. If he gave me this job, he would technically be my boss.

For once in my life, I was going to have to not only listen but obey.

What the fuck had I gotten myself into?

"No music?" I asked.

"Play your own," he said.

"You are boring, Zahariev."

His lips twitched, and he tilted his head back a little. "You don't want to dance to my music, little love."

I could usually ignore the effect of that nickname, but this time when he said it, I had to roll my neck to hide the way it made me shiver. As much as Zahariev accused me of fucking with him, he played the same game, which was fine.

I was about to fuck with him.

I turned and stuck my ass out as I bent to retrieve my phone from my belongings. When I faced Zahariev again, I saw his eyes shift quickly to my face. I wanted to smile, but I didn't want him to steal the little bit of power I'd taken back.

I handed Zahariev my phone.

"Press Play when I tell you," I said.

He took the device, holding my gaze.

"No questions?" he asked.

"I'll ask for forgiveness later," I said, turning away to get into position, keeping my back to him as I cocked my hip to one side. When I was ready, I glanced at him over my shoulder. "Press Play, Zahariev," I said in a breathy voice. I didn't intend to sound so seductive. The truth was I couldn't breathe. As much as it thrilled me to dance and attempt to rile Zahariev, I also desperately wanted this job.

The music began, a slow and sultry beat. It was like the music Coco danced to before her final performance of the night and, according to her, the most important.

It's the one that gets them all wound up, she had said.

I smiled at her words and let the music sink into my skin. I could feel it coursing through my veins. It was a guide that kept me moving.

I enjoyed this. I lost myself in this.

There were very few things in my life that I controlled, but when I danced, I felt powerful. Here, there was no magic, just the simplicity and beauty of a body in motion, and I wanted Zahariev hypnotized.

I let my arms rise, hands gliding over my ass, my sides, my chest, reaching high over my head before floating down, hips swaying as I pivoted to the side, rolling my body slowly. I held Zahariev's gaze, which was easy because his eyes were pinned to me. His chin was lowered, his lips pinched together. It was a look that would have stopped any other woman in their tracks, but I was used to him.

I smiled.

"Don't you ever relax, Zahariev?"

I was breathless as I dropped down, knees wide, my hands sliding along my thighs. He didn't speak, but he uncrossed his legs and adjusted his position. One hand rested on his thigh, the other on the back of the couch.

I kept moving, arching my body as I stretched out on the floor before rising to my feet again.

"When did you learn to dance?" he asked.

"Coco taught me," I said, lifting my arms up over my head, swinging my hips to one side, then the other.

"Of course," he said.

For a second, his tone interrupted my rhythm, and I had to catch up to the music. I felt a brief wave of embarrassment and then frustration.

"Why say it like that?" I asked.

"Like what?" he asked.

"Like you don't approve of Coco," I said.

"Don't infer, Lilith," he said.

There was a beat of silence, and while I knew I should focus on my routine, I couldn't help asking him another question.

"Are you mad?"

I couldn't look at him, which wasn't the point of this at all. I was supposed to maintain eye contact, but I didn't want to see his expression.

"Why do you always ask me that?"

"I don't know," I said. Anger just seemed like the natural reaction to anything I did. The real question was why did I care what he thought?

"Do you expect I will disapprove?" he asked.

I didn't want to talk anymore. His questions made it hard to focus on my work, so I didn't answer and instead focused on the energy in the room. The air felt electric. It always did when I danced, but more so when it was slow and sensual. I liked to imagine I was releasing everything I didn't want—the guilt my mother and father planted inside me, the fear of not being able to survive in this world, the desperation that had sent me to Smugglers' Row week after week.

When I looked at Zahariev again, I didn't feel so lost.

I approached, our eyes locked, and placed my hands on his knees, swiveling my hips as I lowered to the floor before him and rose again, palms sliding up his thighs.

He didn't stop me.

Zahariev was built. I'd seen him without a shirt plenty of times, but feeling the hard edges of his muscles was a different experience. His stomach, chest, and arms were covered in ink. I remembered when he'd gotten his first tattoo and how my mother had disapproved. She considered them to be tasteless and unsuitable for anyone who intended to lead a family, but her disapproval meant nothing to him, and at each event after that, he seemed to have a new piece. Eventually, they crept beyond the edges of his clothing, up his neck and past his wrists to the tops of his hands and knuckles.

I liked them.

He knew it.

I rested my hands on his shoulders and then straddled him, a knee on either side of his body. I didn't let myself rest fully against him, but my nails scraped against the shorn hair at the back of his head until my fingers found and twisted into his longer strands. I pulled, and his head tilted back, my lips hovering close to his.

He didn't move an inch.

I'd never been this close to him before. I didn't expect to grow warm where we touched. Inside, my body was at war, growing soft but taut at the same time.

"Well, Zahariev?" I asked, my voice quiet. "Are you satisfied?"

My lips parted on a gasp when Zahariev's hands cupped my bare ass. He sat up straight, bringing us closer. His eyes darted to my mouth as he spoke.

"You dance in the cage," he said. "You stay masked and keep your clothes on."

His fingers dug into my skin as if to emphasize the point.

"No private dances and no fucking magic," he continued. "*Do you understand?*"

He was trying to sound authoritative, but I couldn't help smiling.

"Are you saying I have a job?" I asked.

The corner of his mouth lifted even as he warned, "Until you break my rules."

I ignored the implication of his words and let out an unholy screech as I threw my arms around his neck. "Thank you, thank you, thank you!"

I squeezed him, and his hands went to my sides. He didn't push me away, but he was definitely trying to keep me at a distance, which was fine. I needed to leave anyway and tell Coco the good news.

I started to pull away, to ask him when I could start, but Zahariev's arm suddenly tightened around me. He threw me to the side, and I landed on the couch, stunned. I watched him rise to his feet and draw his gun just as the curtain to our room was forced aside. Two men stood there dressed smartly in matching dark gray suits and shiny black shoes. One wore a light blue button-up, the other beige.

They each wore a matching gold pin on the lapel of their jackets in the shape of a cross, which basically introduced them as enforcers from First Temple, a kind of law enforcement. I could guess why they were here.

"Calm down, Zahariev," said the man in light blue. He put his hands up, palms flat. He was younger than the one in beige.

"You're in my territory, Burke," Zahariev said. "Don't tell me to calm down."

"We heard a noise," the enforcer explained. "We came to investigate."

"You heard a noise all the way in Hiram?" Zahariev asked.

"We came from Hiram to speak with you. We thought we heard a woman in distress," said the older man.

His gaze slid from Zahariev to me. He nodded. "Miss Leviathan."

Fuck. Fuck. Fuck.

"If you thought that was a woman in distress, I worry about your wife, Koval."

Zahariev lowered his gun. "If you will give us a moment," he said. "We were just about finished."

The enforcers exchanged a look. I wanted to punch him in the liver. He was supposed to deny their accusation, not affirm it.

"Of course," said Burke. He closed the curtain.

I rose to my feet as Zahariev turned to face me.

"Get dressed," he said.

"Don't tell me what to do," I said, frustrated by his command. It was one I didn't need. "Do you think I want to walk out there like this? The way they caught us was bad enough. What if they tell my dad? He's already threatened to kill you once today."

Zahariev raised a brow, but he didn't ask why, likely because he wasn't surprised.

"They aren't going to tell your father anything," he insisted.

"They're enforcers, Zahariev," I said as I stepped into my skirt. "If they don't tell my father, they'll tell the fucking church."

God, what had I been *thinking*?

"They aren't going to tell the church either," he said.

"How do you fucking *know*, Zahariev?"

It was so easy for him to be unconcerned. He was not held to the same moral standards I was. If word got out about this, I would be shamed, not him. Worse, though, I would be forced home and likely locked in my room until my mother and father arranged a marriage.

"Because Burke has been embezzling money from the church for years, and Koval is cheating on his wife," said Zahariev. "They're not going to say a *fucking* thing, Lilith."

While his words brought some relief, his frustration kept me on edge. For a few seconds there, I'd forgotten who he was.

"I'm sorry," I said. "I didn't mean to make you mad. I just..."

I thought I'd just lost everything.

"I'm not mad," he said, but the irritation in his voice told me otherwise. His eyes darted down my front. For a moment, I thought I saw a flash of regret. I wanted to latch on to that and milk it for everything it was worth, but it was gone as quickly as it had appeared.

"Get dressed," he said again.

I hurried to button my shirt and traded my heels for my flats. Despite being more put together than before, nothing was going to ease the embarrassment of leaving this room with Zahariev to face these enforcers.

When I was ready, I approached Zahariev. Now that I was a little more clearheaded, I could think about why they were really paying him a visit.

"What did you do with Ephraim?" I asked.

"Nothing," he said.

"Zahariev," I said, a note of disapproval in my voice, though I didn't think he was lying exactly. He was just avoiding my question.

His lips quirked. "Careful, little love. You're starting to sound like my mother."

He pulled back the curtain, and I stepped out ahead of him but let him take the lead down the hallway. I didn't want to be the first person to greet the enforcers.

81

We found Burke and Koval waiting near the bar. From their expressions, I suspected they had overheard what Zahariev had told me about them.

"What do you want?" Zahariev asked.

"We'd like to discuss a very important matter with you, Mr. Zareth. Privately, if possible."

"It isn't," he replied.

"It isn't proper, Zahariev—"

"Let's not pretend anything about this is proper, Burke," Zahariev said.

I hated blushing, but I couldn't help it. He might not be worried about these two snitching on us, but I really wanted him to stop giving in to the implication.

"You have already wasted valuable seconds of my time. You have one more to answer my question before I have you escorted out of my territory."

"We are looking for this man," said Koval, opening a folder he'd been holding under his arm. He offered a piece of paper to Zahariev.

It was a photo of Ephraim.

Zahariev looked at me. "This is the man from last night?" he asked.

"Yes," I said and looked at the two enforcers. "He said he killed a man."

"He confessed to you?" Koval asked, obviously surprised.

"Need I repeat myself?" I asked.

"Of course not, Miss Leviathan," he said.

I tried not to cringe at his address. It reminded me that he knew who I was.

"Please...could you tell us more?"

I wasn't going to tell the entire truth. It was one thing for them to have caught me half-naked with Zahariev, another thing for me to confess to using my magic without supervision from my father.

I looked at Zahariev, and though we exchanged no words, he understood what I was thinking. He nodded once, encouraging.

"I noticed he had a dagger unlike anything I had ever seen. I asked him where he got it. He told me he killed a man of the church for it. I then told Zahariev about the confession."

"I am sure you understand how imperative it is that we locate this man and the blade he stole."

"Imperative, certainly," said Zahariev. "Just as imperative as your silence regarding what you witnessed when you interrupted my meeting with Miss Leviathan."

I'd never really wanted to die before, but if God decided now was my time, I'd be glad to fucking go. Nothing could get worse than this.

"We would never divulge your personal business, Mr. Zareth," said Koval.

Zahariev stared, waiting.

"Or Miss Leviathan's," Burke added quickly.

He exchanged a nervous look with Koval. They were both sweating, the lights glaring off their foreheads.

"Right," Zahariev said.

The sound of a door closing drew our attention. My gaze shifted to the entrance. Cassius had arrived, carrying a metal case. I assumed the blade I'd taken from Ephraim was inside.

"Gentlemen," said Zahariev. "You are familiar with my second."

"Of course," said Burke, nodding to Cassius.

"He will escort you to your vehicle with the blade."

"Respectfully, Mr. Zareth," said Burke, "we would like to confirm the blade is in hand before we depart."

"There is nothing respectful about your request," said Zahariev.

Silence followed his reply. The air around us grew thicker.

"What about Mr. Caddel?" asked Koval, jumping to change the subject.

"I'm afraid Mr. Caddel did not survive his night in Nineveh," said Zahariev, turning his attention to his second. "Cassius."

It was a command and a dismissal. Zahariev was finished entertaining the enforcers.

"Gentlemen," said Cassius. "If you will be so kind." He directed them to walk in front of him.

Their gazes lingered on Zahariev for a moment. I wondered what they wanted—perhaps to extract the same promise he had asked of them, though that would be both insulting and futile. Unless they gave Zahariev a reason to disclose their secrets, he wouldn't.

Finally, they relented, and Cassius followed them out.

Once the door was closed, I turned to Zahariev. I had so many questions about so many things.

"Ephraim is dead?" I asked.

"We found him in a canal early this morning," said Zahariev.

"Why didn't you tell me when I asked you earlier?"

"I'm telling you now," he said.

"What happened to him?"

"I suspect he fell," said Zahariev. "If Abram died like you said—"

"He did," I snapped.

There was a beat of silence, and then Zahariev continued.

"Blood was pooled in his eyes."

I frowned, brows lowering. I didn't understand. As far as I was aware, there were only two common denominators between Ephraim and Abram: me and the dagger. I hadn't killed them, so there was only one possibility left, but why them?

Or rather, how had Zahariev and I survived?

"What is that knife, Zahariev?"

"Not our problem," he said.

"Zahariev—"

I wanted to argue with him, because it *felt* like our problem.

"Not ours, Lilith," he repeated, his tone stern.

I stared back at him, confused by my own feelings on the matter. He was right. The blade was with the enforcers now. It was theirs to deal with. I guessed what I really needed help with was the guilt. I felt responsible, at least for Abram's death. I had brought him the knife, but that still didn't explain what happened.

I startled when Zahariev's fingers grazed my skin as he brushed a few strands of hair out of my face.

"Let it go," he said. "You had a close call, but never again. Arrive with Coco. You start tomorrow."

ZAHARIEV

I am in so much fucking trouble.

I watched Lilith leave.

Once the door was shut, I reached across the bar where I'd left my cigarettes. I shook one out of the pack and lit it just as my brother returned.

"You wanna tell me what you were doing with Lucius's daughter?"

He only called her that when he wanted to remind me who Lilith was. What he failed to understand was that I never forgot.

I blew a stream of thick smoke from my mouth before I answered.

"I wasn't doing anything with her."

"Bullshit," said Cassius. "I saw how she looked."

"How did she look, Cassius?"

He stared and then shook his head. "You know what? Never mind."

I was glad he chose not to answer. Depending on the direction of the conversation, I might have knocked him out cold.

Cassius snatched a cigarette from my pack. I handed him a light.

"Mom would be so disappointed," Cassius said.

"Can't be disappointed if you're dead," I said.

My brother took a drag from his cigarette.

"You are a harsh motherfucker, Z."

It wasn't harsh. It was just true.

"You should have made more fuss about that fucking knife. We could have extracted something hefty from the church."

"Something you need, Cass?" I asked.

"There's always room for more," my brother replied.

I wasn't interested in filling space, especially if it attracted the attention of the church.

"Greed is the root of evil," I said.

My brother scoffed. "Says the fucking seed."

Cassius was heading into Praise as I was leaving. He was four years older than me and essentially a younger version of Zahariev, though he favored his father more, with the same deep-set eyes that had always unsettled me.

"Hey, Lili-Billie," he said.

"That's not my name," I said, instantly annoyed.

I'd never really gotten along with Cassius, even before I'd moved to Nineveh. Unlike Zahariev, Cassius wasn't as willing to bend family rules. I thought he'd fallen prey to a desire to earn praise from his father. That wasn't unusual, especially from family spares, but Zahari Zareth hadn't applauded Cassius's tendency to just repeat things he'd already said.

To me, it was a sign he couldn't think for himself.

"It's your nickname," he said.

"No one calls me that," I said.

"I do," he said.

I held his gaze as I replied. "Like I said...*no one*."

He chuckled quietly. "You know, my brother has fucked a lot of other women, and none of them act like they own his territory the way you do."

"I haven't fucked your brother," I said.

His gaze swept down my body. "Whatever you say, Lili-Billie."

He stepped past me and disappeared into the club. I wanted to stick my foot out and trip him, but I'd rather just not look at him anymore.

I walked to the curb before calling Coco. Down the street, a man was shouting as he paced. Despite the mild weather, he wore a long trench coat, a scarf, and a beanie.

His name was Tori.

Or at least that was what the locals called him.

He was the opposite of an open-air preacher. He was more of an open-air dissenter, and while he spoke out against the church, the stuff he preached didn't make any sense.

"We are living in a simulation!" he yelled. "The true gods are trapped beneath the mountain. They are knocking at the gates! Can't you hear them? Can't you hear them? Wake up! Wake up! *Wake up!*"

"Lily?"

I was startled at the sound of Coco's voice. I hadn't even heard her pick up.

"Coco," I said as Tori's shouts faded into the background. "Sorry, I—"

"How did it go?" she asked in an excited rush. "Did you get the job?"

I tried to pause and build anticipation, but I couldn't contain my excitement.

"I start tomorrow," I said.

She screamed. "Oh my God! Tell me everything! What did Hassenaah say?"

I should have expected her to ask that question, because she was assuming I had auditioned for her. I hesitated to lie, but I also would prefer going to my grave with no one knowing I'd willingly danced for Zahariev. It was bad enough those two enforcers left thinking we were in some kind of a relationship.

"I don't think Zahariev gave her a choice," I said, which was true and something Coco already knew. "She'll hate me even more now."

"She doesn't hate you," said Coco, but that was because Hassenaah loved her. "But even if she did, it doesn't matter. You have the job! And if she decides to pick on you, just tell Zahariev."

"I'm not going to run to Zahariev every time I have a problem, Coco," I said.

I hadn't even liked involving him in the situation with Abram—I'd *tried* not to—though I didn't think there had been any other option.

"I'm just saying you have friends in high places, Lilith. A lot of us would kill for your connections."

"A lot of people do," I said.

Guilt seeped into my chest, a poison I couldn't shake no matter where I turned. I realized I was lucky to have been born with the status I had. The only reason I was able to behave the way I did was because of it. My life had been far easier than most, but that didn't make it the life I wanted.

"Are you on your way home?" Coco asked.

"In an hour or so," I said. "I want to stop by Esther's."

"Oh, tell her I said hi!" she said. "Text me when you're on your way."

"I will," I said. "Love you."

"Love you, babes!" she said.

I ended the call and dug my headphones out of my purse along with a handful of change and wandered toward Tori, who was still shouting.

"The church is a slave to the gods under the mountain!"

"Hey, Tori," I said.

He paused his oration and met my gaze. His eyes were a startling shade of blue, so light they almost looked white.

"Oh, hey, Lilith," he said.

His voice was warm and friendly.

I held out my hand with a fistful of change. Tori cupped his beneath mine, and I dropped the coins into his gloved palms.

"Bless you," he said.

I offered him a half smile. "Are you doing all right?"

"Yeah," he said. "I'm okay."

There was a childish edge to his voice that made me think his struggles had begun at a young age, which was not at all surprising. There were few resources for people in Hiram who struggled with their mental health, which meant there were almost none in Nineveh. Zahariev had at least tried. He'd started a center near the Trenches, an area also known as Tent City, where those in need had taken up residence.

"Do you hear that knocking?" Tori asked.

I always tried to remain stone-faced when Tori asked questions like this. I didn't want to invalidate what he was experiencing, because I believed he actually heard it, even if it wasn't real for the rest of us.

"I think you have better hearing than I do," I said. "All I can hear is traffic."

"It's getting louder," Tori said. "You'll hear it soon."

"I appreciate the warning," I said. "Take care, Tori."

"Yeah," he said. "You too."

I headed down the street. Behind me, Tori returned to preaching, but his voice drifted away as I put in my headphones. I liked listening to music while I walked, though I rarely got the chance because I was usually out at night and preferred to stay as alert as possible.

Gabriel and Esther lived in an old factory building in Sumer, an area of Nineveh populated mostly by warehouses. Their complex was several stories high and surrounded by a concrete fence that was topped with barbed wire. It looked menacing, but I appreciated the extra security.

I used the call box at the gate even though I had a code to their building, covering the camera as it rang.

"Who is…"

I heard Esther's voice and then dropped my hand, sticking my tongue out.

"Lily!" she said, her voice so bright, it honestly felt like sunshine.

"Hi, my love," I said. "I've come for a visit. Oh, and I brought Gabriel's jacket back."

"I am sure he will appreciate that. Come in," she said. There was a loud click as the doors unlocked.

"I'll be right up," I said, smiling.

I took the elevator to the seventh floor and found Esther waiting for me just outside her door. When I saw her, I broke into a run. I had to rise onto the tips of my toes to hug her. She was taller than me, and her round belly put more distance between us.

"How are you?" I asked, meeting her hazel eyes. I didn't know what it was about this woman, but she literally seemed to glow with an inner light. Everything about her was beautiful—from her dark, curling hair to her warm, brown skin.

As much as I loved Gabriel, I questioned how he managed to land her. She was out of his league.

Fuck, she was out of *my* league.

"I'm good," she said, smiling. "Better now that you are here."

"I missed you," I said.

"You are always welcome," she replied, which again filled me with gnawing guilt. It had been a while since I'd visited, though it wasn't because I hadn't wanted to. I'd been busy trying to make ends meet. "I will want your company, especially after the baby arrives."

My eyes lowered to her belly. "How is my nephew?"

Gabriel and Esther were as close as I would get to having a brother and sister. I was grateful they had claimed me.

"He's thriving," she said. "Me, not so much."

"You look beautiful," I said, because it was true and because I didn't know what else to say.

"You are always so sweet, Lily," she said. I wasn't, but it was kind of her to say. "Come in."

She held the door open for me, and I walked ahead of her to the kitchen. It was open to the living room, which had large, arched windows, brick walls, and exposed metal pipes overhead. Esther liked plants, and she kept a variety of ivies, shrubs, and palms. It was one thing that reminded me of Hiram and probably the one thing I missed about my home district, the beauty of a thriving green garden.

There wasn't much in Nineveh, unless you counted the weeds that grew between the cracks in the pavement.

"Would you like some tea?" she asked.

"I'll make it," I said. "You sit."

She smiled. "You're such a dear."

I moved into the kitchen and found her kettle.

"I was so jealous when Gabe told me he saw you last night," she said, lowering onto the couch as I filled her kettle with water and turned it on to boil.

"Well, it wasn't the best circumstances," I said, retrieving two mugs from the cupboard. "This is much better."

"I heard," she said, frowning. "I worry about you, Lily."

"Don't worry about me," I said. "You have enough on your plate. Besides, I'm fine. Look at me, here in one piece."

I stretched my arms into the air and give her a little curtsy, showing off. I was being silly, but I thought it might make her smile.

It didn't.

"You are," she agreed. "But I will always worry about you."

"Well," I said, her sincerity making me feel awkward, even though I was grateful. "That's why I love you." The kettle began to rumble. "Which tea would you like?" I asked.

"There's ginger in the canister," she said and then rose to her feet again, a hand on her lower back.

"I'll find it," I said.

"I'm not getting up for tea," she said. "I'm getting up for cake."

I couldn't help laughing. "I can bring you a slice," I said. "Or the whole thing, whatever you need. Just tell me where it is."

"Just a slice," she said, breathless, as she took her seat again. "It's behind you."

I turned and saw a half-eaten chocolate cake. It sat on a plate covered with a glass dome and was decorated with purple orchid blossoms. Esther had to make everything look pretty, even at thirty-five weeks pregnant.

"There are plates just above you," she added.

I opened the cabinet and took out two plates before uncovering the cake. Though it had cooled long ago, somehow it still smelled warm.

My mouth watered.

"When did you make this?" I asked.

"Oh, sometime last night," she said. "I couldn't sleep."

I cut two pieces and plated them. If Esther had done it herself, there wouldn't have been a crumb out of place, but since I was chaos incarnate, mine were messy. I assessed them, trying to decide which one was prettier. I went with the left and gave that to her.

I turned toward the island and poured her tea.

"Is Gabriel snoring too loud?" I asked. "You could shove a sock in his mouth."

She laughed softly. "No, he wasn't home. I have a hard time sleeping when he is away."

"He wasn't home at all?" I asked.

"Zahariev needed him," she said.

I paused as I entered the living room, carrying a tray with our tea and cake, realizing I was probably the reason.

"I'll talk to Zahariev. Gabe should be home with you, especially at night."

Esther laughed. I loved making her laugh, but I was serious.

"I do not mind so much," she said. "Especially if he is being called away to take care of you."

I lowered my gaze, swallowing hard. I set the tray down between us before taking a seat opposite Esther. I could feel her gaze on me, but I avoided it, nervously arranging our tea and cake.

"Are you all right?" she asked, her voice full of warmth and concern.

I appreciated it but also didn't want to talk about last night. When I thought about it, all I could see was Abram's ashen face and bleeding eyes.

"I'm fine," I said, taking a sip of hot tea, burning my tongue. "I'm sorry I wasn't able to visit sooner. Things have just been…"

I didn't know how to explain the status of my life. *Difficult* seemed extreme. I still had a roof over my head and food to eat, even though my diet consisted mostly of salty noodles.

"Not the best," I said. "But I think they are about to get better. Zahariev finally gave me a job."

Her brows rose like she was surprised. "That's wonderful. What will you be doing?"

I hesitated, suddenly feeling insecure.

"Dancing," I said, sipping my tea. "At Praise."

"Dancing?" she repeated, almost breathless. "Zahariev agreed to let you dance?"

"You don't approve," I said. Disappointment settled over me, a cold weight sinking into my bones.

"I am just surprised," she said. "I expected him to at least give you a job within the family."

I almost laughed. "Zahariev would never. I annoy him too much."

More relevant, though, was the fact that I was the daughter of a rival. Right now, the families were on good terms, but that didn't mean we swapped secrets. I already knew more about Zahariev's dealings than he probably wanted.

"You don't annoy him," Esther said. "It is Zahariev's honor to keep you safe."

"You are confusing Zahariev with Gabriel," I said.

"Gabriel is very protective of you," she agreed. "But then we all are."

The sound of a key scraping in the lock drew our attention.

Esther's smile widened even more. "Gabriel's home."

A second later, he pushed open the door. He was dressed in the same clothes as last night, and his exhaustion was evident. His eyes looked dim, and the corners of his mouth were turned down, but then he saw Esther, and his expression brightened.

"Hello, beautiful," he said as he entered the living room, leaning down to kiss her before he looked at me and straightened. "It's good to see you, baby girl," he said. "You here to help me put some things together in the baby's room?"

"So that's why you invited me over," I teased, arching a brow.

"Hey, I gotta snag help when I can."

"Shouldn't you rest first?" I asked.

"I'm fine," he said, then let out a groan as he stretched. "You know what they say. There ain't no rest for the wicked."

I rolled my eyes.

"I am going to shower though." He dropped another kiss to Esther's head and then started to walk backward toward the bedroom door. "Don't bail on me now."

"I'm not going anywhere," I said.

"I knew I could count on you," he said, winking before he spun around and disappeared into the bedroom.

I looked at Esther. "I don't know how you put up with him."

"The same way you put up with Zahariev," she said.

"I ignore Zahariev," I said.

"Exactly."

We laughed together and finished our tea and cake. By the time Gabriel emerged from the bedroom freshly showered, I was making more tea for Esther and cleaning a few of the dishes I'd dirtied.

He looked a little less pale, but his eyes were still red. They probably felt like sandpaper. I knew that feeling. I felt that way now thanks to that fucking nightmare.

"You ready, baby girl?" he asked.

"Yes, just let me finish Esther's tea," I said.

The kettle was just boiling.

"Maybe you should move in," said Gabriel, leafing through his collection of records for something to play. There was always music on when he was home. It was his way of decompressing. "I'll pay you to help Esther around the house. You won't have to sell shit on the street."

"Did Zahariev not tell you?" Esther asked.

I instantly felt dread knowing what she was going to say. It was different, telling Gabriel. Maybe because he was like an older brother.

"Zahariev gave her a job."

"Doing what?" he asked. He looked from his girlfriend to me.

I cleared my throat, confidence wavering as I answered. "Dancing."

His brows rose. "Dancing?"

Gabriel and Esther made eye contact.

"What?" I asked.

"Nothing," said Gabriel. "I'm just surprised."

"Zahariev gave me rules," I said, though I wasn't sure why. Maybe I thought it would be more palatable.

"Oh, I'm sure he did," said Gabriel. He turned away to

put his record on and a few seconds later, mellow acoustics echoed in the room.

I wished they'd just say they didn't approve, but I knew them too well. Neither of them wanted to damage my excitement, though it was too late for that.

I brought Esther her tea.

"Thank you, my dear," she said.

"Of course," I said and looked at Gabriel. "Ready?"

He smirked, but there was no sparkle in his eyes. He just looked tired. This version of Gabriel made me sad.

"I've been ready, baby girl," he said.

I followed him into a smaller room on the opposite side of the living area. The walls were painted a calming sage green, and a rocking chair and changing table were arranged around the room. There was a large space left against the wall for the crib, which was still in a box on the floor.

Gabriel pulled a folding knife out of his pocket and began slicing through the tape. I yawned as I knelt beside him.

"Tired?" he asked.

I hesitated to answer because I knew he was exhausted, and that was partly because of me.

"I...didn't sleep very well," I said.

"Bad dreams?"

I frowned. "How did you guess?"

He offered a brief smile. "You are strong, baby girl, but last night was hard."

I swallowed the thickness that gathered in my throat.

"Have you been at Abram's this entire time?" I asked.

"No," he said. "The cleanup was minimal. The autopsy was not."

"Autopsy?"

"Zahariev wanted him examined," he said. "I had to oversee it."

"What was found?"

"Cancer," said Gabriel. "He was full of it."

My brows lowered. "Are you trying to tell me that's what killed him?"

"No," he said. "I'm trying to tell you he would have died anyway."

"Gabriel," I said. I couldn't hide the frustration in my voice. "Do you know what killed him?"

He shook his head. "Dr. Mor couldn't say exactly. He ordered a few tests, said we'd know more in a couple weeks. He suspects something environmental."

"Environmental?" I asked.

"We don't live in the best part of Eden," said Gabriel. "And Abram was older. His shop was *even* older. It's possible he just died from some kind of pollution."

It was hard to accept his explanation because of the timing. In truth, it was far easier to rationalize that he'd died from some sort of toxin rather than the blade itself, but that didn't explain why Ephraim had also turned up dead.

"What's wrong, baby girl?" Gabriel asked.

I shifted my gaze to meet his. "I don't know. I guess I just want to know for certain that I'm not somehow responsible for Abram's death."

"All I can tell you is that everyone knows the risk of living in this part of the world. Sometimes that means someone's gotta die."

"You're talking about self-defense," I said. That didn't apply here, though I supposed it could have. If Abram had survived, I was certain he wouldn't have given the blade back to me. I wasn't sure what would have happened then.

"I'm talking about survival," he said. "Maybe the good Lord took him to spare you."

I narrowed my gaze. "You don't believe in the good Lord," I said.

He grinned. "No, but it sounds good, doesn't it?"

I rolled my eyes and knelt on the floor beside him, focusing on the job at hand. Together, we pulled out all the pieces for the crib. It was basically a pile of wood and an instruction manual with no words, only pictures.

"How are we supposed to know what goes where?" I asked.

"Your guess is as good as mine," said Gabriel. He was holding the manual a few inches from his face and squinting.

"This is going to take us forever," I said.

"You have somewhere to be?" he asked, raising a brow.

I shoved his shoulder a little. "Don't be a jerk."

"It's a genuine question," he said, smiling. "One day, you'll tell me you have a date or something."

"I don't date, Gabriel," I said.

It wasn't that I didn't want to. It was that eventually I'd have to tell any potential boyfriend who I really was, and that would be the end of their interest in me. No one wanted to get involved with a family, especially mine. I didn't blame them either, so I never let things go further than a drink or a dance or a quick fuck, but that was it—one night, no names, and I never saw any of them again.

"You know who else doesn't date?" asked Gabriel.

"If you say Zahariev, I'm going to hit you over the head with this fucking crib leg," I threatened.

"Tsk, tsk," he said. "Hasn't anyone ever told you violence solves nothing?"

"Isn't your job description violence?" I asked.

101

"That's me, baby girl, not you," he said. He was quiet for a moment and then looked up at me. Sometimes the sincerity in his expression made my heart hurt, and I wondered how someone so caring could lead the kind of life he did, but I knew the answer.

He was born into it.

"I just want you to be happy, Lily. That's all."

"I am happy," I said. "Happier than I've ever been."

His answer was a soft smile. "Good. All right, let's put this crib together so my son will have a place to sleep. Hell, maybe by the time we finish, it'll be so late, you'll have to use it."

I smiled, shaking my head at his ridiculous joke.

We spent a good hour assembling the crib. As we worked, the smell of fresh herbs and garlic wafted into the room.

Esther was cooking.

My stomach growled.

Gabriel raised a brow. "You eat today?"

"I had lunch with my dad," I said.

"So no," he said. He knew my father always ordered for me and how much I hated what he chose.

I had never learned to cook. My mother said it was our job to manage, not to execute. She hired chefs and made menus, but she'd never touched a frying pan in her life. When I moved to Nineveh, it was the first time I was responsible for not only feeding myself but also cooking. I'd burned a lot of food, but Coco and I were figuring it out together. Needless to say, I was always grateful for a good, home-cooked meal, and Esther never failed to deliver.

"Oh, it looks wonderful," she said. I turned to look at her. She was wiping her hands on her apron, which accentuated the swell of her belly even more. She looked so cute, it physically hurt. "Will you hang the letters too?"

She opened a dresser drawer and pulled out a set that spelled Liam.

"Only if you tell me exactly how you want them," said Gabriel.

Esther raised a brow. "What are you saying?"

"He's saying you are picky," I said.

Gabriel's head whipped toward me. "Whose side are you on?"

I shrugged. "She's going to feed me."

"I'm *saying* I know you have conjured some kind of vision in that beautiful brain of yours, and I want to get as close to it as possible."

Esther tilted her head back to hold his gaze.

"Just center them over the crib," she said.

They smiled at each other and then kissed. I looked away, feeling like I was intruding on a private moment. I rarely yearned for partnership. I didn't like the idea of answering to someone or having to make decisions *with* someone, but when I witnessed the gentleness between these two, I thought maybe, if it was like this, I wouldn't mind.

I pushed the feeling away quickly. It was a pointless desire. There wasn't a single man in Eden who thought loving me was worth the threat of my father. It was in these moments I realized no matter how far I traveled, no matter how deep the break, I would never escape my family.

So what was I even doing?

"You all right?" Gabriel asked, nudging my shoulder. "You look a little lost."

I met his gaze, relieved when my stomach growled loudly again.

Gabriel chuckled. "Let's get these letters up so you can eat," he said.

We set to work hanging them. By we, I mean that Gabriel did everything while I stood aside with the letters in hand, until he was ready for them. Once they were up, the nursery felt a little more complete, and I realized that the next time I visited, there would probably be an actual baby in here, which was a little hard to imagine even with Esther being so pregnant.

"Thanks for the help, baby girl," said Gabriel as we left Liam's room. "Couldn't have done it without you."

"He means wouldn't," said Esther. She was still in the kitchen but had set the table, which was decorated with eucalyptus and a mix of slender taper and pillar candles, all lit and dripping white wax. The plates were already piled with steaming food—pepper steak, mashed potatoes, and peas and carrots.

"Sit! There is bread in the basket and gravy in the boat," said Esther, approaching with two bottles. "Would you like some wine, Lily? I have white and red."

"Red," I said. "But let me open it."

Esther had already done so much, I could pour my own wine.

She handed me the bottle and a corkscrew. Once my glass was poured, I offered it to Gabriel, but he was in the middle of making himself a Jack and Coke.

"To Lily," said Esther, lifting her glass when he finished. "Congratulations on your new job."

Gabriel stuck his hand out, blocking Esther's glass. "It's bad luck to toast with water."

"Well, I can't have alcohol," she said.

"Here." He rose to his feet and ran into the kitchen for another glass. When he returned, he poured some of his cocktail into it for the toast.

"You and your superstitions," Esther said.

"I'd rather be safe than sorry," he said. "All right. To Lily!"

"To Lily," said Esther.

I smiled as I raised my glass, clinking it against theirs, relieved that despite whatever they thought about my new job, they were still willing to celebrate with me.

We talked and laughed as we ate, and I found myself feeling an overwhelming amount of gratitude for these two people who had invited me into their home without question the moment I'd moved to Nineveh. I was even more thankful because their kindness had nothing to do with my name. Esther and Gabriel, they cared about *me*.

That was more than I could say for Zahariev.

After dinner, I helped Gabriel do the dishes and then got ready to leave.

"I'll call you a cab," he said as I gathered my things.

"I can walk," I said.

"No can do, baby girl," he said. "If anything happened to you, I'd never forgive myself, and Zahariev would also kill me, so there is that."

I doubted that, mostly because my father would have Zahariev's head before he could even give those orders, but I didn't say that.

I hugged Esther and then placed both my hands on her stomach, whispering goodbye to Liam.

"Come back soon," she said. "You are always welcome."

"I will," I said. "Thank you…for everything."

"I'll walk you down," said Gabriel.

Esther followed us to the door. Halfway down the hall, I turned to wave goodbye. "I love you!"

"I love you too, my dear," she said.

In the elevators, Gabriel and I stood on opposite sides. He slouched against the wall with his hands in his pockets like he wasn't able to hold himself up anymore.

"You made her day," he said. "Thank you."

I smiled. "I'm glad I finally—" I couldn't finish my sentence without yawning. Like Gabriel, my exhaustion had finally caught up with me. "Got to visit."

Gabriel chuckled. "I think we could both use some sleep."

"You can say that again," I muttered as the doors slid open.

Hopefully I was done with nightmares.

As we exited the building, the smell of rain slammed into us. I wrinkled my nose. Rain in Nineveh was different from rain in Hiram. In Hiram, because of all the greenery, it smelled earthy and clean. Here, it smelled faintly chemical. Suddenly, what Gabriel had said about Abram dying from something environmental didn't seem so far-fetched.

Maybe the blade was just a coincidence.

Gabriel walked me to the waiting taxi and spoke to the driver, giving him my address.

"Don't leave until she's safely inside," he said, slipping him a few more dollars. He opened the rear door, and I climbed in. "See you later, baby girl," he said.

Just as he slammed the door closed, it started pouring.

The driver looked at me in the rearview mirror. He was an older man with rounded glasses. He wore a gray hat and a light jean jacket.

"Temperature okay?" he asked.

"Yes, thank you," I said.

He put the car into gear, and I settled in for the short ride, grateful the driver didn't seem interested in conversation. I would have listened to my own music, but I liked the sound of the rain tapping against the car. My eyes felt gritty and heavy. I wanted so badly to sleep, but I knew it was a bad idea. Gabriel might have paid this guy extra to get me home safely, but that didn't mean anything. If I fell asleep, I might wake up in a warehouse without a kidney.

I looked out the window into the neon night and tried focusing on things that would help me stay awake. The problem was my mind chose Zahariev and how he'd handled me during my dance.

I could still feel his hands on my ass, his fingers pressing into my skin. I hadn't expected him to touch me, but I wasn't mad about it. I just couldn't let myself think it meant anything. He'd only done it to fuck with me because I'd fucked with him.

Payback's a bitch.

"You're off Providence?" the driver asked as he glanced in the rearview mirror when something darted in front of the car.

"Watch out!" I shouted, but it was too late. There was a loud thump before he slammed on his brakes. My seat belt locked, cutting across my body as I jerked forward.

Then it was over, and for a few seconds, we sat in stunned silence.

I was definitely awake now.

"Are you all right?" the driver asked.

"Yeah," I breathed, though I wasn't exactly sure.

"Stay here," he said.

No *fucking problem*, I thought.

As he went to open his door, I noticed his hands were shaking.

He stepped out of the car and shut the door. I waited in

the eerie quiet, interrupted only by the squeak of the wipers as they dragged across the windshield, dry now that the rain had let up.

I clenched my teeth harder with each grating sound before I decided I could no longer stand it. I unbuckled my seat belt and squeezed between the seats, reaching for the switch that would shut them off. As I did, I looked up and saw the driver on his phone. His back was to me, but then he turned, his face illuminated by the headlights of his car. A second later, I bore witness to his murder.

Two gloved hands shot out of the rainy dark. One gripped the driver's head, while the other drove a knife into his neck over and over.

A partial scream tore from my throat before I clapped a hand over my mouth and fell back into the seat, watching as the attacker released the driver.

I recognized him.

It was Burke, the younger of the two enforcers. He looked different in a way that made me think I was seeing things. His eyes seemed to glow with a faint violet hue. In his hand, he held the gold dagger he was supposed to have returned to Hiram.

I catapulted into the front seat, shaking as I fumbled for the locks. They clicked in place just as Burke slammed his hands against my window. A scream tore from my throat as I tried to move the gearshift, but it seemed to be locked.

I was doing something wrong, but the problem was I couldn't fucking drive. *I wasn't allowed.*

Fuck! I hit the steering wheel with the palm of my hand, and the horn sounded.

Yes! The horn.

I laid on it, letting the shrill sound fill the night.

Burke's pounding ceased, and when I looked, I saw he had drawn a gun. I screamed and ducked. Unlocking the door, I opened it and shoved my foot against it. The door flew into him. He stumbled back but latched on to the window. I grabbed the handle and tried to slam it closed. Despite crushing his fingers, he held on.

I let go of the door and reached for my gun, leveling the weapon at him, but then he jerked me by the ankle, and suddenly, I was out of the car, the back of my head striking the pavement. The pain was instant and numbed my entire body. Briefly, I felt panicked, unable to move as a faint ringing grew louder and louder, but then Burke was over me, and I remembered I had a gun.

My fingers closed around the grip. I aimed at his chest and pulled the trigger.

The shot was loud, and his blood spattered my face. I sat up and scrambled away until my back hit the frame of the car.

Burke staggered and fell to one knee, looking at me. That strange glow in his eyes was gone.

"Kill me," he said. "Please. I don't want to do this!"

I shook my head.

One shot was bad enough. Two would be considered overkill.

"*Please*," he begged, his teeth clenched. "*Please!*"

When I didn't move, he growled, baring his teeth, lunging like an animal. I shot him once more. He landed face down on the pavement and didn't move again.

Despite how badly I was shaking, I rose to my feet. I kept my gun pointed at Burke, even though I suspected he was now dead.

I crept toward the front of the car where I found the dead driver and another man—Koval, the other enforcer.

"What the fuck is happening?" I muttered under my breath, wincing as I turned to look back at Burke.

My head *hurt*.

I started toward the car. I needed my stuff, and then I needed to get as far away from here as I could before I called for help.

As I went to step over Burke's body, I noticed something gleaming beneath him. Before I realized what I was doing and what it was, my fingers had already grazed the hilt of the golden blade. A bone-deep cold took root inside me, and my fingers tightened around the weapon.

As I straightened, I heard a voice.

"Beware…"

And then a thousand more.

Beware, beware, *beware*.

I fell to my knees. The strike made my head throb and my vision blur. I fought the urge to vomit, my stomach roiling, fingers digging into the desert sand. As I waited for the feeling to pass, I became aware of my body. My skin felt tight and chapped, stretched too thin over my bones. I ran my rogue tongue over my cracked and bleeding lips, devoid of moisture. Even my eyes were scuffed from sand, so dry they felt shrunken in my head.

The whispers did not cease, their warning punctuated with the beat of a drum. I didn't know where it came from, perhaps my own heart, pounding, pounding, *pounding* in my chest.

As I listened, words poured from my lips.

Beware, goddess of night,
Mother of the moon.
There is poison on your tongue,
Venom in your blood.

Lie upon my altar,
Bleed upon my steps.
Release me from these bindings,
Break down these carmine gates.

I tasted blood, and as it coated my tongue, I felt restored. When I looked up, I found that I knelt at the mouth of a large cave. The darkness reached for me. I rose to meet it.

ZAHARIEV

"I'm sorry to bother you, Mr. Zareth," Colette D'Arsay said. "But I'm worried about Lilith. She isn't home yet, and she isn't answering her phone."

Unease crept over me, an unsettling shadow. The feeling of fear was like a foreign object in my body. I wanted to expel it but knew there was only one way to do so.

"I'll find her," I said. My throat was tight as I made the promise and hung up.

CHAPTER
SIX

When I woke, it was like rising from a dark pool. I felt myself surface and my body awaken, aware that I was on a bed and my clothes were damp. My head hurt. It felt like my brain was throbbing, growing too large to fit in my skull. It took me a moment to remember what had happened. I had to parse through my memories, which were overshadowed by my strange, desert dream.

It was a continuation of the last one and still so real. My tongue was gritty, my lips dry. I tried to swallow, but there was no moisture in my mouth.

I needed something to drink.

I opened my eyes to a tall, shadowed ceiling. I knew by the light fixture at the center—a rattan globe—that I was in Gabriel and Esther's room. I lifted my head a little and glimpsed Zahariev standing in the corner. One arm was crossed over his chest, the other raised as he mindlessly brushed his thumb across his lips.

I whispered his name, and his eyes lifted to mine, but he

didn't come to me. He dropped his arms and opened the door, speaking to someone. A second later, he stepped aside, allowing an older man to enter.

I recognized him immediately. His name was Luke Morganstern, but everyone called him Dr. Mor. He was an older man with short salt-and-pepper hair and a black mustache. The skin below his jawline sagged, which made him look like he was always frowning, except that he was actually always cheerful.

I'd known about him for a long time, but I'd only met him when I moved to Nineveh. He worked for Zahariev and treated those in his circle. When I was seventeen, I asked for birth control. Well, I'd had to ask him through Zahariev, which was embarrassing, but I got it nevertheless. I wasn't the only woman in Hiram who used his services—or man for that matter.

The church and the five families liked to tell women what they could do with their bodies, but secretly, they'd do anything to suppress a scandal, including paying for abortions under the table.

"Miss Leviathan," Dr. Mor said as he approached. "How are you feeling?"

"Like I hit my head," I said, sitting up slowly. I threw my legs over the edge of the bed, but a wave of dizziness kept me seated. I closed my eyes, trying to find my equilibrium, but even then, I felt like they were swimming in my head. The feeling moved into my gut, turning my stomach.

"Careful," said Dr. Mor. "Any dizziness?"

"A bit," I said, my eyes still closed.

I let out a long breath.

"Nausea?"

I nodded. I didn't want to speak, fearing I really would

114

vomit. After a few seconds, though, the feeling passed. I opened my eyes as Dr. Mor set his bag down on the bedside table and opened it. He pulled out a pair of powder-blue gloves.

"What happened?" he asked.

I glanced at Zahariev, who was still present in the room. I knew he lingered for this reason.

"I was pulled out of a car by my ankle," I said. "I hit the pavement."

"Who pulled you out of the car?" asked Zahariev. There was a grittiness to his voice that made me think he was angry.

I looked at him and regretted it instantly as a sharp pain shot from the back of my skull and into my eyes.

"Fuck," I muttered, reaching to touch the sorest part of my head, but Dr. Mor stopped me.

"Try not to touch it. I'll look in a second. How about we wait until you've had some rest before we inundate you with questions?" he suggested, glaring at Zahariev over his glasses.

"It's fine," I said between my teeth. "I shouldn't have moved." I took a deep breath and let it out slowly. "It was Burke," I said. "He jerked me once, and I was out of the car. It was so fast, I couldn't do anything except land."

As I spoke, Dr. Mor shone a light in my eyes and then felt around the back of my head. The spot where I had hit the pavement was tender, and I inhaled through my teeth.

"No open wound, just a decent knot," he said. "He gave you a nice concussion."

There was nothing nice about it.

"Two days of complete rest. If you're feeling better by then—no dizziness, nausea, headaches—you can return to *light* activities," he said.

I didn't like that he glanced at Zahariev as he spoke, like he was somehow responsible for my *level of activity*.

"After a week, you can return to regular activities *if* you are symptom free. Take something for pain as needed," Dr. Mor continued as he shucked off his blue gloves. "If your headache worsens, your vision changes…call me immediately. Any questions?"

"No," I said. "Thank you, Dr. Mor."

He smiled. "Of course, Miss Leviathan."

The doctor shoved his gloves in the pocket of his coat, zipped up his bag, and left, nodding to Zahariev as he went.

Alone, we stared at each other.

"How are you feeling?" he asked.

"Are you asking because you care or because you want to question me?"

"Both," he said.

He didn't move from his place against the wall. He was dressed down, in dark jeans and a black shirt. His hair was wet and hung messily in his face. I didn't think he'd showered, so I assumed it had been raining again.

I sighed. "I don't know what to tell you," I said. "Gabriel called me a taxi. The driver was fine until he hit someone. It turned out to be Koval. Then Burke attacked the driver once he was out of the car. It was like a setup."

"Maybe it was," said Zahariev.

"But why?" I asked. "And why would they risk it?"

It didn't make sense. They knew who I was. Even estranged, I was still a daughter of Leviathan.

"I don't know," Zahariev said. "But they did."

I frowned. Something about it still didn't seem right.

Burke had begged me to kill him. It was like, he'd been possessed, and in a moment of clarity, he'd begged me to stop him. I considered telling Zahariev what I'd seen—a violet glow to his eyes—but now I questioned if that had been real. It was more likely a reflection of the surrounding neon lights.

"What now?" I asked.

"*You* are going to rest," he said. "That means no work, Lilith, until the doctor says otherwise."

"*Zahariev*—"

"It's a week, Lilith," he said. "A week, and you can start."

I didn't know why I was arguing. I knew I needed rest. I guessed I was just afraid when I was ready, the offer wouldn't be there anymore.

"Don't you trust me?"

I frowned at him, brows lowering. "Of course. Why would you ask me that?"

"Then trust me right now," he said. "I won't rescind my offer."

My face grew hot. I was embarrassed that I had panicked. "Thank you."

Zahariev said nothing and then offered his hands. "Let's get you home."

I took them, aware of his warmth as his fingers closed around mine. I got to my feet and stared at Zahariev's chest until my head stopped spinning.

"You okay?" Zahariev asked, his voice low, almost a whisper between us. It dripped down my spine, making me shiver.

"Yeah," I said, blowing out a long breath, trying to suppress the nausea roiling in my stomach.

"Lilith."

I tilted my head back, meeting Zahariev's gaze.

"What?"

One side of his mouth lifted. "I just want you to look me in the eyes when you lie."

I glared at him.

"I *want* to be all right, okay?"

His expression softened. "It's okay to not be okay."

"It doesn't feel that way," I said. I let my head rest against his chest.

His laugh was quiet. "That's because you do not like to be contained." He paused and then added, "Most wild things don't."

I pulled away. "Are you calling me an animal?"

His quiet chuckle warmed my chest. "No. Let's go."

Zahariev placed a hand on my lower back, guiding me to the door. I blinked against the light in the living room. It made my headache worse, but after a few moments, I was good enough to move. I spotted Esther on the couch, her head awkwardly resting against the arm, asleep.

"Where is Gabriel?" I asked.

Zahariev looked down at me and said nothing, though I didn't need words to know what he was thinking.

Where do you think?

"You can't keep sending Gabriel away from Esther," I said. "She could go into labor at any moment."

"Then Gabriel can tell me," said Zahariev. "As it is, he was more than happy to get a look at the two men who hurt you."

I moved to the couch. I didn't want to wake Esther, but she needed to be in a real bed.

"Esther," I whispered, shaking her gently.

She opened her eyes and then closed them.

"Hey, you need to go to bed," I said, shaking her again.

118

This time, she opened her eyes and actually looked at me.

"Oh, Lilith," she said, taking my face between her hands. "Are you okay?"

"Yes, I'm fine," I said.

"I was so worried," she said, her eyes welling with tears.

"Don't cry," I said. I couldn't handle it if she cried. "I'm fine, really. Zahariev is going to take me home, and you need to rest in a real bed. I'll call you tomorrow, okay?"

"Okay," she said, pulling me into a hug. "Be careful."

"Always," I said, though those words rang false. I'd left here with every caution and still managed to find trouble.

"I love you," I said, kissing Esther's forehead.

"I love you too."

"Good night, Esther," Zahariev said as he guided me to the door, a firm hand on my back. He kept it there even as we headed down the hall to the elevator. I thought he might put distance between us once we were inside, but he didn't. Even with him near, I held on to the bar, feeling a rush of nausea as we made our descent.

"The church is going to come looking for their enforcers," I said.

"I'm counting on it," Zahariev replied.

I looked at him. He was staring straight ahead, so I could only see the sharp edge of his jaw.

"What are you going to tell them?"

He looked down at me. "I'm going to tell them what I found," he said. "Three dead men and a taxi."

"What about the knife?" I asked.

Zahariev frowned. "What do you mean, what about the knife?"

"Burke had the knife," I said. "I saw him use it. I picked it up."

119

I knew I wasn't imagining it either, because as soon as I'd had it in hand, I'd been transported to that fucking desert.

"It might have been there before you passed out," said Zahariev. "But it wasn't there when Gabriel arrived."

"Why would someone take the knife and leave my bag?"

"Maybe they thought it had more value," he said. "I suppose it's just a matter of time before we find the person responsible."

"Do you already have a lead?"

"No," he said. "But everyone who's touched that blade has ended up dead, save you and me. I doubt whoever has it now will be an exception."

I shared the same doubt, but why did Zahariev and I seem to be one?

———————

On the ride home, I lay down in the back seat. Zahariev let me use his leg as a pillow, which wasn't exactly comfortable, but I didn't complain. My head felt like a weight, and it was better than sitting up. I kept my eyes closed but didn't sleep. The ride was too bumpy, and I'd become aware of other injuries I'd sustained in the struggle with Burke. My ass hurt. Maybe I'd broken something other than my head during that fall. It didn't help that Zahariev's hand was resting on my hip, a warm weight that only made me dwell on the ache.

When we arrived, I groaned. I didn't want to feel that rush of dizziness as I sat up again. Zahariev combed his fingers through my hair and I opened my eyes, looking up at his stupidly pretty face. He had to be the only person in the entire world who didn't have a double chin when they looked down.

Fucking rude.

"Are you feeling okay?" he asked.

"I just want to sleep," I said.

His fingers running through my hair didn't help. If he kept it up, I'd be asleep in his lap in no time, especially now that we were stopped.

Zahariev's lips curled. "You're almost there, little love. Do you want me to carry you?"

"That's the second time tonight you've tried to sweep me off my feet, Zahariev."

His smile widened for a moment and then vanished completely.

"I'm sorry," he said.

I frowned, confused by his sudden change in tone. "Why are you apologizing?"

"Because, this should have never happened."

"You're not going to wax poetic about how I'm your responsibility, are you?" I asked. "Because if so, you can save it for another time."

"I wasn't," he said.

"Thank fuck," I said, sitting up. I felt just as shitty as I expected. I hung my head in my hands until the initial ache subsided.

Zahariev was already out of the car, waiting with my bag and jacket draped over his arm.

"Bye, Felix," I said. "See you next time."

"Good night, Miss Leviathan," he said with a nod in the rearview mirror.

I slid to Zahariev's side and started to climb out of the SUV when he offered his hand.

"I'm okay," I said, getting out on my own and shutting the door. "You don't have to hover."

I wasn't frustrated with him, even though I probably sounded irritated. I just didn't like feeling helpless.

"I'm not trying to hover," he said. "I just don't want you to fall."

"I'm not going to fall," I said, though as luck would have it, I found just the right spot on the pavement to catch my foot and stumbled. I managed to steady myself but lost my dignity.

I looked at Zahariev, who was standing with his arms crossed, brow raised.

"Don't say a fucking thing," I warned.

To his credit, he didn't and instead followed me up the stairs to my apartment. I paused there and turned to him. I started to speak, to tell him I was sorry for what I'd said, but the door opened.

"Lilith," Coco said, my name leaving her lips breathlessly. She pulled me into a hug. "I was so worried."

"I'm okay," I said.

She hugged me tighter. Zahariev slipped past us and into our apartment. He headed into my room and left my things on the bed.

Coco pulled away as Zahariev exited.

"Thank you, Mr. Zareth."

"Always," he said.

It took me a moment to put two and two together, but I finally realized the reason Zahariev had found me was because Coco had raised the alarm.

His gaze slid to me. Suddenly, I wanted the other Zahariev, the one who smiled at me and played with my hair. This one had buried all that beneath a mask of indifference. I would remember that the next time I told him not to hover.

"Get some rest," he said.

I watched him leave. As he crossed the parking lot to his waiting SUV, Coco spoke.

"I'm sorry, Lilith. I didn't know where you were, and you weren't answering your phone—"

"I know. It's okay," I said, meeting her gaze. I wasn't mad that she'd called Zahariev. I hadn't even been mad when she'd gone to him about Abram. I'd just dreaded his reaction. "I'm sorry I worried you."

"Don't apologize," she said. "I am just glad you are safe."

I smiled and pulled her into another hug. "I love you."

"I love you too," she said. Her arms bit into my back as she held me tighter.

She made me feel like I was the center of her universe and that my absence would send her entire world out of orbit. If I never got another thing out of this life, Coco's friendship would be enough.

"Let's get out of the breezeway before someone creepy comes along," she said, pulling me into our apartment and bolting the assembly of locks on our door. "Do you need anything?" she asked. "Water, food…pain meds?"

"I'll be fine," I said. "I'm going to wash my face and go to bed. You should get some rest. You have work tomorrow."

"You mean today," she said. "It's four a.m."

"Fuck." I raked my fingers through my hair. "I'm sorry, Coco."

"It's fine," she said. "I have all day to sleep."

I swallowed, and my eyes began to water. I wasn't sure why I suddenly felt the urge to cry. I inhaled through my nose and ran my fingers under my eyes to catch the tears. I thought part of me was overwhelmed, and another part of me just hurt. Literally.

"Oh, babes," Coco said, unfolding her arms and pulling me into another hug. "Whatever happened, I am so sorry."

"It's fine," I said, clearing my throat. "I'll tell you everything tomorrow...today...whatever."

"You don't have to tell me anything," she said.

The thing I loved about Coco was that she never pushed. When we first met at Praise two years ago, she had no idea who I was, and she didn't care. She'd just seen something in me she liked. She was the first person to ever show me kindness, approaching out of the blue to introduce herself. The rest was history.

"I love you," I whispered.

"I love you too," she said, pulling away. "Get some sleep."

I wandered down the hall and made my way to our shitty bathroom. It was painted and tiled in pink. There was rust in the sink and a perpetual colony of mold growing in the caulking around the bath, and if we weren't careful, the medicine cabinet would fall out of the wall, but at least the water was hot.

And I mean scalding.

I looked in the mirror.

I was pale, though the light in this room always made my olive skin look more yellow. My face was smeared with black from my liner and mascara, and my eyes were bloodshot. I looked just about as bad as I felt.

I pulled my hair back and turned on the faucet to wash my face. I let the water pool between my hands until it was warm and splashed my face before massaging cleanser into my skin. I already felt better. Like I was washing away everything that had gone wrong today.

I started to rinse my face when I noticed the water running red.

A tingling sensation spread throughout my body, erupting in my chest. I couldn't breathe, and the edges of my vision blurred, tinged with the same shade of red.

I was going to die in this shitty pink bathroom.

I snatched a towel from the bar and blotted my face as I straightened and peered into the mirror, but there was no sign of blood.

The panic that had filled me so suddenly vanished.

I took a deep breath and let my head fall back. I kept my eyes closed for a moment before opening them to stare at the square fluorescent light in the middle of the room.

What the fuck was wrong with me?

I looked in the mirror again. The woman who stared back was fucking tired.

I threw my towel into the sink and returned to my bedroom. I stripped out of my damp clothes and pulled on a dry tank top and underwear before I threw my coat off the bed and searched my bag for my phone, tossing the heels I'd worn for Zahariev to the floor.

My face flushed at the memory. I was going to have to do some work on those pesky feelings.

Finally, I found my phone at the bottom of my bag. There were several missed calls and texts from Coco, one from my dad.

It was a picture of an invitation to my mother's gala.

The Leviathan family invites you to enjoy a dazzling night beneath the stars.

I rolled my eyes. There were no visible stars in Hiram, but knowing my mother, she'd find a way to have them, even if it meant turning off every streetlight in the city.

125

I plugged my phone in and threw my bag on the floor, freezing at the sight of the dagger on my bed. The rubies in the hilt gleamed beneath my dim lamplight like little eyes, their color matching the bloodstained blade.

I thought Zahariev had said he couldn't find it.

What the fuck was it doing here?

I reached for it but hesitated. It radiated with the same energy that had drawn me the first time, only now I felt...afraid. Whatever power it contained, clearly, it was dangerous. It had killed four people. I was counting Burke and Koval among the dead. I didn't believe they'd returned to Nineveh to assassinate me. At least not by choice.

This blade was capable of possession, and it liked to send me into the desert, a place I wasn't keen to revisit.

"What am I supposed to do with you?" I muttered, as if it might tell me.

I considered calling Zahariev, but I was so fucking tired.

I retrieved a shirt from my floor and took the blade by the hilt.

Opening my nightstand, I dropped it into the drawer and slammed it shut. I'd deal with it tomorrow.

Today.

Whatever.

I needed some fucking sleep.

———

When I surfaced from slumber, my head was pulsing, like my brain had developed a heartbeat. I kept my eyes shut, squeezing them tight when the pain sharpened. Someone could take a knife to my eyeballs, and that would literally feel better than this.

I lay there for a while before gathering the courage to open my eyes. My room was dark, not a hint of light filtering in from the window near my bed. I checked the time on my phone.

It was 4:00 p.m.

I had a few texts, one from Esther and Gabriel asking if I was okay and if I needed anything and one from Coco saying she was headed to work and that she left food in the microwave. My heart squeezed. I'd never had friends in Hiram, not real ones anyway. From a young age, my father had taught me the power of my name.

You will never need an introduction, but you will need discretion, he would say.

When I started to attend social engagements, my father would stand with me in the shadows and tell me whom to befriend among the elite—high-ranking church officials, philanthropists, and a few favorable members of the five families. Zahariev was not among them, yet he was the only one who held my attention.

At first, it was because he looked different from the rest of us. He seemed more mysterious, and I wanted to know his secrets. As I got older, it was because he was hot.

What can I say? I was young, and he was an older man. I watched others watch him too and knew I wasn't the only one feeling the effects of his attractiveness.

One night at sixteen, after my father had set me free, I ignored his instruction to befriend the daughters of Viridian and kept an eye on Zahariev. That was how I knew he'd left the party and wandered to the cemetery behind my house.

"You following me, little one?" he asked as I stepped past a massive headstone.

I whirled to face him. He was lighting a cigarette, the flame igniting the contours of his face.

He'd made me feel things I never had before. They were all forbidden desires, not only because of his name but also his age.

"I thought maybe you were going somewhere a little more fun," I said.

He expelled a stream of smoke and looked off into the darkness of the graveyard. "I just came to commune with the dead," he said.

"Did you really?" I asked, instantly intrigued by the idea, probably because Archbishop Lisk had spent several sermons declaring the practice of channeling and anything associated with speaking to the dead to be blasphemous. This was after he'd executed several women for witchcraft.

Those who commune with spirits commune with demons. The archbishop preached on it often, always wanting to be very clear about what made the Elohai different from witches. Mainly, it was blood. Elohai were gifted magic from God, while witches learned magic by studying craft created by demonic forces.

I'd always wanted to know who these demonic forces were. Where had they sourced the knowledge that allowed everyday people to harness magic if not from God?

I'd never asked those questions though. By that time, I had decided the consequences of questioning the church weren't worth the punishment.

Zahariev chuckled. I guessed he was amused by my interest in the occult. I blushed, both embarrassed and disappointed that he'd been joking. I crossed my arms over my chest, suddenly cold.

"Your old man give you the talk?" he asked.

"The talk?"

"Who's your friend, who's not," he said. As he spoke, smoke poured from his mouth.

My eyes widened a little. "How did you know?"

His smile didn't waver. "It's a rite of passage," he said. "Ten bucks says I'm not on his list."

I hesitated, and his smile widened. He didn't need an answer from me.

I rubbed my arms. "It's stupid," I said. "I don't want fake friends."

"Then don't make them," he said.

I have to, I wanted to say. It wasn't a suggestion; it was an order. But I stopped myself. "You said you had the same talk? Was I on your father's list?"

Zahariev dropped his cigarette, grinding it into the earth with his foot. He took a few steps toward me. At the time, holding his gaze as he approached had been the bravest thing I'd ever done.

"Yeah," he said. "You were on a list. Untouchable."

I'd taken Zahariev's advice.

I didn't make fake friends, which was why I had none at all until I came to Nineveh, the only place in the whole of Eden where anyone was *real*.

I replied to Gabriel, Esther, and Coco, letting them know I was okay, before heading into the kitchen. I filled a glass with water and downed it before filling it again and taking it into the bathroom where I popped a handful of pain meds into my mouth and turned on the faucet. When the water was hot, I showered.

I thought I would feel better, and I did physically, but I couldn't shake the awareness of that fucking blade. I could feel its presence even stashed away in the top of my bedside drawer. Its magic reached for me, curling around my body like the cold, clammy body of a snake. It made me feel stretched thin, like if I didn't take hold of it, I would never be whole again. It was a trick. For whatever reason, it wanted me back in that desert.

I had to get rid of it, and I was going to put it in a place where no one would ever find it.

Freshly showered, I got dressed in dark jeans, a black tank, and my favorite leather jacket, which hid the gun I kept clipped at my waist. I went into Coco's room and searched through her closet until I found what I was looking for: a small backpack she used to carry. I wrapped the dagger in the same shirt I'd used to pick it up last night and put it in the bag. As I shouldered it, it felt heavier than I expected.

I realized it sounded a little absurd, but I thought it knew my intentions. I was further convinced as I headed out into the night, pausing on the top step. For the briefest moment, a sense of dread overwhelmed me. The night felt...*off*, but then it was Sunday, and Nineveh always felt different on Sunday. The crits were gone, having returned to their respective districts, leaving behind a quiet stillness.

It unnerved me, and I almost turned around, but that was what the blade wanted. Its weight had the opposite effect it intended, reminding me I had a greater task ahead. Getting rid of this blade was more important, more pressing than the unfavorable feeling of the night's energy, so I sucked it up and headed down Sinners' Row, which was alight with flashing neon, beckoning in colorful hues of pink, purple, and blue. Few would answer the call tonight and even fewer tomorrow.

Still, Coco worked.

If the girls weren't dancing for customers, they were dancing for Hassenaah.

I might have known what that was like if I hadn't hit my fucking head, and I might not have hit my head if it hadn't been for this fucking blade.

I tightened my hold on the straps of the backpack. It wasn't unusual to be robbed on these streets. The locals typically targeted crits, but I wasn't about to let my guard down.

That's when you become prey, got it? I heard Zahariev's voice in my head, felt his fist in my hair. That was how he'd driven the point home the last time I'd been mugged.

It was probably the hottest thing that had ever happened between us, but I had also understood the warning. From then on, I'd been much more aware of my surroundings and how I carried my belongings. I hadn't been robbed since, and I wouldn't be tonight, especially when I was on my way to rid myself of this fucking blade.

It had irrevocably disrupted my life.

I would never forget seeing Abram die.

I would never forget shooting Burke dead.

And those goddamn nightmares.

I shivered.

I could still feel the wind roaring around me and the sand clawing at my skin. I could feel the tremor of fear in my chest, like every bone was rattling as my eyes teared up with blood.

Maybe if this blade was far enough away, lost somewhere in the depths of the Kurari Sea, all this would end.

I continued down Sinners' Row and cut through Southgate Cemetery to the canal bridge. Beneath, water flowed from the sea into the Nara-Sin Desert. Its creation had been a massive undertaking and happened to be the legacy of my great-great-great-grandfather and the other heads of the five families. They wanted to dig a canal through to the other side of the desert, thinking that a sustainable water supply would mean a better chance at survival as they sent men to mine the desert for minerals and oil.

Eventually, they succeeded, but only after a few hundred died building it.

The irony was that the canal, a resource that had made the five families rich, ran close to what the church described as the root of sin. On the other side of the bridge, carved into the mountainside, was the Seventh Gate. It was said that the evil of the world was trapped behind it, tangled in the roots. The gate itself was massive, a great work of stone the color of blood. Intricate mosaics of twisted serpents were inlaid around the archway in black, and the double doors were sealed with magic.

Or so the *Book of Splendor* said.

Who really knew what was behind them?

I looked all around as I unshouldered the backpack to make sure I was alone before I climbed onto the top of the stone barrier. I took out the dagger, slid it through an opening in the chain-link fence, and let it drop. The blade glimmered before it was swallowed by darkness. I knew it hit the water when I heard a quiet splash.

I imagined it sinking to the very bottom of the canal where it would be swept away, never to be seen again. The tightness in my chest eased.

I jumped down from the ledge.

As my feet touched the ground, a chill slithered up my spine.

It was colder near the mountains, but there was also something unsettling about being within their shadow. I turned to look at the menacing peaks, their angles highlighted red from the light of Nineveh, reminding me of the edge of burning paper.

The night was quiet. I held my breath and listened, seeking an echoing strike from the other side of the gates, but there was nothing save the whistling wind and the burbling canal.

As I released my breath, a flush crept across my cheeks.

I felt silly, though no one was here to witness me as I entertained Tori's ramblings.

I turned on my heels and left.

I considered dropping by Sons of Adam for mozzarella sticks before heading home. My stomach growled at the idea, but the trek would take me across town, and I'd also have to pass Raphael's Relics. I wasn't sure I was ready for that, though I wondered what had become of the merchant's shop. Had Zahariev hired someone to take Abram's place? That was what he would have done if the shopkeeper was executed under his orders. I'd seen it more than once—here in Nineveh and in Hiram.

In the end, the ache at the back of my skull outweighed my curiosity, and I headed north up Procession Street.

I expected to feel a little more at ease on my return without the burden of the blade, but for some reason, I felt even more unnerved. The energy felt unstable, almost violent.

I quickened my pace, eager to put a wall between myself and the outside world, but as I came to pass the first few clubs at the start of Sinners' Row, I paused.

A beanie lay discarded on the ground. I bent to pick it up, recognizing it as Tori's.

Then I glanced down the alleyway and saw four men, their silhouettes dark against the electrified light of the street. They stood in a circle around another figure who lay on the ground, curled into a fetal position.

It had to be Tori.

"Hey, fuckers!" I screamed and charged toward them. "Leave him alone!"

The men turned, and when they saw me, they laughed.

"Keep walking, pretty girl. This ain't about you," said one.

"Is this some dick-measuring contest? You get off on hurting those less fortunate than you? Does it make you feel big?"

They scowled. "We got orders, lady. Now fuck off."

"Orders from who? I know they didn't come from Zahariev."

And if he knew this was happening right outside his club, he'd have all four killed and sent through the wood chipper.

One man stepped toward me, and I drew my gun. He held up his hands.

"Now, now," he said. "Don't get trigger-happy. We're just doing the Lord's work."

Gabriel used that term when he was carrying out Zahariev's will.

"Are you telling me you're here on another family's orders?" I asked.

The man laughed, but there was an incredulous note to it, like he couldn't believe he was dealing with me.

"What are you? Some kind of morality police?" asked one.

"You're hurting my friend," I said. "And you don't belong here. Get the *fuck* out of my district."

"Put the gun down, sweetheart."

The voice came from behind me. I turned toward the

134

sound and came face-to-face with the barrel of a gun. Reluctantly, I dropped my own.

Fuck.

Where had he come from?

"Kick it to my buddies over there, will ya?" he asked.

My eyes shifted from the man to my gun. Technically, it wasn't my only weapon. I had magic, but none of these men were feeling frisky, so I had no way to control them.

Reluctantly, I did as he asked, watching as my only weapon skidded across the pavement. One of the four men picked it up.

"Good girl," the man behind me said, and then his clammy hand came down on the back of my neck. He pressed hard, and I scrunched my shoulders to ease the pain. It might not have been so bad had I not hit my head last night. "Is it done?" he asked the other four.

To my horror, the man who had picked up my gun aimed it at Tori and pulled the trigger. The impact of the bullet jarred his body. I screamed, but then the man's hand clamped down hard over my mouth. I hated the feel of his coarse palm against my lips. I would have bitten him if it weren't for the gun pressed into my back.

"Move," he ordered, and I obeyed.

His rough hand slipped from my mouth and returned to my neck, but the gun never moved as he hurried me to a waiting SUV. The man shoved me inside and got in beside me. The other four men piled into the vehicle, and before the doors could close, the driver gunned it, speeding down Procession Street and out of Nineveh.

"Where are you taking me?" I asked.

"You asked who sent us," one of the men said. "We'll introduce you."

"Bag her," said the man beside me.

A second later, my world went dark as one man slipped something over my head. My hands weren't bound, but the gun was still shoved into my side, so I didn't move. I wasn't exactly afraid but angry and eager to get wherever these fuckers were taking me. If they were working for one of the families, they'd get a huge surprise when they unmasked me, and I wanted to watch the fallout.

Someone turned on the radio to fill the silence. A few minutes into the song, one started singing. Then another joined and another until they were all bellowing around me.

"For fuck's sake," I muttered.

This felt like a prank, except there was nothing funny about how Tori had died.

I curled my fingers into fists, my anger making me sweat. I didn't understand how they could all be so carefree after they'd just committed a horrible crime and against someone who was so…innocent.

I sat through two more sing-alongs before the SUV finally came to a stop.

I was relieved, tired of being squished between these two hairy men, tired of smelling my own breath, tired of being their prisoner.

The man with the gun grabbed me by the arm and dragged me from the SUV. I stumbled, disoriented, in the dark, but before I could fall, he jerked me to my feet.

"Take her bag," he ordered. "And her phone."

I wrenched away, but the man grabbed me and shoved his gun into my jaw. Hands settled on my shoulders and swept down, groping my breasts. I shoved whoever was touching me, but the man tightened his fist in my hair.

"Calm down, sweetheart. All we're gonna do is look," he said, and the two snickered.

A second later, I felt a faint, pulsing desire stir.

My stomach turned.

"The phone is in my jacket pocket," I said between gritted teeth. "On the *left*."

"Go ahead, Kane," said the man holding me.

Kane, Kane, Kane, I repeated in my head. I would remember him.

"Fucking buzzkill," Kane muttered as he slipped his hand into my pocket and retrieved my phone. The contact gave me a better impression of his lust, which felt almost… superficial. Still, I latched on and held it like a leash as I was pushed forward.

"Walk," the man ordered, keeping his hand on my neck.

The ground was flat, thankfully, so I didn't stumble, but at some point, the air changed, and I knew we'd gone inside.

"We brought you a snack, boss," said one man. I thought maybe it was Kane, but his voice sounded far away and a little echoey.

"She wanted to know who we worked for," said another. "So we thought it best to show her."

Suddenly, the hood was gone. I squinted against the light but quickly focused on the man in front of me, and my confidence was knocked out of me like a blow to the stomach.

I hadn't been taken to one of the families.

I'd been taken to Archbishop Alarich Lisk.

My stomach churned, stirring the anxiety that had roared to life as soon as I met his watery blue eyes. I couldn't look at him without thinking of all the terrible things he'd done to me since the moment my mom allowed him to be alone with me.

And I knew by the feel of his own lust he did too.

"Miss Leviathan."

I clenched my teeth as his voice slithered over me. I loathed the way he said my name, with cold judgment. I felt words building up in the back of my throat. They tasted like venom. I wanted to poison him with the same feelings he'd injected into me—guilt and shame and embarrassment—but that wish was futile.

Archbishop Lisk did not feel.

He was a fucking sociopath.

"She interrupted our justice," said one man. "She called the dissenter a friend."

I glared at the one who spoke, a man with short, blond hair and a beard. I tried my best to commit his face to memory, though it was hard to retain anything when I stood in front of the man who had abused me for most of my life.

I knew what I should do.

I should inject my magic into his veins. I should instruct him to cut off his penis and swallow it whole so I could watch him choke to death. Then I would finally know what it meant to feel safe.

Except facing him now, it was as if my power had frozen in my veins, unwilling to mingle with the sickening energy of his lust.

I ground my teeth so hard, my jaw hurt. I hated him in a way that made me want to crumble, but I wanted to hate him in a way that made me rage.

"Tori was harmless," I said, my mouth trembling. I didn't know if it was because I'd watched him die or fear of Lisk.

"You believe it is harmless to speak out against the church?" Lisk asked. His voice sounded thick, like he had spit in the back of his throat. My stomach turned.

"He was *ill*," I argued.

Nothing he ever said made any sense.

"Any dissenter, whether of sound mind or not, can gain a following," said Lisk. "It is a risk the church will not take. I would think of all my pupils, you would understand that best."

A wave of nausea curled through me as memories of his *instruction* surfaced. I could still feel the raw sting of his ruler against my fingers, urging me to write faster. At some point, he decided I needed a different sort of punishment. He'd made me lift my skirt so he could swat me, which evolved into pulling my underwear down, which evolved into him jerking off and ejaculating on my exposed behind.

I fucking hated this man.

"If you had a problem, you should have gone to Zahariev," I said. "Nineveh is his territory."

"That's funny," said one of the men. He had a head of dark, curly hair. "Didn't you say it was yours? When you told us to get the *fuck* out of *your* district?"

I glared at him in the silence that followed.

Lisk took a few steps toward me, and I bristled as goose bumps rose on every inch of my skin.

"I think you have forgotten that my power exceeds that of the families," said Lisk. "Do not forget that you have been allowed this rebellious streak. It is a privilege granted to you by *me*. Your father bought you another year, but your time is up, Miss Leviathan. Return to your family, or there will be consequences."

I held my breath and glared at him, eyes blurring with tears. I hoped he couldn't tell. I hated how I wilted before him.

Lisk's gaze shifted to the man beside me.

"Take her back to where you found her," he ordered.

139

I tensed as the man tightened his hold, preparing to drag me to the car, when Lisk added, "And, Lilith. Let this be a reminder that not even Zahariev can protect you."

ZAHARIEV

"Your girl is bad luck," said Cassius, expelling a stream of smoke from his mouth.

I ignored him, staring at the three new additions to my morgue.

Jonathan Koval. Joseph Burke. Esli Reed, the driver.

This wasn't luck, good or bad. It was something else.

A sickness had taken root in my city, and it had started with that fucking blade.

The doors swung open behind us as Dr. Mor strolled into the room wearing a white coat.

"Good evening, boys," he said in a chipper tone as he strolled to the wall and pulled a couple of gloves from the box on the wall.

"Evenin', doc," said Cassius.

"Put it out," Dr. Mor said, leveling a stern look over his glasses at Cassius, who turned a little red. He moved toward the sink to wet the end of his cigarette. "You know better."

I chuckled but quickly choked on my laugh when the doctor looked at me, disapproving.

"What? I didn't do anything!"

"Exactly," said Dr. Mor. "You're the oldest. You're supposed to keep him in line."

There was definitely a downside to employing a man who'd known me his entire life, and that was the ease with which he parented me.

Cassius snickered, but his expression quickly fell when we both glared at him.

"*As I said on the phone*," Dr. Mor began, directing our attention to the bodies. He snapped his gloves in place as he approached. "Cause of death is apparent, but there is something I wanted you to see."

Dr. Mor pulled back one white sheet, revealing a purple-tinged Burke. A thread of anger snaked through me, and my jaw

clenched. I was eager to know what motivated the enforcer to attack Lilith but also eager to confront Lisk.

The archbishop had given me something to hang over his head, though I didn't think he was aware just yet, but it was clear to me that the dagger Lilith had come into possession of had been in the care of the church.

Dr. Mor drew a pen from the pocket of his white coat and pointed to Burke's discolored mouth.

"This pinkish-purple coloring," he said. "It is a sort of jellylike substance. During his autopsy, it oozed from every orifice. I took a sample, but don't expect results for a few weeks."

"What do you think it is?"

"No clue," said Dr. Mor. "I have never seen anything like it, but I do wonder if it was some kind of magic. Maybe a curse."

For a second, I thought Lilith might be responsible. Maybe she'd used her magic during the scuffle, but I didn't know a single Elohai whose magic had this sort of effect.

"Call me when you have an update," I

said, then looked at Cassius. "Find someone to notify Reed's family of his death."

"What about the other two?"

"They're gonna take a little field trip up north," I said.

L isk's men didn't take me back to where they found me. They dropped me off at the border of Nineveh, beneath the judging eyes of the archangel Zerachiel. Suddenly, all the work I'd done to become a different person—the woman I wanted to be—was useless. Faced with my abuser, I'd become that same scared girl who'd run away from home two years ago.

I pulled my jacket tight around me and started walking.

I wasn't really aware of how I got home. My feet just carried me in that direction while my mind went blank, incapable of thought, crippled by a sense of dread. For a long time, I didn't know what it was like to wake up without anxiety or fear. Those feelings ravaged me now.

When I made it within sight of my apartment complex, I spotted a familiar SUV. Zahariev leaned against its passenger side door. When he saw me, he straightened and threw his cigarette to the ground.

"You're a piece of work, little love," he said. "Don't you ever do what you're told?"

I burst into tears.

I hated crying, but I hated crying in front of Zahariev more.

I covered my face with my hands. I wanted to hide, but there was nowhere to go. Zahariev pulled me close. My fingers twisted into his shirt as my body shook. All the while, I heard my mother's voice in my head, ordering me to stop.

Push it down. There is power in never letting the world know how you feel.

She had never questioned the source of my pain. I used to wonder if she knew but didn't want to face it or thought, in some twisted way, that it might put me on the right track. *Her* track.

As much as I despised her words, I tried to listen. I didn't want to be like this right now. There were other, more important things to deal with.

Like Tori.

Zahariev's hand slid up my back, toward my neck.

"Don't!" I said, shoving away from him. The sudden panic had made me shaky, but I could still feel that man's fingers pressing into my skin.

Zahariev stared at me, eyes wide, mouth agape. After a second, he composed himself and took a few careful steps toward me. He lifted his hands slowly until he held my face between them. His thumb brushed over my cheek.

"What happened?" he asked.

My eyes welled with tears.

"They killed him," I said. "They shot Tori."

A guttural sob tore from my throat.

"Where?" he asked.

"In the alley, at the end of Sinners' Row."

He started to turn, but I reached for his hand. He halted and looked at me.

"Don't leave me," I said, mouth trembling. "Please."

I didn't want to be alone, and Coco wouldn't be home for a while.

"I'm not going anywhere," he said.

He knocked on the passenger door of his vehicle. "Get Cassius on the phone," he said to Felix. "Tell him he needs to get down to Sinners,…"

He looked at me for more direction.

"He's in the alley, between Angel and Reverence," I said.

"Angel and Reverence," he repeated, though I was sure Felix had heard me. "There's been an incident."

Zahariev turned to me and reached for my hand, sliding his fingers between mine. He pulled me along, up the stairs to my apartment door before turning to me. I realized he expected me to unlock the door.

"I…I don't have my key," I said. "They took it and my phone."

Zahariev's mouth hardened before he drove his foot into the door. The wood near the lock and handle splintered as it flew open and hit the wall.

I stared at him, and he gestured for me to go inside. I obeyed, watching as he closed the door and slid the chain into place. It was the only thing keeping it closed.

Zahariev pulled out his phone and sent a quick text before meeting my gaze. I stood in the middle of the room, arms wrapped around myself. I didn't know what to do.

"You'll have a new door before I leave," he said.

"If they access my phone, they will see my texts," I said. "They'll know about…everything."

The knife. The rent. My nickname. They would assume the worst.

"I'll take care of it," he said, and then his gaze dropped to my neck. He pushed my hair away, fingers dancing over a sore spot on my skin.

"I tried to fight back," I said, feeling embarrassed. "But he had a gun."

"Who had a gun?" he asked.

"I don't know his name," I said. "There were four of them, but only one was named. Kane. They work for Archbishop Lisk."

Zahariev's expression hardened.

"Did he hurt you?" Zahariev asked.

I swallowed, unable to clear the thickness in my throat. When I finally answered, my voice was nothing but a whisper. "Not tonight."

I'd never told Zahariev exactly what Lisk had done to me, but my reply said enough. I was thankful he didn't ask questions, and to avoid the possibility, I explained what happened tonight, leaving out the part where I took the blade to the canal. I told him about the men, how they'd shot Tori with my gun, the ride to see their boss, and Lisk's warning.

"Maybe I was stupid to think I could escape my name," I said after a long, miserable pause.

"Someone always has to be first," said Zahariev.

"Being first won't matter if I'm dead," I said.

"No one's going to touch you," said Zahariev.

He didn't say it, but I knew what he was thinking—*and if you had listened to me, no one would have done so tonight.*

"What are you going to do?" I asked.

"What do you want me to do?" he asked.

"I want you to find those men. I want justice."

"For you or for Tori?" he asked.

"Why not for both of us?" I asked.

He studied me in the quiet that followed and then lifted his hand, looping a stray piece of my hair around his finger as he brushed it from my face.

"They won't survive the week," he said.

I shivered despite the warmth of his touch. Those were hands that had killed countless times. I rarely thought about it, but tonight I couldn't escape it, because I'd just ordered the murders of four men.

But what disturbed me most was that I didn't feel an ounce of remorse about it.

"Lisk has to know you will come for his men," I said.

"I imagine he does," said Zahariev. "You are assuming he cares."

"You won't get in trouble, will you?"

He chuckled.

"I guess that was a silly question," I said as heat rushed to my face. "You are the definition of trouble."

His smile widened. "You aren't wrong," he said. "But I appreciate the concern."

There was a knock at the door.

I froze for an instant and hated my reaction. I'd never been afraid to answer my door, but that was before I'd had my gun taken away.

"It's just the carpenter," Zahariev said.

I let my breath escape slowly between my lips before I met his gaze. "I'm going to shower. I need…"

I needed to wash away the feel of those men, but something about saying it out loud felt like admitting that I'd failed, and though it wasn't true, I couldn't stop blaming myself.

"Don't leave," I whispered.

"Wasn't thinking about it," he said.

As I retreated to my bedroom, I slipped out of my jacket and left it on my bed before grabbing a set of clothes to change into. I glanced toward the living room as I returned to the bathroom. Zahariev had taken off his jacket and rolled up the sleeves of his button-down. He was on the phone, rubbing his forehead with his thumb and forefinger like he had a headache.

Or like *I* was his headache.

It was probably the latter.

I disappeared into the bathroom and turned on the shower. As the water warmed, I undressed and inspected my body. I checked my neck first, where Zahariev had noticed something wrong, and found red marks in the shape of fingertips. They were also on my arm—five perfect ovals, dark in color. They would be bruises by tomorrow.

I felt around my ribs where the gun had been jabbed into my side. There was no mark, but the area was sore.

As my hands passed over my skin, I was reminded of how those men had handled me, how Kane had touched me and kindled his lust. I thought about how they had brought me before my first abuser, and suddenly I felt like I was shaking from the inside out, and a terror I had buried long ago roared to life.

I climbed into the shower, body vibrating, and scrubbed myself until all I could feel or focus on was the stinging pain of raw skin. I didn't know how many times I washed and rinsed, but at some point, Zahariev knocked on the door.

"You okay?" he asked.

I could feel the thickness gathering in the back of my throat, the tears welling in my eyes. I tried to swallow the feelings so he wouldn't be able to tell I was breaking down, but when I spoke, my voice was still hoarse.

"I'm fine."

There was a pause. "Do you need me?"

His question broke me, tore open my chest, and brought me to the floor. I slid to the bottom of the tub, drew my knees to my chest, and sobbed.

"Lilith?"

There was another pause, and then I heard Zahariev open the door. I got to my feet and pushed the curtain aside. I fell into him, and he caught me as I wrapped my arms and legs around him, clinging to him like I never had before.

"I've got you," he said, his voice a fervent whisper.

I believed him. I knew him.

He was constant.

For a few brief moments, I felt out of control, shaking as each guttural sob rippled from the most damaged parts of me.

And then it was over, like a tap had been turned off.

Maybe I had nothing left. I wasn't really sure.

In the aftermath, I became aware of myself, the way I'd wound my wet and naked body around Zahariev, but I didn't have the energy to be embarrassed.

"I'm sorry," I whispered.

"Don't be sorry," he said. "Better?"

I nodded before pulling away, and Zahariev let me slide to the ground. I wrapped my arms around myself, not to hide but because I was cold. Zahariev handed me a towel.

"I'll wait outside," he said.

Once I was alone, I turned off the shower, dried, and got dressed.

When I left the bathroom, I found Zahariev sitting on the

151

edge of my bed. He was shirtless, the sound of our shrieking dryer filling the apartment.

"It's probably going to take three hours for your clothes to dry," I said.

"I don't have anywhere to be," he said.

"You're a liar, Zahariev," I said.

"If you say so, little love." A brief smile touched his lips, but then his eyes shifted, narrowing on my arm. He had spotted my other injuries. I tried to cover it as I approached and crawled into bed. Zahariev didn't move, but he also wasn't looking at me. His jaw was popping, his anger renewed.

"Are you going to tell my father?" I asked.

"No," he said, his voice quiet. "But he'll find out... eventually."

My stomach churned at the thought, and I rolled onto my side, curling into myself. I felt Zahariev's eyes on me, and after a moment, he reached to turn off the lamp. I thought he was going to leave, but then he stretched out beside me.

We didn't speak. We didn't touch.

The silence thickened the air between us. I was on edge, my skin tingling. I couldn't decide why I felt this way. Maybe it was because in all the time we'd known each other, I'd never been this vulnerable with him before.

Or maybe it was because I wanted him to touch me.

Not in a sexual way. I just wanted to be held by someone who actually cared.

My skin was on fire, burning from the embarrassment of what I wanted to ask.

I took a breath but lost my nerve and stayed silent.

"What's wrong?" Zahariev asked.

"Nothing," I said.

"And you say I am a terrible liar," he replied, but even in the dark, I could tell he was amused.

I didn't argue, silent for only a few seconds before I finally asked.

"Will you...hold me? I just..."

My words dried up. I didn't really know how to explain why I wanted this. I just did. I needed it.

Zahariev was quiet, but I could feel his gaze.

"You don't have to ask," he said.

I shifted closer to him, and as I rested my head on his chest, he wrapped his arm around me. His other hand closed over mine.

"Is this all right?" he asked. There was a breathy edge to his voice, like the words had come from some unfamiliar place inside him.

"Yeah," I said, pausing before I whispered, "Thank you."

He didn't speak, but beneath me, he felt tense, building a wall between himself and my gratitude.

I could hear the words he didn't speak—*don't thank me.* They were words he'd said hundreds of times.

I'm not just saying it, I'd said, recognizing that the expression had little meaning given our backgrounds. All our lives, we'd been taught to express thanks—to our parents, to the church, to God, none of which had given me a fraction of what Zahariev had.

I know, but I don't need it. Not from you.

I didn't understand then, and I didn't understand now, but I still felt like it was important to say it.

Zahariev's warmth eased the tension in my body. I pressed the palm of my hand harder against his chest so I could feel the beat of his heart and relaxed against him, my eyes growing heavy.

"Did Cassius find Tori?"

"He did," Zahariev confirmed.

"He never hurt anyone," I said, whispering now. I was so tired.

"It wasn't about hurting anyone," said Zahariev. "It was about what he said."

"Everyone knows what he preached was nonsense," I said.

I expected him to agree, but even his silence felt conflicted.

"Zahariev?" I lifted my head to look at him, even though it was too dark to make out much of his expression.

"Maybe it isn't nonsense at all," he said.

"What are you saying?"

Zahariev's answer was to brush his fingers through my hair, the way he so often did.

"Nothing," he said, letting his hand drop, taking his warmth. "Go to sleep, Lilith."

His voice had changed. He had retreated into his icy shell again. I just didn't understand why. I shifted closer, trying to regain some of that heat, grateful when his hold tightened, except that I could still feel the distance between us, like our bodies were made up of uneven edges.

We no longer fit together.

———————

I dragged my feet over the dusty ground, inching my way through the darkness of the cave. Behind me, the desert roared, mourning the loss of my bones. I could not call this place a shelter. I had traded cutting sand for cutting stones. My body bled. There was something in the air, a scent that smelled slightly sulfuric. I could barely breathe, too afraid to fill my lungs with whatever dark essence haunted these high caverns, yet I kept going.

The air grew colder as I descended. I shook so hard, I felt like the earth was vibrating beneath me. Still I continued, crawling over jagged pillars and squeezing between narrow gaps in the rocky formations that barred my way…to what, I didn't know.

But there was something here, and it called to me.

She called to me. Her words lingered like cold tendrils of air, shivering down my spine.

Dark mother,
Reverent queen,
Wear your darkness like a shroud.
Make your descent through crimson caves,
Coil at their tangled roots.
Drink sweetly from the grail,
The holy blood, the venom, the ecstasy of night.
Awaken the sacred fire and rise to strike,
Unleash your fury, your eternal wail.
Break these chains, these binding gates.

I took a step and felt something tap my ankle. It was like I'd passed by a branch or twig, or maybe I'd kicked up a rock. I kept walking and felt it again, higher this time. I reached to brush my leg when something latched on to my hand, and a cold, clammy serpent coiled around my arm. I screamed, seizing the creature. Its venomous fangs shredded my skin as I jerked it free and threw it into the dark.

I staggered, holding my arm to my chest, and then sank to the ground, paralyzed by a burning pain that set my blood on fire, shattering everything inside me.

Then I felt the serpent's fangs sink into my skin again. It had returned, and my pain turned to rage. My fingers brushed the edge of a nearby rock, and I reached for it. Lifting it over my head, I brought it down upon the serpent, crushing it again and again and again.

It writhed, agonized by each blow, yet I did not stop. I couldn't. I was no longer tethered to my body but standing outside myself, a spirit who had abandoned humanity.

I put all my strength behind my final strike, and my arms trembled with the impact. I released the rock, letting it remain atop the serpent, and fell back. My breathing came in shallow gasps, perspiration beaded off my body, my arms hurt—all of me *hurt*.

My vision blurred, and suddenly, the bloody remains of the serpent were gone.

I had taken its place, and embedded deep in my chest was a gold and gleaming blade.

—————

I woke up on a gasp, rising into a sitting position, clutching at my chest. I inhaled air like I'd just been given life for the first time. My lungs were burning, my heart was racing, and my entire body *ached*.

I twisted onto my side and turned on my lamp, opening the drawer to my bedside table, half afraid I'd find the blade, despite having thrown it into the canal.

A cold wave of relief flooded through me when all I discovered was a tangle of charging cords.

I shut the drawer and shoved my fingers through my still-damp hair.

Zahariev was gone.

I wondered when he'd left.

Rising to my feet, I started to reach for my phone to

check the time when I remembered I didn't have it anymore. My stomach flipped at the thought of Lisk having access to my messages. They weren't overly incriminating, though my exchanges with Zahariev were always flirtatious. If the archbishop decided to share them with my father, I was going to have a hard time convincing him nothing was going on between us.

Thank fuck I'd never sent nudes.

Not with that phone at least.

And never to Zahariev, though after last night, I couldn't say that he had never seen me naked. It didn't matter that it had nothing to do with sex. If my father found out, Zahariev was a dead man.

Except he'd known that, and he'd stayed anyway.

A warm flush crept into my cheeks, and my heart beat a little harder. I'd never been so vulnerable with another person before. I felt a collision of emotions inside me, a heady embarrassment I wasn't sure I liked.

I took a breath and exhaled, tilting my head toward the ceiling. For a few seconds, my embattled emotions vanished, returning with a vengeance when I thought about everything that had happened last night, particularly the way Zahariev had just...*been there*. He had cared enough to check on me, cared enough to hold me, cared enough to stay with me until he was sure I wouldn't be alone. Now all I could think about was how solid he'd felt against me, how warm his skin had been against mine, how good he'd smelled, bold but sweet. I couldn't place it. I just knew I liked it.

And I hated that I liked it.

It wasn't like I'd never thought about kissing Zahariev. I had. *Look* at him. He was hot. Everyone I'd grown up with wondered what it would be like to fuck him. Some of them had. I knew because the women who had made it into his bed told me how good he was.

I hated that too.

But I hated the jealousy that ravaged my insides more.

The problem was Zahariev wasn't for me because I wasn't for him.

Untouchable.

That was my list, and this? It was just the remnants of my schoolgirl crush, surfacing in the aftermath of a night that had made me feel like a child again.

I left my bedroom to use the bathroom. The nightmare left me feeling like I was covered in a layer of silt. I washed my face, noticing the water in the sink turning brown.

For a moment, I thought it was coming from the faucet, but as I cupped my hands beneath the stream, the water was clear. I frowned and then ran my wet hand over my forearm, feeling sand grind against my palm as brown droplets fell to my pink tiled floor.

I looked in the mirror and dragged the same hand over my chest. My fingers left paler slashes in the dust on my skin.

What the fuck is happening to me? I muttered.

Did I sleepwalk?

Coco had never said anything. Maybe it was a recent development. Maybe that was why I'd started having such weird dreams.

Or maybe Zahariev's boots had been really fucking dirty.

My stomach stirred. My body knew that wasn't true.

I left the bathroom to grab a set of clothes, but as I entered my room, it felt different. Like someone had been here and looked through my things. I approached my bed, each step making my heart beat faster and faster. I gripped my comforter, noticing the sand on my sheets, and dragged it to the floor.

There, gemstones gleamed in a golden hilt, its blade buried deep in the springs of my mattress.

ZAHARIEV

I waited until Colette was in the shower to leave.

I didn't want to startle her or have to explain why I was here. I'd leave that up to Lilith.

I pulled my shirt from their shitty dryer and slipped it on, not bothering to button it up. The sleeves stuck to my arms, still damp.

As I left the apartment, my phone vibrated in my pocket. I waited until I'd cleared the steps to take it, lighting a cigarette as I went.

"Yeah?" I answered, crossing the parking lot.

Felix was still waiting.

"You got a present," said Cassius. "Want me to open it?"

"Five minutes," I answered.

I hung up and climbed into the passenger seat.

"What the fuck are you listening to?" I asked.

Felix turned the music down. "It's orchestral. Keeps me awake."

I looked at him with a raised brow. "You're a fucking monster, Felix."

He chuckled, but it grew quiet quickly.

"Where to?" he asked.

"Home," I said. "Cassius got me a gift."

I sat in the living room, cocooned in a blanket. I'd turned on the television, just to have some sort of noise in the background. That was all it was good for anyway since the church controlled the networks. I'd flipped through biblical education channels for children and reruns of Archbishop Lisk's past sermons, finally landing on the news.

After that nightmare, I didn't want to sit in silence. I hadn't even pulled the blade out of my mattress. I left it there and covered it with my blanket.

How the fuck had it gotten back to me?

I was half tempted to ask Zahariev to drag the canal, but I knew he wouldn't find a thing. I knew because I recognized the feel of this blade. I'd tasted its magic the first night I'd touched it, metallic on the back of my tongue, though it had been subtle enough then that I'd mistaken it for the tang of Ephraim's lust.

I wondered why the church was so desperate to have it back. It was possible it was only a relic, something that had belonged to some saint, but whose magic possessed the blade, and why was it killing men left and right? Why had it left me and Zahariev unharmed?

I felt as though I had two options. I could return the blade to the church myself and endear myself to Lisk by placing it right in his hands, but I didn't want his praise.

I wanted his fear.

I wanted leverage.

I wanted to know what I had, but I needed to be careful. I couldn't bring the blade to a collector or a dealer without possibly killing them. I also didn't trust anyone on Smugglers' Row to appraise it without trying to steal it or outing me to the fucking archbishop. They might hate the man, but if there was money to be made, they'd worship at his feet.

I had to find another way to get the information I needed.

"Hey, babes, are you all right?"

I startled, my head snapping up to meet Coco's gaze. She stood at the end of the hallway, her hands cupped around something small, black, and fuzzy lying against her chest.

"Sorry. I didn't mean to scare you, but you looked a little out of it."

I heard what she said, but I was too distracted. "Coco... is that a cat?"

She grinned and held her up in both hands like an offering.

"Isn't she adorable?"

"*Coco*," I groaned. "If Paul finds out, he's going to evict us."

"I thought about that," she said, kneeling on the couch and sitting back on her heels. "But I figured since Zahariev punched him in the face, he probably won't fuck with us."

I tried to stay strong in the face of the feline's innocent, copper-colored eyes.

"You know, some nights we can barely feed ourselves," I said. "How are we supposed to feed her?"

"With all the money we are going to save over the next three months now that we don't owe rent." She held the kitten up and nuzzled its nose as she spoke in a higher pitch. "Isn't that right? You can thank Uncle Z, yes, you can."

My brows rose, amused by the thought of Zahariev holding this tiny kitten and letting Coco call him uncle. I wasn't sure he even liked cats. If his household was anything like mine growing up, it was likely he was never allowed pets. My mother said dogs were too dirty and cats were too destructive. Plus, she didn't want to risk either pissing or shitting on her silk rugs.

"What did you name her?" I asked.

Coco's smile was sly, her eyes brightening with a flash of pride.

"Angel," she answered.

I almost snorted. "You can't be serious, Coco."

"What?" she asked. "Just look at her! She's small and sweet. She is an angel!"

"*Cherubs* are small and sweet," I said. "Angels are… something else."

If the statues around Eden were anything to be believed, they were terrifying, but I didn't want to voice my fear aloud.

"Then we'll call her Cherub!" Coco declared, turning her attention to the kitten. "What do you think?"

She offered a high-pitched meow in response.

"See? She likes it!"

I shook my head but couldn't help smiling. I had to admit I enjoyed seeing Coco with a pet. I also liked the idea of coming home to something, especially when Coco was still at work, but I felt guilty about allocating money to something so soon after Zahariev had gotten us out of a hole. I still wanted to work on paying him back, even though I knew he didn't expect it.

"Is she supposed to be that little?" I asked.

"She's probably the smallest of her litter," said Coco. "But she'll grow with time and lots and lots of love."

She snuggled the kitten cheek to cheek.

"Do you want to hold her?" she asked.

I was a little reluctant because she was so small.

"What if I drop her?"

"You won't drop her," said Coco. "Besides, cats are resilient. They land on their feet."

I wanted to argue that I didn't think that was always true, but Coco was already leaning toward me. I took the kitten, though it was strange to hold a living thing in the palms of my hands. I lowered her to my lap and scratched behind her soft ears. Soon she was curled up and vibrating like a little motor.

"See?" said Coco. "You're in love already."

I arched a brow at her. "Nice try."

We sat in silence for a moment before she spoke.

"So," she said, drawing out the word. "Are you going to tell me why we have a new door?"

I hesitated, pausing my rhythmic caress of Cherub's silky ears.

"Zahariev kicked it in," I said. "I lost my key."

Normally, I would tell Coco everything, but I didn't think I was emotionally stable enough to recount what happened last night without spiraling. I'd save it for another day.

When Coco didn't comment, I looked up and found her watching me. I didn't like the suspicion in her eyes.

"Do you ever wonder why Zahariev drops everything for you?"

"Coco—"

I didn't want to go down this road. I knew what she was going to suggest.

"Zahariev," she interrupted. "Zahariev *freaking* Zareth, the literal head of the most powerful family in Eden. The man probably has drugs to sell—"

"Zahariev doesn't sell drugs," I said.

"People to kill," she continued.

I didn't argue with that one.

"But you lose your *key*, and he's here to break down doors for you?"

"It was one door," I said, and it was more than a lost key, but I didn't say that. "And yes, because he made a deal with my father to watch out for me."

And Zahariev obliges because he likes leverage. I wasn't about to get it twisted.

"I've seen the way he looks at you, Lilith," said Coco.

"He looks at me because he's watching, probably to see if I'm going to steal."

Coco shook her head. "No, Lily. That man wants to fuck."

I almost laughed. "Coco, I *know* when men want to fuck me. You know what radiates from Zahariev ninety-nine percent of the time? *Annoyance.*"

"Doesn't mean that one percent isn't aroused by you," she countered. "Admit it. You've thought about fucking him."

"*Everyone's* thought about fucking him," I said.

"But have *you*?"

"Of course I have!" I said, frustrated. My face flushed.

I felt like I'd confessed some deep, dark secret, but really, I just didn't like admitting that I lusted after Zahariev out loud. I took a breath and shook my head. "I mean, *look at him*. He's fucking hot. *You've* probably thought about fucking him too."

"He's not really my type…you know, since he's a man and all."

I laughed at the way her nose wrinkled in mild disgust, easing a bit of the tension that had built up around this conversation.

Coco sighed. "I'm not trying to make you mad. I was only curious."

"I'm not mad," I said. "Trust me, I've tried to get a rise out of Zahariev. I like fucking with him. He *never* bites."

I wasn't sure what I would do if he ever did, honestly. We had known each other so long…would we remain friends, or would it tear us apart? Maybe I didn't want to find out.

"He will one day," she said. "When you want him to."

My brows lowered. *When I want him to?*

I considered asking her what she meant, but I decided I didn't want to give her any reason to continue this conversation. Coco seemed to get the hint, because she turned her attention to the television.

"What are you watching?"

I followed her gaze. It looked like some sort of children's show, but all the characters were weird hand puppets. I was about to answer that I had no clue, but a knock at the door interrupted us. We exchanged a look before she hopped from the couch.

"Speak of the devil," she said as she peered through the peephole before opening the door.

All of a sudden, my heart was racing, and I didn't know why. Zahariev had visited a million times, and I'd never had this reaction.

It's because of last night, I told myself. *A lot of things happened last night.*

"Good morning, Mr. Zareth," said Coco.

"Good morning, Miss D'Arsay," Zahariev said, his eyes connecting with mine as soon as he walked into view.

I wondered how much sleep he'd gotten. He still looked tired, but he was freshly showered.

"Good morning," he said.

"Hi," I said, though my voice sounded small and breathless. I blamed Coco for that, because now I couldn't look at Zahariev without thinking about sex.

This was a new low. I needed to get laid.

I glanced at Coco, noticing how she pressed her lips tight to keep from smiling.

"I'll just…uh…be in the bathroom," she said.

I wanted to roll my eyes but didn't, noticing Zahariev's attention had dropped to my lap where Cherub still slept. Before he could ask about her, I spoke.

"What are you doing here?"

"I brought you a gun," he said, holding up a black case. I hadn't noticed it before. It blended almost seamlessly with his long jacket. "I also brought you a phone."

He pulled the device from his pocket and handed it to me. It was new and shiny, and it made me feel anxious.

"What about my old one?" I asked.

"Disabled," he said.

I felt a little better, but there was a part of my brain that wondered if it was too late.

Zahariev set the gun case on the coffee table and then

168

stared at me. I felt like he wanted me to say something. I thought about apologizing for last night, for breaking down, for asking him to hold me, for being an inconvenience, but I knew he would reject it, and I also wasn't sorry.

"How are you feeling?" he asked.

"I'm fine," I said, probably too quickly for it to really be true.

I couldn't handle holding his gaze, so I dropped it to the fur ball in my lap. The couch dipped with Zahariev's weight.

"When did you get a cat?" he asked.

"Apparently this morning," I said. "Coco brought her home sometime last night."

"Are you keeping her?"

"I...don't know," I said, glancing at him.

He held out his hand as if to pet her but hesitated. "Can I?"

I nodded.

She was so small, he could only stroke her with the tip of his finger.

"She's beautiful," he said, meeting my gaze again.

"You like cats?"

He shrugged one shoulder. "I don't mind them."

"Do you want to hold her?" I asked, but he withdrew his hand.

"I should probably go. I have a few things to take care of today."

"Anything of interest to me?"

He knew I was asking about Tori's killers.

"Plenty," he said but didn't clarify and likely wouldn't unless I showed up at his compound, but I didn't feel the need. It was enough to have confirmation that he'd started the hunt.

Zahariev rose to his feet and paused at the door, turning to look at me.

"I gave your dad your new number," he said.

My brows lowered. "Why?"

"Because he called."

"So you're besties now?" I asked. After last night, I didn't want to be reminded that Zahariev's actions were a favor for my father.

"We're not," Zahariev said with just as much frustration in his voice. "He asked me to make sure you were scheduled to attend your mother's gala. He said you haven't responded to his request."

"So you told him what? You'd make me?"

"When have I made you do anything you don't want to?" he asked.

I looked away. I felt like a pouting child, especially when my dad tried to manipulate me through Zahariev.

I took a deep breath, trying to quell my misplaced frustration. This was why I hated feelings.

"Are you going?"

"Wouldn't miss it," he said flatly.

I appreciated the sarcasm because it meant he dreaded the event as much as I did. He was only going because he had to, just like my mother only sent him an invitation because *she* had to. We were all fucking sheep.

"I don't know why he's so persistent," I said. "He knows this is going to piss my mom off."

Zahariev shrugged. "Appearances."

"Is that why you're going?"

He didn't answer.

I scoffed, shaking my head. "You're such a fucking crit, Zahariev."

His brows rose, and the corner of his mouth lifted in a cold smile.

"You have a pretty mouth, little love, but you say the ugliest things."

His words actually hurt, but it was fair, given what I had said.

"If you decide to go, I'll take you," he continued. "Lisk will be there, and I want him to know you're with me."

"I don't think that's a good idea," I said. "What if the commission thinks you and my father made some kind of deal behind their back?"

"I don't give a *fuck* about the commission. I would think you'd understand that by now, but I guess you're too busy assuming the worst to actually fucking *listen* to me."

I stared at him, stunned by his reaction. He was *mad*.

So this is what it's like, I thought.

I went hot all over, both embarrassed but also angry. I didn't assume the worst, and I *did* listen to him, but he also quoted their fucking rules like it was the *Book of Splendor* itself, so to act like he didn't throw their judgment in my face was a *lie*.

He paused with his hand on the door, and his eyes fell to Cherub.

"Keep the cat," he said. "Learn to let someone love you."

I fumed in silence after he left, scrambling to make sense of what had just happened between us. What had he meant by *learn to let someone love you*? I let plenty of people love me. Coco. Gabriel. Esther. *He* was the one who constantly kept everyone at arm's length, *including* me.

God, I fucking hated him sometimes.

Except I knew that wasn't actually true, and right now, my stomach churned with guilt. I had gone too far. Calling

Zahariev a hypocrite was next level, and I should have known better.

I am such a fucking disaster, I thought, letting my head fall into my hands. My eyes dropped to Cherub, who was still asleep in my lap, oblivious to my turmoil.

"So," said Coco, returning to the living room, her wet hair wrapped in a towel. "Zahariev said we should keep the cat?"

I gave her a withering look. "How much did you hear?"

"Enough to know that he thinks she's beautiful," she replied. "Unless he was talking about you, to which I agree."

I sighed, though I wasn't sure what I was reacting to: Coco's eavesdropping or her comment about my appearance. I wasn't exactly irritated by either, just not surprised.

"He was definitely not talking about me," I said.

The only time Zahariev had commented on my appearance was when I'd danced for him, and that had felt more like judgment.

Oh, and just now when he'd let me know what ugly things came out of my pretty mouth.

"Do you work tonight?" I asked.

"No, but Hassenaah wants us to be at the club around six for rehearsal," she said. "She decided our routine was stale and wants to change it up."

"What?"

Coco's eyes widened a little. It was like she forgot Zahariev had hired me.

"Don't worry, babes!" she assured me. "I'll teach you everything!"

It didn't matter if she taught me. I wouldn't be able to practice for another week and by then, I'd be behind.

"You know she's doing this on purpose," I said. "She's pissed Zahariev went over her head."

"Maybe," said Coco. I could tell by the tone of her voice she didn't agree. "But I don't think she's wrong. My tips have been shit."

A flush crept over me, and my chest felt a little tight. I knew Coco wanted to believe Hassenaah, but this was intentional.

"Why don't you come watch tonight?" she suggested. "At least you'll get a sense of the new numbers."

"What about Cherub?" I asked.

"She'll be fine for a couple hours," she said.

I'd already been planning to be gone for more than a couple of hours this evening. After last night, I had a list of questions that were likely going to send me into some pretty seedy parts of Nineveh, which was saying a lot, because the entire district was sketchy as fuck.

"I don't know if I trust myself to be in the same room as Hassenaah," I said, though a part of me wanted to gloat. "I might punch her in the face if she calls me an ungrateful child one more time. I don't think Zahariev will appreciate that."

Especially since he was actually mad at me this time.

"Probably not," said Coco. "But he'll forgive you."

"I'll think about it," I said.

"Well, whatever you decide, I'd love to see you there."

Coco wandered down the hall to her room to finish getting ready. Alone save for Cherub, who was still sleeping in my lap, I checked my new phone. I had one message from my father. He'd resent a picture of my mother's invitation to the gala with a single note: *do more than think.*

Fuck my life.

ZAHARIEV

My lungs burned.

Sometimes I thought I could feel them disintegrating as they filled with smoke, but I powered through. Smoking kept my mind busy. Occupied.

Without it, I craved other things.

Untouchable things.

"Wait. Please! I'll tell you everything. Just please don't kill me!"

Judas Fischer III.

He was the one wailing.

One of four responsible for Lilith's kidnapping.

The second recipient of my vengeance. Lilith's justice.

The first was Jadon Chavara.

"We got a list and orders from Lisk, see?

Eliminate the threats. Your girl, she was in the wrong place at the wrong time."

I took one more drag from my cigarette.

"Thank you," I replied before I lifted my gun and pulled the trigger.

CHAPTER

NINE

After Coco left, I spent about an hour sketching. I wasn't an artist by any means, but drawing a picture of this blade seemed like the safest way to carry it around without actually having it with me or taking a picture, which, thanks to Lisk, was now out of the question. If anyone got suspicious about my inquiries, I would just claim I had a client interested in something with its particular design.

I bore down on the page as I filled in circles representing red gemstones. Afterward, I wrote a description of the blade and drew arrows pointing to different parts.

It wasn't perfect, but it would work.

While I was at it, I wrote as many details as I could remember from my nightmares. They hadn't started until I had come into possession of the blade, so I suspected they were related.

I scribbled down what I could remember about my surroundings and lines from whispered prayers.

Drink sweetly from the grail,

The holy blood, the venom, the ecstasy of night.
Unleash your fury, your eternal wail.
Break these chains, these binding gates.

I thought about Tori's warnings.

I didn't think it was a coincidence that my dreams and Tori had warned about the gates. I might not have thought that had Lisk not had him killed, but it made sense to me that the archbishop would want to eliminate anyone who drew attention to whatever was locked behind those doors, especially if it threatened the power of the church.

Maybe it was demons.

Maybe it was gods.

But I was going to find out.

When I was finished writing out my notes, I got ready to leave.

"It's just you and me, kid," I said, staring down at Cherub, who wasn't listening. She was too busy battling a loose thread on my comforter, not that I thought she actually understood anything I was saying. I'd been talking to her since Coco left, and her responses fell into two categories—staring and sleeping. Playing was new.

I sighed, resting my hands on my hips as I watched her.

I had no choice but to bring her with me, which wasn't ideal, but I couldn't leave her here alone.

I looked around my room for something I could use to carry her.

After some digging, I found a long scarf and fashioned a type of sling so I could keep her in front of me. I half wondered if it was a good idea to have her tiny claws so close to my boobs, but it wasn't like she had much to grab on to, so maybe it'd be fine.

"All right, little one," I said, then winced at how easily I'd used Zahariev's former nickname for me. I kind of wanted to wash my mouth out with soap. "Let's try this."

I picked her up and slipped her into the fold of the scarf. She sat still, almost like she was confused by what was happening, her furry head peeking out from the opening.

I turned to look in my full-length mirror and laughed.

"We look ridiculous," I said.

Cherub looked up at me as if to ask *who are you calling ridiculous?*

"Okay, fair. *I* look ridiculous."

And I sounded ridiculous too, but honestly, of all the things that had happened in my life the last few weeks, this was the most normal of all of them, and I kind of liked it. It was grounding.

"Let's pack you some water and food," I said.

Lisk had taken Coco's larger backpack, so all I had was a small one I'd used as a purse a few times—until some stealthy pickpockets stole my wallet. At least if they tried to steal this time, all they'd get away with was some cat food.

I slipped on my jacket and then the backpack.

I holstered my new gun. I was anxious about carrying it because I hadn't used it yet, though I imagined Zahariev—or one of his men—had cleaned it and fired a few shots. The point was I wasn't used to it, and I didn't really like that, but at least I had a weapon, because I wasn't about to go into Gomorrah unarmed or carry that fucking knife.

I glared at the top drawer of my nightstand. I hoped it could feel my disdain.

I left my apartment with Cherub. She was quiet as I headed down Procession Street. The sidewalks were a little more crowded than the night before, mostly people living with addiction who couldn't stay away from the clubs for more than a day or so. A few cast me looks, anywhere from quizzical to amused, but no one tried to talk to me, for which I was grateful. It probably had something to do with my expression. While I didn't know exactly what look I was giving, I knew the energy. I was determined and a little pissed thanks to Zahariev, ready to shove anyone out of my way if needed.

I crossed Procession Street and took Twelfth, passing the mossy stone walls of Southgate Cemetery, which took me into the southernmost part of Gomorrah. Abram wasn't my only customer, but he usually bought what I had, even when he gave me a hard time. Others weren't so easy. A few had clients, crits in Hiram and Temple City who wanted certain artifacts, things that sent me to sketchy shops to deal with sketchier people.

It wasn't my favorite way to make money, but desperate times called for desperate measures.

This part of the city was a maze. The only road into the area was Smugglers' Row. Beyond that, shops and residences were accessed via a series of narrow alleyways that zigzagged between derelict buildings. I'd learned the safest routes the hard way, though like all things in this district, *safe* was a stretch.

As I slipped down one dank passage, I wrapped an arm around Cherub and kept the other close to my gun. There were pockets of brightness from windows or open doors, but anything could happen in the gaping darkness.

A woman stood in a slice of light ahead, a length of fabric wrapped between her hands.

"A scarf for you, madam?" she asked.

I ignored her and the curse she spat at my back as I continued, passing a man who sat cross-legged on a blanket, ringing a series of bells. A handmade sign read HEALING BELLS, TUNED TO THE FREQUENCY OF THE ANGELS.

I wondered what that meant and how many people believed his claims, though I doubted anyone in need of true healing sought it in Gomorrah.

Nothing here could save you.

I made a few more twists and turns, winding through the alleys, passing more unfortunate shops—one that sold exotic animals, another selling illegal pharmaceuticals—before rounding the final corner and coming to a stop.

Ahead, a man stood in a flood of yellow light, smoking. He looked to be about Zahariev's age. His hair was dark and his face carved by the cut of his beard. He took a drag from his cigarette before dropping his hand to his side, smiling.

It wasn't an unpleasant smile, but it wasn't warm either.

"Well, well," he said. "Look who it is."

"Baal," I said in acknowledgment.

His eyes glittered in the half-light and fell to the sling around my body, his thick brows rising. "Is that a baby?"

"It's a cat," I said, parting the fabric so Cherub could poke her head out.

"It sure is," he said, taking a drag from his cigarette. "It's been a while, serpent. What are you up to?"

"I have a new client."

"Replacing Abram already?"

I stiffened. I didn't like his tone and wondered what rumors were going around about Abram's death, but I wasn't curious enough to ask. I didn't like Baal. He gave me the creeps, and not for the usual reasons. Baal didn't lust after me, though I sensed waves of attraction. I suspected I was too old for him.

"Money's tight," I said.

"Ain't that the truth," he said, flicking his cigarette into the darkness before heading into his shop. It was a narrow room and overcrowded with shelves displaying icons haloed in shining gold, statues of saints in pewter and bronze, and hand-jeweled religious books. They were items that were popular with the devout but not what he was known for, at least in my circle.

Baal specialized in procuring religious relics and not just bits of bone or scraps of clothing. He'd sold the mummified heads of saints, their tongues and jaws, reliquaries full of blood and hair.

I was usually a skeptic when it came to the authenticity of relics. They were easy to fake. I knew five people who thought they owned the skull of Saint Innocence, but Baal was different.

He was probably the slowest concierge on the market. It could take him a year to secure items for his clients. If a patron wanted something that already belonged to someone else or didn't exist, he said so. He also kept detailed physical records of the items he found and sold.

Were they real? I had no fucking clue, but it was his attention to detail that made me think he at least thought so.

"What are you looking for?" he asked.

"My client is looking for a knife," I said. "But all he gave me was a description."

I pulled out my notebook and laid it flat on his counter so he could see my horrible drawing.

"What the fuck is this?"

"I *told* you," I snapped. "All my client gave me was a description. I did my best."

He gave me a look, as if to say *this is your best?*

"Just tell me what he described."

I rolled my eyes and swiped my journal off his counter. "A blade with a gold-plated hilt. It's set with red gems."

There was a beat of silence. Baal's brows rose. "That's it? That's all he told you?"

I flushed. I didn't know if I was frustrated or embarrassed.

"If that is all the information your client gave, I'm afraid he is wasting your time."

"He told me to keep it sheathed when I found it," I said. "Unless I wanted my eyes to bleed."

He chuckled. "Now I am certain he is wasting your time."

I stiffened. I thought for sure that would spark something. "What do you mean, I'm wasting my time?"

"Sounds like your client believes in a myth," said Baal.

"Which part is the myth exactly?" I asked.

I had to change my tone halfway through my question. I sounded too defensive, like I knew better.

Because I did.

"There's a belief that the unworthy cannot behold truly sacred things," he said. "But what makes something sacred other than the human belief that it is important?"

"Maybe it has nothing to do with veneration," I said. "Maybe the blade's cursed."

Baal looked amused. "Maybe," he said. "But I have handled many sacred things and passed them on to many unworthy people. I have never witnessed their eyes bleed."

I narrowed my eyes. "I think you're right," I said, taking a step back. "If you had ever handled anything truly sacred, you would definitely be dead by now."

I turned to leave when Baal called out to me.

"Your client," he said. "It's not Zahariev Zareth, is it?"

I looked at him, surprised by the question. "Why would it be Zareth?"

"Word on the street is you were seen with him outside Abram's shop the night he died," said Baal. "All that seems a little coincidental."

"I didn't know you were a gossip, Baal," I said.

"The network's suspicious, Eve," he said.

Eve was the name I gave my contacts. There were a lot of reasons I didn't want to give my real name.

"About what?"

"No one wants to make deals with someone associated with the families."

"Do you really speak for everyone in the network?" I asked. "Or are you just afraid Zahariev will find out you're a pedophile?" Baal's features hardened, and I laughed. "I think it's the latter. Good night, Baal. Thanks for nothing."

I left his shop, only quickening my pace once I was out of his sight. I didn't want him to think he'd gotten under my skin, but now I wondered how many of my contacts had heard the same rumor.

My next visit answered that very question.

Mistress, a severe woman who kept her hair in a bun so tight, it pulled the skin on her face, took one look at me and told me to get out. I tried to argue even though I had no grounds to do so, and she threw a paperweight at me.

The security at Ellesar's Gold and Gemstone Gallery turned me away as soon as I gave my name, and when I tried to buzz myself into Joakim's Emporium, he yelled at me through the speaker and said he didn't do business with *rats*.

I turned away from the door and took a long breath, tilting my head up toward the red-tinged sky.

Why did Zahariev ruin everything?

As soon as the thought crossed my mind, I felt guilty. It wasn't a fair thing to say, but there was a reason I hadn't called him when Abram died.

"Fuck."

Cherub meowed.

"I know. I'm sorry," I said. "This isn't going the way I planned."

I had one more option before I hit a dead end, and I'd saved it for last because I was really hoping I wouldn't have to go. Gomorrah was bad, but the Trenches? They were worse.

There were rules for patrons on Sinners' Row, rules for operating on Smugglers' Row. There were no rules for those who ventured into the Trenches.

Once known as Southgate, it had become uncharted territory when a fire broke out years before Zahariev was born. Since then, it had become a home to those in need and to those who did not feel like they belonged in Nineveh. It was a place I only ventured when I had to, like when I needed to sell something my usual buyers wouldn't take, even though the people who lived there didn't often trade in money. They traded in things—crumbling books, serpentinite pieces, the *bone of an angel wing*, things I'd just have to take back to Gomorrah to sell.

It was a waste of my time, and as I passed through the entrance, marked by two scorched pillars, I didn't think this visit would be any different.

I followed cracks in the broken asphalt, overrun with weeds. It was the only greenery here. Nothing else had survived. Some buildings and homes were still intact but dilapidated and smoke stained; others were nothing more than skeletal silhouettes. Still, if it had a decent roof or a concrete wall, the locals would use it as shelter, often scavenging wood, brick, and metal from other parts of the area.

I once asked Zahariev why he hadn't rebuilt. He had enough money. He could give everyone here a nicer place to live.

If I gave them a new area, it would no longer be theirs.

At first, I didn't understand what he meant, but it didn't take long to learn. A week in Nineveh, and I had watched those who had take from those who had less and those who had less take from those who had nothing.

I shouldn't have been surprised. The foundation of Hiram's wealth had begun in Nineveh with the canal, the desert, the mines. I just never expected to see the same abuse on a micro level, but sometimes people were worn so thin, all they could do was survive.

Overhead, the darkening sky ignited in a blaze of light, followed by a deep, sonorous roll of thunder. It made the ground quake, like the storm had awakened some sort of monster deep in the earth.

Fuck. I hadn't expected rain on my walk.

Cherub meowed with as much dread as I felt. I didn't like being out in the rain. It felt like being poisoned.

As the first few droplets fell, I finally found the street I was looking for, memorable because of the wash lines that crisscrossed between blackened windows, some still heavy with clothes. Here, the buildings were less damaged and terraced.

There were a few people out and about, a man smoking outside his convenience store, another digging through bags of trash piled on the street. While neither of them paid me any mind, I couldn't help feeling uneasy. Maybe it was the rain, but the few times I'd been here, the area had been far more active.

The shop owners brought their merch onto the sidewalk and bartered into the early morning. There were no streetlights, so they strung lanterns from the clotheslines. It felt like another world, and I guessed, in some ways, it was. No one else outside this place ever tried to barter with angel bones, save the woman in shop 213. I stared up at the fading numbers over her door. I thought it had once been blue, but the paint was so faded, there was only a hint of color left. She had also carved symbols into the wood. I didn't know what they meant, but I was certain the church would think it was some kind of witchcraft.

I walked up her slippery steps and knocked on the door. As I stood on her tiny porch, it began to rain harder. I crowded closer, trying to fit as much of my body beneath the short overhang as possible, knocking harder, but there was no answer. Cherub was meowing.

"I know, kid. I'm sorry," I said.

I tucked her inside the scarf and folded my jacket over her, gritting my teeth as I felt her claws against my skin.

This sucks.

I looked around for some way to peer into the building, noticing a pillar beside the porch that would give me a view inside.

I climbed it, pressing my face to the window as the rain rolled off my hooded head and back. I could see a woman inside standing behind a counter, her face illuminated by candlelight.

She looked serene and focused.

Maybe she hadn't heard me at the door.

I knocked on the window.

Her head snapped in my direction, eyes narrowed. If looks could kill, I'd be a dead motherfucker.

"We're closed," she said. I could barely hear her muffled voice.

Closed? No one here ever closed.

I knocked on the window again. I was desperate. I'd been ostracized by my other contacts, and this was my last one.

Her response was to blow out the candle.

"Hey!" I yelled. "I know you're still in there!"

It was like she didn't understand object permanence.

I dropped down from the pillar and knocked on her door. I had to hand it to her though; this lady was a trooper. It took me five full minutes of knocking before she came to the door.

She was probably close to my mom's age, with graying blond hair. She kept it low and twisted into a bun at the back of her head, though a few unruly wisps had torn free and floated around her head.

I had forgotten her name, though it was possible she'd never given it.

She glared at me, just as angry as she had been when I knocked on her window. I couldn't really blame her. I was being annoying as fuck, but I needed help.

"I said *we're closed*."

She tried to shut the door, and I tried to pull a Zahariev and shove my foot in the opening but quickly pulled it out as a sharp pain went straight to my brain.

"Mother. Fucker!" I said through my teeth, hopping on one foot as I rode each throbbing wave of pain. That was the last time I tried to do anything like Zahariev.

The woman cracked a smile before shutting the door in my face.

"No, no, no," I said, slamming my palms on the door. "Please!"

I hated begging, and I felt ridiculous. I doubted the woman could even hear me, but I refused to give up just yet.

I slid my backpack off my shoulder and dug inside for my journal.

"Look, I'll trade whatever, but I need some information."

I slipped the journal under the door, open to the page with the blade. I let it stay there for a few minutes. Just when I was about to give up and take the book back, she yanked it from my fingertips.

I waited, barely breathing.

What were the chances she kept it and never answered?

I started to consider the odds pretty favorable when I heard the knob turn. She opened the door again, eyes assessing as she sized me up.

"Who are you?" she barked.

"My name is Eve," I said.

She narrowed her gaze like she didn't believe me, but I wasn't about to give her my real name.

"Interesting choice," she said. "Did your mother think it was pretty? Or did she intentionally name you after the woman who committed the first sin?"

I shrugged. "I guess that depends on what you believe."

The irony was that my mother did believe the story, and she used it to remind me of my place when she felt I was anything but submissive.

We partook of the apple. This is our punishment, she would say.

It was the justification written in the first few pages of the *Book of Splendor*. From a young age, I had been taught that I was responsible for Eve's so-called sin. I was made to

189

feel guilty for how easily she had been tempted to disobey God and for her temptation of Adam.

Now that I was older, I suspected either Adam was just as responsible, or he had never been capable of critical thinking. Given my experience with most men, I couldn't dismiss the latter.

Now that I thought about it, choosing Eve as my alias was fitting. My mother used her story to indoctrinate me, but what she'd really done was free me.

Cherub chose that moment to fight her way out of the sling, ears popping up as she freed her head.

The woman's expression softened briefly.

"What's her name?" she asked.

"Cherub," I said.

"Cherub," she repeated, bending so she was face-to-face with my cat. "Aren't you precious? My name is Saira."

I was trying to decide if it was weird that she that only addressed my cat, but then her gaze lifted to mine, souring again, and I decided I didn't care, so long as I got what I came for.

She straightened and stepped aside, allowing me to enter her shop. The candle was lit again, and it smelled earthy, probably because she had so many plants. They were everywhere, hanging in baskets from the ceiling, trailing along the walls like garland. With the candles, it almost felt homey, if it weren't for all the weird shit she kept on display—jars of graveyard dirt, brackish water, and dead things floating in discolored liquid.

They were things that outed her as someone who practiced witchcraft, or at least someone who sold items to those who did. It was a dangerous way to make a living, but this was probably the safest place to do it, deep within the

Trenches of Nineveh. If the church found out, they would persecute not only her but her clientele.

The woman walked past me, still holding my journal.

"You've never been closed," I said as she made her way behind the counter.

"There's always a first," Saira said, holding up the journal. "What's this?"

"My dreams," I said.

It wasn't exactly a lie, but I also wasn't about to give her the whole truth.

"Your dreams," she repeated flatly, dropping the journal on the counter. I could tell by her tone I'd lost her.

"I know what it sounds like, but I need answers," I said.

"I don't interpret dreams," she said.

"You opened the door for a reason," I snapped. "Why?"

She glared at me, angry. I knew it was going to take time for her to trust me. The problem was I didn't have time. Not with that fucking knife in the drawer of my bedside table.

After a few tense seconds, she opened the book to the page where I'd drawn the blade, jabbing her finger at the picture.

"What do you know about this blade?" she asked.

"What do *you* know about it?"

"It's my shop. I'll ask the questions."

"I don't know anything about it," I said, frustrated. *"That's the fucking problem."*

She stared, waiting for me to continue. God, she was as bad as Zahariev.

"I dreamed I found it in the desert," I said. "Nothing's been the same since."

"What else?" she asked.

"What do you mean, *what else?*" I asked, confused by her question.

"I mean, what else do you see in your dreams?" She spoke between her teeth.

I thought you didn't interpret dreams, I wanted to say, but I decided that wouldn't get me very far. I realized we hadn't met on the best terms. She had every right to be annoyed with me, but the fact was she'd opened the door, which meant I had something she wanted.

"I think this was a mistake," I said, reaching for my journal, but she snatched it away, holding it against her chest. This was why I hadn't brought the actual blade—this, and it seemed to want to kill anyone other than me and Zahariev.

I wasn't going to fight her for a notebook when I could just get another one and fill it with the same shit, so I started to leave.

"Wait."

I paused and stared at her.

"How do I know you aren't from the church?" She tried to hide the quaking of her voice, but I could hear it. A subtle fear.

"Because I'm not."

"You think that's sufficient?"

"You think an agent of the church would come here with a cat strapped to their chest and a journal of shitty drawings and ask you for help?"

"I think the church will do anything to maintain power, even send me a girl with a disdain for the *Book of Splendor.*"

"I don't know what you want from me," I said. It wasn't like enforcers had identifying marks aside from how they dressed.

She looked at me for a few long seconds before dragging

a candle closer. It was a simple black taper. She lit it using the flame of another and set it between us. I knew she was using magic, but it differed from mine. This wasn't innate; it was learned.

She was a witch, as I'd suspected.

"Before the nightmares started, what happened?"

"One of my buyers died in front of me," I said.

"Abram Elkin."

I shouldn't be surprised that she knew him. I had hoped word wouldn't reach this far. Unlike Baal, though, she didn't ask about Zahariev.

"What did you bring him the night he died?"

I hesitated, and her brows rose.

"That blade wasn't just in your dreams."

I stared at her, unable to take a breath.

"What is it?" I asked.

"*Where* is it?" she countered.

I clutched at Cherub, hand hovering over my gun.

She put up her hands. "I'm not asking because I want it."

"Well, you'd be the first," I said, and I'd be stupid to believe her.

"So there are others who know you have it?"

"Not anymore." I let the weight of my words settle in the silence between us before asking again. "What is it?"

She watched me, and I wondered if she was silently cursing me or planning some way to keep me from leaving.

"I'll tell you," she said at last. "But I require something in return."

"Why does that not surprise me?"

"There is a price for trust," she said.

"Don't make it sound grand," I said. "It is what it is, payment. What do you want?"

"Jade," she said.

My brows rose. "*Jade*? As in the drug, jade?"

She just stared.

"Do you have an addiction?" I asked.

She narrowed her eyes. Despite her obvious irritation, it was a valid question, not that I expected her to tell me the truth.

"I do not," she said. "I use it to induce visions."

"How do you know they are visions and not hallucinations?"

"I just know," she snapped, coming around the counter. Her sudden approach put me on edge but also made Cherub hiss. At some point, she must have freed her little paw, because she swiped at the woman. She was too far away to do any damage, but her reaction caused the woman to halt. Surprisingly, she smiled.

"You have an excellent familiar," she said.

"She's not a familiar," I said and immediately regretted it.

The woman offered a crude smile. "Not so disentangled from your beliefs as you'd have me think," she said.

My face grew hot. It was true. Her use of the word had frightened me though. I didn't know what it meant, save that it was related to witchcraft and considered a crime against God.

"I... What is a familiar?" I asked.

"Your church calls them demonic spirits," said the woman. "Creatures controlled by the evil behind the Seventh Gate, but they are just guides, only harmful to those who threaten their charge."

I watched her, wary.

"If familiars are not demonic spirits," I said, "then what is a demon?"

"There are no such things," she said.

I frowned, but the woman offered a small, humorless smile.

"Not the answer you wanted, is it? Consider that before you return. Nothing I have to tell you will be comforting."

Right. Okay.

"You promise," I said. "If I bring you what you've asked for, you'll tell me about this blade."

"I'll tell you more than you've ever wanted to know," she said. "Just get me the jade."

I felt uneasy about her request, but I wanted answers.

"Fine," I said. "I'll see you in a few days."

I didn't give her a solid timeline, mostly because I didn't know how long it would take me to secure the drug. While Zahariev had stolen my father's shipment, it was possible he'd already destroyed it. If that was the case, I would have to organize a drop, which would prove difficult since my name had been sullied.

As hard as I tried, I couldn't help feeling angry at Zahariev for making my life just a little more difficult.

I started toward the door.

"Wait. Take this," said the woman, handing me an umbrella, adding, "For your familiar."

"Thank you," I said, because though she'd made it clear her kindness wasn't for me, I was still grateful.

I stood outside her door for a few seconds, zipping up my jacket to keep Cherub warm. It had grown colder since I'd been inside, the rain a steady, miserable drizzle. I took a deep breath, inhaling burnt air. The sharp smell grounded me as I deployed my umbrella and left the Trenches.

By the time I arrived at Praise, my jeans were soaked, but at least Cherub was dry.

Since the club was closed, I went around back and left my umbrella at the door. It was cold inside, and I shivered as I made my way across the carpeted floor toward the stage, my socks squelching in my boots. Luckily, no one heard my approach over the vibrating music.

Coco's smile widened when she saw me.

The downside was that it also drew Hassenaah's attention to me.

She was standing before the stage, one hand folded just below her chest, the other propped into the air. Her head and upper body twisted toward me, eyes flashing to mine. She was a beautiful woman, probably a little older than Zahariev, with dark hair, thick arched brows, and prominent cheekbones.

She looked me up and down like she was disgusted by my very presence and then turned toward the stage.

"Again," she snapped, her voice hitting the air like a whip.

The music stopped, and the girls took their places, some hurrying offstage. When it began again, I focused on Coco. I loved watching her dance. Her movements were always so controlled and graceful. If she'd been born in Hiram, she would have been put in the National Ballet.

I wandered closer to the stage, one step behind Hassenaah.

I knew she was aware of me by the way her shoulders rose. It took her a few minutes, but she finally spoke. She couldn't help herself.

"If you think you can go over my head for a place on my stage, you are mistaken, Miss Leviathan."

"I didn't go over your head," I said, a flush of warm hatred twisting through me.

"Don't lie, Miss Leviathan," she said. "You got what you wanted the way you get everything you want: with your name."

"Actually, I danced for him," I said.

Hassenaah's head snapped toward me, her shocked gaze falling to mine. I probably should have kept my mouth shut about that particular truth, but she pissed me off. She was so eager to throw my name in my face, she couldn't even acknowledge when I worked hard.

"What would your father think about that?"

"Are you threatening me, Hassenaah?" I asked.

"It's a fair question. To my knowledge, the families aren't allowed intimate relationships."

"Who said anything about intimacy?" I countered. "It was a dance, nothing more. Maybe you need to consider why it makes you jealous."

She jerked her head back to the stage and waved her hand, signaling the sound guy to cut the music.

"Practice is over," she said. "Stretch tonight. We start tomorrow at six p.m. sharp."

Hassenaah strolled away, and the girls dispersed. Coco ran up to me as she pulled on a long-sleeved shirt.

"Everything okay?" she asked. "I saw you talking to Hassenaah."

"Yeah," I said. "Everything's fine."

"What did she say?"

"Nothing nice," I said.

"Lilith." My name was almost a whine as it left her mouth. "You didn't make things worse, did you?"

"Why am I the one who always makes things worse?" I asked, frustrated. "She hates me, Coco. She doesn't like my family, and she wants to fuck Zahariev."

197

"Okay, okay," Coco said, glancing around like she was embarrassed by the possibility that someone might hear me. "I'm sorry. I just...*want* this for you, Lilith, and if you can't get along with her, it's going to make everything harder."

"I've *tried*!"

I had tried *so* hard. I had tried harder with Hassenaah than anyone else in my life. Nothing about me impressed her, not kindness, not bitchiness, not talent.

She hated me.

And the fact that Coco insisted otherwise hurt.

I looked away and pulled Cherub out of her sling before slipping it over my head.

"Are you heading home?" I asked.

"Yes. Aren't you?"

"I need...to find Zahariev."

I lied because I couldn't really tell her I was going to search for a few grams of jade.

"What time will you be home?" she asked.

"I don't know," I said. "Late, I imagine."

She stared at me. I knew she didn't want me to go. She wanted to talk through this tiff, make sure everything was all right between us, but I didn't feel like talking, not about Hassenaah anyway. I had other, more pressing matters to deal with.

"Okay," she said, her voice quiet.

She held out her hands for Cherub. I lifted her up, looking into her coppery eyes.

"You're a great sidekick," I said, handing her over.

She meowed at me, and Coco lifted a brow, trying not to smile.

"What?" I asked.

"Nothing," she said. "I just thought you didn't want a cat."

"She grows on you," I said, reaching to scratch behind Cherub's ears. I lifted my gaze to Coco's. "I'll see you later."

"Be careful, Lily."

I left Praise the same way I'd entered, through the back. As I reached for my umbrella, my phone vibrated. I pulled it out of my pocket to see Esther was calling, and my heart rose into my throat. Had she gone into labor? Why wasn't Gabriel calling me instead?

"Hello?" I answered.

There was silence on the other side.

"Esther?" I asked. I took a few more steps before I came to a halt, pulling my phone away from my ear, just to check that the call hadn't dropped. It was still active and tracking the seconds. "Esther, is everything all right?"

Maybe she dialed me by accident, I thought, though something about that didn't feel right. Reluctantly, I ended the call, checking my texts to see if she'd sent anything, but there was nothing.

I started walking, but I only made it a few steps before my phone rang again.

"Esther?" I answered, but again there was silence. "Esther!"

I spoke louder, hoping she might hear me if she had accidentally made the call, but there was nothing. Again, I pulled the phone away from my ear and stared at the screen. That feeling of unease deepened, and I changed directions heading toward Sumer. There was nothing wrong with double-checking that everything was all right...right?

I kept the call connected as I headed toward their apartment. At some point, I discarded the umbrella and broke into a full-out run.

I told myself I was just being overly protective. It was likely that Esther had fallen asleep on the couch like she had the night I was attacked. She probably had her phone under her. That was how I imagined finding her. Perfectly fine, asleep.

I just needed peace of mind.

By the time I made it to the apartment, my lungs were burning from exertion, and my hands were a little shaky. I entered the code to her building and headed up the elevator, which seemed to take a century to reach their floor. The doors were barely open when I slipped through and hurried down the hall to their apartment. I didn't knock.

If Esther really was asleep, I didn't want to disturb her rest. Instead, I used my key.

As soon as I was inside, I knew something was wrong. There was spilled tea and shattered ceramic on the floor of the kitchen, like she'd been in the middle of making tea when she'd dropped her mug. It was a mess Esther would have never left untouched, even at the end of her third trimester.

I drew my gun.

"Esther?" I called, jumping over the shattered cup.

That was when I saw the blood. It was just a few bright drops, but it was leading toward the bedroom.

Maybe she'd cut her hand.

"Esther!"

My voice reached a pitch I didn't recognize. Hysteria rose inside me as I made my way into her bedroom. It was also empty, but the door to her bathroom was ajar, and through it, I could see a foot.

"Esther!" I screamed, holstering my gun as I charged into the room.

My vision was suddenly red.

Blood was *everywhere*—on the sink, the toilet, the bathtub, the floor—and in the middle of it all was Esther. She lay on her side, her hand near her phone, one finger extended and curled, hovering over a dark screen. The other rested on her round belly.

"No, no, no, no."

My hands shook so badly as I pulled out my phone, it slipped from my hands, clattering to the floor, sending blood spattering across my shoes and the bottom of my jeans. I picked it up and wiped it on my shirt, eyes blurry with tears. I managed to get enough off the screen to dial emergency services.

When the dispatcher answered, I screamed the address into the phone.

"912 Sumer Road, Unit 716. My friend is unconscious and bleeding. She's pregnant."

I could hear the woman on the other side, clicking away.

"You said the patient is a female?" she asked.

"Yes! A female, thirty-five weeks pregnant." I could barely speak because I could barely think. "She's bleeding everywhere. There is blood everywhere!"

"Is she breathing?"

I couldn't tell.

I lowered to my knees and put my ear to her chest.

"Y-yes! Yes!"

Relief flooded me. She was alive. There was hope.

"Esther!" I screamed, shaking her. "Esther, please wake up!"

"Ma'am. Ma'am. Do you know where the blood is

coming from?" The dispatcher was also yelling. "Did she hit her head? Is she hemorrhaging?"

I couldn't comprehend her questions. How was I supposed to know where the blood was coming from? It was everywhere!

"Ma'am?"

"I don't know. *I don't know.* I'm not a fucking doctor. Just get someone here, please. *Please!*"

"I've already dispatched an ambulance," she said. "Asking these questions will not slow them down at all. I need information for the paramedics."

I detested her calm voice. I didn't care that it was part of her job. It put me on edge. It made me feel like she didn't understand how important Esther was to me. How important Liam…

"Ma'am?"

"What?" I snapped.

"I need you to let the paramedics into the apartment," she said.

Oh.

I rose to my feet and went to the door. When I opened it, there were two men on the other side. They were already wearing gloves, and one carried a large bag.

"Somebody call for an ambulance?" one asked.

"Yes, she's in the bathroom," I said.

I hurried ahead of them, showing them to the room.

"Oh, sweetheart," one said under their breath. "What happened?"

"I don't know," I said. "I found her like this."

They wasted no time getting to work.

"What's her name?" one of them asked.

"Esther," I said.

"Esther," the man said, tapping her face. "Wake up, sweetheart. Can you open your eyes for me?"

"How far along is she?" the other one asked.

"Thirty-five weeks," I said.

The man spoke into his two-way radio, repeating the information I had given and more, mentioning hemorrhaging, her blood pressure, heart rate, and a million other things that faded into the background as I watched Esther from the corner of the room.

Eventually, they got her on the gurney and wheeled her out. I followed, riding down the elevator with them. She was facing me, lying on her side. She wasn't conscious, and an oxygen mask covered her face. I didn't like how the elastic bands were pressing into her skin. I wanted to reach out and touch her, but I had blood on my hands. Instead, as I stared at her, I willed her to wake up.

Wake up. Wake up. *Wake up.*

"Are you related?" one of them asked.

"She's my sister," I said.

It might as well be true.

"Do you have a way to get to the hospital?"

I shook my head.

"You can ride up front."

"I can't be with her?"

"It won't be long," he said.

As soon as the doors opened, they were out. I followed, but my steps faltered, and I watched from a distance as they rolled her into the ambulance.

Something deep inside told me I'd never see her alive again.

ZAHARIEV

"I heard you touched my girl," I said.

She wasn't mine. She wasn't anyone's.

But I was the dealer of her justice. Her vengeance was mine.

"I didn't know she was yours, man." His voice quivered. "I didn't mean anything by it!"

This one was called Christian. Christian Masters.

He was number three.

The fourth would be here soon.

"Are you saying you had no intention of assaulting her?"

"Assault? Is that what she said? I barely touched her! Dude, you have to believe me."

"I believe you," I said.

His shoulders relaxed. I let him feel that relief before I punched him in the face.

My knuckles connected with his jaw, and he went slack.

As I pulled back, I heard Cassius over my shoulder.

"*Your girl* is calling."

I cast him a cold look. "Do you want to join him?" I asked, snatching my phone away.

The fight left me when I answered.

"Zahariev," Lilith said, my name leaving her mouth on a sob. "It's Esther. I don't... Where is Gabriel?"

My throat felt tight. "Where are you?"

"In an ambulance on the way to the hospital. Zahariev," she said, and a horrible sound came from somewhere deep in her throat. "I don't know if she'll make it."

CHAPTER
TEN

A team of doctors and nurses was waiting when we arrived at the hospital. Before I even climbed out of the ambulance, they were wheeling Esther through the sliding doors and rushing her down the hall. I followed along, but no one really noticed me until I tried to enter her room.

"You can't be in here," said a nurse in blue scrubs.

I heard her, but I didn't really understand. Esther had called me, which meant she needed me. What if she woke up and she was alone, surrounded by all these strangers? I had to be with her.

I stared at the nurse and then Esther, but I could barely see her beyond all the activity.

"There's a waiting room down the hall. Someone will come get you when she's stable." The nurse pointed and then shut the door in my face.

I stood there, staring at the wood grain until my vision blurred.

Did she say stable? I thought. That sounded promising.

I turned away and looked up and down the hall. It was empty. Quiet. The opposite of what was happening in Esther's room.

The opposite of what was happening in my head.

I wandered in the direction the nurse had pointed and found the waiting room. The fluorescents glared off blue vinyl seats and the grayish floor. It was so bright, my eyes watered.

Or maybe I was just crying.

I chose a seat away from everyone else and sat with my arms around me, trying to hold myself together. I wondered how long it would take for Gabriel to arrive. I didn't want to be alone. What if something terrible happened?

Please, please, please.

I didn't know whom I was pleading with: maybe Esther, maybe God.

I realized this wasn't the best time to ask a god I resented for mercy, but if she survived this, I'd do anything.

I'd go home.

I wasn't there long when a nurse called for Pomeroy. That was Esther's last name. My stomach roiled with dread. At the same time, my chest rose with hope. I wanted her to tell me I could see Esther, but instead she told me she was there to escort me to another waiting room.

"Your sister's going into surgery for an emergency C-section."

"Is she okay?" I asked. "Is the baby okay?"

"I don't have any details," she replied. "But someone will be out to give you updates when they can." Her eyes dropped to my bloodstained hands. "Are you hurt?" she asked.

"No," I said, holding out my hands, palms facing up.

"It's...my sister's blood. I...had to see if her heart was beating."

"Oh, sweetie," she said, frowning. "Let me show you to a bathroom where you can freshen up."

As I followed her down the hall, I looked up to see a familiar black trench coat. Before I could think, I broke into a run.

"Gabriel!" I was relieved to see him, but when his head swiveled toward me, I almost stopped. I had never seen him frown so deeply. Even in serious situations, there was always a glint in his eyes, but the ones that gazed back at me, they were dead already.

"Lilith," he said.

I collided with him, and he squeezed me tight. I didn't want to let him go. I was afraid he would disappear.

"I'm so sorry, Gabriel," I said. I didn't want to cry, but I couldn't contain my emotions. It had been building in the back of my throat since I arrived at their house and erupted the moment I made contact with him.

"It's all right, baby girl," he said. "Everything's going to be all right."

I wanted to believe him. In my head, I let myself imagine what it would be like to return to their apartment to visit Esther and the baby, but my heart...it was breaking into a million pieces.

I pulled away and wiped my eyes, realizing suddenly that he had not arrived alone. Cassius was with him...and so was Zahariev. Our eyes met. I couldn't make sense of his expression, but then again, I couldn't make sense of my feelings. There was a part of me that wanted him to comfort me. Another part of me wondered if we would be here right now if he'd done like I'd asked and let Gabriel stay home with Esther until after the baby arrived.

I looked away quickly and wrapped my arms around myself when a different nurse approached. "Mr. De Santis?"

"Yeah?" said Gabriel.

"If you'll follow me, I'll take you to your private waiting room."

"Where is my wife?" he asked.

"She's in surgery," said the nurse. "Once I show you to your room—"

"How is she? What about my son?"

"Mr. De Santis, I can call the OR for an update once I show you to your room."

"Gabriel," I said, wrapping my arm around his. He dropped his gaze to mine. "Let's go."

His eyes lingered on my face. I didn't know what he was thinking, maybe nothing and everything all at once.

I tugged him forward, and he followed. We fell in step behind the nurse. The suite wasn't far, just down the hall and behind a windowless door. The room itself was spacious but still screamed hospital with modular seating and laminate wood tables. One wall was painted green, and they had traded fluorescents for table lamps.

"Someone will be with you shortly," said the nurse before he left, closing the door quietly behind him.

A heavy and horrible silence settled between us. Gabriel sat on the edge of the couch with his head in his hands. Cassius glanced at me before crossing the room to the coffee machine.

Zahariev touched my arm. I looked up at him.

"You should wash your face," he said. My eyes narrowed, but before I could ask him what was wrong with my face, he added, "And your hands."

My eyes widened.

Zahariev took a step back and opened the door to the adjoining bathroom. I slipped inside and went straight to the sink, turning on the hot water. I pumped too much soap into my hands, hating how the suds turned red with Esther's blood. The water was steaming, and I inhaled sharply when it touched my skin, but I didn't care. It made me feel somewhat clean.

I hadn't realized that Zahariev had followed me into the bathroom until he came up behind me and turned the cold water on.

"Stop!" I snapped, turning it off.

"You're hurting yourself," he said, turning it back on. I reached for it again, but he kept his hand there. "Lilith, *stop*."

I turned and pushed him. He took a step back, though I knew he'd done that purposefully, to put some space between us. I hated the way he looked at me, his gaze almost glassy, like he hurt *for* me, and it pissed me off. He didn't get to care after he'd decided to ignore me.

"None of this would have happened if you had listened to me."

His jaw tightened. "Lilith—"

"Fuck. You."

I pushed him again, and he let me. Maybe there was a part of his brain that realized he deserved it. When his back was to the wall, he grabbed my wrists.

"Let go!" I said between clenched teeth. I tried to free myself, but he pulled me closer, and then his hands were on either side of my face, fingers pressed hard into my scalp. He was so close, I could feel his breath on my lips. His eyes were watering.

I'd never seen him like this. I wished I wasn't seeing it now.

210

"I'm sorry," he said. "I should have listened. I wish I had. I'm sorry."

"I don't want you to be sorry," I said. "I want you to *fix* it."

He shook his head ever so slightly, as if to tell me there was nothing he could do.

"Lily—"

"You *don't* get to call me that!"

There was a knock at the door, and Zahariev released me. I turned in time to see Cassius poke his head into the room, but I already knew what he was going to say. I knew because I could hear Gabriel's deep wail from the other room.

"Liam made his arrival. They're stabilizing him," said Cassius.

My mouth quivered. "Esther?"

Cassius just shook his head.

I covered my mouth as the first sob bubbled to the surface. Once it started, I couldn't stop.

I crumpled, and Zahariev followed me to the floor.

———

Esther is gone. Esther is gone.

Esther is gone.

I repeated the words over and over again, waiting for the moment when they would feel real, when I would understand.

That was the problem. I didn't understand.

How did this happen?

I saw her two days ago. She'd been happy and smiley. She'd baked a fucking cake.

And now she was dead.

"She called me eighteen times," said Gabriel.

211

He was in the same spot he'd been in since they'd led us to this fucking suite, leaning forward, elbows on his knees. The only difference now was that he held his phone in his hand.

I sat in a chair, angled away from him, but glanced in his direction when he spoke. I couldn't look at him for too long, because I felt too many things I didn't like.

"Eighteen times." Gabriel's voice broke.

Where was your fucking phone? I wanted to ask. Instead, I ground my teeth. I wished he wouldn't talk, at least not about this. As angry as I was with Zahariev, Gabriel was the one who'd decided to leave Esther knowing the risks... though none of us had expected this.

Maybe that was the problem.

We hadn't prepared for every possibility.

But why the fuck was *this* even a possibility?

What was the point of a god if he couldn't save the most virtuous among us?

I didn't understand.

I just didn't fucking understand.

There was a knock on the door, and a young nurse entered.

"Mr. De Santis?"

"Yes," Gabriel said, getting to his feet.

"I'm Victoria," she said.

Her voice was high and too cheerful. It went straight through me, an arrow to the chest. How could anyone be so happy when the brightest light in the world had been snuffed out?

"I'm going to help you prepare to meet your baby boy. If you'll follow me?"

The baby.

Liam.

A nervous excitement built inside me. It was confusing given Esther's loss, but it felt wrong to only mourn when her son had lived. His light had only begun to burn, and I looked for it now because I wanted to follow it. I needed it to guide me.

I wondered who he looked like, Gabriel or Esther? Would I even be able to tell?

"Once I have Mr. De Santis settled with the baby, I'll be back to get you, family. Don't worry!"

She held the door open for Gabriel to exit, and then they were gone, and I was alone with Zahariev and Cassius. Without Gabriel, the only sound was a clock, reminding me how long we'd been here. Each second that ticked by brought us closer to daylight and I didn't want to face it without Esther.

I grew more and more tense. Zahariev wasn't helping. He was watching me. I was so used to the feel of his gaze, I could even tell when he looked away and then back. It was like he thought I was going to crack at any moment, which meant he was preparing for one of two things: He was either going to hold me back if I ran or catch me if I fell.

It was always one of two.

The clock kept ticking, and I ground my teeth harder.

We shouldn't know each other so well.

Vulnerability is a weapon for an enemy's arsenal, my mother used to say, and I'd handed mine over without a second thought.

I ground my teeth harder.

And that fucking clock...

I was out of my chair before I realized what I was doing. I climbed on the couch and ripped it from the wall, flinging it

213

to the ground with all the strength I could muster. Jumping down, I strolled over to where it lay and stomped on it again and again and again.

No one held me back.

No one caught me.

Each time the plastic crunched beneath my boot, a little more fight left me.

When it was gone I took a few deep breaths and returned to my seat.

"You know," Cassius said, "you could have just asked one of us to take the battery out."

I didn't look at him as I stuck out my arm and flipped him off.

"Your girl's a fucking menace," Cassius said.

"I'm not his girl," I snapped. "And you're the fucking menace."

Cassius's lips twitched. I wanted to claw his eyes out.

He downed what was left of his coffee. "I'm going to go smoke."

"What kind of monster smokes before meeting a baby?" I asked.

"Any normal person would need a fucking cigarette after dealing with you," said Cassius. "Why do you think Zahariev smokes so much?"

"Cassius," Zahariev snapped. "Take a walk."

"On it, boss," he said, offering a mock salute.

When he was gone, I spoke.

"If you haven't introduced him to Hassenaah, maybe you should. They can bond over how much they hate me."

"Why do you think Cassius and Hassenaah hate you?" he asked.

"Because they think I'm an ungrateful, spoiled brat," I

said. "And Hassenaah wants to fuck you, or maybe she has fucked you and she can't shake it. I don't really know."

"Cassius doesn't hate you," said Zahariev. "He thinks you distract me. He hates that."

"Sounds like the same fucking thing," I said.

Zahariev didn't respond to that. Instead, he changed the subject.

"Would you like me to fire Hassenaah?"

I turned to look at him, surprised he would ask. "You can't," I said. "Coco loves her."

"I can do whatever I want," he said.

"Yeah, except they would both know you fired her because of me, and I don't want that kind of reputation."

Zahariev raised a brow. "What reputation is that?"

"If you swoop in to save me every time something goes wrong, I'm just going to look like a rat, and everything they say about me will be true."

Running to Zahariev was the equivalent of running to my dad to get me out of trouble, and there were just some things that weren't worth that kind of debt.

We fell into an uneasy silence, but most of that came from one unanswered question. He hadn't denied sleeping with Hassenaah, and that just ate away at my insides. I couldn't stop imagining them together, and the more I thought about it, the more my frustration grew.

I didn't even know why I needed to know.

Maybe it was because I saw Hassenaah as my enemy.

My anger ebbed and flowed, rising higher and higher, and just when I was about to speak, there was a knock at the door.

I thought the cheerful nurse had returned to take us to see Liam, except it wasn't her. It was an older doctor with a few wisps of hair on the top of his head. He wore scrubs and a white lab coat. I instantly disliked him. I'd rather see Dr. Mor, but he wasn't for traditional medicine.

He didn't follow the rules set by the church.

"Mr. Zareth," the doctor said.

I looked from the doctor to Zahariev, who nodded in acknowledgment.

"I have some information I think you might be interested in concerning Esther Pomeroy," he said. "We ran her labs upon arrival at the hospital. She had high concentrations of Commiphora myrrha in her system."

"What does that mean?" I asked.

The doctor glanced at me but then looked at Zahariev. So he was one of *those* men.

"She asked you a question," Zahariev said.

The doctor's eyes widened. "Apologies, madam—"

"Miss Leviathan," Zahariev corrected. "You have the pleasure of being in the presence of Miss Lilith Leviathan, Dr. Marlow."

His eyes widened further. "Apologies, Miss Leviathan. I...I didn't know."

The worst part was that if I were anyone else, he wouldn't have cared.

"You were saying what you found in Esther's system," I reminded curtly.

"Y-yes," he said, clearing his throat. "Commiphora myrrha. She had a high concentration of the herb in her system. In high doses, it can cause preterm labor."

"Are you...trying to say she was poisoned?"

"I can tell you she took a large dose and all at once. That is what caused the bleeding."

I started to speak, to argue that she would never do

216

something like this. She would never put Liam in danger like this, but the doctor continued.

"By the time she made it here, she had lost a significant amount of blood and went into cardiac arrest on the operating table." His gaze shifted to Zahariev, and so did mine. "I thought you would want to know and perhaps…deliver the news."

Zahariev nodded, though he wasn't looking at the doctor. He was looking at me. I heard the door close behind me.

"She would never, Zahariev!"

For a moment, I thought he was going to disagree with me, but then he pushed away from the wall where he'd been leaning and said, "I know. You aren't the only one who knew Esther, Lilith."

I blinked, and as my face flooded with heat, I dropped my gaze. I knew I was acting like the only person who had lost someone tonight, but it was hard to think beyond my personal pain, especially when I had been the one to find her.

Zahariev touched my chin, guiding my head back until I met his gaze.

"I know you want an enemy here," he said. "But I'm not it, little love."

I felt his thumb brush the corner of my mouth, and there was a part of me that wanted to bite him and not in a sexual way. I bared my teeth and jerked away from him. "You don't get to decide who my enemies are, Zahariev. I'll make you one if I want to."

His eyes darkened, and I wondered what he would have said had the cheerful nurse not returned at that moment to take us to see Gabriel and Liam. I gave Zahariev the most withering look I could muster before I left the room, discovering Cassius waiting outside.

"How long have you been out here?" I asked.

"Since I left," he said. "I didn't want to walk in on something I would never be able to erase from my memory."

"I wish I could erase you from my memory," I muttered.

The nurse either didn't hear our exchange or she was trying really hard to ignore us, because she smiled brightly and motioned for us to follow her.

"This way!"

She took us through a large door, past a registration desk, and into another hall of patient rooms. When we arrived at Gabriel's, she paused and knocked, announcing as she opened the door, "I brought family!"

I entered first but found that my feet wouldn't carry me beyond the entryway. Gabriel was holding Liam to his bare chest. I couldn't see more than the baby's profile, but he was small and pink and perfect.

Gabriel looked up and smiled at me.

"Lilith," he said. "Come see…he looks just like her."

I thought those words would make me happy, but they went through me like ice. Zahariev touched my arm. He had yet to enter the room, the same with Cassius. They were waiting for me.

Except I couldn't move.

All I could focus on was how hard my heart was beating. Zahariev's touch turned firm. I looked up to find him frowning, his brows lowered.

Lilith?

His mouth was moving, but I couldn't hear anything he said. His grip tightened, and I looked down at where he held me. His fingers immediately loosened.

"Lily?"

Gabriel's voice broke through the fog. I turned my head

and met his gaze. I couldn't handle any of it—not the way he said my name or the strange euphoric pain in his eyes. I couldn't handle meeting Liam without Esther.

I tore free of Zahariev and ran.

And ran.

And ran.

At some point, I was aware of someone following me.

"Lilith, will you fucking stop?"

It was Zahariev.

Somehow, I found it in myself to run faster, and I didn't stop until I was at Gabriel and Esther's apartment building. I was hot. My hair stuck to my sweaty face. My lungs fucking burned, but I didn't care. The pain of this day wasn't so bad when all I could do was concentrate on breathing.

It wasn't until I tried to punch in the code to the building that I realized I was shaking. Still I managed, and the door clicked open just as Zahariev approached. He reached for it and held it open. I didn't look at him as I slipped inside. He followed me to the elevator, his arm brushing mine as he came to stand beside me. I resisted the urge to put distance between us. There was a part of me that wanted him to hold my hand the way he did last night after I'd returned from Archbishop Lisk's, but he didn't, and when we got on the elevator, we stood on opposite sides, watching each other.

"You don't have to do this right now," he said.

"There is only now," I said.

Because later, I might not be strong enough to come back. I wasn't sure I was strong enough now, yet when the elevator doors opened, I stepped into the hall and returned to Esther's apartment.

When I entered this time, I recognized the smell. It wasn't just spilled tea on the floor. It was myrrh.

Zahariev walked past me and bent to pick up the most intact piece of the shattered mug, which just happened to be the part with the handle. He flipped it over, twisting it one way and then the other.

"What are you doing?" I asked.

"The myrrh sticks to the ceramic," he said and then showed me. Amber-colored rivulets clung to the surface.

"Do you think Lisk did this?"

It was a question I'd wanted to ask from the start, a suspicion I couldn't shake. It didn't seem like a coincidence that the archbishop had started to target dissenters, and now Esther was dead. Not that I'd ever heard her utter a word against the church, but maybe he'd killed her since he couldn't kill me.

"No," said Zahariev.

A hot wave of anger rose inside me at how fast he shut down my theory.

"Lisk wouldn't risk being deposed by the commission," he continued, "which is what would happen if he targeted anyone in my family."

"Except that he thinks his power exceeds the commission's," I said. "He told me that."

Zahariev placed the broken piece of ceramic on the counter, his gaze sliding to me. I got the impression he wanted his hands free, and I didn't like that.

"He might have said it, but that doesn't make it true. The commission appointed Lisk. The commission can remove him."

"Talk to me like I'm fucking five, Zahariev. Why is it so hard for you to believe Lisk would do something like this?"

Zahariev turned fully toward me. "You are making this personal."

"This is personal," I gritted out.

"You think Lisk targeted Esther because of you," said Zahariev. "But he has no reason to hurt her, even if she is important to you."

I turned away from him, scanning the kitchen. "I hate when you defend him."

"I'm not defending him, but you're missing the mark."

"I can't listen to you anymore," I said.

"It's not like you do anyway," he countered.

I winced.

"I'm not saying Lisk doesn't deserve your hate," Zahariev said. His voice was quieter this time. "But your rage belongs somewhere else, and I want to make sure you unleash it on the person who deserves it most."

My eyes were watering again. God, I fucking hated this.

I cleared my throat. "I just want to know what happened."

"That's why we're here, isn't it?"

I glanced at Zahariev as he made his way into the living room, pausing to look at something on the floor. I assumed it was Esther's blood and promptly turned my attention to the kitchen, crossing to where Esther kept her tea. I started opening containers, looking for any sign they had been tampered with, but found nothing like the substance on the mug.

When I was finished with the tea, I decided to go through the entire kitchen. I searched every cabinet and drawer, opened every labeled and unlabeled jar to smell what was inside. Esther liked to can things, especially different kinds of pickles. By the time I was finished opening them, my hand hurt, and all I could smell was vinegar.

"You're going to give yourself a headache," said Zahariev.

I turned to see him leaving Esther and Gabriel's room,

and I realized he had been in the bathroom. He looked a little pale, and his eyes had changed. At least his gaze felt different to me. Maybe now he understood why I was a little more unhinged than usual.

"I've had one since yesterday," I said.

Zahariev frowned, but he also looked a little frustrated. "You need to rest like Dr. Mor told you to do in the first place," he said. "I can do...whatever it is you're doing."

"I'm fine," I said. "I'm not leaving any room for doubt."

It was bad enough that the doctor at the hospital implied Esther had done this to herself. At least I could say with certainty I'd searched the house and found nothing like the substance in her mug.

"Did you check the medicine cabinet?" I asked.

"Lilith," Zahariev said, a note of disapproval in his voice.

You saw the bathroom, I wanted to say. *Why can't you understand why I need to do this?*

"I'll check," I said, leaving the kitchen, but Zahariev cut me off. I tried to step past him, but he wouldn't let me.

"Zahariev," I snapped.

"You don't need to check," he said. "Because you aren't going to find anything. All you're going to do is retraumatize yourself."

"You just offered to help," I said. "And now you're being a jerk."

"I'm not being a jerk," he said.

I started to shove him out of the way when he moved, slipping his arms around my waist and lifting me off the ground.

"Zahariev!" I wrapped my arms around his neck and my legs around his waist. It was instinctual, my body's response to feeling like he was going to drop me. He

222

didn't. Instead, his hands shifted beneath my thighs as he carried me, planting my ass on the dining room table.

"You don't fucking listen," he said.

"You don't fucking listen!" I tried pushing him away again, but he basically welded my hands to my thighs with his grip. So I tried to kick him, but I wasn't very successful considering he was standing between my legs.

"Are you done?" he asked. His jaw was tight, his masseters popping.

I glared up at him. He was already over a foot taller than me, but sitting beneath his frustrated gaze made me feel like a kid.

"I'm not a fucking child, Zahariev," I snapped.

"Then why are you acting like one?" he asked.

His words felt like a slap to the face. I physically recoiled. Zahariev didn't even blink. I jerked my hands free and crossed them over my chest, averting my gaze as I tried to keep myself from crying again.

"Lilith," Zahariev said, but I refused to look at him.

I felt his fingers graze my temple. I closed my eyes, taking a shuddering breath.

"I'm trying to protect you. Why won't you let me?"

I opened my eyes and met his gaze. I sort of hated the way his features softened, like he was trying to make me forget he'd called me a child.

"I don't need you to protect me."

"You need it," he said, unable to keep that tender facade. "You just don't want it from me."

"Oh, fuck off," I said. "Don't act like you've done anything for me out of kindness. We both know my father asked you to keep tabs on me."

Zahariev's brows lowered, and I swear his eyes became a

brighter shade of blue. I recognized I was playing with fire, but I wanted to burn.

"You don't think I have been kind?" he asked.

There was a rough edge to his voice. It scraped against my skin, making me shiver. As he spoke, he leaned closer. I had to hold on to his arms to keep from falling. His biceps were solid muscle, and I was reminded of how it had felt to be held by him after my run-in with Lisk.

My grip tightened as my body grew taut, almost uncomfortable. There was a heat pooling between my legs that made me feel swollen and empty all at the same time. I wanted to press my thighs together, but Zahariev was between them, once again keeping me from the thing I wanted.

"Kindness doesn't mean anything if you're doing it for favors, Zahariev."

For a second, he was still as stone, but then the corner of his mouth lifted in a mocking half smile before his eyes dropped to my lips.

"Oh, little love," he said. "You have so much to learn."

I felt like he was laughing at me, and the desire to make him suffer coiled tightly within me. I slid my hands around his neck and pulled him to me, our mouths colliding in a hot, too-simple kiss before parting for a few breaths. At the same time, I tightened my legs around Zahariev's waist and drew him closer. He was exactly how I'd imagined, hard and thick.

I almost moaned.

"Lily," Zahariev warned, his voice low and rough.

My fingers tightened in his hair. "I thought I told you not to call me that."

"Everyone calls you Lily," he said.

"My friends call me Lily," I said.

"Am I not your friend?" he asked.

I rocked my hips, reminding him of our current circumstances. Zahariev's breath hitched.

"Are you interested in fucking your friends?" I asked.

His hands shifted, spanning my rib cage. It was like he wanted to put distance between us but couldn't gather the courage to do so. Selfish prick. "I didn't mean for this to happen."

I blinked, my hold on him lessening.

"Are you saying you didn't mean to get hard?"

He stared at me, his mouth tight, his body rigid.

"Why are you making this so difficult? You know this can't happen."

"I'm not making it difficult," I said. "You act like this has to mean something. Sex can just be sex."

He'd fucked plenty of women with those same expectations. The only thing keeping him from doing the same with me was my name.

Zahariev released me and took a step back. I watched as he shut down whatever part of him had given in to temptation. That cold stab of rejection brought me back to reality.

I bolted for the bedroom.

"Fuck, fucking, fuck, Lilith!" I heard Zahariev shout behind me, but he couldn't stop me this time. I was in Esther's room before he reached me, pushing open the door to the bathroom.

I hadn't expected it to look worse than what I remembered, but now the blood had dried. It was no longer a glaring, bright red but a crude black, thicker in some places than others. I could see all the places she'd touched—the shower wall, the faucet, the countertop. It was like reading her panic in the minutes before she'd called me.

I held on to the frame of the door as I slid to the floor.

Zahariev came up behind me and sat, his arms encircling me, his knees caging me. He dropped his face into the crook of my neck.

I expected him to say something—one day, you'll learn to listen to me.

But he didn't.

He didn't say anything at all.

ZAHARIEV

I stepped into the hall to call for cleanup.

I needed a fucking cigarette, something to distract from the ache in my fucking balls, but I also didn't want to think long or hard on what Lilith had said in the dining room.

You act like this has to mean something.

Fucking brat.

She meant everything.

CHAPTER
ELEVEN

*Z*ahariev stepped into the hall. I knew he was calling for cleanup, though he didn't say it aloud, which I was grateful for. It was one thing to know it was happening, another thing to hear it said.

I wasn't sure how long we sat on the floor in Esther's bedroom, but eventually, Zahariev convinced me to leave. I was surprised he was still willing to deal with me. I was a fucking catastrophe, and I'd been very mean. I didn't really have an excuse, except that I had been awake for almost twenty-four hours and didn't have a good hold on my emotions right now.

I felt volatile. I felt reckless.

I would have fought him. I would have fucked him. I'd have done anything to do something other than what I was doing right now, which was *thinking*.

I rose from my position on the couch, pulling Esther's blanket around my shoulders, and crossed the room to Gabriel's record collection. I flipped through them, searching for something familiar to fill the silence, when I heard a noise coming from Liam's room.

I paused and looked toward the door. It sounded like something had fallen. I took a moment to pull out the record I'd chosen and then headed toward the room. As I opened the door, I tried to turn on the overhead light, but it looked like Gabriel had been in the middle of changing it out, because there was an empty hole in in the middle of the ceiling and a ladder nearby.

Entering this room felt like stepping back in time. I wondered if this was what Gabriel was working on before he was called away to deal with…well, whatever Zahariev had called him to do.

My chest tightened at the thought, but I shoved those feelings away.

I left the door propped open. The light from the living room was enough to see the last letter in Liam's name had fallen off the wall. I started to look around the crib when I noticed something inside it.

I jumped, my brain scrambling to register exactly what I was seeing. At first, I thought it was some kind of toy, but as I leaned closer, I realized it was something else. Like a large pulsing glob.

"What the *fuck*…" I pulled out my phone to get a better look, but as soon as the light hit the creature, it gave a high-pitched screech and *launched* itself into the air. I scrambled back, knocking into Liam's dresser as the creature grew tentacles, its pulsing mass alive with threads of purple electricity.

I reached for my gun just as Zahariev burst into the room, weapon drawn. The creature gave another high-pitched shriek and then spun itself toward him. Zahariev fired, and the creature screamed, falling to the floor. It seemed to writhe, pulsing with violet light. Its tentacle-like arms shot out toward the window, shattering the glass as it catapulted itself outside.

For a few seconds, everything was quiet.

Zahariev looked at me. "You okay?"

I nodded, though my heart was still beating a mile a minute.

Zahariev moved toward the window, his gun still drawn. I followed, but as I looked over the edge, all I could see was broken glass glimmering in the yellow security light.

"Where did it go?"

"There," said Zahariev, nodding toward the fence.

The creature had landed on the rolled barbed wire, blobs of its gelatinous body dropping to the ground, and it no longer glowed with that strange, purple light. Was it dead?

I pulled away from the window, leaving Liam's room and heading for the front door. I wasn't surprised when Zahariev followed. We headed down the hall to the elevator.

"I thought I imagined it," I said, still a little breathless. My heart hadn't stopped beating out of my chest. Zahariev looked at me.

"What do you mean?"

I met his gaze. "The night the enforcers attacked, I thought Burke's eyes were glowing with that same violet light."

"Why didn't you *say* anything?"

"Because I hit my fucking head," I said, not to mention what I'd seen had been there one minute and gone the next. "Don't act like you would have believed me! Look at that fucking thing!"

Zahariev didn't say anything, but we both knew I was right.

We made it to the ground floor and headed outside.

Zahariev drew his gun, but as we neared the wall where the creature had fallen, most of it was gone. A few pulsating globs remained, crawling through the grass like strange, glowing slugs. They must have sensed our approach, because they shrieked in unison, projecting several short, sticky limbs. Unlike the larger one, they only managed to roll in the grass like tiny wheels.

"Are you telling me that thing was a *mother*?" I asked as Zahariev squashed them with his boot.

"Not a mother," he said. "But it can definitely multiply."

"Then stop squishing them! What if you're making *more*?"

"You think they can come back from this?" he asked, lifting his boot. The sole was covered in slime.

My stomach flip-flopped. "Gross."

Zahariev scraped his shoe in the grass, leaving behind a trail of jelly.

"Do you think we can catch it?" I asked.

"No, I don't think we can *catch it*," Zahariev snapped, his voice raised. "What are we going to kill it with? I probably just infected my entire city with some goddamn alien virus."

"I realize I've given you a lot of reasons to yell at me, but I am just trying to solve a fucking problem, unlike you, who made this *a million times worse*!"

There was a moment of silence before Zahariev spoke. "I'm sorry. I didn't realize I was yelling."

"It's fine," I said, suddenly feeling the weight of my exhaustion. It had been a long twenty-four hours.

"I should get you home," Zahariev said, looking at his watch, but neither of us moved. The thought of returning to my apartment felt almost foreign, especially with so many unanswered questions. I shifted my gaze to the slime-covered grass.

"Do you remember when Lisk would preach about demons in church?" I asked.

I knew the witch said demons didn't really exist, but I thought these things made a pretty good argument to the contrary.

"Are you telling me you actually paid attention?"

"I didn't become a heathen until my magic surfaced," I said. "What's your excuse?"

"I was born this way," he said.

"*My point is*," I said in an effort to redirect the conversation, "what if that creature is a demon? Lisk said demons were spirits that could possess people. Those things possessed Burke and probably Esther too."

I paused.

"What if…what if *I'm* the reason it was even in their apartment?"

"Stop," Zahariev said, but the terror of that thought was already clawing at my throat. He took my face between his hands. "You can't go down this road, Lilith."

"I'll never forgive myself, Zahariev—"

"Yeah, well," he said, brushing my tears away. "Forgiveness is overrated. It's just something churchgoers shove down your throat so they can beg for it when they sin."

I gave a breathless laugh. "You're not cynical at all."

"It's how we were raised, little love," he said, dropping his hands to my shoulders. "Let's get you home."

He led me to the front of the apartment complex and placed a call to Felix. By that time, the cleanup crew had arrived. I wandered away from the commotion and found a spot to sit on the cold sidewalk, pulling my knees to my chest.

I jumped when I felt Zahariev drape his jacket around my shoulders. It was only then I realized I was shivering. A second later, he sat beside me, and I leaned my head against his shoulder.

"How am I supposed to do this?" I asked.

"What do you mean?"

"Go home. How do I go back to normal?"

"No one is expecting you to go back to normal," he said. "You go home, you sleep. You wake up in a different world. People will tell you it gets easier, but it never does. There are good days, and there are days when the pain hits like a fucking freight train."

I swallowed around the thickness gathering in my throat. Zahariev had never talked to me about losing his father, but listening to him now, I suddenly realized how hard it must have been. Not only had he lost his father, but he'd immediately succeeded him as head of his family.

"What do you do then?" I asked, looking up at him. "When the pain hits that bad?"

Zahariev's eyes dropped to mine.

"I just suffer through it until it's over," he said. "It's just life, little love."

"If this is life, then I don't know that I want to live it."

"Don't say that."

"Why not? I mean it. What am I even doing, Zahariev? I came here to escape a life I can't escape. Eventually, I will have to go home. I'll have to marry some asshole my dad chose just so he can stick his dick in me. All women in our world are just glorified breeding machines."

Zahariev's jaw popped. I wasn't sure which part he was

reacting to, but I didn't imagine he liked being called a breeder any more than I liked being called a machine. He knew his responsibility was the same—produce heirs, carry on the line.

"Promise me something," he said, still watching me.

"What?"

"If you ever feel like you don't want to do this anymore… tell me. Give me the chance to bring you back."

I wanted to kiss him.

For a brief moment, I felt like I'd never wanted anything more in my life. I found myself leaning toward him, tilting my face so our lips would meet at just the right angle.

"Lilith."

He said my name like a warning, but it wasn't the same as earlier when I'd felt him rock against me. This one was cold. It told me to behave.

"I'm sorry," I said. My laugh was hollow as I turned my head away. "I almost forgot who you were."

God, I really need sleep.

We fell into an uneasy silence. I thought it was more because I was embarrassed than anything else, but soon Felix arrived. Zahariev offered his hand when I went to rise, but I didn't take it. For now, I was done touching him. Felix exited the vehicle and held my door open. His face was drawn, his frown deep.

"I'm sorry, Miss Leviathan," he said.

I didn't know what to say. I was sorry too.

I climbed into the back of the vehicle. Felix slipped into the driver's seat and then rolled down my window. Zahariev stood outside it.

"You aren't coming?"

I hated the way my heart dropped, but he usually saw me home.

"There's a lot to be done," he said.

"I know you aren't going to be on your hands and knees scrubbing blood off the floor. So what else is there?"

He gave me a sad, half-hearted smile.

"Get some sleep, Lilith," he said, stepping away from the vehicle.

"Wait!" I said, shoving off Zahariev's jacket. I bunched it up and threw it out the window at him. He caught it, eyes blazing.

"I know you don't care," I said, "but if you do this without me, I'll never forgive you."

He didn't move a muscle, which made me think he knew how serious I was.

Good.

I meant every word.

I turned away, and Felix rolled up the window, sealing us in from the outside world. The cabin was warm, and classical music played quietly in the background. I let my head rest against the seat and closed my eyes.

———

Someone touched me.

I startled awake, jerking hard, sending a sharp pain straight through my already pounding head.

God, I felt awful.

It took me a moment, but I realized we'd arrived at my apartment complex. Felix stood with the door open, waiting for me to exit.

"Apologies, Miss Leviathan," he said. "You're home."

"Thanks, Felix," I said. I was so tired, and my mouth was so dry, I could barely bring my voice above a whisper. I slid out of the back seat, blinking. I felt like I was moving in slow motion. Maybe I was.

"Will you be all right?" Felix asked. I'd never heard true concern in his voice before, and honestly, it felt too late to ask.

"Coco's home," I said. "I'll be fine."

I didn't look back as I headed up the concrete stairs to my apartment.

Inside, it was quiet and dark except for the television, which was projecting light on the opposite wall and couch. A rumpled blanket lay to one side. It looked like Coco had just gotten up to go somewhere. She wasn't in the kitchen, so maybe the bathroom.

I pulled my boots off at the door and then headed down the hall toward my room when I noticed there was no light on in the bathroom and the door was ajar.

Something about that set me on edge.

I approached and pushed it open, relieved and also anxious when I found it was empty. Swallowing around a knot in my throat, I turned toward Coco's room, discovering the same.

A sense of dread overwhelmed me as I neared. The tips of my fingers were cold, and my heart raced as I pushed the door open.

Coco was in bed, and Cherub was curled into a ball on the pillow beside her head.

I released a shuddering breath.

"Hey," said Coco. Her voice was a little hoarse, like she'd just woken up. "Are you just getting home?"

I nodded.

She frowned and sat up, her long hair spilling over her shoulder. "What's happened?" she asked. "What's wrong?"

For the first time in my life, I found myself wishing I was like my mother and had armor around my heart. Maybe this was how it happened, one painful blow after the other, until one day, you woke up and felt nothing at all.

My throat tightened, and I tried hard to blink away the tears, but there was something about Coco's voice that tore it out of me. I crawled into her bed and lay down beside her. I felt her fingers comb through my hair.

"Lilith?" Coco whispered.

"Everything," I answered with a sob.

ZAHARIEV

With Lilith safely on her way home, I pulled out my phone and placed a call to Dr. Mor.

"It's early for you, Zahariev," he said.

"Yeah, well, it's been a long night," I said. "I need you to arrange pickup of Esther Pomeroy from Nineveh General Hospital within the hour. We need a full autopsy."

I could feel the shock in the silence that answered. "Of course."

He didn't ask what happened. He'd know soon enough.

"And those samples you took from Burke's corpse, " I added before hanging up. "The jellylike substance?"

"Yes?"

"I know what it is."

PART II

THE
HARROWING

CHAPTER
TWELVE

Sons of Adam was busy.

The bar was packed, and every table was full. A thick haze of smoke hung in the air, which made the entire dining room seem darker. Now and then, someone would rise and wander down the hall. A few were just going to the bathroom, but others were going to the warehouse, where Samuel kept an arsenal. He had everything from small knives to an actual flamethrower.

What are you going to do with that? I'd asked when I'd gone to buy my first handgun.

Look at it, he replied.

I kind of believed him. He seemed like a collector who had started by selling a few items on the side. Despite this, he took his business seriously. The process of obtaining a weapon was actually far more extensive than just showing up at Sons of Adam. He required background checks and gave in-person classes and written tests.

If you don't wanna go through with the requirements, then you don't need a weapon, he'd said.

Did Zahariev have to do this? I asked, a little sullen, mostly because my father had already taught me to shoot.

Who do you think taught Zahariev?

Until that moment, I'd assumed it was his father.

Though I whined, I appreciated Samuel's gatekeeping. Very few people here should have weapons, though that didn't stop them from trying to buy them elsewhere or making their own. I didn't know how many times I'd heard reports of stabbings on the street with some kind of sharpened piece of plastic or metal. It was a problem, but not the kind it might turn into if anyone could get a gun...or a fucking flamethrower.

I sat in the corner of the room at a round table. I'd been here for two hours, and I'd had four strawberry daiquiris and only half my mozzarella sticks. After my third drink, they'd started to taste like rum and sugar, which was fine. I didn't really have an appetite.

After Felix had dropped me off, I slept all day. When I woke up, Coco made soup, and I drank the broth. It wasn't that I felt nauseous exactly. I just didn't feel hungry.

I didn't feel much right now aside from a need to find out what happened to Esther in that apartment.

A waitress dropped by my table carrying a tray of empty glasses and pitchers. Her name was Shelley. She had fluffy, blond hair and coal-black liner smudged around her eyes. She smelled like cigarettes and talked like her lungs were on fire. She'd served me since I arrived in Nineveh. Sometimes, she'd slip me an extra order of mozzarella sticks *for the road*, she'd say.

"You want another drink, darlin'?" she asked.

I looked at my empty glass, trying to weigh just how buzzed was too buzzed to fight a demon.

That was what I'd started calling the blob creature I'd found in Liam's bedroom. It seemed like the most fitting name, considering I was pretty certain it had possessed Koval, Burke, and now Esther.

My eyes watered at the thought, which was how I knew I wasn't buzzed enough.

"One more," I said, handing her the empty glass. "Thank you, Shelley."

"You got it, darlin'," she said, heading off into the crowd.

I hadn't come here to drink. I hadn't even come here for mozzarella sticks, but Shelley delivered them shortly after I sat down.

"Jack started makin' them the moment you walked in the door," she said.

I had to swallow the lump in my throat, unprepared for how the smell would make my stomach churn, but I didn't want anyone to ask me what was wrong. If they didn't know yet, they would soon. I suspected the only reason news of Esther's death hadn't reached the streets was because the funeral hadn't been announced.

I was dreading that day.

I let my magic unwind, opening myself up to a barrage of lust around me, but the feeling was fuel. It overpowered my despair, and I used it to tease.

"Tell Jack I owe him one," I said.

"Oh, honey," said Shelley. "You don't wanna owe that man nothin'. I'll just tell him you said thank you."

I grinned, but as soon as she turned her back, I dropped my smile and the charade.

I leaned forward, resting my elbows on the small table, and picked up one of the mozzarella sticks. I dipped it into the marinara sauce, twisting it one way and then the other. I had no intention of eating it. I just needed to keep my hands busy. It was a habit my mother abhorred and when she'd catch me, she'd kick me under the table if we were in public or slap my arm if we were at home. It got to the point where I'd flinch whenever she lifted her hand, even if it was to pick up her silverware.

That just made her more angry.

And my father wondered why I didn't miss her.

"Hey, firecracker," said a voice.

It was familiar, so I didn't even look up, but I stopped playing with my food, returning the mozzarella stick to its basket.

"I'm not in the mood, Abel," I said.

"You're never in the mood," he said.

I looked up, glaring at the older man who was also Sam's brother. He wasn't creepy like others who frequented Sons of Adam, but he liked to give me a hard time, and I usually gave it right back. I just didn't feel up to a verbal sparring match tonight.

He took a seat.

"You wanna talk about it, firecracker?" he asked.

"How many times have I told you not to call me that?"

"There are worse nicknames," he said.

"There are also *no* nicknames."

He chuckled but fell quiet, unfazed by my prickly behavior. After a few moments, I took a breath.

"I'm just not having a good day, Abel."

"Nothing wrong with a bad day," he said. "We're allowed one now and then."

"You be nice to her, Abel," said Shelley, sliding a fresh drink to me. "She's having a hard night."

"Is it really that obvious?"

244

"Considering you haven't finished your mozzarella sticks or convinced some poor sod to pay for your food and drinks, yes. It's very obvious," said Abel.

Damn, am I that predictable? I pursed my lips.

"I think I know what's got you down," he said.

"You do?" I asked, dread pooling in my stomach. If he brought up Esther, I wasn't sure how I would react. I'd probably burst into tears.

"You heard about Tori, didn't you?" he said.

"I more than heard about it." I paused to swallow. "I found him."

"I knew it was comin'," Abel said.

I frowned. "What do you mean?"

"He's not the first to be executed for talkin' about gods under the mountain," he said. "You know that's why Southgate got destroyed...too many people started believing in other gods."

I frowned. I hadn't actually known that.

"Who are these other gods?" I asked.

"They're just stories that didn't make it into the *Book of Splendor*," he said. "Now and then, they surface, and the church stomps them out. At some point, you gotta wonder why they're so afraid of something if it's not true."

"What do you mean there are stories that didn't make it into the *Book of Splendor*?"

Abel stared at me like he couldn't believe I was so ignorant, but I was raised within the walls of First Temple in Hiram. There were no stories outside the ones in the *Book of Splendor*.

"The *Book of Splendor* was curated by men. They came together at a council back when we had kings to decide what stories should go in their so-called sacred book. They claim they were 'divinely guided,' which is a funny way to say politically motivated."

"Do you know the stories?" I asked. "The ones that didn't make it into the book?"

He shook his head. "Not fully. They don't exist in written form anywhere that I know of, but I bet you can find someone who thinks they know the truth of it. The gist is what you've already heard. People believe there is more than one god and that they are trapped behind the Seventh Gate. They claim there are signs the gate is weakening, that their magic is slipping through the cracks, making the weather harsher, the people sicker and more violent, but if you ask me, that's just people looking for an explanation for something they can't explain."

"So you don't believe any of it?"

Abel shrugged. "Gods under a mountain aren't any more unbelievable than a god in the sky. What does it matter?"

"It matters because people are being killed," I said.

"People have always been willing to die for their beliefs."

"Tori wasn't willing," I said. I didn't think he knew what he was saying half the time. "He was targeted and murdered because the archbishop is a fucking coward."

For some reason, the noise in the restaurant dipped, and my voice carried over the crowd. There was a beat of silence, and I felt like every eye in the room was on me.

I looked around. "Mind your own fucking business," I snapped.

It was slow, but soon people shifted their attention away from me, though I couldn't help feeling like some were still listening.

Abel leaned across the table.

"You know how some of us live so long? We know when to keep our thoughts to ourselves."

"Maybe if more people weren't afraid to speak up, Lisk wouldn't feel like he could just kill us."

"You have sweet dreams, firecracker, but in our world, when people get too mouthy, they die, and when a lot of them get too mouthy, they burn."

"Are you telling me to let it go?"

"I'm just telling you, you can't do anything if you're cold in the ground. You think it's bad now? It's gonna get worse."

I frowned, brows lowering. "Why do you say that?"

"Because I've seen this before," he said. "Right before the fire that took out Southgate." Abel downed the rest of his beer, letting out a wet sigh as he stood. "I'll get your tab, firecracker," he said, throwing a handful of dollars on the table. "Keep your head down and your eyes open, and watch the rich."

"Watch the rich?"

"They'll abandon the area," he said. "Lisk isn't gonna let them die. It takes money to start again."

"Who's rich in Nineveh?" I asked.

"Well, the Zareth family, for one," he said. "But I never said they would only target us. There are plenty of sinners all over Eden." He paused and knocked on the table. "I'll tell Sam to get you back."

I watched Abel wander away, pausing at the bar to clap friends on the back, laugh, and make jokes. It was like he hadn't just been talking about a possible end to the world, though maybe he felt like he'd survived one and could again, or maybe he wasn't afraid to die.

I couldn't decide if I was afraid of death or the end of the world. I'd never really thought about it, not even when

I'd attended church regularly and Archbishop Lisk would preach about the promise of paradise. It was a gift for the righteous, for those who believed God sacrificed his only son for our sins, but that always seemed too simple.

Shouldn't paradise be granted to people who were inherently good? That was assuming an afterlife even existed, except that if it didn't, it would mean that Esther no longer existed, and I didn't think I could handle that.

"Sam's ready for you, honey," said Shelley, dropping by the table to leave a glass of water and a handwritten receipt.

I stood, briefly overwhelmed by dizziness as the alcohol went straight to my head. I paused, steadying myself with a hand on the table. I downed the water. It was so cold, it almost tasted sweet, or maybe I was just dehydrated.

I headed down the dark hall. At the end, there was a door with a sign that read EMPLOYEES ONLY. I pushed it open and found myself in a familiar warehouse. It was full of shiny cars and looked more like an auto shop than a place to buy weapons.

A couple of men were trying to guide a tow truck into an open bay while another group gathered around the hood of a compact pickup truck. They had some kind of machine rolled under the front of the vehicle and were attaching chains to parts of the engine.

Sam stood behind a metal podium, looking through a stack of papers. He was tall and thin and sported a perfectly manicured goatee.

"Pretty car," I said as I approached.

He looked at me and grinned. "Wanna take it for a spin?"

"I wish," I said. "You know I can't drive."

"I got an ole beater and an empty field with your name on it whenever you're ready to learn," he said.

248

"Thanks, Sam," I said, though I wasn't sure I'd ever take him up on that offer. It wasn't like I could afford a car anyway.

"What can I do for you?" he asked.

"I need a stun gun," I said.

"What for?"

"To stun people," I said.

He chuckled. "Anyone in particular?"

"You didn't ask me this many questions when I bought a gun," I said.

"When Zahariev Zareth gives you a call, you don't ask questions," he said.

"I never got that memo."

"I imagine very few rules apply to you," he said, shoving his paperwork into a folder.

"What's that supposed to mean?"

I expected him to say something about my name. He'd never broached the subject of my family, though he was aware.

"Men are useless in the face of a beautiful woman," he said. "Something just short-circuits in their brains."

I raised a brow. "You sure it's the brain?"

Sam chuckled and stepped away from the podium.

"Come on," he said. "I'll hook you up."

I followed him into his office, which was small and square. Inside, he had a simple metal desk with a laminate wood top. Behind it was a long cabinet with different doors and drawers, each one locked. Sam unhooked a ring of keys from his belt loop and searched through them until he found the one he was looking for.

"How do you know which is which?" I asked.

"A really great memory," he answered as he unlocked

one of the drawers, pulling out a black plastic case and an additional box. He set the items on his desk before closing and locking the drawer again.

"You ever use a stun gun before?" he asked, opening the case.

"How hard could it be?" I asked. "Just point and shoot."

The corner of his lips lifted, but he soon turned serious as he instructed me, taking the stun gun from the box.

"Cartridge attaches to the front of the gun," he said. "Squeeze the tabs, and keep your hand clear of the front of the cartridge. There's a sight at the top and a laser. That's where the top prong hits. The second shoots below. Turn the safety off, laser comes on, aim for center mass. Trigger."

As he spoke, he demonstrated.

"What's center mass?"

"Midsection," he said. "Got it?"

"Got it," I said.

Seemed simple enough, though I wasn't exactly sure what *midsection* meant for a demon blob. I was only here because I had a theory, and I needed a stun gun to test it.

I hoped the current from the gun would overwhelm whatever electricity coursed through the demon and kill it. Of course, it was possible the currents would combine and make it stronger. If that was the case, my backup was the blade, which I had in my backpack. I realized it wasn't the best plan—hunting for demons without knowing for sure what weapons might work against them—but I didn't really care. It had killed Esther, and I was willing to do just about anything to destroy it.

Sam started packing up the stun gun.

"You don't have to repack it," I said, sliding my backpack off my shoulder.

"You planning on using it tonight?" he asked.

"Just leaving prepared," I said.

Sam studied me and then asked, "You aren't thinking about going after members of the church, are you?"

"No," I said.

Not yet anyway.

"You understand that would be a suicide mission no matter whose daughter you are," he said.

I smiled, eyes narrowing slightly, and teased, "Are you afraid of the church, Sam?"

"Yes." His tone was matter-of-fact and stole the humor right from my body. "And if you knew what was good for you, you'd be too."

I thought he might reconsider letting me have the stun gun, but he handed it over, along with two additional cartridges.

"How much?" I asked.

Sam laughed like I had just told him a joke.

"I'll put it on your tab."

I flushed, embarrassed because he knew I didn't have the money. I shoved the cartridges into my backpack, already heavy with the blade. I wished it had never caught my attention. Maybe I'd be dancing on stage tonight, making my own money. Maybe Esther would still be alive.

I shoved those thoughts aside. I had to focus on the here and now, and part of that was hunting down these fucking demons.

"Thanks," I said.

"Stay out of trouble," he said.

Suddenly, there was a loud crash, like metal slamming into metal. I turned to look out the office window. One of the chains had come loose from the engine of the truck, causing it to collide with the edge of the vehicle and then the cement floor.

"Motherfucker," Sam muttered, stepping past me. He left the small office, yelling, "Were you fucking born yesterday!"

I followed him out, taking that as my cue to leave, pausing as I heard one of the mechanics speak.

"It's not our fucking fault!" he said, flinging something to the ground, a familiar gelatinous substance.

"What the fuck is that?" another asked.

"I don't know, but it's oozing out of the engine."

I inched toward them, noticing the small glob of light pink goo on the ground. It wasn't moving. I wondered if it had been churned to mush when the engine had started. Was I going to have to run every fucking one of these demons through a wood chipper?

"Where did you pick up the car?" I asked.

"Off Tenth and Tyre. Wouldn't start. Obviously found the problem."

I left, slipping out one of the open bays into the back alley. It was lined with dumpsters, overflowing with trash. A rivulet of unknown origin and substance snaked its way down the asphalt road. I followed it until I found myself at Fifth Street, which intersected with Smugglers' Row into Gomorrah. The mechanic had said Tenth and Tyre, which was a few blocks down from Gabriel and Esther's apartment. I guessed part of the demon had taken refuge in that truck after fleeing. I wondered if the others were near and if they would be on the move now that it was dark.

It occurred to me that I was being reckless and a little unfair to Zahariev. I'd made him promise not to investigate

Esther's death without me, and here I was hunting demons, but this felt better than sitting at home crying.

As I headed away from Gomorrah, the night was less busy. The area here was more industrial, a mix of residential apartment buildings and factories. Some of them still burned coal, which made the air hazy and heavy. It settled in my lungs like stones. I hated everything about it, hated knowing that the people who lived and worked here were sick from it and would die young all so the elite in Hiram could wear cashmere.

Until I'd come to Nineveh, I'd never known what it took to supply that kind of fabric, but that was a theme in my life.

I followed Fifth to Tyre, then headed south to Tenth. The smell of mildew and floral detergent wafted into the street from an open laundromat door. Customers wandered out and into the nearby liquor store or the deli a little farther down the street. There was a part of me that envied these people completing their everyday tasks while I was on a mission to kill the thing that had stolen one of my dearest friends.

I came to the intersection of Tenth and Tyre. Ahead, there were greater pockets of darkness from broken street-lights. Those that worked flickered. Most of the shops on this street were closed or abandoned, their windows boarded. I blamed the graveyard, which was just another block south. Its eeriness cast a wide net, ensuring the only businesses that survived were a monument and grave marker company, an undertaker, and a celestial shop.

I stopped in front of it. The window was lit with a string of lights, illuminating an astrology map painted in gold. Through the glass, I could see shelves of candles, crystals, and cards, things forbidden by the church—things that made me curious. I wondered if people came here seeking something to believe in because religion had hurt them too.

Those were heavy thoughts, and I wasn't ready to add them to the burden of my grief.

I turned away from the window, looking up and down the street. I'd come to the right place, but as I scanned the pavement, I didn't see any sign of the glowing demon blob or its many children.

It was possible it was too bright. I assumed by the way it had reacted to my flashlight it preferred the dark. I wandered a little farther down the sidewalk when I heard a noise coming from the alley between the celestial shop and another abandoned building.

I shifted, my boots grinding on the concrete as I pressed myself against the front of the shop. I slid my backpack off and took out the stun gun and my only two cartridges, shoving one in each pocket, before peering down the alley. There were dumpsters and round metal trash cans overflowing with garbage. It was mostly dark, save for a greenish-blue light blazing over a shadowed side door.

For a moment, I saw nothing, but then I noticed a lid leaning against one of the trash cans, wobbling. I inched closer, readying the stun gun, though I'd have to put some distance between me and the demon if I wanted to do any real damage.

As I neared, I didn't feel afraid but angry, determined to see these fuckers hurt as much as they'd hurt me, though I didn't think that was possible.

I kicked the lid aside, only to find a large rat. Its eyes were hazed in violet, and when it hissed at me, black tendrils unfurled from its mouth, fluttering like a forked tongue.

An undignified shriek left my mouth. Before I could

think, I jumped back and pulled the trigger of my stun gun, but the rat made its escape, diving between the trash bags where the two darts had landed.

Fuck!

I retrieved a new cartridge from my pocket. My heart was still racing as I tried to make sense of what I'd just witnessed.

A rat. You just saw a rat possessed by a demon.

For now, I didn't let myself think about what that might mean for Nineveh—for Eden. With my new cartridge loaded, I shoved the bags aside and kicked over trash cans. Not that I expected the rat to still be there or that I could use the stun gun on it, but I had to check.

Call it due diligence.

I even shoved the dumpster, but nothing scurried out.

It had probably slipped into a drain. I wondered if the demon could reproduce on its own, if that single rat could infect multiples. There were millions of rats in the city, which meant millions of ways for that demon to travel.

Maybe that was how it had gotten into Esther's house.

"Fuck!" I yelled as I kicked one of the fallen trash cans.

I stood in the silence, anger winding through me, feeling completely helpless. How was I supposed to fight something like this?

Rat poison?

I shrugged. It was worth a shot.

Honestly, I'd try anything, so long as I eradicated this *thing* responsible for Esther's death. Though I wondered if that would be enough. As much as I wanted to annihilate them, I also wanted to know where they came from. They looked like something that had escaped from a sci-fi movie or a mad scientist's evil lair, and while I called them demons,

I didn't think they were the ones Archbishop Lisk warned us about.

Maybe it was some kind of curse gone wrong or a spell cast by learned magic.

Whatever it was, I had to find the source.

I took a breath and let it escape slowly between my lips before turning to leave. I suspected I'd made enough noise to chase away anything holed up here, and I knew from last night that those demons could move incredibly fast for something that looked like a slug.

Then a drop of water hit my face.

Or at least, that's what I thought it was until I reached up to wipe it away.

That's when I realized it wasn't water at all but gel.

I tilted my head back. Against the neon-tinged sky, I saw the pulsing mass of a demon stretched across black wires overhead. It had yet to ignite, appearing gray instead of violet, until it realized I had spotted it. It gave a horrifying cry that made my ears ring and then lit up like lightning in the sky. As it did, sparks erupted from the lines where it nested, and the light behind me flickered.

I stumbled back, raising the stun gun as the demon launched itself at me, black limbs bursting from its pulsing body. I pulled the trigger, but only one of the darts hit my mark, sinking into the demon's gelatinous body.

It let out an awful cry, but I didn't think it was in pain.

I thought I pissed it off.

One of its tentacles wrapped around my wrist, tightening as a serpent would, burning my skin. I screamed and tried to jerk my hand away, but the limb remained tight. I drew my gun, having no other option, and shot at the creature. Its unholy howl echoed in the narrow passageway, but it released me, leaving behind an oily substance on my skin that burned.

"Fuck!"

I realized too late how unprepared I was for this fight. I kept my gun pointed at the demon as it pulsed, growing in size, using its tendril-like arms to glide effortlessly toward me. I had one more cartridge in my pocket, but I needed time to load it.

So I fired, and as my bullets sliced through the demon, chunks of it tore free. The creature shrieked, and the sound was like nails on a chalkboard permeating my entire body. I gritted my teeth against it and kept firing as I put distance between us.

When my clip was empty, I holstered my gun and took out the stun gun and cartridge.

My hands shook, though I didn't think it was so much from fear as it was from pain. The spot where the demon had touched me still burned.

I kept shifting away, maintaining distance, even as I loaded my final cartridge. The demon was quivering and bubbling, almost like it was boiling. Maybe it was. I imagined it was angry. It wasn't until something shot out of it and flew past my head that I realized what it was doing— returning my fucking bullets.

Goddammit!

I dove behind the dumpster as more followed, making an awful high-pitched sound as they struck, and managed to shove the new cartridge into my stun gun. Finally, there was silence, at least from the demon. *I* was fucking *loud*, my breath haggard and uneven.

Slowly, I peered around the dumpster, but the demon was gone.

"Are you fucking kidding me?" I whispered.

I leaned farther out just as another bullet slammed into the dumpster near my face.

I screamed and fell back but caught a glimpse of the creature glowing violet as it unleashed another bullet. I reached for the trash can lid. Using it as cover, I stepped out from behind the dumpster. As the demon glowed, preparing to launch another bullet at me, I aimed and fired.

This time, both darts hit their mark. I squeezed the trigger, as if the current might increase the harder I pulled.

The demon pulsed and flashed, lighting up like a Christmas tree.

I shuffled toward my backpack, which I'd stupidly left near the opening of the alleyway, and withdrew the blade. The creature's shrieks grew louder at the sight of it.

"Does this scare you, fucker?" I asked.

I'd never fought with a knife before and didn't know how to hold it, but I wasn't afraid, because the current running through the demon kept it frozen in place. I neared, lifting the dagger, my hand fisted around the hilt, and shoved it into the demon.

The cut was easy, and I thrust so hard, the tip of the blade hit the asphalt, causing my hand to slip. I readjusted my grip and continued my frenzied attack, fueled by anger.

When I was done, it seemed too quiet, but maybe because everything had been so loud.

I sat on my knees, breathing hard, watching its pink-tinged body wither into blackened ash.

Then I looked at the knife.

It had basically melted that creature. Like it had been *made* to do so.

"What are you?" I muttered, turning the blade over in the muted light.

As I staggered to my feet, I was certain of one thing.

I needed to get that jade, and soon.

ZAHARIEV

Archbishop Lisk's home sat opposite First Temple, a smaller, no less striking version of his coveted church. It was a sprawling mansion with a gleaming marble facade, stained-glass windows, and a spired rooftop.

It was a shrine dedicated to his greed.

I rapped on the door and rang the doorbell in quick succession before taking a drag from my cigarette.

I waited until Lisk answered to let the smoke roll off my tongue into his face.

"Alarich," I said.

"Mr. Zareth," his voice thick, his frown deep. "What can I do for you?"

"I brought something that I think... belongs to you," I said.

I watched him stiffen, and his expression

became almost hopeful, eyes shining with an inner light.

Feet shuffled behind me, and I stepped aside as Cassius and three soldiers lugged two bodies down Lisk's pristine stone walkway before depositing the corpses on his steps.

Lisk's face turned bright red.

"I believe you know them? Jonathan Koval and Joseph Burke," I said, using my foot to roll them onto their backs so Lisk could get a good look.

"This is obscene!" Lisk seethed, the words slipping between his teeth.

I moved my tongue over the inside of my cheek and laughed.

"Come on, Lisk. You've seen worse. You've done worse...haven't you?"

The archbishop looked up at me, scowling. I took a deep draw from my cigarette.

"If you've come here to threaten me, Zareth, I'll—"

I released a plume of smoke directly into his face again and leaned closer.

"You'll what?" I asked.

Cassius and the three soldiers returned with two more bodies.

They were Christian Masters and Judas Fischer III.

I dropped my cigarette to his marble steps, crushing it beneath my foot.

"How dare—"

"How dare I what? Threaten you?" I smiled. "I'm not making a threat. I'm laying your sins at your feet."

Cassius and the boys brought the final two bodies. Jadon Chavara and Kane Hoyt.

"You recognize them? They all have one thing in common with you. They hurt someone under my protection."

Someone very important to me, I thought.

Lisk remained silent, almost stoic.

I shifted closer, placing a hand on his shoulder, leaning close.

"I know your secret," I said, my fingers tightening, digging into his skin. "If you harm one hair on her head, I'll end you."

I took a step back, holding his gaze. It was as though his crimes had suddenly

caught up with him. They pulled at his face, aging him.

"And just so we're clear, that's not a threat. It's a promise."

The apartment was dark when I returned home, which meant Coco was asleep. I relaxed a little, relieved that I wouldn't have to explain my ruined clothes or the visible cut on my hand.

I didn't like hiding things from Coco, but what happened tonight felt impossible to explain. It would also cause her to worry and not about the demons, which should be her real concern.

Instead, she'd fret over me. I was grateful to have someone who cared about me, which was why I didn't want to burden her. The things I'd seen, they were better left unsaid. At least for now.

I wandered into my bedroom and turned on the light, throwing my backpack on the bed and shoving off my jacket, grinding my teeth as the fabric slid over my burned hand.

It stung. The skin was blistered, shining red, yellow, and a little brown. I wondered how to make it stop hurting. Right now, it felt like it was on fire. The entire thing throbbed, touched only by air. I was going to have to figure out how to treat it until I could make it to Dr. Mor, though I knew once I did, he would inform Zahariev of my visit.

I sort of resented that I couldn't do anything without Zahariev finding out, but it was better than my father knowing, so I'd have to take the lesser of two evils.

I stepped out of my boots and then searched through the clothes on my floor for something to sleep in when I heard the toilet flush.

Fuck. Coco *was* awake.

I wondered if I could turn my light off in time to go unnoticed, but as I swiped a shirt off the floor and straightened, Coco was already standing in my doorway.

She looked me up and down.

"Did you have to fight a bear to get those mozzarella sticks?" she asked.

I swallowed before I spoke. "They were busy."

Coco just stared. I didn't really know what to say. There was a part of me that wanted to tell her about my night, but I didn't even know how to begin. *Remember during church when the bishops would lecture about demons? When they claimed that sin led to possession? They lied. Even the pure of heart are vulnerable.*

"Why are you up?" I asked instead, changing the subject.

"I had to pee," she said, pausing before adding, "You got a delivery today."

I frowned. I hadn't been expecting anything, but then I wondered if Gabriel had sent along something to get my attention. I hadn't answered any of his texts.

"From who?"

"Zahariev," she said.

"Send it back," I said.

265

"You don't even know what it is!"

"I don't need to know," I said. "I don't want it."

She frowned at me. "I know you're angry with him right now, but don't let that get in the way of accepting a perfectly new dryer."

"A *dryer?*"

"I've already done four loads of laundry in record time," she said. "And warmed my towel for my bath."

I wasn't going to lie, that sounded really nice, especially when winter hit. The bathroom was poorly insulated, and there were no vents, so the only warmth came from the steam of hot water, and that didn't last long when it was below zero outside.

"I just…don't want to feel like I owe him," I said, though I knew Zahariev didn't expect anything in return, it didn't feel right to let it lie. I wanted to pay him back for the rent, and now I wanted to pay him back for the dryer.

The list was getting long.

"He isn't asking for anything, Lilith," she said. "He just…cares about you."

"Coco," I said, stopping her. I didn't want to think about Zahariev caring. I'd crossed some boundaries with him the night of Esther's death. I blamed our familiarity. It was easy to seek comfort from him, but now that I was on the other side, I realized the mistake I'd made.

"I'm just saying, he's trying to help," she said.

"You just don't want to give up warm towels," I said.

"You won't either once you try it," she said. "I'll put one in now."

I didn't argue, because it honestly sounded wonderful.

So did a shower.

Coco vanished to retrieve a towel. I left my room, pausing

just outside to open the door to the laundry closet. The new dryer was bright white with a large window and sat on top of our yellowed washer. It had a digital display and buttons, not dials. It was also much larger.

"Isn't it nice?" she asked.

It was definitely a far cry from the one Coco and I had pieced together at the junkyard. I'd used my magic to coerce the owner into helping us scavenge for parts over the last few years. It wasn't ideal, but it worked far better than making our way down to Sumer just to do laundry every week.

"It sings to you when it's done," she said, nudging me out of the way so she could throw my towel in.

I smiled. "Coco, are you in love with a dryer?"

"I've never had anything this nice, Lilith," she said. "I mean…not that it's mine."

My heart squeezed at her comment. Sometimes, I forgot that Coco hadn't grown up with the same comforts I had, and I hated myself for that.

"It *is* yours," I said, looking at her. "I won't say anything to Zahariev."

There was a moment of silence, and then she said, "He asked about you. I told him you were sleeping."

I wondered if he believed her. I doubted it.

"Thanks," I said, pausing to take a breath. Suddenly, I realized why it was easier to be out in the night, hunting Esther's killer, whether it turned out to be the demon in Liam's room or not, because in here, within the walls of my apartment, the reality hit too hard. Pressure built behind my eyes, and I swallowed hard. "I'm going to take a shower."

"Holler at me when you're ready, and I'll bring your towel," Coco said.

"Go to bed, Coco," I said. "It's late."

"It's *early*," she said. "And it's fine. I'm awake anyway."

She seemed decided, so I didn't argue and made my way into the bathroom. I scrubbed every inch of my body, feeling as though I was covered in a thin layer of grit. I was careful with my burn, though it stung under the steady stream of water.

When I was finished, I cracked the door and called to Coco. She was right about the warm towel. It was heaven, especially after the shock of leaving the scalding shower and stepping into the chilly bathroom.

I kept it wrapped around me until it was cold and I was dry, using the time to bandage my burn with gauze and medical tape.

When I was finished, I changed into a long-sleeved top and shorts.

Before climbing into bed, I emptied my backpack, storing the dagger in the top drawer of my bedside table. The gems in the hilt glared back at me.

"Don't look at me like that," I said aloud, realizing I sounded a little irrational, but I couldn't help it. I felt like the thing was judging me for having used it on a demon without knowing anything about its origin. Usually, that wouldn't bother me, but this dagger was different. It had magic apparently only I could feel, and it was stalking me, having returned to me twice, once through the enforcer and then from the bottom of the canal. I couldn't even escape it in my sleep, because it starred in my nightmares.

I missed the days when I was disturbed only by the occasional sex dream in which Zahariev usually appeared, though I should probably refrain from allowing my mind to go down that road given how he'd acted when I'd kissed him.

"If you can call that a kiss," I muttered to myself.

It hadn't at all been what I'd dreamed—a basic peck, a

268

brush of the lips. I hated that he was so restrained, so withdrawn. How had he managed to put a lid on his desire? I'd felt it fully against my own.

"Why are you even thinking about this?"

"Thinking about what?" Coco asked.

I jumped and shoved the drawer closed, turning to look at her, hiding my hand behind my back. Her eyes darted to the nightstand. I recognized the suspicion darkening her gaze. I was going to have to find a different hiding spot for my blade.

The blade, I corrected myself.

Not that I didn't trust Coco. I just didn't want to explain how I'd come to possess it. In this case, the truth sounded a lot like a lie, and it would mean explaining other things that might upset her. What was happening to me was new and strange and almost unbelievable. I don't think I even had words to describe it.

"Just…something Zahariev said," I explained and then quickly asked. "What's up?"

"I figure you'll still be asleep when I leave for work, so I wanted to let you know in case you had plans, you're on Cherub watch tonight."

"Got it," I said. I did have plans, but I'd taken Cherub into the Trenches. I could take her to the docks too. She was turning out to be a true sidekick. "Anything else?"

Coco started to speak but hesitated and then shook her head. "Get some sleep, Lily."

———

I sat on the ground, knees drawn to my chest. I was cold despite the fire before me. It gave off no heat but burned if touched. I knew because the tips of my fingers still stung,

269

blistered by the flames. I was somewhere deep inside the cave, the sound of the roaring desert wind long gone, replaced by an almost solid silence.

Maybe it was not so much the silence that had mass but the darkness that settled on my back like a heavy stone. I could not escape it, even this close to light.

Somewhere behind me lay a corpse.

She looked like me but was not me.

Not anymore.

Something cold slithered across my foot, up and around my leg.

It was a serpent, but unlike the other, this one did not bare its fangs or bite. It hovered just above my knees, staring. I reached out, touching its smooth skin, just below its rounded head.

It slithered along my arm and then around my back and waist. The firm press of its body became a hand on my belly.

"What do you seek, goddess mine?" he asked, his lips pressed into the hollow of my neck, gliding toward my ear.

I tensed, feeling him all around me now—his chest against my back, his legs braced around mine.

"I seek what calls to me," I said. "It is buried deep."

"Is it deep?" he whispered. His fingers shifted beneath the chain of my necklace, raising the hair on the back of my neck. His other hand remained on my stomach. "Or are you afraid to find it?"

I turned my head, but I could not see the man's face. The light did not touch him, but I knew him. He felt familiar, like the darkness I had woken to in the womb.

The warmth of his mouth hovered near. I wanted to feel him against my lips.

"Only darkness would accuse the light of fear," I said.

He chuckled, and his hand shifted to my breast. It wasn't exactly what I wanted, yet as he rolled my nipple between his thumb and forefinger, I gasped.

"But you tremble."

"I tremble out of need," I said between my teeth.

"Then take, goddess," he said. "Desire is only a weakness when it's starved."

My hand snaked around his neck, and I brought his lips to mine. His mouth was firm, and I parted mine so that I could taste him, but it was not enough. In this moment, I was a desert, and he was the rain. We were two creatures not long meant for each other, yet only he could cool the scorched parts of my body.

It had always been that way.

Goddess mine, his voice rumbled.

He was inside my head.

"You are a serpent," I said aloud.

My lips were aflame as they parted from his. I shifted onto my knees and pushed him to the ground. I mounted him, sliding down his thick cock. He filled me up, made me whole, and as I moved, I whispered words, maybe a spell, maybe a prayer, which I did not know, but they fell from my mouth and into the space between us.

Give me your venom, your holy blood.

I will take your poison, your silver tongue.

Drink deep from my body, taste darkness on my lips.

Worship me within my temple, on the steps of my altar.

Bring forth my rapture, my violent end.

I felt his power beneath my hands, and then it was inside me, rising until I could not see or breathe.

You are brilliant, I heard him say. *Open your eyes, little love.*

I did and found Zahariev beneath me. We were not in a

cave or even my bed, but whatever was under us was soft, cushioning my knees as I straddled him. I rocked back, feeling his balls press against my ass. His hands slid from my thighs behind my knees, and he frowned.

"What's wrong?" he asked.

You will regret this, I wanted to say, but I couldn't. I wanted this too much. I shook my head and let my hands slide up his tattooed chest.

"Nothing," I said, and as I kissed him, he began to thrust into me with a practiced rhythm that made my eyes roll. "Don't stop," I begged.

"Wasn't planning on it," he said and took me over the edge.

I woke up on my stomach with an ache between my thighs. I was hot and rolled onto my back, pushing the covers off me. They felt too heavy, and I needed to breathe. I lay there letting the chill air blanket me, hoping it would ease this unearthly heat.

Fuck. I hadn't felt like this in a long time. I was empty, desperate to impale myself on anything that would make me feel stretched and full. I blamed Zahariev—or rather myself—for thinking about him before falling asleep.

I pressed my thighs together, deepening the tension. I was trying to decide if the short-term release was going to be worth the effort of masturbating when I heard Cherub meow and abandoned the thought entirely.

She was basically my child, so that was a hard no.

I sighed and sat up. She was sitting on the floor amid piles of dirty and clean clothes, staring up at me.

"I guess you heard," I said. "It's just you and me, kid."

She meowed, and I checked my phone. I had a few messages, and each one gave me a different kind of anxiety, save Coco's, which was just a reminder that there was soup in the fridge.

One was from my father, reminding me of the gala tomorrow night.

One was from Zahariev, asking if I was all right.

And then there was one from Gabriel. Several from Gabriel, actually. I'd just ignored them.

The morning following Esther's death, he'd texted:

Hey baby girl. Just want to check on you. Come by the hospital anytime. Liam and I will be here for another day. He's excited to meet his aunt.

Then yesterday:

Tried calling. Left a voicemail. Just wanted to let you know Liam and I are heading home tomorrow. You are welcome anytime.

Later that day:

I know this hurts. I'm sorry.

His most recent message had come sometime this morning.

Funeral is tomorrow at 10 a.m.

The invite deadened my lust instantly, and a needlelike numbness consumed me.

A funeral.

I'd known this was coming, but I hadn't let myself think about it. They were going to put her in the ground. That wasn't exactly shocking. Everyone in Eden was buried or entombed in great mausoleums except criminals, who they burned as a punishment so that their souls could not return to their bodies upon the second coming.

I had never believed in the second coming. I'd had too many questions about how it worked. How did the dead, buried deep, rise from their graves? Were their bodies miraculously restored? Why did God delay such a grand promise just to test the loyalty of the people He claimed to love so deeply?

It didn't make sense to me, but it was possible Esther believed it, and if that was the case, I wanted her to have the option of returning to her body, even if I loathed the thought of seeing her buried in the cold ground.

I guessed I should just be glad I had a place to go when I wanted to visit her.

I didn't acknowledge Gabriel's messages. I didn't know what to say to him. Despite finding that *demonic* creature in their apartment, I still blamed him for Esther's death. If he'd been there…well, I didn't really know what might have happened, and it wasn't fair to say she might have lived when there was a real possibility that I could have lost both of them.

I just wasn't ready.

I hated myself for it, but that was the truth, and I'd rather wait until I knew I could face him so I didn't ruin what I had left.

I set my phone aside and brushed away a few stray tears on my cheeks before getting dressed for the evening and packing my backpack. I slipped Cherub's scarf over my head and looked down at her.

"Ready?" I asked.

She didn't answer or look at me, too busy licking her paw.

"Hey," I said, snapping my fingers near her head. That got her attention, and she swatted at me like I was playing. I picked her up, staring into her copper eyes. "If you're going to be my sidekick, I need you to be alert, got it?"

She meowed as if accepting my instruction. I settled her in the sling and then slipped on my jacket and the backpack.

"Let's go steal some drugs," I said as I headed out the door.

I didn't necessarily think this counted as stealing. Technically, the drugs I was taking from Zahariev had belonged to my father, so they were mine, but I wasn't going to argue the semantics until I had to.

I still wondered what he planned to do with the shipment. I knew for a fact Zahariev wasn't involved in the drug trade, and he forbade any of his men from making or distributing substances. If they were caught, they were immediately dismissed. I wondered what Zahariev would do if—*when*—he found out what I was doing. I was used to his disappointment so that didn't scare me, but I did wonder if I was pushing his limits.

I guessed I'd find out how big a mistake I was making soon.

I headed east, toward the port of Nineveh, which took up most of the coast, with only a small portion dedicated to a beach that was often trashed. Ironically, it was a hangout for users and often dangerous, littered with spent needles. Zahariev had made attempts to clean it up, but the cycle began anew. I thought it was one reason he detested drugs so much and likely why he'd stolen the shipment from my father, to prevent it from filtering into his city.

The port technically belonged to the church, but the families oversaw the sale and distribution of the goods received there, which were things like vehicles, cranes, and other industrial machinery, all produced by penal colonies on the Kurari Sea Islands.

Most of the port was enclosed by a tall chain-link fence, which I would normally climb, but it was topped with barbed wire, so I was going to have to use one of the actual entrances. The challenge was that there were many, since various goods belonged to different corporations, and I didn't exactly know which section belonged to Zahariev.

It was just more information I was going to have to pull out of the poor soul who stood guard tonight, though interacting with the security wasn't ideal. The port wasn't actually guarded by Zahariev's men. It was guarded by enforcers, which meant I wasn't breaking Zahariev's rules, I was breaking the church's rules.

It wouldn't be the first time, but I wondered when Zahariev would stop saving me from the consequences of my actions.

I headed across Procession Street to Gomorrah and turned down Fourth Street. It was mostly dark, save for a bluish glow from the port ahead. The ground sloped downward steadily and then wove through a stretch of grassy field. I was glad there was no traffic, though I suspected at this time of night, it would be rather desolate until early morning when shipments came in and moved out.

I came around the final curve. Ahead, there was a small guardhouse with darkened windows and a red-and-white reflective beam barring the entrance. As I approached, I spotted several cameras aimed in every direction, including at me, so I wasn't surprised when a man emerged from the guardhouse.

He was wearing dark clothes and a jacket, which was irritating, because I couldn't see what sort of weapons he carried. His hat spelled out SECURITY, with the T stylized to look like a cross. He was what I expected—young, fit, round-faced.

"Can I help you?" he asked in a firm tone.

I smiled at him. "Just going for a little stroll."

"Not around here," he said. "You can just stroll back the way you came."

"Someone's grumpy," I said.

The man frowned at me. He wasn't going to make this easy.

"You wanna pet my pussycat? It might make you feel better."

The man's eyes widened and then narrowed as I parted my jacket to reveal Cherub sitting stoically in her sling.

"I'm allergic." He scowled and then pointed down the darkened road from where I'd come. "Go."

I scratched behind Cherub's ear, never taking my eyes off him.

"Maybe you aren't allergic to pussycats," I said. "Maybe pussycats are allergic to you."

The guard reached for something at his belt. I assumed it was a gun, but I wasn't actually going to stick around and find out, even though I was armed. I didn't want to die any more than I wanted to kill someone over a drug I didn't even take.

"Okay, okay," I said, turning on my heels.

I'd find another way in.

I retraced my steps, returning to Gomorrah and taking a different road to the port. This entrance was a little bigger, made specifically for large vehicles. A guard was already standing in front of the barrier, his arms crossed, like he was waiting for my approach. It had not occurred to me that perhaps the thing the other guy was reaching for was a radio, but now I suspected he had warned the other officers of my loitering.

Despite this, the man smiled as I neared and dropped his arms to his sides. Clearly, he didn't see me as much of a threat. That was lucky considering the warning could have had the opposite effect.

I took a quick inventory of his person. Unlike the other guard, he wore a bulletproof vest and a belt heavy with his gun, extra ammunition, a stun gun, and a flashlight.

"I hear you have a pussycat," he said.

I let a smile curve across my lips. I kept Cherub within sight in her sling and scratched behind her ears.

"Word gets around," I said.

"It ain't everyday we get visitors, and never one with a pussycat," he said, his eyes dropping to Cherub—or maybe he was looking at my breasts, judging by the spike in his desire. It wasn't the darkest or most violent I'd ever felt, but it still made my stomach roil.

"What a shame," I said, keeping my voice low and breathy, stoking his hunger. I had yet to reach for it with my own magic. I needed it to be a little more intense to get exactly what I wanted, which was entry to the port and the location of Zahariev's zone. "This must be your lucky day."

"That all depends on you, princess," he said.

He was so close, I could feel his breath on my face. It was uncomfortably warm and smelled faintly of onions. Still, I managed to smile, my gaze darting to his name, which was embroidered on a patch affixed to his bulletproof vest.

"Well, Nathaniel," I said, lifting Cherub from her sling,

pressing a kiss to the top of her head. "Would you like to hold my pussycat?"

The guard's eyes flitted to Cherub. He offered a quiet chuckle, almost like he couldn't believe he was having this conversation. I couldn't believe I was, either.

He answered all the same.

"Nathaniel's my last name," he said. "But sure. I'll hold your pussycat. I'll hold whatever you want."

Cherub meowed as I handed her to the guard. He tucked her into the crook of his arm. She looked at me, the pupils of her copper eyes narrowing. I scratched her head, hoping it would ease her frustration a bit. I needed her to play along for two seconds.

"You got any plans now that your hands are free?" he asked, his eyes trailing down my body. I tried not to shiver. It wasn't a good shiver either. His lust turned my stomach—he'd started fantasizing.

It had taken a lot of time, observation, and direct questioning to assign meaning to each feeling—what gave me a headache or made me feel dizzy versus what made me want to vomit. Age was also a factor. Younger men usually thought about sex more frequently, and their lust had more power, but that also meant they were far easier to control.

The man in front of me was older, but his lust was strong. I suspected it had been a while since he'd seen any action.

"Oh, I have plans," I said, smoothing my hand down the guard's arm. He wasn't muscular, really, but I also found myself comparing the feel of him to Zahariev, which was unfair and also frustrating. I didn't want to get into the habit of comparing men to the one I literally couldn't have.

That wasn't the point of the touch anyway. The connection allowed my magic to sink into him and take hold.

"Which zone belongs to Zahariev Zareth?" I asked.

The man blinked, confusion clouding his gaze as my power pulled the answer from his mouth.

"M-40 to 45," he said.

"What does that mean?" I asked.

"Bay M, numbers forty through forty-five," he answered.

"And where is that?" I asked.

"About a mile south," he said. "The letters are spray-painted on the ground."

A mile?

"Can I get there from here?"

"Yeah, you can get there from here," he said. "But why would you want to?"

"He's got something that belongs to me," I said.

"Baby, don't fuck with the family—ouch! She bit me!" he shouted suddenly, dropping Cherub. She landed on her feet and bolted right under the gate.

Fuck.

"Cherub!" I shouted, running after her. "That was rude!"

And not part of my plan, I thought as I chased after her, ducking beneath the red-and-white bar blocking the entrance, but whatever. I was going to take it.

"Hey! Come back!" the guard called. "*Stop!*"

"Sorry!" I said. "I have to get my cat!"

I kept running. Ahead, I could see her just sitting in the middle of the road, all stoic with her tail curled over her feet.

"You little fucker," I said. I barely stopped as I scooped her into my arms, holding her close as I ran. I felt like I was jostling her so hard, her brain was probably bouncing around in her skull.

I didn't stop until I was hidden among the maze of shipping containers all stacked at different heights. The guard hadn't followed me, but I wasn't stupid enough to believe he'd let me continue to trespass. I was certain he'd radio the other guards. I just hoped when they came in search of me, they wouldn't use dogs, for Cherub's sake.

M-45, I thought as I jogged down the long corridor created by the shipping containers, searching for anything that might give me an indication of where I was in relation to Zahariev's zone when I spotted a number on one of the container doors.

A-36.

Are you fucking kidding?

I was going to have to jog to *M*?

"We wouldn't be in this situation if you had just let him hold you," I said, shoving Cherub back in her sling. She gave a drawn-out meow. "Don't argue with me. You're not the one who has to walk there. If you'd given me more time, I probably could have convinced him to drive us."

I'd be lucky to make it halfway before security descended.

On the flip side, this place was huge. I could probably hide just about anywhere and long enough to make them think I'd given up my task, though the thought of being shut inside one of these containers for an hour didn't appeal to me in the least.

If all else failed, I'd call Zahariev, but he was my last resort.

I made it to row E before I saw lights ahead and darted into the shadows, peering around the side of the container. They were still some distance away but approaching fast, pausing only to shine their flashlights down each aisle. I turned away and walked down the dark passage, hoping that one of these containers had enough space for Cherub and I to slip between, but they were too perfectly stacked.

I could try climbing and hiding out on top.

I hurried down the bay until I found a single container amid the towering tiers. I slid my backpack off and unzipped it before settling Cherub inside.

"It's only for a little while," I whispered, though she didn't protest like I'd expected.

I left enough of an opening at the top of the bag so she wouldn't be completely closed off. Rising to my feet, I hefted her onto my back and started to climb. I felt clumsy, learning which parts of the container would hold me, but the locking mechanism provided me with a place to put my feet. I slid my hands up the cold rods and then used the hinge that jutted out from the side as a step, rising higher until I could reach the top of the container.

Gripping the edge, I hoisted myself up, chest landing flat on the roof. I swung my legs over until I could get my knee under me and then crawled to the middle of the container where I slid my backpack off, opening it fully to check on Cherub.

She looked up at me, her pupils wide, almost swallowing the color of her eyes.

"I'm sorry, little one," I whispered. "Just a little longer."

With Cherub settled, I shifted to the edge of the container again and rested on my stomach, watching. Now that I was still, I was painfully aware of my throbbing wrist. I checked it, finding blood on the gauze.

It felt like forever before I saw a flash of light at the end of the bay. I pushed back from the edge of the roof and flattened as a bright beam of light slowly scanned the darkness.

The only sound came from the guards, who were chatting as they patrolled.

One of them sighed. "I hate these fuckers, wasting our time."

"What do you think she wants?" asked the other.

"Who really knows? Rich said she mentioned Zahariev Zareth, but I'd bet my left nut she thinks she can stow away with the cargo. Probably believes in that conspiracy going around, that the church has been building some kind of paradise at sea."

I hadn't heard of that conspiracy before, but I didn't doubt the rumor or people's belief in it.

"Wait until she finds out there's nothing out there but hell on earth."

The guard chuckled in response, and then the light was gone and their voices faded.

I didn't move immediately. Those men would be back, patrolling in the opposite direction. As I bided my time, I thought about what had brought me here, the witch's promise of knowledge. I desperately hoped she was trustworthy.

When I felt like I was in the clear, I climbed down from the container and returned Cherub to her sling. I made my way down the remaining rows to M and walked the bay until I found what was supposedly Zahariev's section.

I felt my phone vibrate, and when I checked it, I saw that Zahariev was calling.

My irritation spiked as I declined the call.

He sent a text immediately, almost like he'd written it before he'd even called.

Answer the fucking phone, he said and called again.

I could hear his tone. *Pissed*, which usually didn't bother me, except this time, my scalp tingled.

"What?" I snapped.

"I don't like trespassers, little love," he said.

"That's ironic," I said. "Aren't you their king?"

"Lilith," he said, a note of warning in his voice.

"How do you even know where I am?" I asked, irritated, though I could guess.

"I got a call," he said and paused. "Are you wearing your cat?"

"You can see me too?"

I held up my middle finger.

"Cute," he said.

"You are such a fucking stalker," I said, deciding I wasn't going to let him keep me from what I came for. I unlatched the first of his five containers, which held boxes and furniture. Not at all what I expected.

"You're in my territory," he said. "And snooping through my things."

"None of this looks like yours," I said, scanning the overly ornate furniture.

"It wouldn't," he said. "Seeing as how everything there belonged to my mother and father."

His comment made me feel cold.

I closed the door and moved to the next, but it was more of the same. I started to wonder if all I'd find here were his parents' old things.

"What are you looking for?"

"Something that definitely doesn't belong to you," I said.

There was a pause, but I knew he'd guessed. He didn't speak it aloud, and neither did I—we knew better.

"And what are you planning to do with it?"

"It's currency, Zahariev," I said, opening the third container. Inside was another, smaller one.

Bingo.

"What are you buying?" he asked.

"That doesn't concern you," I said.

"It concerns me," he said. "You are breaking my rules."

"Not the ones you gave me," I said. "See you, Zahariev."

I hung up and opened the second container. Inside, there was a row of four pallets, stacked with blocks of wrapped white jade.

I set my backpack down and pulled out a plastic bag. I wasn't about to carry around a brick of this stuff or hand that much over to a complete stranger. I withdrew my blade and shoved it into the side of the shipment. It was a lot like stabbing a bag of sugar. Once my knife was free, it came pouring out in a stream of white.

I didn't take much, what I considered to be about a spoonful, before I closed the bag and shoved it into my pocket, letting the rest spill to the floor. I didn't care to save it.

I didn't care if Zahariev destroyed it tomorrow.

I only cared that I'd gotten what I came for.

ZAHARIEV

I stared at my phone after Lilith hung up.

She knew how to piss me off and liked doing it, but this felt different. She wasn't breaking into my storage container to make me angry. She was up to something, and she wasn't telling me.

Maybe that was really what pissed me off: the secrecy.

I could call her back, but I knew she wouldn't answer a second time. I could head to the port, but she'd probably be gone by the time I arrived, so I'd have no way of tracking where she was off to with a pocket full of jade.

"Everything all right?" Gabriel asked when I entered his apartment again. I'd gone into the hall to make the call to Lilith.

Once Liam had been discharged, I brought them home from the hospital and stayed to help Gabriel get settled.

"Yeah," I said. "Just trying to keep tabs on Lilith."

It wasn't unlike her to go looking for a thrill, but this seemed reckless even for her.

"You talked to her?" Gabriel asked.

"Barely. She's in avoidance mode," I said.

Gabriel dropped his gaze, twisting his fingers one way and then the other.

"It's my fault," he said. A second later, he was sniffing and dragging his hands over his face. "I should have been the one to find Esther. She'll spend her whole life running from that nightmare."

The thing was, I didn't think Lilith was running at all.

And maybe that was the problem.

She was diving headfirst into danger.

L eaving the port had almost been too easy, though I assumed that was because Zahariev had made a few calls after our chat. I half expected him to be waiting outside the gate, eager to reprimand me in person, but he wasn't.

I pulled up my hood and kept my head down, doing my best to go unnoticed as I took a maze of darkened side streets to the Trenches. The area was busier than before, and there were a few shops open, though 213 was not one of them. In fact, when I made it to Saira's door, I found she had covered her windows with paper so that no one could see in, a move I assumed she made shortly after I left, which felt justified but also kind of rude considering I was bringing her the drug she'd asked for.

I knocked, glancing up and down the street to gauge who was watching, though no one seemed to pay me any mind. I realized I was paranoid, expecting Zahariev to show up at any moment and ruin everything the same way he'd ruined my reputation in Gomorrah.

He would think he was protecting me, but really, he would just keep me from the information I really needed— the information *he* needed, though he didn't realize that yet, which was my fault. I hadn't told him my plans, though to be real, I'd just played all this by ear, which was evident by the throbbing burn on my wrist.

I pulled my gaze away from the street and knocked again. It was another minute before the door opened. All I could see was a sliver of Saira's face, her eyes widening a fraction before she spoke.

"You're back," she said. "I hoped you'd come."

I was both surprised and a little suspicious. Was she hopeful because of what I'd brought or another reason entirely?

Then she added, "I was talking to the cat, by the way. Come in."

She stepped aside to let me enter.

Of course. The cat.

The woman's shop was as I remembered it, only darker now that the windows were covered. I pointed at them with my thumb. "Is this because of me?" I asked.

"You, spies, enforcers," she said as she locked the door.

"One of those things is not like the others," I said.

"We'll see," she replied, giving me a hard look. "Do you have it?"

"Really?" I asked.

"I gave you a task," she said. "I assume you would not return if you didn't have it."

I stared at her, trying to read her expression, but really, she just looked mean. Maybe the jade would take the edge off.

I pulled the bag out of my pocket. She snatched it from

my hands and moved farther into her shop. Bypassing the counter she'd put between us last time, she went instead to a small table at the back of the shop. It was low to the ground and seemed almost intended for a child.

She took a seat, pulling a rectangular box toward herself.

From it, she took out a round, silver container and what looked like a micro spoon. She poured what little jade I had brought into the container before scooping a small bit onto the back of her hand to sniff.

When she was done, she looked up at me. "Sit."

I did as she said, lowering into the small chair.

She turned to retrieve something behind her. When she faced me again, she had my notebook in hand. She set it on the table in front of us, pointing to my crude drawing. "This blade is one of seven."

"*Seven*?" I asked, surprised. "You're telling me there are seven of those motherfuckers floating around?"

"Yours is the only one *floating around*," she said. "Three are with the church. They used to have four. I suspect the one you possess now was stolen from them."

That checked out, considering Ephraim said he took it from a priest. Suddenly I understood why no one seemed to be too upset about the murder. It was because he'd taken the blade.

"They were once one blade," she continued. "A sacred sword of fire called the Deliverer."

There was that word again.

"What does that even mean?" I asked. "Sacred?"

It seemed to me the word had a different meaning, that in one sense, it was just a title applied to things people found worthy. In the other, it was like a curse, punishing those deemed undeserving, whatever that meant.

"In the context of the Deliverer? It means the sword was made by the true gods."

"The true gods," I repeated flatly.

Had the jade already taken effect? Suddenly, I expected Saira to rise to her feet and begin preaching about living in a simulation like Tori.

"You mean the ones locked behind the Seventh Gate?"

She didn't offer any kind of confirmation, just stared. "What do you know about them?"

"Very little," I said. "Only what I heard preached on the street."

Can't you hear them? Tori had said. *They are knocking at the gates.*

What I didn't say aloud was that I thought I could, but only in my dreams. It was a distant rhythm, a steady thrum that matched the beat of my heart.

"They've started executing us again," she said. Her voice was quiet, nearly a whisper. "The ones who speak the truth."

"What is the truth?" I asked.

Her gaze returned to mine. She turned to a blank page in my notebook and plucked a pen from her box.

"Have you ever wondered why the Elohai have magic?"

My brows lowered. I hadn't, mostly because I'd always been told our magic was granted to us by God, and it made sense that some higher power would have the ability to bestow magic. What I did wonder was why the gift only manifested in women, but I didn't say any of that aloud.

"The Elohai are descendants of the Elohim," she continued. "The Elohim are Eryx and Ashur, the creators of humankind and the true gods of our world. They are trapped beneath Mount Seine, behind the Seventh Gate, and have been for thousands of years."

My mouth felt dry as I processed the information she had just shared. I reached into my backpack and withdrew the bottle of water I'd packed for Cherub, taking a drink before pouring some in her bowl.

As I took her out of the sling and set her on the table, I asked, "If these two, Eryx and Ashur, are the true gods, how did they become imprisoned?"

"The god your church worships, the one they call the Messiah, he is an invader." She wrote as she spoke, but it was in shorthand, almost like she was taking notes and couldn't keep up with what she was hearing. I probably wouldn't understand any of it later. "He saw what Eryx and Ashur had created and wanted it for himself. There was a battle, and the Messiah was bound in chains. As his execution neared, the Messiah promised knowledge if humankind would aid in his rescue. They conspired and forged a blade, the Deliverer, which cut through his chains and burned with fire. He used it against Eryx and Ashur and drove them behind the Seventh Gate, where they were trapped beneath a net over which the Messiah summoned peaks of great stone. With the true gods defeated, the Messiah ruled, but the knowledge he had promised was never given. Over time, he grew bored. He abandoned us. After that, man saw an opportunity. They made rules for humankind and appointed men to measure morality and choose ethics. They made claims that this was the knowledge the Messiah had imparted, that he'd lived among us so long only to choose those worthy enough to carry his message. These men— these prophets—they were the descendants of Eryx and Ashur, the ones you now call the Elohai."

I sat in silence, trying to keep track of what she was saying, but at the end of her explanation, my head hurt, and my only thought was how ironic it was that Saira claimed the Messiah had left without imparting knowledge.

It was obvious he'd taught humanity deception.

"What does all this have to do with the dagger?" I asked. "You said there were seven and that they were once this sword?"

"The Deliverer," she said. "It is relevant because reforged, the sword can open any of the seven gates."

"Why was it...unmade?" I asked. I didn't know what term I should use, but it seemed like a valid question.

"It was broken by the prophets who shared the seven pieces," she said. "As the Deliverer, it posed a threat to their power."

I considered asking how they'd all been able to handle the blade without dying, but I thought I could guess—it was their blood. *My* blood.

I drew my tongue over my bottom lip. Suddenly, it felt harder to breathe.

"You said the church has three blades and I have one. Where are the other three?"

She had to guess I would ask, and she went rigid, her lips pursed.

"They are with the Order of the Serpent," she said.

I raised my brows. I'd never heard of such a group. "And who are they?"

"Your church would call us witches, but the magic we practice is no different from the magic they steal from the Elohai. It is only witchcraft when it does not serve the archbishop."

Well, that hit close to home.

"We are women who are tired of giving away our power," she said. "Aren't you tired?"

I straightened. I thought about asking her how she knew I had magic, but I realized she knew because I hadn't died handling the blade.

"Tired, sure," I said, trying to sound nonchalant. I didn't want her to know that her question had made some deep part of me ache with the desire to be free. "But what does all this have to do with the blade?"

"If we remake the Deliverer," she said, "we can free the true gods."

I sat in confused silence.

"Why would we do that?" I asked.

"Because they have promised to serve us if we can open the Seventh Gate."

"How can they make promises when they are trapped beneath a mountain?"

"I told you we are witches," she said. "They have chosen us to save them."

I laughed. I couldn't help it. "You're serious? Can't you hear yourself? You sound just like the Elohai who claimed to be prophets."

She scowled. "We are not like them. They *enslaved* us."

"How do you know it is a god who speaks to you from under the mountain? It could be…anything."

"You sound like a woman raised in the church," she said.

I clenched my jaw.

"Has it ever occurred to you that the prophets who wrote the *Book of Splendor* warned us against communicating with unknown entities so we would not heed the pleas of our true gods?"

"As plausible as that might be, how can you trust their word?"

"Faith," said Saira.

I scoffed. "I'm not interested in the belief required for faith."

"Then believe in a world where we are not subservient to men."

I could do that, but I didn't like the idea of handing over that dream to gods I did not know.

"Why must we rely on gods to create that world? Why can we not do it on our own?"

"If women believed in their power, perhaps we could," she said. "But you cannot rouse the downtrodden without a show of great power. The gods under the mountain have promised that."

I sat across from her, uncertain. I believed there were gods under the mountain, or at least some kind of powerful magic, but I didn't trust what they promised. Would these Elohim just give us another book, create another religion?

"If I cannot convince you," she said, "then let me introduce you to the women of the Order of the Serpent."

"In exchange for what?" I asked. "The blade?"

"I am offering because they want *you*," she said.

I almost scoffed, but then she added, "You should accept their invitation. If they only wanted the blade, they could have killed you already. That's the only thing about witchcraft the *Book of Splendor* got right. It's dangerous."

I started to ask why they wanted me. What did they know about me other than I had one of the seven blades and that I was an Elohai? But a knock at the door interrupted me—though *knock* was a generous word.

Whoever was on the other side slammed their fist against it, shaking the glass in the window.

We both froze.

"Enforcers," Saira whispered.

I snatched my journal from the table and wrapped an arm around Cherub as I rose to my feet. Saira followed, slipping the silver tin of jade into her pocket and grabbing a candle.

"Come," she said.

I followed her into the back room where she approached the wall and felt around until part of it gave way to reveal a hidden door.

She ushered me inside and followed, sliding a lock in place.

She turned with her candle, which provided no light, save to illuminate her drawn face.

"You mean to tell me you have an escape tunnel but no flashlight?"

She narrowed her eyes and stepped past me, blowing out the flame. A second later, a bright light shone into my eyes. I held up one hand to shield my face and used the other to cover Cherub's.

"Careful what you wish for," she said, shifting the light away. She reached up and retrieved another flashlight, which was leaning on a metal pipe secured against the wall. She handed it to me. "Let's go," she said.

Behind us, there was a crash. The enforcers had made entry. I wondered how long they'd been watching and if they'd seen me enter.

"Will they destroy your shop?" I asked.

"Likely," she replied.

The silence was heavy.

"I'm sorry," I said.

She didn't acknowledge my apology, and I didn't blame her. My words were meaningless in the face of such a violation.

We were quiet for some time. The only sound was our feet scraping over rotting wood as we made our way through the dank tunnel. I took a few seconds to shine the flashlight up and around, finding that the walls and ceiling were reinforced with brick and wooden arches.

"When was this built?" I asked.

"Before the fire," she said. "We knew the end was coming, so we prepared."

I suddenly understood why she seemed so unbothered about losing her shop and her home. It wasn't the first time.

I didn't ask any more questions, though they floated around in my head. If there were really gods behind the Seventh Gate, what was behind the other six? The church had always said the second, third, and fifth gates held fire and the first, fourth, and sixth gates held water.

Supposedly, during Armageddon, the gates on the west would open first and release fire, destroying the world. After, the gates on the east would open to cleanse the world with water, and an era of peace would follow.

But was that true or did something far darker lay locked behind them?

Did the church know about the Order of the Serpent and that they had possession of three other blades? Lisk had clearly valued mine enough to send enforcers to retrieve it. Was he aware of this alternate history and the Deliverer?

We came to the end of the tunnel where Saira paused and prodded the ceiling, causing dirt to loosen and fall. She pushed hard, opening a makeshift door. She centered an old crate beneath the opening and used it to climb out, then bent, holding out her hand as I rose onto the crate.

I reached for her hand, but she slapped mine away.

297

"Not you," she said. "Give me the cat. You can't crawl out with her hanging around your neck."

I glared at the old crone, before pulling Cherub from her sling. I kissed the top of her head and whispered in her ear, "It's okay if you bite her."

"I can hear you," Saira snapped.

"You should have thought about that before you slapped me," I said as I handed Cherub over.

I was shorter than Saira, so I had to jump, pressing my palms flat into the earth and bringing my knee up as I crawled out of the hole. Once I was on my feet, I found that the opening of the tunnel had let us out beneath a massive tree, perched high upon a hill overlooking the ocean, the coast illuminated by the burning glow of the harbor.

It had been a long time since I'd thought anything in this world was beautiful, but this gave me pause. The feeling was short-lived, however, when I caught sight of an orange haze in the distance. Her shop was on fire.

"Here," said Saira, handing off Cherub.

I settled the kitten into her sling while the witch covered the opening of the tunnel, first with the makeshift door and then with loose foliage.

When she was finished, she straightened and looked at me. "If you want to meet the members of the Order of the Serpent," she said, "meet me here in four days, on the night of the new moon, not a minute past midnight."

I didn't acknowledge her invitation and instead asked, "Where will you go?"

"I have places," she said.

I nodded, uncertain of what to say, so I just turned and started down the hill.

"Eve," she called, and I paused, turning to look at her.

"There is no future where this world doesn't end. The sooner you accept that, the better off you'll be, but hurry. Time is running out."

Well, that was fucking cryptic.

"I think the jade's kicked in, Saira," I said, turning away, hugging Cherub close. "You might wanna hydrate."

I couldn't hear what she said as I left, but I didn't really care. Her warning was enough.

If her intention was to scare me, it had worked.

I was terrified.

———————

When I got home, I took Cherub out of her sling.

"You're a great sidekick, kid," I said as I set her on the ground.

She meowed.

"I know, I know," I said, heading into the kitchen. I grabbed her bag of treats from the top of the fridge.

She meowed louder and made a figure eight between my legs.

"I'm working on it," I said, my fingers slipping on the plastic. "Patience is a virtue, Cherub."

When I finally got the bag open, I gave her two treats and then refilled her water bowl before heading to my room. As I pushed open the door, I froze, finding Zahariev sitting on the edge of my bed. He looked amused, the corners of his lips tilted up.

"How the fuck did you get in here?" I demanded.

"I put the lock on your door," he said, as if it were obvious.

"So you took that as permission to drop by anytime?" I asked.

"I would have knocked, but I didn't think you'd answer even if you were home."

"That's usually a sign you aren't exactly welcome," I said, letting my backpack slide off my shoulder. I set it on the ground.

"We have a few things to discuss," he said.

I didn't look at him and instead scanned the clothing on my floor for something to sleep in. I really needed to do laundry.

"*Things* are discussed during business hours," I said.

"Apparently all your business is conducted between the hours of midnight and five a.m. so I guess I'm right on time."

"I'm ignoring you," I said.

"When don't you?" He countered, a tinge of bitterness in his voice. It gave me pause, and part of me wanted to argue, but I thought he wanted that, so I decided not to give in.

"Fuck you, Zahariev," I said, leaving for the bathroom. I wanted to slam the door, but I didn't want to wake Coco up, so instead, as I undressed, I hurled every piece of clothing to the floor. By the time I was finished, I felt more silly than frustrated. I didn't even really know what I was angry about, except that my plans to come home, crawl into bed, and sleep had been interrupted by the man who'd starred in my sex dream last night.

It was all highly inconvenient.

After I washed my face, I felt a little more calm and considered entertaining whatever Zahariev had come here to say.

That was until I returned to my room and found him sitting with my backpack between his legs, my blade in hand.

"Wanna tell me where you got this?" he asked.

"Stop looking through my things!" I snapped, bolting

across the room. I had every intention of snatching the dagger away from him, but he held it high and wrapped an arm around my waist, keeping me anchored to his body.

"You looked through mine," he said.

"I didn't *look* through anything," I said, shoving my hands against his shoulders. I let out a small yelp as he fell back onto the bed, taking me with him.

I scrambled back, straddling him as I sat up, hoping I'd be able to reach for the blade, but both of his hands had moved to my thighs.

"Where is it?" I demanded, my palms planted firmly on his chest.

He arched a brow at me. "I guess you'll have to search for it."

I narrowed my eyes, wondering what he was playing at but very aware of where our bodies touched.

"It's not like you to play games," I said.

"This isn't a game," he said. "I asked you a serious question you still haven't answered."

I could just tell him how the blade had come back to me, but I wanted to be difficult.

"What will you give me?" I asked.

"What do you want?"

This motherfucker, I thought.

"You aren't brave enough to give me what I want," I said.

My voice was quiet, a warm whisper between us. I let my eyes leave his, following the lines of the tattoos on his neck until they disappeared beneath his collar. I decided I wanted to see them all and started undoing the buttons of his shirt.

He didn't stop me as I neared the bottom and shifted back, inhaling as I settled over his prominent arousal. His hands were still on my thighs, his fingers pressing harder into my skin.

"Lilith."

There was a rough edge to the way Zahariev said my name. I kept my eyes closed as a violent desire twisted through me and exhaled slowly.

"Hmm?"

His hand curled around my wrist, the uninjured one, and I met his gaze. His jaw was tight, his pupils blown.

"What do you want?" he repeated.

"Do you really want to know?" I asked as I stretched over him, my lips hovering a breath away from his before whispering, "Kiss me, Zahariev."

I held my breath, waiting for him to *say* something, to *do* anything.

But he didn't.

All I could manage was a hollow laugh.

"I knew it." I'd hoped to sound teasing instead of hurt, but I couldn't hide the inflection in my voice as I tried to pull away.

Then Zahariev's hands splayed across my waist, shifting to my ass as he sat up, holding me tight against his cock. I wrapped my arms around his neck. For once, he had to tilt his head back to look at me, but his burning gaze fell to my parted lips, and then he kissed me.

To say I wasn't prepared for the way he would feel against me was an understatement. I expected him to end this before it really began, except he didn't. He kissed me like he owned me, something I'd never wanted before but suddenly realized I could live with, especially if it meant feeling like this every second of every day—high out of my fucking mind, on fire from the inside out, and not a single goddamn drug in my system.

Maybe I was just desperate, or maybe for once in my life, my desire wasn't overshadowed by the feel of another's.

His tongue slid over the curve of my bottom lip, and I opened my mouth to receive him. I always thought he would taste like cigarettes, but he was warm and sweet, and when I sucked on his tongue, he groaned into my mouth.

"Fuck," I breathed as his lips left mine, trailing down my neck, nipping lightly at my skin. My shirt rose as his hot palms slid up my ribs to my breasts, squeezing, teasing my peaked nipples with his thumb and forefinger. His mouth followed, and my breath caught in my throat at the warm pull against my skin.

I gripped his head, holding him to me, savoring the dizzying heat building inside me with each brush of his lips, each swirl of his tongue. I wondered how much more I could take before I begged him to make me come.

Turned out not much.

"Zahariev," I whispered—pled, really, grinding against his swollen cock. He groaned, and his hands tightened around me, and then suddenly, I was on my back, and his knee was between my thighs as he hovered over me on the bed.

Our gazes met.

His skin was flushed and his lips a delicious shade of dark pink. His eyes scanned my face, and I hoped he was making a similar assessment and not thinking about lists.

I drew my knees up, one at a time, so they braced his body.

"What are you thinking?" I whispered.

He shook his head once. "That you've fucked me up, little love."

I didn't have time to comprehend what he'd said or even smile teasingly at his words because he kissed me again.

His body came to rest against mine, sealing us together. My hands grazed down his back beneath the waist of his jeans where I squeezed the hard muscle of his ass. It wasn't until I tried to reach between us, to smooth the palm of my hand against his naked flesh, that he stopped me. Gripping my wrists, he planted them firmly above my head.

I might have found it hot if it hadn't hurt, but he'd unknowingly touched the burn on my wrist.

I gasped in pain, and it was like dousing him with a bucket of ice water. He stopped immediately and sat back on his knees, eyes wide with shock.

"Fuck," he said. "I'm so sorry, Lilith."

I blinked up at him. I was just as startled as he was. I hadn't thought twice about my injury since the moment he kissed me, though now I couldn't ignore the sharp stabs of pain slicing through the haze of my desire.

"What did I do?"

"Nothing," I said. "I'm fine."

"You're holding your arm," he said.

Oh. I hadn't noticed, but now that he pointed it out, I realized I had both hands pressed to my chest.

"It's nothing," I said, but I didn't think he even heard me. His eyes were locked on my wrist as he tugged the sleeve of my shirt down, exposing the wound.

"What the fuck is this, Lilith?" he asked.

I flinched at his tone, so different from the heady rasp he'd used moments before. It made me angry, and I pushed him off as I sat up.

"I *said* it was nothing," I snapped.

He gripped my jaw, tilting my head back.

"What did I tell you?" he asked. "At least look me in the eye when you lie."

304

"It's a burn," I said between my teeth, shoving his hand away.

"How did you get it?"

I glared at him, and a part of me wondered how we'd gone from almost fucking to fighting.

"I went hunting for demons," I said.

His brows lowered. "Demons?"

"The jelly monster that killed Esther," I said. "I went hunting for it. I found it. I killed it…well, most of it."

"With what?" he asked.

I just stared at him.

"The knife," he said, answering his own question.

"And a stun gun from Samuel," I added.

He stared at me, incredulous. After a moment, he pulled out his phone.

"What are you doing?"

He didn't answer, but I could guess.

I rose to my feet and reached for his phone, but he turned away from me.

"I'm going to Dr. Mor tomorrow!" I said, my fingers twisting into the fabric of his unbuttoned shirt as I tried to pull him back. I didn't want him to bring the doctor here tonight. He would probably wake up Coco, and then all she would do was worry.

"Tomorrow is Esther's funeral," he said.

"I'm not going!" I yelled, angry that he had brought it up. Why had he brought it up? He looked at me, and I felt pressure building behind my eyes. I ground my teeth against it. I didn't want to cry. I took a breath, but that didn't stop my voice from shaking as I spoke. "I can't."

I turned away.

"Dr. Mor," I heard Zahariev say. "Lilith has promised me

she will come see you tomorrow around noon. If she doesn't arrive, I expect a call."

There was silence. I tried to get a handle on my emotions, but I didn't exactly understand what I was feeling. Everything was all tangled up, impossible to unravel. Then I felt Zahariev's hand on my shoulder. I turned into him, wrapping my arms around his waist. He held me tight.

"I'm sorry," I whispered.

It was easier to apologize to him this way, enclosed in his warmth.

"It's all right," he said, though I wasn't sure I believed him.

I wondered what he thought about earlier and how long it would take him to say something along the lines of *that can never happen again*, but it turned out he wouldn't have to say anything.

He *showed* it by dropping his arms the moment my door opened. I tamped down the disappointment, eyes falling to Cherub as she meowed, wandering into my room.

I smiled softly but felt little happiness as I bent to pick her up. I sat on the bed and held her close, comforted by her rhythmic purr. Zahariev remained standing, watching.

"You can go," I said.

His expression was neutral.

"You never answered my question," he said. "Tell me about the knife."

I heard what he didn't say—*I gave you what you wanted*. I swallowed around the lump in my throat.

"The night the enforcers attacked me, you said it was missing, but after I got home, I found it in my bag. I didn't want it. It had already caused so many problems, so I threw it in the canal. That was the night Tori died." I paused. "Later, after you left, I woke up to find it stabbed into my mattress. So to answer your question, I don't know how I got it. It just keeps coming back to me."

Even knowing that my blood was the reason I could carry the blade without dying didn't answer the question of why it had chosen me.

I'd just have to add that one to my list of unanswered questions.

"Why didn't you tell me?" Zahariev asked.

I shrugged. "I don't know. I guess I got distracted."

I didn't need to say why. He knew I was talking about Esther.

"And tonight?" he asked. "Where were you?"

"You know where I was," I said.

"You weren't at the port this whole time. What did you do with the jade, Lilith?"

"I don't think you have time for the explanation that requires," I said.

"For you, I have all the time in the world."

"Well, I don't. I want to *sleep*," I said.

"Sleep," he said. "I'll be here when you wake up."

I looked away and took a frustrated breath, needing to get my thoughts in order and decide where to begin.

"When the blade came back, I decided I wanted to know what I had. It seemed important to the church, which meant it was important to Lisk. I thought maybe, if I could figure out why, maybe Lisk would do anything to get it back, like let me stay in Nineveh."

I couldn't place the look on Zahariev's face as I spoke. His eyes were unchanging, but his mouth was tense, his jaw popping. I explained how I'd visited my contacts in Gomorrah and how they'd shut me out.

"Turns out someone saw me with you the night Abram

died," I said. "I had one final option, a contact in the Trenches I rarely used."

His frown deepened when I told him about Saira and the jade, then morphed into a strange anger when I explained what she'd said about the true gods, the Messiah, and the sword she'd called the Deliverer.

I even told him about the Order of the Serpent.

When I finished, he was quiet. The longer he went without speaking, the more fidgety I felt. I rubbed Cherub's ears to the point that she swatted my hand away.

"Well?" I asked, finally unable to handle his silence. "Is your world imploding, or am I the only one?"

"Not imploding," he said, scrubbing his face with the palm of his hand before crossing his arms over his chest.

"Do you believe it?" I asked.

"Which part?"

"Any of it," I said.

I had struggled with religion for years and questioned the teachings of the church, but I'd never expected to have my entire belief system, the thing I'd built my values and ethics on, destroyed. I certainly hadn't expected to face another possibility altogether, which was the existence of multiple gods.

"The stories come from somewhere," he said. Again he was quiet, dragging the edge of this thumb over his bottom lip.

"You won't give the blade back to Lisk, will you?" I asked.

I didn't think he would, but I still had to ask.

"I wasn't planning on it," he said. "But I'd like to know why he wants it."

I lowered my brows. "What do you mean? It's in his best interest to keep them a secret, maybe even destroy them. He loses his power, his credibility, if the world finds out there are other gods."

Although he deserved that and more.

"Or maybe he gains more power if he reforges the sword," Zahariev said. "The witch said the blade can open the other gates. Lisk would have a key to end the world."

"That's only if the other six doors actually hold fire and water like the *Book of Splendor* says," I said.

"I'm betting Lisk knows for certain," said Zahariev. "He knew enough to start collecting the daggers. He's targeting people who speak openly about these gods. He has a lot of information for someone who preaches about the existence of only one god."

That was true and something I'd been suspicious about when he'd targeted Tori.

"He'll be at the gala tomorrow night," I said. "Should we make it interesting and ask?"

"I don't think he'll talk without some encouragement," said Zahariev.

"I could make him," I said.

The suggestion hung heavily between us. I couldn't lie; it made me sick to think about. It meant that I would have to harness the desire this man—*this monster*—had for me, the same desire he'd had for me when I was a *child*.

But now I could use it against him.

I could ruin him.

"No," Zahariev said, his voice firm and final.

"Why not?" I asked. I felt a little defensive about how quickly he shot me down. "It's the quickest way to get the truth and not as messy."

"Maybe I want to punch him in the face," said Zahariev. "And I'm not letting you do that."

"*Letting?*"

Oh, I hated that word.

"I won't ask," he said.

"You aren't. I'm offering."

"Lilith—"

"Zahariev—"

"I said no!" he roared.

My spine straightened, and as I blinked away my shock at having been *yelled* at by Zahariev, I watched as he squeezed his eyes shut and covered his face with his hand.

"That man," he said, but his voice broke, so he stopped and tried again. "That man *hurt* you. I couldn't protect you from him then, but I can now, and I refuse—" He paused again and swallowed. "I *refuse*."

I thought there was going to be more to that sentence, but that was where he left it.

My chest hurt.

"Zahariev."

All I could do was whisper his name. He wouldn't look at me.

I rose from the bed, letting Cherub jump to the ground, and went to him. Before I could think, I was already moving, dragging his mouth to mine.

I didn't know if he'd kiss me back, if he'd had time to realize this wasn't supposed to happen, but his reaction was immediate. He kissed me hard and deep, parting my mouth with his tongue. His hands burned as they pressed into me and drew us together. He was still hard, and I was desperate to touch him, to taste him.

But as soon as I reached for the button of his jeans, his hold on my shoulders tightened, and he ended the kiss, his forehead resting against mine.

"Lilith."

My name was a rasp on his lips. It was like he wanted me to believe he was desperate for me, even though he'd rejected me twice.

I guessed this was what obligation looked like, and while it was clear he'd break a lot of rules for me, this wasn't one.

I took a step back, almost tripping over a pile of clothes. Zahariev reached to steady me. "*Don't*."

He froze, and I crossed my arms over my chest.

"Don't touch me."

His arms fell limp at his sides as he stared, but I didn't want to see the regret in his eyes.

"I'm sorry," I said.

"I'm not," he said.

"You're a terrible liar, Zahariev," I said.

"It's not a lie."

"Then you're an asshole," I said. To that, he said nothing. "I think you should leave."

"Yeah," he agreed. "I should."

He didn't move, so I did.

Retrieving the dagger from atop the rumpled covers, I returned it to my bedside drawer before wrapping my blanket around my shoulders and sitting cross-legged on my bed, waiting for Zahariev to leave.

He adjusted and buttoned his shirt.

I probably should have let him go without a word, but I was angry, and I felt like stoking this flame.

"Can I ask you a question?"

He paused with his hand on the door and looked at me, waiting.

"I know you fuck," I said. "So why not me?"

I expected some speech about the importance of our

roles and the value of the system our forefathers created. It was bullshit, lofty language with no substance, like our religion, and we both knew it.

But that wasn't the path he took.

"You really want to know?" he asked.

I tried not to fidget, but it was difficult beneath his stare. It was like he'd let his mask drop, and the force of his desire hit me hard.

Or maybe I was just horny.

"Someday I will have to watch you marry another man, and it will be far easier to do if I never fuck you."

ZAHARIEV

That was a lie.
It was never going to be easy.

CHAPTER

FIFTEEN

I couldn't sleep.

I was too desperate for rest, or maybe just desperate to escape my thoughts, which were fixated on Zahariev and his stupid reason for not fucking me.

I wished he'd just lied.

I would have rolled my eyes. I would have called him a coward and a fucking crit, but at least his answer wouldn't have basically been *it will be easier on me*.

Selfish prick, I thought.

What he failed to consider when he'd made that decision was *me*. What if *I* wanted *him*?

I rolled onto my back for the thousandth time and stared at the ceiling. The darkness felt heavy, like it was beckoning, reaching for me with claws, desperate to pull me under, but I knew what waited on the other side, and I was not eager to return to that everlasting nightmare.

I hadn't told Zahariev about the dreams. It was the one thing I'd kept to myself. Though they'd haunted me since the night I'd first touched the blade, my pilgrimage through the cave and desert didn't seem relevant. Although I wondered if the blade could choose to come back to me, was it leading me somewhere? And if so, what was it trying to show me?

There was a part of me that didn't want to know.

I gave up on the idea of sleep and took a bath instead. I hissed as I sank into the scalding water, but it felt good, or maybe it just felt better than all the messy feelings Zahariev had stirred inside me. After years of relentless teasing, Zahariev had given me exactly what I deserved.

The agony of desire.

I took a deep breath and let my head rest against the back of the tub, wondering what had changed between us over the last week, but I knew the answer. At some point, I'd decided I wanted Zahariev Zareth to want me.

"You are in so much fucking trouble," I whispered to myself before I held my breath and let myself slip beneath the water.

———

There was a knock at my door.

I looked up from where I sat on my bed. I knew it was Coco. I'd heard her get up about an hour after I left the bath. She'd just gotten out of the shower, her hair and body wrapped in a towel.

"Are you going to the funeral today?"

Her voice was quieter than usual.

"No," I said. "But I think I will go see Gabriel and Liam this morning."

I'd been toying with the idea, but there was so much about going that made me anxious. It wasn't just about facing the shame I felt at having abandoned Gabriel. My last visit was fueled by adrenaline and a determination to prove Esther had been murdered. This time, I had nothing to distract me from the truth.

Coco's shoulders fell, empathy etched into the furrow of her brows and the press of her lips.

"I'm sure he would love to see you," she said.

I swallowed hard, not nearly as certain as Coco.

"Do you want me to go with you?" she asked.

"No, that's okay," I said. Selfishly, I wanted to go alone in case I lost the courage and backed out. "You should finish getting ready."

"Okay," she said, smiling gently. "If you change your mind, let me know."

"Thanks, Coco," I said. "You're the best."

When she left, I got myself together. Once I laced my boots, I slipped into my holster, which was more like a vest made from leather straps. I didn't always use this one, but it had space for me to loop the dagger. Now that I knew what it really was, I didn't feel comfortable leaving it behind when I wasn't home.

Though I never left my apartment unarmed, there was something strange about reaching for my weapons when I was only going to see a baby. Still, I pushed through my discomfort, knowing the real danger was the walk there and back.

I put on my jacket and gave Cherub a couple head scratches before heading out.

It had rained at some point, and the sidewalks were slick. The clouds still hung low, heavy with the threat of another storm. As fitting as this weather was, Esther deserved sunshine for her last day on earth. If I could control the weather like the matriarch of the Viridian family or her daughters, I would part this dark sky as a final goodbye, but I had nothing to offer, at least in the way of magic, and asking for a favor was out of the question.

The Viridians were rule followers. Even if there was potential to save hundreds of lives, their matriarch would not act if her husband and Archbishop Lisk said no.

Plus, they hated me.

At the sound of thunder rumbling somewhere in the distance, I pulled my hood up and walked with my head down. I made it to Gabriel's building just as it began to rain and let myself in. As soon as the elevator doors closed, my heart started pounding.

I knocked when I arrived at his door and waited in the musty hallway. I couldn't hear anything from inside the apartment and wondered briefly if Gabriel was even home, but then the lock clicked. I held my breath as the door opened, thinking it might keep me from bursting into tears.

Except it wasn't Gabriel who answered.

It was Zahariev, and I had an entirely different reaction to him.

My whole body *blushed*.

"What are you doing here?" My voice was sharper than I intended, but honestly, I'd hoped to avoid him until the gala tonight.

"I'm trying to help Gabriel so he can get ready for the funeral."

"Oh," I said. Of course. Because he was actually a good friend. "This is probably a bad time—"

"It's not a bad time," Zahariev said, interrupting me. "Come in."

He held the door open for me, and I only hesitated for a second before slipping past him, pausing in the entryway.

The apartment was darker than usual. Gabriel had

drawn the blinds, something Esther rarely did, especially on rainy days. She preferred the view and the natural light. It also smelled different, but that was probably because every time I visited, Esther was cooking or baking or making something.

I knew she was gone, but the changes were a harsh reminder that this was no longer my safe place.

"Are you all right?" Zahariev asked. His hand came to rest lightly on the small of my back.

"I just need a moment," I said.

I thought Zahariev would move past me, but he didn't, and I wondered if he stayed behind me to keep me from fleeing.

"Is it Livie?" Gabriel called from another room.

"Livie?" I asked, looking up at Zahariev, curious.

She was the teenage daughter of one of his soldiers. I'd had little interaction with her, save for the few family-friendly parties Zahariev had hosted at his compound. She'd been sweet to me initially, but as the years passed, she'd developed a crush on Zahariev and decided I was the enemy.

"She's going to watch Liam," Zahariev explained.

At that moment, Gabriel walked into view. He wasn't even ready yet, wearing a stained T-shirt and a pair of blue plaid pajama bottoms. His blond hair was a mess, sticking out in all directions like he hadn't put a brush through it in days. I suspected he hadn't even showered.

When he saw me, he froze, and his eyes widened a little.

"Lily," he said, taking a breath. "It's good to see you."

My mouth was already quivering. I pushed away from the wall and went to him, slipping my arms around his waist. He hugged me tight.

318

"I'm sorry, Gabriel," I whispered as a few stray tears trailed down my cheek.

"There's nothing to be sorry for, baby girl," he said. His voice was warm and gentle. It made me feel at home, even though everything had changed.

After a few seconds, I smelled sour milk and pulled away.

"Gabriel," I said. "I mean this in the nicest way possible, but you smell."

"Which is why he's supposed to be in the shower," said Zahariev.

He was standing behind me, leaning against the kitchen island, arms crossed over his chest, looking pointedly at Gabriel.

"I'll take a shower," he said. "Hey, but first, do you want to meet Liam?"

"Yeah," I said with a nod. My smile still felt shaky.

"You have twenty minutes," Zahariev warned.

Gabriel dismissed him with a wave as he headed toward Liam's room. "Plenty of time!"

I laughed quietly at him, even as I wiped at the tears on my face.

"You okay?" Zahariev asked.

I turned to look at him. He was standing in the kitchen, rolling the sleeves of his shirt up to his elbows. On the counter in front of him sat a canister of formula.

"Are you making a bottle?" I asked.

"Yeah," he said. "You wanna help?"

"I don't think that's a two-person job," I said.

The corners of his lips twitched. "You're probably right."

"When did you learn to make a bottle?"

I was curious. It wasn't something I expected him to

know, given his status, even with the instructions written on the container.

"I had two younger brothers," he said.

"Two?" I asked. "Why have I only met Cassius?"

"Because my youngest died," he said.

"I'm sorry." I wished I hadn't asked, but I also didn't like that I hadn't known something so important about him.

"It's fine," he said. "I didn't expect you to know. He was ten years younger than me… You were what? Two?"

"Don't say it that way."

"What way?"

"I'm only two years older than your youngest brother?"

He stared at me like he wasn't comprehending what I was saying, and maybe he didn't get it, but I didn't really want to think about how young I'd been when he was twelve after he'd had his tongue down my throat last night.

"Here we are," Gabriel announced as he returned to the living room, cradling a swaddled Liam in his arm. "Do you want to sit down?"

"Yeah," I said, moving toward the couch. I had never actually held a baby before and didn't feel comfortable standing with him.

I took a seat as Gabriel bent close, placing Liam in my waiting arms.

"Just make sure you keep his head supported," he said.

"Is this okay?" I asked. His head rested in the crook of my elbow.

"Yep, that's perfect," he said, adjusting his little hat. A few feathery hairs peeked out from beneath the cap, golden in color.

I couldn't stop looking at him, amazed by his detailed features. His lips were pink, perfectly bowed, his nose already looked like a smaller version of Gabriel's, and his lashes were blond, fanning across, heavy, rosy cheeks.

I was in awe of Esther, who had literally grown this perfect human. As I held him, I couldn't understand how women, mothers especially, were treated like second-class citizens. This was a miracle. It was magic. This, I would worship over an absent God.

"I can't believe he is here," I whispered. I was afraid to speak too loudly. I didn't want to disturb him. He was already twitching in my arms.

"Hey," Zahariev said, snapping his fingers at Gabriel before pointing to the bedroom. "Shower. Now."

"I'm going," Gabriel said, thrusting his fingers through his hair. It was so stiff, it stuck straight up. "Just...if you need anything...."

"We're fine," Zahariev said, rounding the counter, a bottle in hand. "Go."

"Right. Going," Gabriel said, disappearing into the bedroom.

I glanced at Zahariev. "You're such a daddy."

"You only get to call me that when you behave," he said.

My gaze snapped back to him. His expression was serious, which made me feel like he wasn't joking.

"The day I behave is the day you fuck me, Zahariev," I said. "Two things that will never happen."

He raised a brow and handed me the bottle. "Not in front of the baby."

"Why are you handing me this?" I asked.

"You need to feed him," he said.

"But he's asleep."

"Feed him anyway," he said.

I hesitated, but Zahariev wrapped his hand around mine, guiding the bottle to Liam's lips.

"Hold it here, and see if he latches," he said. "The nipple goes all the way in his mouth. Just keep the bottle tilted. Perfect."

He took a seat opposite me when he was finished with his instruction.

"Maybe you should do this if you're such an expert," I said.

"You'll have to learn someday."

"Why?" I asked. "I'm not having children."

At least, that was my goal if I managed to stay in Nineveh.

"What makes you so sure?"

"Why does everyone want to argue when a woman says she's not getting married and she doesn't want children?"

"I'm not arguing," he said. "I just asked a question."

"I wouldn't make a good mother, Zahariev," I said. The question frustrated me. The answer was obvious. "Mine isn't exactly a great role model."

"That's what will make you a great mother," he said. "Your desire to be better than her."

"Do you want to be a father?" I asked pointedly, but the question didn't seem to bother him the way it bothered me.

"Maybe," he said. "If I find the right woman."

I scoffed. "You think you can find the right woman when your marriage is going to be arranged?"

"You might try to burp him," said Zahariev, changing the subject, though I wasn't surprised. He didn't like when I talked about marriage.

Guess we were even.

"I don't know how to do that," I said.

Zahariev stared before rising to sit beside me.

"Give him here," he said.

I didn't know how to hand off a baby, but Zahariev acted like he'd done this a million times, slipping one hand under his head and the other beneath his bundled legs. He sat him up, his large hand splayed across Liam's chest as he patted his back until he made a quiet gurgling sound.

"There you go," he said, chuckling quietly. After, he cradled Liam in his arm.

It was a sight, and suddenly, my uterus didn't even belong to me. I wouldn't say I wanted a baby, but I definitely wanted to fuck, and if Zahariev were mine, I'd jump his bones the second we were alone.

I looked away.

Silence stretched between us.

"Did you tell Gabriel about the demon in Liam's room?" I asked.

"Let's get him through the funeral first," said Zahariev.

"You shouldn't let him stay here," I said. "You should tell him it isn't safe and that he needs to move. This place is cursed."

I was surprised when Zahariev's hand landed on my thigh. I stared at the letters etched on his knuckles before meeting his gaze.

"I have invited Gabriel to the compound," he said. "He hasn't accepted yet, but I won't force him out of the home he shared with Esther. It's safe here for now."

"You can't know that," I said.

"I think I do," he said. "I'm pretty convinced your so-called demons are after those seven blades."

I furrowed my brows but didn't have time to ask why he thought that, because Gabriel returned to the living room.

"Can one of you help me with this fucking tie?" he asked.

I jumped at the sound of his voice.

"Of course," I said.

As I rose to my feet, Zahariev's hand slipped from my leg.

"I hate these things," Gabriel said as I took each length into my hands.

Coco called this one of my hidden talents. Really, I'd just been forced through etiquette training. I'd learned how to make menus around special occasions, pair the perfect wine with each dish, arrange flowers into a stunning bouquet, and knot a neck or bow tie, which ever my husband chose.

I'd have rather learned how to cook or even drive a car. Those were practical skills.

"You don't have to wear it if you don't want to," I said, glancing up at him. I noticed his eyes were rimmed with red, and I suspected all he'd done in the shower was cry.

"I know," he said, his voice quiet. "But I think Esther would like it. She always told me she did."

"Well, it's only a few hours. Then you can come home and change into your smelly robe," I said, tightening the knot at his neck before letting my hand rest on his shoulder. "For now, though, you smell better."

His laugh was almost like a sigh. "Thanks, Lily."

"Five minutes," Zahariev called.

Gabriel flipped him off as he headed into his bedroom.

I turned and found Zahariev watching me. I couldn't place the expression on his face, but it made me feel self-conscious.

"What?" I asked, just as a knock came at the door.

"You want to get it, or should I?" he asked.

"If it's Livie and you don't answer, I think she will be very disappointed."

He raised a brow but rose with Liam, approaching me. "Hold him."

The transfer didn't feel as awkward as it had the first time, though he made a few quiet noises before yawning and going still. I watched him as Zahariev went to the door.

"Hey, Livie," I heard him say.

"Hi, Mr. Zareth," she said shyly.

I looked up as she entered the living room and smiled at her.

"Livie, you remember Miss Leviathan," Zahariev said.

"Yes," she replied with a note of quiet disappointment.

It didn't bother me. I knew what it was to be her age and have a crush on an older man. Even knowing the impossibility of anything happening, the jealousy was hard to quell.

Being a teenager was hard.

"How are you, Livie?" I asked.

"Good," she said, letting her eyes drift to the floor.

"We just fed him, Livie. He should be good for a couple of hours. Gabriel!" Zahariev called. "Livie's here!"

A few seconds of silence passed before Gabriel left his bedroom.

"Hey, Livie," he said. "Let me show you where everything is."

While Gabriel gave her a tour, I kept my gaze on Liam. Tears came to my eyes. I felt silly, but I was so in awe of him and so proud of Esther. How was it possible to already love him so much?

Zahariev neared and placed his hand on the top of Liam's head, pressing a kiss to his forehead. I met his gaze as he straightened, a single tear sliding down my cheek.

Zahariev brushed it away with the backs of his fingers. His touch lingered, and I wondered why he was torturing me.

"You have my number if you need anything," Gabriel was saying as they returned to the living room. "We should be back by two. There's plenty of food in the fridge if you get hungry."

"Thank you, Mr. De Santis," said Livie.

"We should go," said Zahariev, glancing at his watch.

I looked down at Liam and pressed a kiss to his forehead. "Be good for Livie, little one," I said and handed him off.

Zahariev and I waited at the door while Gabriel searched frantically through the house for his keys. After a few more minutes, he found them, and we slipped into the hall and headed down the elevator.

Without Zahariev fussing at Gabriel, there was nothing to distract from the weight of our collective sadness. None of us spoke until we were outside the complex where Felix waited. I slowed to a stop on the sidewalk.

"Gabriel," I said. "I'm sorry I can't…"

"Hey, remember what I said?" he asked. "Nothing to apologize for."

I swallowed hard as I nodded, taking a shaky breath.

"There's something I want you to have," he said. He reached into his pocket and pulled out a small plastic bag. Inside was a pendant. It was round, a greenish stone encased in gold.

I opened the bag and let it slide into my hand. It was heavier than I expected, and as I studied the stone, I noticed there was some kind of liquid encapsulated within. It gave off a faint energy, though I didn't recognize it as magic exactly. It felt like Esther. Perhaps she had carried it so long, the stone had absorbed her essence.

I wondered if Gabriel knew.

"Esther called it a protection amulet," he explained. "I

don't know if I believe in that sort of thing, but she always wore it when she left the house."

"Are you sure you don't want to save this for Liam?" I asked, though I was already holding it tight within my grasp.

"I wouldn't have offered it if I wasn't sure," he said.

"I love you," I said, slipping my arms around his waist.

"I love you too, baby girl," he said, returning my hug. "Come back anytime."

He pulled away and gave me a smile. It was not as bright or as wide as it once was, but it gave me a little hope that things might end up okay. He climbed into the SUV, and my gaze shifted to Zahariev.

"We can drop you off at Dr. Mor's," he said.

"I can walk," I said.

He nodded once. "Behave, little love."

I arched a brow in challenge. He knew what I was saying. He didn't need the words.

Fuck me, and maybe I will.

ZAHARIEV

"I love you like a brother," said Gabriel once the door was closed. "Which is why I am telling you this. Lilith deserves commitment."

"I know what she deserves," I said. "I'm just not sure she wants it."

You act like this has to mean something, she'd said the night Esther died. *Sex can just be sex.*

"Maybe she doesn't think that's possible with you," said Gabriel.

I ground my teeth. That was exactly what she thought, because it was true, but I would break every rule for her if she said she wanted more.

CHAPTER
SIXTEEN

Dr. Mor cleaned and dressed the burn on my wrist.
"If it swells or you develop a fever, call me," he
said. "Take something over-the-counter for the
pain."

It was raining hard when I left his office, so I made a
couple stops on my way home to have a break from the
downpour, dropping by Sons for a to-go order of mozzarella
sticks and a pharmacy for a bottle of painkillers.

By the time I returned to the apartment, it was around
two. Esther's funeral would be over. I tried not to think
about what that meant. I realized she was gone the moment
she passed at the hospital, but with her body buried in the
cemetery, it felt final.

I took off my jacket and holster before returning to the
kitchen to warm a couple of mozzarella sticks in the microwave. Cherub was purring loudly and rubbing against my
legs.

I gave her a treat while I waited for my food. When it was
done, I carried it into my room and sat in the middle of my

bed. I didn't eat in here often, but today, I felt like it. When I first moved to Nineveh, it felt rebellious.

Growing up, my mother planned three meals a day—two when I was in school—and they were all to be taken in the dining room. It was the one rule even my father wasn't allowed to break.

It wasn't until I came to Nineveh that I learned some people actually ate in their living room while watching TV.

I bit into my first mozzarella stick, and hot cheese exploded in my mouth. I'd left them in the microwave too long. After managing to cool the bite enough to chew and swallow, I was more careful with the second, though I couldn't really taste it since I burnt my mouth all to hell.

When I was finished, I set my plate aside. I had a couple of hours before I had to start getting ready for the gala. I hadn't even decided what I was going to wear, though I only had two choices: one that would please my father and one that would please me. Neither would please my mother.

But I wasn't going for her.

I sighed, got to my feet, and made a path through my clothes to the closet, where I pulled out both dresses. One was black with a square neckline. The other was a red silk gown with a plunging neckline and thigh-high slit.

"Which one, Cherub? This one that says I'm going to the morgue or *this* one that says I'm going to hell?"

As soon as I asked, the lights flickered. I stared up at my ceiling light and then at the lamp.

"I didn't mean literal hell," I muttered. I crossed the room, nearly tripping on a tank top I hadn't pushed far enough out of the way. I tossed both dresses on the bed and then turned and looked at my floor.

My room was a direct reflection of what had been going

330

on in my life. Things were messy, chaotic, and a little embarrassing. I decided I should probably clean since I had the time and didn't feel sleepy enough to nap.

I never intended to be someone who didn't keep up with laundry. It had just happened over time as our washer and dryer became more and more unreliable. To keep from having to go to the laundromat, I'd gotten in the habit of wearing everything—sometimes multiple times—before I made time to wash my clothes.

I dragged my overstuffed basket of clothes into the hallway. Once I had a load in the washer, I returned to my bedroom to collect more clothes from the floor. In the process, I found a pair of heels I'd lost a few weeks ago and decided to wear them tonight.

They were gold and had straps that wrapped around my calf. They were a favorite of mine, though my mother would disapprove and say they were ugly. She liked to comment on my appearance as often as she could, even when I dressed according to her wishes.

I hated that after all this time and distance, I still let her judgment give me doubt, but it was that anger, that resentment that fueled most of my decision-making and why I would wear what pleased me to the gala.

It seemed Cherub agreed, because when I was finished cleaning, I found her curled up on the black dress, sleeping.

"Glad we both agree," I said, and then my phone buzzed loudly against the nightstand where I'd left it. My father messaged me with what I would consider a warning:

Be on your best behavior tonight, and please dress appropriately.

If I hadn't already decided on my outfit, *this* would have pushed me over.

My father had given me a lot of leeway over the years, and I was grateful he'd let me escape to Nineveh, because that was what he'd done. He'd let me. He knew it, and I knew it.

But I didn't think he expected the freedom to push me further away from who they wanted me to be. I'd done my best over the years at our biweekly lunches to respect him. I'd dressed according to family rules. I'd avoided topics of work and friendship. For a time, I'd even let him think I'd returned to reading from the *Book of Splendor*, but I was done pretending.

Saira had given me a different type of freedom. As skeptical as I was, the possibility of other gods had unraveled what little faith I had in the teachings of the church. I'd only held on out of fear of not believing in something. What was the point of life without the promise of eternal paradise?

But that was the great lie, wasn't it?

Life was life. It was as meaningful as I made it.

I moved my laundry from the washer to the dryer and started another load, then took a shower. By the time I was finished, I felt even more determined to show my parents who I had become. As much as my father had begged me to attend tonight, I knew the truth. He didn't really want me. He wanted the daughter I'd been five years ago, but she didn't exist anymore, and it was time he realized it.

I wiped fog from the mirror and stared at my misty reflection. My sleep schedule was catching up to me. My eyes were puffy and a little dark. I could also use some drops to lessen the redness, lest my mom think I was high.

When I opened the cabinet to retrieve them, everything fell.

Motherfucker. I stared at the sink full of medicines. I considered putting them in a box and leaving them on the floor, but after a deep breath, I began arranging them.

I was surprised to find a pair of metal scissors amid the bottles. They belonged to Coco. I'd just forgotten they were in here.

I left them for last, and when I picked them up, I shut the cabinet door and looked at myself in the mirror.

I had always wanted bangs. Coco used to get excited when I'd talk about it. She offered to cut them, and once, she'd made all the necessary parts before I'd backed out. Now, when I mentioned it, she didn't even react.

I had always hesitated because they were such a drastic change and also because, as much as I fought conforming to the expectations of my parents and the church, some things gave me more anxiety than others, and one of those things was my appearance.

I'd never made a change my mother liked. It didn't matter if I thought it looked better. She claimed it was a sign I was becoming vain. She didn't recognize her own hypocrisy.

I started parting my hair. I didn't know what gave me the confidence to do this on my own. Maybe because I'd watched Coco do it a million times before. Maybe I was just being reckless. Whatever the case, I continued combing a section of my hair forward. I folded it back to see if I liked the way it looked and to assess where I wanted the bangs to land.

Then I reached for the scissors, and with no hesitation, I made the first cut. It was a straight, horizontal line, and the bangs landed just past my brow bone. I dried them and made a few additional snips until I was happy with their shape.

333

For the first time in a long while, I felt like me.

Moving on to makeup, I painted on dramatic wings. As I leaned close to the mirror, the electricity surged again. When the light came back on, it buzzed loudly.

Maybe the wind had gotten bad near the coast.

I hurried to finish my makeup, finishing with a bold red lip my mother would hate, and then slipped into my dress. I was trying to zip it on my own but couldn't manage it past a certain point when I heard a knock.

"Coming!" I called, still fiddling with the closure as I made my way to the door. I assumed it was Zahariev but checked to make sure. Instead of greeting him as I answered, I requested his help. "Can you zip this for me?"

I didn't wait for him to respond. I just gave him my back, shivering slightly as his knuckles brushed against my spine. He was finished in seconds, and I turned, intending to thank him, but the way he was looking at me produced a different response.

"What?" I asked.

My first thought was that he hated the bangs, but then his gaze dropped, lingering on the plunge of my neckline and the curve of my hips, which were exaggerated by the fit of this dress. Zahariev never looked at me this way. That he was doing so now, and so openly, made my stomach coil tight.

"You look nice," he said when his gaze finally returned to mine.

I raised a brow, challenging that word.

"That's the best you can do? Your jaw's on the floor, Zahariev."

He smiled, tugging gently at my bangs.

"I like them," he said.

334

The compliment made me blush. But simultaneously, I wondered if he was lying.

"Thank you," I said, realizing I hadn't even registered his appearance.

He was always well-dressed, but there was something about seeing him in a three-piece suit that did things to me. This one was particularly stunning, fitted to his slim frame. The black fabric had a warm tone, and I couldn't tell if that was because of its shine or the cream color of his button-down. His tie brought the whole look together, a paisley pattern in black and gold.

"I like your suit," I said.

"Thanks," he said. "Fawna said I had to wear color tonight."

Fawna was Zahariev's housekeeper, but she had opinions on everything, including appropriate dress.

"So you chose...cream?"

Zahariev glanced down at his tie. "And gold," he said defensively.

I pressed my lips together to keep from smiling.

"Are you ready?"

"Just let me get my heels," I said.

As I made my way to my bedroom, Cherub left, sauntering into the living room for a look at Zahariev.

"Well, hello," I heard him say, and she meowed in return.

I slipped on my shoes, winding the straps around my calves, then retrieved a set of black lace gloves, a fur stole and a small beaded bag from my closet. I hoped the gloves might hide the bandage on my wrist. The stole and bag were two of only a few things I had left over from my previous life in Hiram, and I'd kept them for this reason.

When I returned, Zahariev stood in the middle of my

living room, cradling Cherub, massaging a spot on her chest. Her head flopped toward me, and I pursed my lips.

"You are such a tease," I said.

"Me or the cat?" Zahariev asked.

"The fact that you had to ask for clarification says a lot."

I walked up to him and took Cherub, holding her at eye level.

"Be good for Coco," I said before kissing her head and lowering her to sit on the arm of the couch.

I wrapped the fur around my shoulders and followed Zahariev to the door. As I stepped out onto the balcony, I noticed the streetlights flashing. It was eerie, made worse by the dark and the heaviness in the air. I almost wished it would rain again. Maybe it would ease the weight.

"That's been happening all day," I said.

"It's probably your mother," said Zahariev. "Using up all the energy for her fucking party."

I laughed but pulled the stole tighter. A chill had settled on my skin, and I was eager for the warmth of Zahariev's SUV.

He held the door open for me, and I slid inside.

"Evening, Miss Leviathan," said Felix, turning to look at me. He let out a low whistle. "Well, aren't you a vision?"

My face warmed at his comment, and I smiled. "Thank you, Felix."

"No need to thank me for saying something true," he said as Zahariev entered the vehicle on the other side.

"You know where to go," Zahariev said, though he didn't sound any more enthused than I felt.

"Yes, sir," Felix said, boosting the volume on his music, filling the space with a mournful, almost ethereal lilt.

"How is Gabriel?" I asked.

"Hard to say," said Zahariev.

I glanced at him and found he was looking at me.

"How are you?" he asked.

"I'm fine," I said, though even I knew I'd failed to deliver that lie convincingly.

The truth I didn't want to face was that I was afraid, and not just of blades and demons and gods behind gates.

Tonight, I was basically subjecting myself to a firing squad of overt judgment and backhanded compliments in a space where my trauma was born and gluttonously fed.

It didn't matter how much I had changed or how brave I felt. In my parents' home, I was a child again, hurt and desperate for love.

As we headed north on Procession Street, I stared out the window. Now and then, the lights would flicker. Maybe there was something to what Zahariev had said about my mother using up all the available electricity. It wouldn't be the first time something like that happened, but it was usually during situations when the weather was bad.

I wasn't sure why it bothered me so much either. It just felt like a very bad omen.

I swallowed a lump in my throat as the SUV slowed, coming upon a line of cars, all inching their way into the hills of Hiram. My family home was nestled at the very top of those winding, narrow roads, surrounded by aged oaks and white pines.

I didn't miss the life I'd had here, but there were things I had loved, like trees and the smell of the earth after rain. They were things I'd taken for granted, never once assuming people in other districts lived without them. It was only later, once I'd come to Nineveh, that Zahariev had explained the deforestation of his district by one of his great-great-grandfathers.

He'd had reasons—they'd needed the lumber for businesses, housing, and furniture. Then they'd needed wider roads and space to build more clubs and hotels.

As he'd explained the systematic decimation of his district, he'd also taken the magic of mine.

You think men build houses around all those pretty trees high on your hill? He had laughed at my ignorance. *There isn't a single part of Hiram that wasn't made to look the way it is now.*

It wasn't what we'd been taught, but it made sense now that I had been deprogrammed. Hiram was the closest district to the Garden of Eden. By default, it meant that only the godliest could reside there, but it also meant that the landscape had to reflect its proximity. What would it say about God or sanctity if the district closest to evil was more beautiful?

The irony now was that if what Saira said was true, Nineveh was actually closest to true divinity.

I took a breath, trying to ease the pressure building in my chest as we neared, when I felt Zahariev's touch. It was a graze at first, just down the inside of my arm as he sought to lace his fingers with mine. A wave of heat rushed to my face and quickly receded. It was dizzying and delightful in a way that other, more erotic things weren't.

I looked at him.

"I've got you," he said. His voice was quiet and coaxed another swell of pleasing heat to the surface of my skin.

"I know," I said.

We stared at each other, and a quiet tension built between us. It made me want those other, more erotic things, so I looked away. I would experience my fair share of rejection tonight, and I didn't need it from the one person who constantly saved me from the storm.

I knew we were close when Felix turned down his music and glanced at us in the rearview.

"If you really don't want to stay, I can back into one of you with the car. Bam! Perfect excuse to leave."

"That won't be necessary," said Zahariev. "But stay close."

I felt strongly that by the end of the night, we'd regret not taking him up on the offer.

Zahariev let his fingers slip from mine as Felix came to a stop and I pulled on my gloves.

An attendant waited and opened Zahariev's door. He stepped out, pausing to button his jacket before offering his hand. I took it and let him help me out of the car, but he didn't move once I was on my feet.

"Need to adjust anything?" he asked.

"When did you become such a gentleman?"

Though I teased, he didn't smile. "I'm not asking to be a gentleman."

I parted the stole and slipped one of the thin straps of my dress back in place, then ran my hands over my hips and stomach to smooth out the fabric. When I was finished, I looked up at Zahariev. By the heat of his gaze, I got the sense he'd tracked every movement I'd made.

I arched a brow. "I think it might be your turn, Zahariev."

He smiled, lips pulling back from his teeth. Anyone watching us probably thought I said something funny instead of implying that the head of the Zareth family had a hard-on for me.

He stepped to the side, and it was the first time I had really gotten a good look at my childhood home. It was a grand mansion, a delicate mix of sharp angles and round edges. After living here so long, the house had felt small, but that was only because I had gotten older and the things I needed to hide from were bigger.

I had rightly guessed my mother's plans to bring her theme of *an evening beneath the stars* to life. Hundreds of shimmering lights hung from the trees outside our home, unpolluted by the yellow-tinged glow of streetlamps.

Zahariev offered his hand, and though I didn't really need help navigating the three short steps that led to my parents' front door, I accepted anyway.

It wasn't the intimate hold we'd shared in the dark cabin of the SUV, but the curl of his fingers around mine was grounding in a space where I felt untethered.

Zahariev looked at me before we crossed the threshold.

"Do your thing, little love," he said, and the part of me that could be harmed by disapproving looks and cruel words held her breath and vanished. It was just in time too, because at our appearance, the murmur of quiet conversation echoing in the foyer went silent.

A smile danced across my lips as I surveyed the crowd, recognizing the faces of family bosses, matriarchs, their children, and associates. I felt their disdain, and it only grew as I slipped my fur stole from my shoulders. I was the only one in red—the only one in a color that wasn't some sparkling shade of silver, champagne, or black.

There must have been a dress code.

Oops, I thought with little remorse.

I felt someone tug on my stole. It was Zahariev, taking it and my purse to check. I relinquished them with a seductive curl of my lips before returning my attention to the crowd.

This time, it was easy to find my parents amid the sea of sparkling gowns, mainly because I could feel my mother's disapproving gaze, though I could hardly take offense. Her icy eyes rarely melted for anyone other than the archbishop.

She stood stoically beside my father, dressed in a black gown with silver beading. The neckline was high and one-shouldered. She was a slight woman but no less powerful, even dwarfed by my father.

Looking at her was like taking a blow to the chest, and it had nothing to do with her disdain.

It was because I saw myself in every part of her, from the sharp curve of her eyes to the pinched dissatisfaction of her mouth. I wondered if she hated it as much as I did.

I turned fully to them and smiled.

"Father," I said with breathless joy as I crossed the room. He accepted my embrace and then held on to my hands as I stepped back.

"Lilith," he said. "Look at you."

His comment was not praise but the equivalent of showing him a piece of art and the only thing he could think to say was, *yep, that's red*. It was the best I could hope for. The worst would come later when he dragged me into his office to scold me for ignoring his *one request*.

"Mother," I said, my tone considerably colder than when I'd addressed my father. I didn't hug her but braced my hands on her upper arms as I leaned in to mimic kissing her cheeks.

"Darling," she said tightly.

I expected her to voice some kind of backhanded compliment. Usually, it was something along the lines of *what a charming necklace*, even though I hadn't taken it off since my father gifted it to me. Tonight, however, she couldn't even manage that.

Luckily, she was saved from having to find something

to like about me by the approach of a man I didn't recognize.

He was older, probably in his forties, and handsome. His skin was burnished, like he'd recently spent a lot of time in the sun. I'd bet he had a yacht off the coast in the Kurari Sea. I could picture him there, dark hair blazing against a pale sky.

He wore black, but there were elements of his suit that made it unique—velvet lapels and a sequined black tie.

"Lilith, darling, I'd like you to meet Mr. Macarius Robert Caiaphas."

I raised a brow at my father's use of his full given name.

"A pleasure, Miss Leviathan," he said.

"Do you go by all those names, or may I call you Mr. Caiaphas?" I asked.

His smile was warm and genuine. "You may call me whatever you'd like."

"That is a brave offer," I said. "What if you don't like what I choose?"

"Lilith—" My mother's voice was a chiding whisper. Her hand came to rest on my forearm, squeezing tight, but Macarius laughed, and she released me.

"Lucius said you were clever. I am happy to learn he did not exaggerate."

"I'm sure he meant it as more of a warning," I said, delivering my line as if it were a joke, though everyone knew it wasn't.

Still, we laughed.

I was sure it was a perfect shot for the photographer who stood nearby, snapping candids. Before the night ended, my mother would review every still and every video, approving only the best footage for the media. It was just one way she controlled our family's image and probably the only reason she hadn't sent me packing the moment I walked through the door.

"So what do you do, Miss Leviathan?" Macarius asked.

The color wasn't even finished draining from my face before my mother jumped to answer his question.

"Lilith is proselytizing in Nineveh," she said, placing her hand on her chest as if she were somehow emotionally invested in my life. "You know how lost some of those souls have become."

Macarius's eyes shifted to me, shining with admiration.

"That is a noble endeavor," he said. "You both must be proud."

My mother made a noise. I thought it was supposed to be the hum of an agreement, but it sounded more like someone had kicked her in the shin.

"Of course, but we miss her dearly."

I could tell she'd turned to look at me. I met her gaze, wanted to see if she looked as sincere as she sounded.

She didn't.

"Luckily," my mother continued, "she will be returning to us *very* soon."

Her threat straightened my spine, but I donned a bright smile.

"So she says every year," I said, turning my attention to Macarius as I gushed. "Yet my parents are never willing to deny my passions. Isn't it a rare gift to be born into such a spectacular family?"

Fuck me. I hadn't lied this much in my entire life.

Macarius's eyes did not waver from mine, and for the first time since I'd been introduced to him, I felt uneasy beneath the intensity of his gaze. "Rare indeed," he agreed. "You are very lucky, Miss Leviathan."

My father cleared his throat and placed a hand on Macarius's back. "Perhaps we should leave the ladies and continue our earlier conversation in my office?"

"Of course," Macarius said, his attention sliding back to me as he inclined his head. "It was a pleasure, Miss Leviathan. Mrs. Leviathan."

He and my father ascended the stairs, and I maintained my smile, even as the tips of my mother's nails dug into my injured wrist.

She leaned in, her voice low and lethal.

"How *dare* you embarrass me," she hissed. "Arriving on the arm of Zahariev Zareth and in *that* dress!"

"And to think I praised you for being such a supportive mother," I said.

"You are not the child I raised."

I flinched and looked at her, the corner of my mouth lifting in a snide smile.

"Do you know what's funny?" I said, jerking my arm from her hold. "I *am* the child you raised."

"Lower your voice!" she hissed.

I ignored her command.

"But you can't accept that," I said. "Because it would mean that you are to blame for the person I've become. What would people think if they really knew the pious matriarch of the prestigious Leviathan family gave life to a demon?"

My mother slapped me.

The sharp sting of her hand against my cheek shocked me, yet I almost laughed as I stared back at her. Her eyes were wide and watery, her cheeks flushed with anger. I had hit a nerve.

It was a few more seconds before my mother came out of

344

her trance and realized what she'd done. She dropped her hand and straightened as her gaze drifted to the crowded room. I was certain she was embarrassed, but only about losing control in front of people, not because she'd hurt me.

No one cared about that.

"It's hard looking in a mirror, isn't it, Mother?" I asked.

I left the foyer and headed down the hallway to the bathroom. It was as large as my bedroom and had a built-in vanity where my mother's guests could touch up their makeup before returning to her festivities.

When I slipped inside, I was startled to find a young woman seated on the bench in front of the mirror.

She scrambled to her feet, hiding a phone behind her back.

"I'm sorry," she blurted out.

I gave her a small smile and locked the door. "You don't have to apologize. You can keep texting whoever it is you're texting. I just came in here to get a break from out there."

And to look at my face, though I could already see the outline of my mother's fingers on my cheek.

The girl noticed too.

"Did your mother hit you?" she asked.

"Oh, did she ever," I said dryly.

I pulled off my gloves as I moved into the main part of the bathroom where the lights were brighter. The wound on my wrist throbbed, and the bandage was stained with fresh blood. I thought about unwrapping it but felt it was probably safer if I waited. I just wished I'd thought to bring something for the pain.

My eyes shifted to the mirror. The red outline of my mother's hand was far harsher under this light.

"Does that mean it will never end?"

The question surprised me but also hurt. I knew the girl was asking because her mother hit her too. I glanced at her and turned on the cold water.

"I wouldn't say never," I said, though I didn't want to make any promises. "But I think we have two options as daughters of the five. We either behave, or we take the beating. I can't tell you which is the right decision, and I wouldn't blame you if you chose the first."

I ran one of the thick paper towels beneath the water and pressed it to my face. The cool water soothed my stinging skin.

"How did you know I was a daughter of the five?"

I smiled wryly. It was a sign of her immaturity that she didn't realize we all knew one another, even those who were older.

"The same way you know me," I said. "We are made to be aware. You are Sienna, right? The youngest of the Sanctius siblings?"

She nodded.

I threw the towel away and turned off the water. "Your mother's scary," I said. "I think she might be worse than mine."

Her name was Marguerite. Her family came from money, having discovered oil in the Nara-Sin Desert almost sixty years ago. It was the wealth that had allowed her to marry into the Sanctius family, the same wealth that gave her a superiority complex.

"She hates me," said Sienna. "I never do anything right. I'm starting to think I shouldn't even try."

I smiled a little. "I think you probably do many things right," I said as I slipped on my gloves. "But you are a little too careless with the things you do wrong."

346

I moved past her, heading for the door.

She followed. "What do you mean?"

I paused and looked at her. "A word from the wise," I said. "If you're going to be a rebel, be smart about it. Lock the door next time."

I left the bathroom, pausing to run my hand over a wet spot on my dress, hoping it might dry faster, and smiled when I heard the lock click into place even as my chest tightened. It was possible I'd just failed her. She was young and impressionable, and her willful spirit could still be beaten out of her.

Maybe I should have told her to behave.

"There you are."

I looked up as Macarius approached, brows drawn. I was confused because there was a familiarity to his words we didn't have, considering I had just been introduced to him.

"I've been looking for you," he said. "Your father wants to speak to you."

"Oh," I said. Now I was even more confused. "He could have found me himself. I am sure you have better things to do."

I also didn't appreciate being approached right outside the bathroom.

Macarius smiled, but I got the sense that he only did so to be polite.

"Not at all," he said. "I'd much rather fetch a beautiful woman than engage in polite conversation with a bunch of people I don't like."

I couldn't decide if he was being sincere or just saying something he thought I wanted to hear. Maybe I just had trust issues.

"Thank you, Mr. Caiaphas," I said and started down the hall.

"I'll escort you," he said, falling into step beside me.

"That really isn't necessary," I said, heading up the stairs, letting my hand rest on the cold rail of the banister. "This is my childhood home. I know well where I am going."

"Of course," he said. "I confess, I wanted an excuse to continue talking."

"I'm not really all that interesting, Mr. Caiaphas."

At least I didn't want to be interesting to him.

"But you are," he said. "I'd like to hear more about your time proselytizing in Nineveh."

"There isn't much I can say about it," I replied.

"Really, after two years?" he asked. "You have nothing?"

I didn't respond. He was annoying, and I really wanted him to go away.

"Could it be that instead of turning people toward God, you spent all your time with Zahariev Zareth?"

I glanced at him but didn't let his question stall me. He wasn't smiling, but I got the sense he was proud of himself for catching me in what he thought was a lie.

"Zahariev is a good friend," I said.

"Is that how you're choosing to describe your relationship?"

I paused as we came to the top of the steps and turned fully toward him. I wanted to push him down the stairs. I still might, depending on what he said next.

"I don't see how my relationship with Zahariev concerns you, Mr. Caiaphas," I said.

"I think it's my right to ask my future wife if she's fucking the head of the Zareth family, don't you think?"

I went cold, staring at him in disbelief.

"Excuse me?"

Macarius's lips lifted in a mocking half smile. "You

348

should run along," he said. "You don't want to keep your father waiting."

I whirled and marched down the hallway to his office. I shoved the door open so hard, it hit the wall with a loud bang. My father stood near the fireplace, a large cigar in hand.

He only smoked when he was celebrating.

"Tell me it isn't true," I said.

I hated that my voice quaked, that I already had tears in my eyes.

"Lilith—"

"Tell me!" I roared.

His expression turned stony, his eyes cold. I watched him go from caring father to the stoic head of the Leviathan family, and I'd never despised him more than in this moment.

"I will secure the future of my legacy," he said. His tone was firm and final. "You have known your duty since you were young. The time you spent away has muddled your mind."

"You *wish* my mind was muddled," I spat.

"Watch your tone," he said, the words slipping between gritted teeth.

"Or what? Are you going to hit me? Go ahead. I barely flinch anymore."

My father paled. I'd chipped away at some of his hard edges.

"You've spent the last two years lying to everyone. You told the archbishop I was just going through a phase. You promised him I would return and witness for him, but you never asked me *why* I left."

"You and your mother weren't getting along, I thought it best—"

"Don't tell me *why* you think I left," I snapped. "*Ask me.*"

He stared. It was probably hard for a man so used to getting his way to take orders from a woman, especially his daughter.

"Ask me!" I screamed.

He cleared his throat. "Why did you leave?" His voice cracked.

I straightened, refusing to cower.

"I left because your beloved archbishop *raped* me," I said. "I left because you never once considered that maybe the reason I'd wavered in my faith was because the man in charge of it had touched me. I left because I didn't *trust* you to protect me. You never have. Not from Mom, not from the church, and not from this fucking world."

"Lilith—"

He whispered my name, a desperate plea, but I couldn't stand it and cut him off, shouting.

"*Two years!* Two years and all you thought about was who would succeed you, because despite being your own flesh and blood, I am still not worth as much as a man, even the one who hurt me." I paused, lifting my chin. "When you think of your legacy, I hope you remember this moment and how you failed me."

As soon as the words left my lips, the power went out.

ZAHARIEV

I was outside when Hiram went dark. I wasn't surprised, given how spotty the electricity had been today. I bet Lilith's mom was furious; her evening under the stars was ruined.

I chuckled at the thought.

It was really what she got for being such a shitty parent.

I felt my phone vibrate in my pocket and checked my messages. I thought Lilith might be texting to ask where I was, but it was Cassius.

Power's out. Generator's up.

I was about to put it away when another message came through. It wasn't

a number I'd saved in my phone, though
I knew exactly whom it belonged to—
Alarich Lisk.

CHAPTER
SEVENTEEN

The power stayed out.

In the confusion that followed, I went unnoticed as I slipped outside. It was colder than before, and the air was heavy with the smell of rain.

Without the glare of city lights, the dark was uninterrupted, save for a few glowing solar candles holding vigil for the departed in the cemetery below. From here, they cast shadows on ghostly monuments, and in this deep dark, every smooth curve and carved edge was visible.

It was a little unnerving, but then terrible things were born on nights like this.

Maybe I am that terrible thing, I thought as I made my way down the hill behind my parents' house. Maybe I should have had more remorse for my father who I'd left, stricken and alone in his office, now burdened with my secret.

In the aftermath of my confession, we'd both become new people. I was stronger than before, more sure than I'd ever been in my life, but my father, he was weaker, a little less of the man he'd been when I'd walked in, and I didn't care.

He deserved to know the truth. He deserved to break beneath it the way I had.

The ground was soft, and I paused halfway down the hill to remove my gloves and shoes, wandering barefoot into the open cemetery. I had walked this path a thousand times in my youth, though now it was hard to tell. The once balding grass had grown fuller in my absence. Still, I found comfort here among the dead, in a place that was silent and judgeless.

As I wove effortlessly between the maze of monuments, my thoughts raced and raged. I was on the verge of bursting into tears or screaming into the void. I didn't know which would come first or feel better. For now, I let them battle.

Finally, I found what I was looking for—a towering marble cross. Twelve years ago, I'd followed Zahariev to this very spot, and it was where I found him now, lit by the white glow of a spotlight.

He was smoking, the cherry of his cigarette burning brightly as he took a long drag. When he saw me, he exhaled, and the smoke coiled through the air, twisting like a serpent.

"Hey, little love," he said, straightening from where he lounged against the monument.

"I want to go home," I said.

I wasn't able to keep my voice from trembling. Zahariev's mouth tightened, and his eyes narrowed. He dropped his cigarette to the ground and closed the distance between us. I stared at his chest as pressure built behind my eyes.

I resented this, crying over something I thought I'd conquered.

He tilted my head back and then took my face between

his hands. I held his gaze, even as my eyes filled with tears. He brushed them away, one after the other, and asked no questions.

"We can go home," he said.

He let his hand slip to the back of my head and drew me close. It was my undoing.

I dropped my shoes, wrapped my arms around his waist, and crumbled within his embrace. I cried hard but not long, and still Zahariev kept me locked in his arms. Maybe it was because he was waiting for me to pull away, but I wasn't ready. This was where I felt safe.

"You want me to do something about it?" he asked.

"You can't," I said. "Not without starting a war."

"I would go to war for you," he said.

I ceased breathing, thinking that I'd misheard him. I pulled back and met his gaze. He was usually so composed, but there was something unfiltered in the way he looked at me now—a raw confession of devotion.

"What did you say?"

His mouth lifted in a soft half smile as he swept his thumb over the edge of my lips.

"I would go to war for you," he said again. "I would fight endlessly to keep you if that's what you wanted."

Again, I felt the threat of tears, but for a very different reason. I couldn't ask this of him. War was serious, far too serious to be fought over one rebellious daughter. I couldn't bear the burden of lost lives.

"I am not worth everything you would lose, Zahariev," I said.

"You are worth it," he said. "But I'll wait until you ask."

I would never ask, but his offer meant everything to me. I wondered if he could tell by the way I whispered his name or the way my fingers twisted into his shirt. I thought he knew because his eyes darted to my lips, and I rose onto the tips of my toes to kiss him, only to shriek at the sudden sound of earthshaking thunder and bury my face in his chest.

Zahariev's arms were still around me, and I could hear him laughing softly.

"I'm so glad I amuse you," I said, pulling back. Though I glared at him, I wasn't actually upset about the laugh. I couldn't be, because it made him even more beautiful. Really, I just wanted him to kiss me and never stop, but another bolt of lightning arced across the sky, followed shortly by a long, low rumble of thunder.

"Come on," he said, bending to pick up my discarded heels. "Let's get up the hill before it rains."

We made our way out of the cemetery. I walked ahead of Zahariev, who fell behind texting. I assumed he was letting Felix know we were ready. I would have waited for him once I reached the top of the hill, but it started raining, so I ran ahead, taking cover beneath the shallow overhang of my parents' home.

It wasn't long before Zahariev caught up and we walked together to the edge of the house but not any farther.

"I'll get your things," he said.

"No, it's fine. I don't want them to know I'm leaving."

They weren't worth the fight of retrieving them. I now knew my father's insistence on me attending the gala had nothing to do with his wish to see me. He had planned to introduce me to his chosen heir, announce our engagement, and lock me in my room until the wedding.

I'd always known this day would come, but I'd never let myself think too long about what it meant.

Tonight, I had to face it. I had been a breath away from

never seeing my friends again. It made my heart ache for home, and suddenly, all I wanted to do was go back to my shitty apartment, soak in my shitty bath, sleep in my shitty bed, and cuddle my perfect fucking cat.

"Is Felix almost here?" I asked. I was cold and anxious.

I glanced up at Zahariev, who was frowning down at his phone.

"The barrier won't open because the power's out," he said. His gaze slid to me. "Can you walk down?"

"I'll do anything to get out of here," I said.

We started across the yard, which was a void of darkness without my mother's starry lights. We were almost on the road when a terrifying boom erupted.

I heard Zahariev say my name over a high-pitched ringing in my ears. Then somehow I was crouched on the ground with his body wrapped around mine as rain and debris fell around us. I watched it pile up: shards of glass, pieces of wood, and mangled metal.

Slowly, I lifted my head to see that the windows of my childhood home had been blown out and there was a gaping hole where my father's study had once been.

The explosion had been a bomb.

I squeezed my eyes shut, thinking that maybe things would be different when I opened them again, but nothing changed.

Zahariev said something as he dragged me to my feet, but I only understood one word—*run.*

I didn't question him. I let him pull me down the dark and winding road. It was an endless spiral, and the rain made it slippery. The descent took all my focus, but once we were on even ground, the reality of what had happened on the hill started to sink in, and it was like those thoughts awakened the pain in my body. I realized how much my chest ached and how badly my feet hurt.

"I can't, Zahariev," I said, breathless.

My hand slipped from his as I came to a stop. He turned back and gripped my face hard between his hands, like he was trying to hold me together even as I broke.

"You *can*," he said, his eyes boring into mine. They were the only bright thing about this night. "It's not much farther. I promise."

I took a deep breath and nodded, rallying for this final push. He tugged on my hand, and we raced together through the streets of Hiram. When we came within sight of the entrance, I could see the flashing red lights of the SUV just beyond the barred gates.

Zahariev slowed as he approached and pushed against it, testing the give.

"Come here," he said. "As soon as you can, go."

Then he shoved harder, forcing a gap big enough for me to slip through. It was a tighter squeeze for Zahariev, but he managed it, and once we were free, he pushed me toward the SUV.

"Go!" he snapped, even though I didn't need the order.

I opened the door and climbed into the cabin.

"The compound, Felix," Zahariev barked, shoving into me as he followed me into the back seat.

Felix slammed on the gas before the door was even shut.

For a few seconds, the only sound was our harsh breathing, and then I realized I was shaking, and everything that had happened crashed down on me in one fierce blow.

A terrible cry tore from my throat and then another. I couldn't stop, even though I wanted to because this hurt in ways I'd never hurt before.

Zahariev wrapped his arm around my back and slid the other under my knees, shifting me onto his lap. I turned into him, burying my face in the crook of his neck.

"I've got you," he whispered.

He kissed my hair and held me tight, like he was trying to keep my soul from splitting, but it was too late. I'd fractured the moment Esther died, and this had shattered me.

On the way to Zahariev's compound, I oscillated between uncontrollable sobbing and quiet contemplation. I cycled through the same two thoughts—*my parents can't really be dead* and *no one could have survived that...right?*

It felt unreal, not only that they were gone but the way it had all happened.

A bomb.

Someone had planted a bomb in my father's office. The one I'd been in moments before. In the house I wasn't supposed to leave tonight.

"Is everyone dead?" I asked. My throat felt tight, and my words were thick, falling heavily from my swollen tongue.

Zahariev took a moment to answer, his arms tightening slightly. "Are you asking about your mother and father?"

"Everyone," I said. "The families, their children?"

"They were gone, Lilith," Zahariev said. "When the power went out, Lisk messaged the families to return to their districts."

It took a moment for those words to settle.

"I was supposed to die," I said.

"Don't, Lilith." There was a broken quality to his voice, but he needed to know.

"You don't understand," I said, pushing away from him.

I had to see his face, to look into his eyes when I told him. "My father chose an heir, Zahariev."

He stared back, gaze hard and heated. I didn't add that it also meant I was technically engaged. He already knew what it meant.

"Who?" he asked.

"You aren't listening," I said. Or maybe I wasn't saying it right. It wasn't about the man. "I was supposed to be in that house tonight. I wasn't supposed to leave. Someone knew that. *Lisk* knew that."

The commission might propose a betrothal, but the archbishop always had the final say. He would have been privy to my father's plans for the gala.

"It's convenient that the power went out, that the families were sent home, all before my house exploded," I said. "Even you have to admit it."

"I'm not denying it," he said.

"But you don't think Lisk was responsible?"

His brows lowered, his eyes a little angry. "You are so quick to jump to the conclusion that I am not on your side. When have I not chosen you?"

My face grew hot, and I could feel my throat swelling. I dropped my gaze.

"I'm just afraid," I said. "And I know I was wrong about Esther...but I'm not wrong about this."

Lisk had grown tired of my father's passivity and my defiance. Our family had made a joke of his law, and we had to pay.

Zahariev's hands framed my face, forcing our eyes to meet. I didn't want to look at him because I'd started crying again.

"I don't think you're wrong," he said, brushing the tears

360

away. "But Lisk never arrived at the gala, so that means someone else is involved. Who is the heir?"

"Macarius Caiaphas," I said.

Zahariev's mouth tightened. "Do you know if he brought your father anything?"

I shook my head. "He was there before we arrived, so it's possible. You could check security...if anything survived the explosion."

Or the erasure Lisk had likely ordered to scrub evidence of his plot.

Zahariev looked out the window, quiet and contemplative. I watched him briefly, noting the hard set of his jaw, before settling against him, but I was on edge, anxious that I had missed something.

I felt like I should have expected the retaliation. I had witnessed Lisk's attacks on Tori and Saira. He had been systematically destroying anyone or anything in conflict with his ideals, but I'd never expected him to target a family.

We were Elohai.

We were the blood of God.

But the blood only mattered if we were faithful to him.

If he couldn't control us, then we were a risk.

I was a risk.

"What happens when Lisk finds out I survived?" I asked.

"Then he will know he has failed," said Zahariev.

I tried to take a subtle breath so he wouldn't hear my voice shudder. "He's just going to try again," I said.

Zahariev's arms tightened around me. "I'll kill him before he has the chance."

———

When we arrived at the compound, I was passed off to

Fawna, the housekeeper, who took me to a room where I could shower and rest. I might have argued, but Zahariev made a few promises I couldn't refuse—he would get in touch with Coco and bring her and Cherub to the compound, and he wouldn't keep me in the dark.

"We're in this together," he said. "So we're doing this together, right?"

I nodded. The words were a reminder we were on the same side and not to do anything alone, unlike before when I'd gone rogue hunting demons, but in my defense, I needed something to focus on after losing Esther. Killing jelly monsters had worked. Even the burn it had left behind was a distraction.

I just didn't know what I was going to do now that my parents were dead too.

I occupied myself with a hot-as-fuck shower.

If Zahariev had caught me, he would have accused me of trying to burn my skin off, but he was just sensitive to the heat.

When I was finished, I searched through all the cabinets and drawers for something I could use to redress my wound, freshly opened thanks to my mother's nails. I found a roll of gauze and wound it around my wrist then crossed into the bedroom, discovering Fawna had left me extra towels, a robe, and an oversize shirt to use as a nightgown.

I slipped it on and climbed into the bed. It felt like a vast sea compared to my narrow twin. I thought it would be easier to fall asleep without a spring sticking in my back, but I remained awake, staring at this strange room with its straight edges and perfect lines. It was like every other part of Zahariev's house: methodical and precise. I wondered if it reflected what went on in his head and if it ever got messy.

At some point, the darkness hovering over me started to feel overbearing and I rolled onto my side, curling into a fetal position. I was cold and alone, and all I wanted to do was rewind this horrible night and never replay it again, but I couldn't stop the spiral.

It was a cruel irony that on the very evening I'd felt most like myself and dropped all pretense of conforming, everything went to shit.

My mother would have called it divine justice. I could *hear* her saying it in that cool, condescending tone. Even dead, her doctrine haunted me, and my anger roared to life. I wished it was powerful enough to overwhelm the bone-deep sadness around me, but it clung to me, and I didn't understand how I could mourn someone I'd spent the majority of my life resenting.

I recognized that most of this was probably for my father, yet when I thought of him, a different sort of ache took over. Maybe it was the way we had left things. It wasn't that I regretted what I said. He deserved to know that the words and guidance he called gospel had come from the mouth of an abuser, a liar, a fake.

It was just that he was dead now, and I had no way of knowing if he would have finally chosen me.

It was the last thing Lisk would ever take from me. I'd make sure of that.

I heard the door open and shut quietly. I let Zahariev think I was asleep, just to see what he would do, but he didn't come to me. Instead, he took a seat near the window.

My eyes began to water. I'd overwhelmed myself by thinking of my parents. I took a breath and spoke, hoping I didn't sound like I was crying.

"Have you talked to Coco?" I asked.

"Cassius has," he said. "She is safe. She'll arrive in the morning."

"And Cherub?"

"Cherub too," he said.

I was quiet, struggling with my tears.

"Gabriel's here with Liam," Zahariev said after a moment. "He asked to see you, but I told him to wait until tomorrow."

I smiled softly, but my face ached.

"Thank you, Zahariev," I whispered.

There was a beat of silence, and then the bed shifted with his weight as he settled behind me and pulled me close. I guided his hand to my chest, holding him around me. If I could sink into his skin, I would.

I took a deep, shuddering breath.

"Do you think they suffered?" I asked.

"Would it help to know?"

"I don't know," I said. I just knew one answer would feed my grief and the other would feed my revenge.

"You should know before you ask," he said. "Sometimes knowledge like that isn't worth the burden."

It sounded like something he knew from experience.

"Hold me tighter, Zahariev," I whispered, closing my eyes.

His legs twined with mine, and he buried his face in the crook of my neck. "Anything for you, little love," he said.

I let myself drift in his warmth.

———

The darkness beckoned.

I could feel her prodding at the edge of my mind, her touch as coarse as the desert sand. At first, she was kind.

Dark mother? she whispered, but I did not answer.

Revered queen, she murmured, but I did not stir.

Goddess? she crooned, but I did not rise.

Then all at once, she became a howling wind, whirling around me, shrieking.

Beware the serpent and his poisonous tongue.

He will take your flesh on the steps of your altar.

He will lie in your crimson blood.

Beware the deceiver and his silver tongue.

He will turn your temple into his monument.

Beware the awakening, the heat of this fire.

It will bind you beneath bleeding gates.

I weathered her tide, but even then, I did not wake.

ZAHARIEV

Hold me tighter, Zahariev, she'd said.
If I did, could I keep her from breaking?

CHAPTER
EIGHTEEN

I jerked awake and found someone leaning over me. It took me seconds to realize it was Zahariev and much longer to calm my pounding heart.

"Hey," he said with a small smile on his face. "I have a few things to do this morning. Coco's arrived. She brought your backpack and some clothes. I left them on the dresser for you."

I frowned up at him, partly because my brain was still trying to come to terms with the fact that I was awake. I blinked, fighting the grogginess.

"Where are you going?" I asked. My throat was dry. I swallowed to wet it, though what I really needed was water.

He took a seat on the bed.

"I am meeting the other heads at your house. We'll be briefed about what the enforcers have found so far, and then I will meet with Dr. Mor."

He didn't need to explain that visit. I knew what it was about.

"You're letting the enforcers investigate?" That little

nugget of information woke me up real fast, and I sat up. "You know they won't be fair."

"It's not my choice, Lilith," he said. "This is protocol. We'll hear what they have to say, and if we don't like it, we'll go from there."

I hated protocol, especially when it was going to waste our time. Still, I reminded myself, this wasn't the way I was going to get back at Lisk anyway. No one was going to publicly accuse him of killing an Elohai, not the enforcers or the commission.

"When will you be back?" I asked.

"In a few hours," he said. "But you will have plenty to occupy yourself between Coco and Gabriel."

"Is that your way of telling me I can't leave the compound?" I asked.

"I think it's best to wait a couple days," he said. "At least until we see how Lisk will react to discovering you're alive."

"He doesn't know yet?"

"It depends on how much progress the enforcers have made at the house," said Zahariev.

I knew what he didn't say—they'd know when they found the bodies.

A part of me wondered if there was a world in which Lisk didn't have to know I lived, but then why did that somehow feel like letting him win?

"The electricity came back on overnight," Zahariev said, rising to his feet. "So there's that."

"Has anyone said what caused it?" I asked, holding his gaze.

"It's being investigated," he said.

"Of course," I said, rolling my eyes.

He chuckled quietly and touched my chin.

"Behave," he said.

My eyes instantly narrowed. "You don't have what it takes to make me."

He maintained that infuriating half smile as he moved his hand to my throat, squeezing lightly. My body straightened, uncoiling eagerly beneath his hold.

"You sure about that, little love?" he asked.

"You have yet to prove otherwise," I said. I deserved a fucking medal for challenging this man under these conditions.

He was still smiling, but there was something harder about it. It was a good sign, a weakness in his armor.

"You are such a brat," he said, his eyes locked on my lips.

"I think you like it," I said. I braced my hands against the bed, using the leverage to inch closer. "I think it makes you hard."

"I like it," he said. "You know what makes me harder? When you obey."

He bent forward and kissed my forehead, increasing the pressure on my throat ever so slightly before pulling away.

"I'll see you later, little love," he said. There was a note of amusement in his voice as he strolled to the door. Unfortunately, my reply came after he closed the door.

"You're pretty smug for a man with a boner," I said aloud, though I was being just as arrogant considering how he'd left me.

I didn't know what stunned me more, that he'd actually acknowledged out loud I aroused him or the way he'd communicated his desire to dominate me. Maybe what surprised me most of all was how badly I wanted it.

Coco's arrival motivated me to stay awake, but I could have slept for another twenty-four hours. When I actually dragged myself out of bed, I regretted it instantly. My body felt heavy, and my eyes stung. I just wanted to keep them closed as I staggered into the bright bathroom to shower.

When I was finished, I used the robe Fawna had left and moved into the bedroom to go through the bags Coco brought. I started with the duffel, which was full of clothes, all folded neatly and organized by type. I wondered if she'd delayed her arrival at the compound just to finish up my laundry.

The answer was most likely yes. I felt a mix of overwhelming gratitude and guilt. I loved Coco, and I didn't deserve her one bit.

After pulling on a pair of jeans and a tank top, I went through the backpack she had also brought, but it only contained my journal, a small bag of cat food, and a bottle of water.

I half expected to find my dagger inside, since it had a proven habit of manifesting wherever I went, but it wasn't among any of the items Coco had brought. I wondered if Zahariev would take me to get it later when he returned. It was probably safer here anyway, and I'd rather have it close, given what it was and who wanted it.

I left the bedroom, entering a long hall with dark walls and dim lights, interrupted only by colorful pieces of fine art. It led into a lavishly decorated foyer that Zahariev would clear out or rearrange for parties. Several rooms branched off from the space, including a library, a parlor, and a family room.

It was there I found Coco and Gabriel. They were sitting on opposite ends of a large sectional. Gabriel was bent awkwardly to the side, head resting on his arms. An unexpected wave of emotion hit me as I observed it to be the same position I'd found Esther in the night Burke and Koval attacked me.

It was a strange thing to get emotional about, but it was a chain reaction. When I was reminded of her, I was also reminded of her absence.

"Good morning, Miss Leviathan."

I jumped at the unexpected voice and whirled to find Fawna standing at a respectful distance. She wore a navy dress that had buttons down the front and a sash tied at the waist.

"Apologies," she added. "I didn't mean to startle you."

"It's fine," I said.

"I came to see if Miss D'Arsay or Mr. De Santis needed anything," she explained. "Can I get you something? Coffee, perhaps?"

"Coffee would be great," I said. "Thank you, Fawna."

She smiled. It wasn't sincere or fake. It was just polite acknowledgment.

"I'll return shortly. Please, make yourself at home," she insisted.

That saying had a range, and I got the sense Fawna didn't mean it in the same way Esther meant it, which was fine. I just wouldn't put my feet on the couch or throw pillows on the floor.

I wasn't sure I could get that comfortable here anyway, even in a space that belonged to Zahariev. In truth, the house didn't feel like him, but I don't think he spent much time in other areas outside his office or bedroom.

Coco must have heard my exchange with Fawna, because when I turned back to the family room, she was on her feet, waiting and watching.

We crossed to each other and met in the middle.

"Lilith," she said, pulling me into a tight hug. "I'm so sorry."

I hugged her back, wishing her words hadn't brought tears to my eyes. I was tired of crying, but I guessed this was going to be my new normal for a little while.

We continued to hold on to each other, even as we pulled away.

"What can I do?" she asked.

"Coco, you have done enough already," I said. "I should be asking how I can repay you."

"There is nothing to repay," she said. "I only want you safe, though that's turning out to be a difficult ask."

My laugh was a breathless exhale. She wasn't wrong. I swallowed a hard lump in my throat.

"I'm sorry I brought this on you," I said.

"You didn't bring anything on me," she said. "You can't help your name, Lily."

"But I knew the consequences of my name, and I have been in denial for a long time."

"I think you've just been hopeful," she said. "And there's nothing wrong with that."

But that was exactly where I had gone wrong. I had hope in a world that punished me simply for existing, yet I'd been under the delusion I could somehow escape the consequences.

I was a privileged brat, and now my parents were dead.

Something brushed against my legs.

"Cherub!" I said, scooping her into my arms. I held her close, eased by her rhythmic purr. "I missed you."

Coco smiled. "She was the best decision ever, right?"

"Truly," I said.

372

An alarming cry erupted from somewhere in the family room. Coco turned, and we watched Gabriel throw the baby monitor as he startled awake. It took him a moment to get his bearings. Then he rose from the couch, swiped the monitor off the floor, and turned it down.

That was when he noticed me and smiled.

"Hey, baby girl," he said. "It's good to see you."

"Hey, Gabe," I said.

"Let me get Liam, and I'll be back to hug you," he said.

He headed down a hallway on the opposite side of the room while Coco and I found a place on the couch. Cherub curled up in my lap.

"It's not like our apartment at all, is it?" said Coco.

"No…it isn't."

"Although I guess you're used to these…nice things?"

"I think what we have is just as nice," I said. "Better even."

I'd spent a lot of my life in places like this, and it was where I felt the most exposed and uncomfortable. Our apartment wasn't the best, but it was cozy, and it was where I could most be myself.

Fawna returned with my coffee, and Gabriel shortly after, carrying a bundled Liam. He had a bottle with him and a cloth tossed over his shoulder. He actually looked adorable.

"What's got you smiling?" Gabriel asked.

"I just think you make a cute dad," I said.

Esther would say the same, I thought, keeping the words to myself. I didn't know how prepared he was to hear something like that, and I didn't want to trigger him.

I sipped my coffee. It was bitter, but it made me more alert. Coco turned on the television and flipped through the channels.

"Wait," I said. "Go back."

She did as I asked and returned to the station that had caught my attention. It was a segment on the power failure.

"Officials have not confirmed what caused a mass outage across Eden last night. Footage shows a purple aura over a power station in Galant."

The screen transitioned from the reporter to a grainy video. The only thing visible was the dark silhouette of pine trees against a violet-tinged light.

My stomach turned, and I set my coffee aside.

"We're told this type of discharge is typically caused by high volts of electricity coming into contact with conductive air. Officials have not confirmed this as a cause of the outage but say last night's storm likely contributed."

All that sounded really scientific for something I knew wasn't science but some kind of cursed magic.

That violet glow came from demons. Multiple demons.

I should have put two and two together. I thought back to the one I'd fought near the celestial shop and how it had been hanging out on the powerlines. Maybe I had found it while it was trying to supercharge itself and that was why the streetlights were out.

Maybe the only reason my stun gun had subdued it was because it had been weak, which begged the question: What were they capable of when they were at full capacity?

I touched the healing burn on my wrist. My tiny-ass dagger was nothing against a stronger version of the one I'd battled.

A sword would be better.

I doubted Saira would appreciate my desire to see her precious Deliverer reforged to fight jelly monsters in the night, but we were motivated by different things.

When the segment ended, I told Coco to change the channel. I didn't want to risk seeing anything about the destruction of Leviathan House, though I wasn't sure if it would make the news this soon. The commission usually decided when and how to communicate about deaths in the families. It was possible they would keep the details vague to discourage copycats. Since they couldn't hide a house explosion, they would probably attribute the cause to a gas leak, though I didn't plan to lie about the way my parents died.

I wanted everyone to know they'd been blown apart and by whom, but I was going to need some concrete evidence before I made any kind of accusation.

We sat in the family room for a few hours together. Despite what was going on in my brain, I was happy to be near two of my closest friends. Coco and I took turns holding Liam, trading off when our arms got tired, until Gabriel took him into the other room to change him.

It was at that point Fawna announced lunch was ready. I was surprised, but only because I'd grown so used to fending for myself, unless I was at Esther's. She led us into the dining room where she had set the table. Though she hadn't gone formal with her setup, it was still more dishes than we would need.

"I have prepared chicken salad and a squash soup," she said. "There is extra bread in the basket and whipped butter beside it. Can I get you anything to drink?"

"The water is fine," I said. "Thank you, Fawna."

"Water's great," Coco added. "And thank you. Everything is so beautiful."

"Thank you, Miss D'Arsay," Fawna replied, smiling. It was a little more sincere than the one she'd given me earlier this morning, and I realized, despite having distanced myself from the grandeur of my family, there was a part of me that still just expected this. It wasn't that I dismissed the effort. I just didn't think about it, and that made me feel like a huge asshole.

"If you need anything, I'll be just through here," she said, disappearing through the adjacent doors.

Coco and I took seats.

"Do we serve ourselves?" Coco asked. "What if I get soup on the tablecloth?"

I smiled at her. "No one will care if you get soup on the tablecloth, Coco. That's what it's for."

"I don't want to make more work for Fawna," she said.

"Give me your bowl," I said. "I'll serve you."

"This is another one of your hidden talents," she said as I ladled soup into the bowl. I stopped short of saying it wasn't a talent, which was my usual answer, because I resented basically everything my mother had taught me.

Gabriel joined us, but he was quiet and barely touched his food. I wondered if it was because he didn't like it, or maybe the presentation reminded him too much of Esther, and the thought also stole my appetite.

As we were finishing up, I heard the front door open, and I bolted from the dining room into the foyer, thinking that Zahariev had arrived, but it was Cassius.

I stopped dead in my tracks.

"Ugh. What are you doing back?" I asked.

"Apparently, I am a glorified errand boy," he said. "Zahariev sent me to return your phone, but maybe I should keep it since you don't appreciate the deliverer."

I narrowed my eyes. "I take nudes with that phone."

Cassius sighed as he reached into his pocket. "Just another thing I didn't need to know about you."

I snickered as I reclaimed it, but my mood shifted once I had it in hand. As unlikely as it was, I'd hoped to see a message or missed call, something from my father that showed he'd tried to reach me before he died, but there was nothing.

"You're not going to cry, are you?" Cassius asked, a note of panic in his voice.

"She can cry if she wants," said Gabriel, entering the foyer behind Coco. "She just lost her parents, asshole."

I winced. No one had actually said that aloud yet.

"I wasn't trying to be an asshole. I was trying to do a good fucking deed."

"Is that really true, errand boy?" Gabriel countered.

I couldn't tell if they were seriously fighting or just fucking with each other, but that was how I felt around Cassius all the time.

"I'm *fine*," I said, cutting them off quickly. "Thanks for bringing my phone, Cassius."

I glanced at him before leaving the foyer.

"Lilith—" Cassius called after me.

"Just let her go, man," said Gabriel.

I retreated to my room and set my phone on the dresser, hand hovering, trying to decide if I should text Zahariev, but knew it would get me nowhere. Whatever he'd learned today, he would only tell me in person. I was going to have to be patient, a virtue I didn't possess.

Coco waited for about an hour before she came to my door with Cherub, knocking softly. By then, I'd taken a long bath and changed back into the shirt Fawna had given me.

"Is Zahariev back?" I asked.

"Not yet," she said as she climbed into bed beside me.

We were facing each other with Cherub curled up

377

between us. I was looking out the window at the fading daylight.

"Do you know what I can't stop thinking?" I whispered.

"What?" Coco asked.

"If my parents are in paradise, then Esther cannot be."

"Why not?" she asked, brows lowering.

"Because it will mean that the *Book of Splendor* is correct and that there is only one way in."

She was quiet for a moment and then asked, "Is it not possible that they all made it? That instead of only one, there are multiple roads to paradise?"

I stared at her for a moment and then snuggled close, saying, "Sounds like a sweet dream."

ZAHARIEV

"The bomb went off near his face," said Dr. Mor. "I'm guessing he opened something on his desk, maybe a drawer." He paused and then asked, "You're not going to let her see him like this, are you?"

I met his gaze as we stood on either side of Lucius's body. He was in a bag.

"Wasn't planning on it," I said, though at least if she asked about suffering again, I could say truthfully he didn't.

I stepped away from the body.

"You wanted to show me something else?" I asked.

"Just another one," he said.

I thought he meant body until he pulled the sheet back. Then I realized what he was really saying.

It was a body, but the same pinkish-purple jelly he'd found on Burke and Koval was oozing from the man's eyes, ears, mouth, and nose.

"This one's a utility worker. He was found deceased on the ground at a substation in Nineveh," he said. "I think it's the same creature you told me about before. What does Lilith call them? Demon blobs?"

"Yeah," I said.

Fucking demon blobs.

CHAPTER
NINETEEN

I opened my eyes, instantly awake.

It was like I'd been startled, but the only sounds were Coco's and Cherub's quiet breathing.

At first, I thought I had just closed my eyes, but when I rolled over to check the time, I found it was midnight. I'd been asleep for a few hours.

Given my haphazard schedule, I wasn't surprised my body seemed to think it was daybreak.

I rose quietly, wondering if Zahariev had returned, though it was also possible he was asleep. I wanted answers badly enough, I'd probably wake him if he was.

I checked his office first, which was on the other side of the house. The door was slightly ajar, a blade of light cutting through the dark hallway. As I neared, I heard the low exchange of voices and soon recognized both: Zahariev and Cassius.

"So what are you going to do?" Cassius asked.

"Ask her what she wants," Zahariev said.

"You're going to *ask* her?" he repeated. "Zahariev, this is a decision you should make. You are the head of this fucking family."

"I have decided. You just don't like it."

"Because I know what she will choose, and then we'll be at war over a fucking woman who decided she was too good for her own family."

I heard a thud. That was when I pushed open the door and saw Cassius holding his nose. His gaze was angry and his eyes watered.

"You want to ask me something?" I said, looking at Zahariev.

"Just in time, little love," he said, talking around the cigarette in his mouth while he shook his hand out, like he was trying to get rid of the sting. "Have a seat. Cassius."

It was clear Zahariev was dismissing his brother, who stormed out and slammed the door behind him. The sound made me tense. I gripped the back of the chair, not really eager to sit like Zahariev had directed.

"Well?" I prompted.

He wasn't looking at me. I didn't think he was looking at anything, maybe a speck of dust on his desk as he held his cigarette poised between his thumb and forefinger. The silence worried me. Finally, he spoke.

"Your fiancé went to the commission to petition for Hiram," he said.

"Don't call him that," I said, bristling at the word.

"It turns out Macarius thought you were dead. Now that he knows otherwise, he has asked for your return and for Archbishop Lisk to grant a quick wedding."

"Couldn't he have waited until my parents were in the fucking ground before staking his claim to my father's district?"

"It's not every day an entire district is up for grabs," said Zahariev. "A lot of men are going to come out of the woodwork to claim ownership, but that all disappears if there's proof Lucius chose an heir."

"*Is* there proof?" I asked.

"Macarius says your father died before any contract could be finalized and signed, but Lisk confirmed he knew of the arrangement."

"And you've accepted his word?"

Zahariev's mouth tightened. "They believe Lucius told Lisk of his plan for the engagement, but the commission was not informed, which is unusual when selecting non-blood heirs. They have decided to delay their decision until after your father's funeral."

I curled my fingers into fists. "You mean my *parents'* funeral? I know the commission only acknowledges women when they want to eat and fuck and use their magic, but my mother died in that explosion too."

And she might have been terrible to me, but she was dedicated to their shitty system and deserved their respect.

"Your mother isn't dead, Lilith," said Zahariev. "She's missing."

The blood drained from my face. "What do you mean she's missing?"

"Her remains weren't in the house," he said.

"Then where is she?" I demanded.

"We don't know," he said. "Maybe she was taken by whoever planted the bomb in your father's office."

I shook my head. "The bomb was planted on Lisk's orders. If anything, he would have…"

I went quiet as the realization hit home.

My mother did everything Lisk asked, believed everything

he said. He would never risk losing such a devout follower, especially one with magic.

If anything, he would have *protected* her.

Another thought occurred to me, though I tried to push it out of my mind. I decided maybe, if I said it out loud, it would go away.

"Do you think she did it?" I asked. "Do you think she planted the bomb?"

She was the one with the most access, but she also had the most to lose. I knew my mother, and she valued her position in society. If it came out she was the one responsible for my father's death, she would be ruined, and I didn't think she would take such a risk.

But then where was she?

"We can't rule her out," Zahariev said. "But we can't rule anyone out at this point."

I sat quietly, trying to process these new emotions, but it was overwhelming. It felt safer to push the feelings away, to watch them battle from a distance while I distracted myself with other things.

"Are you okay?" Zahariev asked.

I lifted my gaze to his and then stood. "Will you take me to get my knife?"

His brows rose.

"It's midnight," he said.

"So? We're both awake, and I don't feel comfortable leaving it at the apartment."

His gaze dipped, roaming over my shapeless T-shirt like it was just as hot as the dress I'd worn to the gala.

"You want to change first?"

"Why? We're just going from here to my apartment. Unless you want to hunt demons after?"

"Hunt demons? With your tiny-ass blade?"

"You can stun and I'll stab," I said.

"No," he said. I didn't think he would agree, even though I thought it sounded fun. Zahariev was practical. "And you shouldn't hunt them until we can find out more about them."

"That's why I know what I do about them," I said. "You know they were responsible for the power outage. The video they showed on the news? The one with the glow over the substation in Galant? Those were demons. I think they feed off energy. If they're weak, a current can overpower them. I'm not sure what happens when they are fullypowered."

Zahariev didn't look happy with my news.

"I'd rather it not be you who finds out," he said.

I rolled my eyes as he put his cigarette out on a tray on his desk before opening a drawer and pulling out a set of keys.

"Let's go," he said.

I followed him out of his office to the garage, where a sleek sedan was parked. Zahariev unlocked it as he headed around to the driver's side. I slipped into the passenger seat. The leather was cold against my skin.

"Would you ever consider teaching me to drive?" I asked.

Zahariev glanced at me. "I'd teach you," he said. "But let me buy a helmet first."

"Fuck off," I said, pushing him.

He chuckled, laughing at his own joke.

We were quiet as we left the compound, but there was nothing comfortable about the silence. It was razor-sharp, digging into me from all sides. All I could think was that this car was too small to contain what was between us.

"The conversation you were having with Cassius," I said as Zahariev turned left onto Procession Street, only to make a quick right on Providence. "You never asked me what I wanted."

"I didn't?"

I looked at him, but he stared straight ahead.

"You know you didn't," I said. "So why don't you ask me now?"

Zahariev waited until he was parked in the lot outside my complex.

"I don't need to ask a question I already know the answer to," he said.

It was true we had discussed this in the cemetery outside my parents' house. I wouldn't let him go to war over me. If it came down to it, I would return to Hiram to save him and everyone I cared about from a nightmare.

"That's the answer to what I will *choose*," I said. "Not the answer to what I want."

"Because what you want doesn't matter if you're going to choose something else."

I ground my teeth against the pain of his words and got out of the car. Zahariev followed. If I could have gone into the apartment and locked him out, I would have, but I didn't have my key, so I had to wait for him to open it.

Zahariev entered first, scanning the place for anything suspicious, but there was nothing untoward. I went to my bedroom and opened my nightstand drawer, finding the blade where I left it.

"Couldn't make this convenient for me, could you?" I muttered as I picked it up.

I turned with it in hand, pulling the blade from the sheath, glaring at Zahariev, who stood just inside the doorway.

"You gonna stab me?" he asked.

"Would it make you talk?"

"I guess it depends on how you used it," he said.

I stared and then shoved the blade into its sheath before sliding it onto the table behind me.

"You are a coward, Zahariev."

His jaw ticked and his eyes darkened.

"If I were a coward, I would have walked away from you a long time ago."

"You think you're brave for handling me?"

"No one handles you, Lilith," he said. "Good fucking luck to the man who tries."

My eyes burned, but I couldn't tell if it was with rage or pain. Maybe it was both.

"I don't want another man to try," I said. My face flushed so hot, I thought I might pass out. "I want you."

He stared, silent, like he was waiting for more, but I had nothing else. I couldn't be any clearer. So instead, I took off my shirt, dropping it to the floor. It was the only thing I had worn, and now I stood naked before him.

His eyes raked down my body, hands flexing at his sides. It took everything in me to stay upright, to not collapse beneath the weight of his gaze. He had never looked at me this way before, and I felt like maybe I had won, except that he remained still.

I scoffed quietly, shaking my head. "I can't ever seem to get under your skin."

Just fucking once, I wanted to know what it was like for this man to lose control.

His brows rose slightly as he crept close, crowding me. I tilted my head back to maintain his gaze, the only part of us that was connected.

"You don't think you are under my skin?"

His voice set my heart on fire. Slowly, he threaded his

387

fingers into my hair, tightening his hold at the base of my skull. I let out an audible breath.

"You don't think I carry you wherever I go? You are unshakable. A *menace*. Sometimes, I think I would do anything to fuck it out of you, this goddamn defiance, even though it won't work. Even though it's what I adore most about you. I guess I just think it would be fun to try."

I smiled, soft and teasing, though inside I felt like I was melting, and let my gaze drop to his lips, whispering, "Then maybe you should."

He gave a breathless laugh, and I saw the moment he broke. It flashed in his eyes, a brilliant spark, just before our mouths and bodies collided. We staggered into the nightstand, but Zahariev caught us before we could fall. He dragged me up his body and moved us to the bed, grinding into me as we kissed. He was hard between my thighs, and it felt unfair that I was so naked and he was so clothed.

I tried removing his jacket, but he was in his own fucking world, devouring my mouth and the skin of my throat. I reached between us, fumbling for his belt, but he chose that moment to suck on my breast. I gasped, arching against him, capturing his head between my hands.

"Zahariev," I breathed.

He glanced up and then released my nipple, pulling back, first to his knees, then to his feet.

I rose onto my elbows and watched him. I kept my knees bent and my legs parted, an open invitation to return. Zahariev stared with a raw sort of fascination. No part of me would go unwitnessed by him tonight.

"What's wrong, Zahariev?" I teased. "You've seen me naked before."

He met my gaze, and I regretted my words, suddenly unable to breathe as he replied, "Not like this."

He took off his jacket and shirt, then tried to come back, but I stopped him, pressing my foot against his chest.

"Take them off," I said. "Or are you afraid to show me your cock?"

He raised a brow, and his hands moved to his belt. I dropped my leg as he removed the rest of his clothing, and when he was completely naked, I sat up and reached for his swollen length, but Zahariev gripped my hand and then my jaw.

I glared up at his stupid, smirking face.

"I knew you'd be greedy," he said, brushing his thumb over my pouting lips. "But I'm going down first."

"Who made you the boss?" I asked as he kneeled on the floor beside the bed.

"In this room," he said, jerking me toward him, "I'm always the boss of you."

I could have fought him for that position, but right now, I'd take anything he gave. I watched him press kisses against my inner thigh, inching closer to my aching flesh. Anticipation coiled through me, and I grew tense and warm, waiting.

"Fucking beautiful," Zahariev murmured right before he kissed me, followed by the soft slide of his tongue. I moaned like no one had ever gone down on me before, but there was nothing like receiving it from someone I had wanted for so long.

He took his time tasting every part of me, licking and sucking. His method was deliberate and practiced, and it was either really fucking good, or I'd gone too long without sex, because I was panting and writhing on the bed. My hands were everywhere: in my hair, twisted in the bedding, kneading my breasts.

I reached for him when he sucked my clit into his mouth and held him there, whispering words I couldn't even comprehend. They were on the tip of my tongue, freed each time another hot wave of pleasure wove its way to my brain.

Zahariev must have liked the sound because he bore into me and thrust deeper, his skilled pace disrupted. His hands tightened around my thighs, fingers digging into my flesh. He wasn't trying to keep me in one place; he was riding the wave with me, seeing this through to the very end.

I didn't have long. I was almost there. All it took was another delicious pull of his mouth, and I erupted. My head fell back, eyes rolling. My hips came off the bed, and Zahariev followed, rising from the floor. I came so hard, I froze in an arch. I couldn't keep my eyes open, body shuddering relentlessly. When it was done, I had no choice but to relax. My limbs were too heavy to lift.

I kept my eyes closed until Zahariev stretched over me.

He kissed me deeply. It was the taste of my come on his tongue and the hard press of his cock against my swollen sex that roused me again. I couldn't wait to be crammed full of him.

He pulled back, and our eyes met. Nothing made me feel more vulnerable than the way he was looking at me now. I wasn't even sure why. He'd just had his face shoved into the most intimate part of my body, and I hadn't thought twice about it, but the physical act was always easier to brave than the emotional one. Right now, I was beneath the man whose devotion knew no bounds, and it scared me.

"Are you good, little love?" he asked.

"Yeah," I whispered, smiling at him. I let my finger trail across his lips. "You?"

"Fucking glorious," he said. He kissed my breast and sucked on my nipple. I trailed my fingers down his chest, sliding my hand over his hard length. He didn't stop me but inhaled when I rubbed my palm over the crown of his cock, coating my hand with sticky precum.

"Is it my turn?" I asked.

"If you want," he said.

"I want," I said.

His smile broadened, and he kissed me again before rolling on his back. He propped himself up against the pillows at the head of my bed while I knelt between his thighs.

I didn't immediately go down on him, though the thought was making me salivate. I'd never wanted to put a dick in my mouth the way I wanted his, but my gaze was drawn to the tattoo on his left thigh, a black-and-gray image of an angel of death. I had never seen it before, but that was because I had never seen him like this.

"When did you get this one?" I asked, letting my finger trail along the curve of a wing.

"It was my first," he said.

Discovering this now frustrated me. It was the second new thing I'd learned about Zahariev this week.

"And here I thought I knew you best," I said, letting my nails trail up his thighs.

"You do," he said. "Better than anyone."

I crawled over him, kissing down his stomach until my chin brushed his cock. He gathered my hair into one hand, and I looked up at him as I licked him from root to tip, giving a breathy laugh. I didn't know why. There was nothing funny about the way he stared at me, like I'd turned his entire world upside down, but I felt giddy, and I was having fun.

I took him into my mouth and swirled my tongue over the tip. He tasted like salt, and I loved it, but probably because it was *him* and I had wanted to do this forever.

Zahariev inhaled.

"Holy fuck," he muttered, his fingers tightening in my hair.

I took him deeper, trapping the smooth head of his cock between my tongue and the top of my mouth. I sucked him gently, and his head fell back as he groaned. He let go of my hair to grip the pillows beneath him.

"Fuck," he hissed.

The word slithered through me and settled low in my stomach. I was aroused before, but this was a new level. There was nothing in the world like hearing unfiltered pleasure from Zahariev Zareth's mouth and being the one responsible.

I released his cock and took him into my hand, jerking him up and down a few more times before I rose to my knees and straddled him. He felt so good between my thighs, and I wondered what it was like for him.

Zahariev gripped my waist, bringing us close, and I wrapped my arms around his neck. He was still reclined, so he had to tilt his head back to look at me.

"I knew you'd find a way on top," he said.

I smiled as he kissed me and cupped my breast. I loved the time he took during sex to explore me. It was like he wanted this to last forever, like he wasn't at all desperate to come.

"You will love it," I said between the languorous twining of our tongues.

I positioned him at my entrance. He was thick, and I

almost laughed because I thought this would be easy, a fucking slip and slide. Instead, I inched my way down him, gripping his forearms as he held my waist.

I savored every fucking second.

"God, you feel so good," I whispered.

"Yeah?" he asked, gripping my ass. He rocked my hips back and forth.

"Yeah," I said, smiling as I reached for his hands, moving them to my breasts. "Do I feel good?"

A strangled laugh tore from his throat, probably because I'd just started riding him. My movements were slow. I knew I wasn't long for this. It was tiring, and Zahariev was going to want control.

"Yeah, little love," he said. He was playing with my breasts, but our eyes were locked. He looked so out of his mind, eyes glazed but bright. "You feel fucking great."

I laughed, breathless, as I bounced on his dick, and he bit his fist, groaning deeply. It was the hottest sound I'd ever heard him make. His fingers flexed, like he couldn't decide if his desire to interrupt me was worth whatever impulse he was fighting.

"Do you want me to go faster?" I asked. I leaned forward, using the headboard for support. Zahariev kept his gaze on mine despite having my breasts in his face, my nipples grazing his chin. His hands smoothed down my back to my ass, gripping my flesh. It felt punishing, but in a good way.

"No," he said, but his hold on me tightened. He rocked me back and forth while thrusting into me. I didn't know if it was how well he filled me or the angle, but fuck, it felt good.

"Holy shit," I gasped, feeling lightheaded and so fucking high.

Zahariev chuckled, and the sound made me feel warm all over.

He sat up, and I wrapped my arms around his neck, rocking against him. I nipped at his ear and sucked on his skin. I liked the way his grip tightened, the way his breath hissed as I played, though he gave just as much.

Then he moved, positioning me on my back, hovering over me. He kissed me hard and then sat on his heels, pushing my knees into the bed. He gripped his cock, stroking himself.

"How many times have you gotten off to the thought of me?" I asked.

"More than you could count," he said, teasing my opening with the tip of his dick. I let my head fall back as I closed my eyes.

"Zahariev," I whined.

I just wanted him inside me again.

"I love the way you say my name," he said.

"Only when I'm begging though, right?"

"No," he said, staring down at me. "I love it all the time, even when you're pissed. Especially when you're pissed. It makes me hard. It makes me want to fuck you."

He thrust into me, gripping my thighs, holding me in place as his hips moved at a brutal pace. I gasped, arching against the bed, fisting the blankets. This pleasure was unholy, and I was possessed, utterly altered from the inside out.

Zahariev watched me with heated eyes, his expression different from before. He took fucking me seriously, and I felt every intention.

"I'm going to come," he said.

I was wrong. That was the hottest thing I'd ever heard him say.

"Yes," I breathed.

"Where?" he asked.

"Anywhere," I said. "I just want to watch."

I wanted to see what I'd done to him. I'd let him fill me with it later.

He grinned, and it was wicked. He bent and kissed me.

"You first," he said.

He'd already gotten me close, so all it took was rubbing my clit a few times, and I burst. The orgasm hit me hard. My entire body locked around him.

"Fuck, fuck, fuck!"

Zahariev tore away, and I opened my eyes in time to watch him come. The first release was a fucking jet. It spattered across my stomach and breasts. The second was much less intense, and the final was a few drops. He groaned through it all, and the sound made me want to fuck him again, but I didn't think my body would cooperate, at least not this soon.

When Zahariev had finished, he looked at me.

"God, you are so fucking hot."

He leaned down and kissed me, tongue driving into my mouth with the same desperation he'd had at the start of this. He rolled onto his back and brought me with him.

He held me tight, and we stayed like that, languidly kissing and touching. I liked it more than fucking. It was unhurried appreciation. It was worship between two lovers. It was a language I had never known before this moment but said everything I couldn't.

That was when I realized I was wrong, that there was no difference between what I wanted and what I would choose.

The answer had always been Zahariev.

———

Zahariev left the bed first. I was almost asleep, which was why it startled me. I assumed he was headed to the bathroom, so I didn't ask what he was doing, but then I heard the loud gush from my high-pressured faucet, and I knew he was running a bath.

Despite feeling like I literally had no bones, my curiosity got the best of me, and I dragged myself out of bed.

Zahariev was sitting on the edge of the tub, dipping his hand into the water.

"What are you doing?" I asked.

"I thought we should take a bath before we head back," he said.

I raised a brow. "We? Zahariev, *you* will barely fit in that tub."

"Then I'll just have to hold you real close," he said.

I smiled at him and approached. He wrapped his arms around my waist, and I ran my fingers through his hair, dragging his mouth to mine. I wondered if our intimacy would continue beyond these apartment walls. There was too much between us to share just one night together.

Zahariev turned off the water and got into the bath first. He'd filled it too full, so when I sat between his legs, it spilled over the edge.

"We'll probably fall through the floor in a few minutes," Zahariev said as I settled against his chest.

"Hey, no one's allowed to insult my apartment except me," I said.

Zahariev chuckled, his arms tightening around me.

"I'm not insulting it," he said, kissing my neck. "I'm quite fond of it."

"Even the bed?" I asked.

He'd bitched earlier about a spring digging into his shoulder blade.

"Only because it's where I fucked you first," he said.

He moved his hands to my breasts. I arched against him, resting my head on his shoulder. He captured my mouth in a slow kiss. Every slide of his tongue reached a different part of me—coaxing, kindling, feeding desire. His hands moved over my slippery skin, down my stomach to my knees, which he pulled apart and brought to my chest.

"You are unreal," he said, smoothing his hands between my thighs before sliding his fingers up and down my labia. His middle finger grazed my opening, from the base of my clit to the very bottom. With each pass, he went a little deeper.

Unlike his kiss, which had enticed me to unwind, this had my muscles tensing. Everything became hard and swollen with need.

"I can't stop wondering how often you've been this wet for me." His tone was low and rough, grazing my skin with every breath.

"It's not like I wasn't obvious about it," I said. "I begged you to fuck me."

"You did," he said. "But you are also a vicious tease, and I wanted to know you were serious."

"I *was* serious," I breathed.

I didn't know how I could have made it more obvious, but then he had been obvious too and still rejected me.

My breath caught as he slipped his finger inside me. It felt so good to have him there, gently caressing the slickest part of me. Then he used that wetness to circle my clit and I became tense and supple all at once.

I gripped the back of his neck, kissing him despite the awkward angle.

It was a slow and sensual build, like Zahariev was taking time to learn what I responded to most, but right now I'd react to anything because it was him doing the touching, the teasing, the exploring. All of it felt good but some of it felt great, and that's where I begged him to stay.

"Yes," I whispered. "There. There. *There.*"

My feet were pressed against the tub, and I rose on my toes, back arching as my shoulders dug into Zahariev's chest. Everything inside me contracted, contributing to the high of this sweet pleasure.

It helped that Zahariev's mouth was near my ear, that I heard every groan and growl as his body rose with mine.

My orgasm hit so hard, I felt like I'd been split in half. I shook uncontrollably, probably because my soul had to find a way back into my body. Zahariev rode it with me, each splintering wave, releasing me only when I relaxed against him.

Finally, I opened my eyes. If I had kept them closed, I would have gone to sleep. We were quiet, catching our breaths. I wasn't sure what changed, but the silence that followed felt like a chasm opening up between us. Zahariev must have felt it too because his arms tightened around me.

"We should get back soon," he said.

"I know," I whispered, though I didn't want to leave. I felt selfish, but I had loved our time together. There would never be another like it because it had been our first. I wasn't usually sentimental about that sort of thing, but then I'd never had sex with someone I cared about in this way.

Unfortunately, Zahariev's comment turned my thoughts to reality and what would happen in the daylight now that my dad was dead and my mother was missing.

"We should spy on Lisk," I said.

Zahariev chuckled. "That's what you're thinking about right now?"

He cupped my breasts as if to emphasize the point.

"You're the one who mentioned going back," I said. "I'm just throwing out ideas. Don't you think it would be helpful to know the company he's keeping?"

"Sure," he said. "Can you manage surveillance without trying to kill him?"

"I have self-control, Zahariev."

"Self-control goes out the window when emotions are high."

"Your faith in me is so reassuring," I said dryly. "I understand the greater goal here."

"I'm not asking because I don't have faith in you," said Zahariev. "I'm asking because Lisk isn't an ordinary demon. I'm not sure even you can predict how you will react when you face him again."

Last time, I'd frozen.

But last time, I hadn't been prepared to face my abuser.

"This is just surveillance," I said, though my voice sounded weak. What would I do if I witnessed Lisk with another victim? I wasn't sure I could keep myself from reacting, even if it meant dire consequences.

"It's Sunday," said Zahariev. "Lisk will be at the cathedral most of the evening."

I perked up. "So his house will be empty?"

"Unless he's holding people captive in the basement," said Zahariev.

I wouldn't be surprised to discover that was true.

"We should search his house while he's at service," I said. "Maybe we'll find the blades or something to blackmail him with."

I'd take either, or better yet, both.

I turned my head to the side, adding. "Unless you have a better idea?"

"I have a better idea, but it's not near as productive," he said. I could hear the amusement in his voice and shivered as his breath brushed my ear.

I craned my neck to meet his gaze.

"So…you aren't opposed?"

I didn't want his approval exactly. I just wanted to know I wasn't alone in my desire for justice.

"No. Even if I were, you'd go anyway, and I'd still follow." He paused. His gaze was gentle, thoughtful as he studied my face. "I'd follow you anywhere."

His words tangled in my chest, their truth drawing us together for a different sort of kiss. It wasn't born out of desperate need or years of longing. It was a vow, sworn and sealed.

We didn't need anything else.

ZAHARIEV

It was just getting light when we returned to the compound. We slipped inside from the garage, finding the house quiet.

Lilith paused in the hallway and faced me, clutching the blade to her chest with both hands. She looked so tired but so fucking beautiful.

"Are you going to bed?" she asked.

The corner of my mouth lifted. "Are you asking because you want to come with me?"

Please come with me, I thought. If she did, I would stay up just to fuck her and every time I woke up after.

"Do I need permission?" she asked.

"Never," I said. I bent to kiss her and then drew her close. She wrapped her arms

around my neck and her legs around my waist, and I carried her to bed.

CHAPTER
TWENTY

I woke unclothed in the cave.

The man was gone. The serpent too.

All that remained were a few dying embers in the fire and a frail piece of shriveled snakeskin. I took it as an offering and wrapped it around my wrist. I continued on, moving through the darkness differently, like I had been born of it.

I could sense the nearness of the cave walls and mineral formations. I could feel the movement of water but also its stillness, and somewhere below, tangled in the root, something burned.

But burned was the wrong word.

It wasn't fire. It didn't move the same way, dancing in colorful ribbons. This felt contained, an energy on the fringe of bursting.

It was distantly familiar, but I couldn't place why.

I only knew it was the answer I had been seeking. It was what whispered to me in the dark and drew me near.

Holy woman,

Mother of the dark world,
Hold tight to your anguish, carry it deep
Revel in the burn, that sweet agony
Make your mark and open your mouth,
Fill the night with your sacred screams
Shatter the earth and never know peace.

The fire seared my skin and torment twisted through me, a force I could not fight as it parted my lips and drew from my body an earthshaking shriek.

———————

I woke to the same piercing cry, only it didn't come from my lips.

It was Liam.

He was wailing. It was so loud I thought he must be in the room with us, but when I opened my bleary eyes, I realized it was just that shrill. I checked the time. I felt like I'd just fallen asleep, but it was late in the afternoon, so it had at least been a few hours. I didn't want to move, but I was also worried about Gabriel. Liam didn't sound okay.

I stretched, and Zahariev's arms tightened around me.

That was when I knew he was awake.

"Hey," I said, my voice quiet as I turned to face him. His eyes were closed, but I touched his face, his jaw rough with stubble. "I think Gabriel needs help."

"I'm coming," he said, though his voice was thick with sleep.

I kissed him and then extracted myself from his arms, rolling out of bed to dress. Zahariev was a step behind me, pulling on a pair of shorts.

In the hallway, Liam's cries sounded even sharper, and I instantly felt on edge.

"He's inconsolable," said Zahariev.

"Gabriel?" I called, knocking on his door. I didn't wait for an answer to enter and found him sitting on his bed, holding Liam. He was crying too. His face was drenched, and so was his shirt. How long had they both been sitting here like this?

"Oh, Gabriel," I whispered.

I didn't even know what to do or how to help.

"He won't stop," he said. His voice was so hoarse, I could barely hear him. "I don't know what to do, and I really...I need Esther."

Zahariev moved past me and took Liam from Gabriel.

"Let me try," he said.

"He won't take a bottle. I tried burping him. He won't take a pacifier."

Gabriel had to pause between words to catch his breath, almost convulsing.

"I got it," said Zahariev. "I think you need a break. I'll take him into the living room."

Zahariev caught my gaze as he headed past. He was tense, and I didn't know if it was from Liam crying or seeing Gabriel like this, probably both. He paused and kissed my temple before leaving the room, closing the door.

The barrier gave us some peace. Gabriel dropped his shoulders and slumped against the headboard.

I sat down and smoothed his hair out of his face. He had been so composed over the last few days, it was easy to forget this turmoil was living inside him.

"I tried so hard," he said, covering his face with his hand. His body shook. "And when nothing worked, I thought maybe I wasn't trying hard enough or that I wasn't even good at this. If Esther were here, she would probably have him asleep in no time."

405

"Gabriel." Hearing him made my heart ache. I touched his arm. "Esther is magic, but I think even she would find this challenging."

He dug the heels of his palms into his eyes. "I just feel guilty. He's all I have left of her, and I'm going to fuck him up."

"You're not going to fuck him up," I said. "Anyone would feel overwhelmed by this."

I felt overwhelmed, and I'd only heard a minute of those keen cries. On top of that, he was grieving.

He was quiet, sitting with his hands in his lap.

"I just," he said, taking a few stuttering breaths, "really miss her, you know? And there are days when I don't think I can do this without her, when I don't *want* to do it, and I feel so guilty, because who thinks that while holding their fucking newborn?"

I shifted so I could sit beside him and took his hand.

"I think a lot of people feel that way," I said. "Having a baby is a big change, and you're doing this without the love of your life. No one's expecting you to be okay."

There was a quiet lull while Gabriel worked to control his breathing.

"The night Esther died," I said, "Zahariev made me promise I would tell him if I didn't want to be here anymore. He asked me to give him a chance to bring me back. Can I ask the same from you?"

He looked at me. His eyes were swollen and almost shut.

"Yes," he said. "Of course I would tell you."

"Thank you," I whispered, because I couldn't speak any louder. My mouth was quivering, and my eyes were blurry. I tried to hide it by resting my head on his shoulder, but I gave myself away when I sniffled.

"Not you too, baby girl," he said, adjusting so that his arm was around my shoulder. "I didn't mean to make you cry."

I wiped my eyes but to no avail.

"It's not you," I said. "Everything's just sad."

"Oh, not everything," he said. "I saw that kiss Zahariev gave you, and I don't think I'm wrong in assuming you were together last night with the way you both came walking in."

My face flushed.

"Wow, why does this feel so embarrassing?"

He laughed. "I'm not trying to embarrass you," he said. "I'm happy for you. Esther would be too. She always said this would happen."

"That what would happen?"

"You and Z," he said. "I was the one who had doubts."

"Why did you have doubts?"

"I just didn't think he would put you in that kind of situation," he said. "You know as well as I do he won't be the one to suffer any consequences if you're found out."

"Zahariev didn't put me in this situation," I said. "We chose it."

"I know," he said.

"Do you think we're wrong?" I asked after a quiet moment. I whispered the words, feeling too guilty to speak them any louder.

"No, baby girl," he said. "Nothing's ever wrong when it's love."

―――――――

I spent a while with Gabriel until he decided he should probably take a shower. I left to check on Zahariev. He was in the living room with Liam, who was now asleep on his chest.

"Hey," I said quietly.

"Hey," he said. "How is he?"

"Okay," I said, sitting down beside him on the couch. "Overwhelmed."

Zahariev nodded and then bent to kiss Liam's covered head. It was such a sweet thing, one he did without thinking. It made my chest feel tight, and a warm flush blossomed in the pit of my stomach. I hadn't changed my mind about having children, but my body was a fucking traitor.

Thankfully, my thoughts were turned from my awakening desire when Coco shouted from somewhere in the house.

"Cheater!" she yelled.

"All you have to say is cheat," Cassius returned. "And you *don't* have to yell it."

"It's *cheater* because I'm calling *you* one, dip wad!"

I looked at Zahariev. "What is happening?"

"All I know is they've been playing cards for about an hour and neither of them like to lose," he said.

I bet I could guess how that started. Coco had proposed a game and taunted Cassius until he gave in to prove a point. I kind of hated that it sounded like his arrogant ass was winning.

It wasn't long after that Cherub wandered into the room, and I felt happier just seeing her. I picked her up and dragged a blanket from the back of the couch, resting my head on Zahariev's shoulder while Cherub curled up between us. I yawned so deep, my eyes watered.

"You should go to bed," Zahariev said. "You'll need more sleep if you want to stay awake for tonight."

"What's tonight?" Coco asked.

I met her gaze as she came into the living room. Her

cheeks were a little flushed, frustrated with Cassius if I had to guess.

"Did you give up on your game?" I asked.

"She didn't give up," said Cassius, joining us. "She lost."

"I lost because you cheated!" she snapped, taking a moment to glare at Zahariev's brother before falling into the seat beside me.

"Whatever makes you feel better, Coconut," he said, slipping a cigarette from behind his ear. "I'm gonna go smoke. Zahariev?"

He said nothing, and when I turned to look, his eyes were closed. He'd fallen asleep. He looked so cute with Liam resting on his chest. I had it bad for this man, and I was pretty sure he knew it.

"You two had a long night," Cassius said.

"I didn't think you'd want details, Cassius," I said, meeting his gaze. "But since you seem interested, it's only right to tell you about all the mind-blowing sex we had."

It wasn't exactly how I planned to tell Coco, but I didn't think she cared. She'd wanted this to happen for a long time.

"I don't need you to tell me," he said. "Because you woke me up this morning *moaning*. If you're going to fuck, at least give us a warning *and* some earplugs."

Given Cassius's comments about me last night, I expected a little more anger over this, but really, he just seemed to be teasing.

"I'm not sure I can get them by the next one," I said. "So this is your warning."

"I'm moving to the other side of the house," said Cassius as he left the living room.

"Oh no, you don't!" Coco called after him. "That's *my* side!"

"You don't even live here!" he called back.

Coco looked at me.

"I'm going to murder him," she said.

I pressed my lips together but couldn't help smiling. "I'll help you bury the body."

"As a true friend would," she said.

We smiled at each other and then fell silent. I dropped my gaze to Cherub, feeling a little awkward for not addressing the elephant in the room, though I should have known Coco would not let it go.

"So," she said, drawing out the vowel. "Zahariev finally took a bite, huh?"

I laughed, breathless. "It was more than a bite."

Coco pressed her lips together. "All night?"

"Mostly," I said.

"No wonder you're tired."

I was tired because I'd gone without sleep for about a week, ever since this fucking blade came into my possession. It had really been the catalyst for so many terrible things. The worst part was I still didn't exactly understand what we were dealing with. I just knew I didn't want the dagger to leave my hands and partly out of spite. I didn't want Lisk to have any more power, but I also didn't want to see the Order of the Serpent release a couple of ancient gods we knew nothing about.

I still felt like I should meet Saira tomorrow night. I would like to know more about the Order of the Serpent. If they were really a formidable force or just a handful of women who truly believed they were talking to a divine entity. Either way, I was going to need their trust to get my hands on their three blades.

As we lounged in the living room, the electricity surged.

"That's been happening all day," said Coco. "The news said the commission might enforce rolling blackouts to minimize the strain on the power grid if it doesn't get better."

Fucking demons, I thought.

The sooner I found those blades and forged that sword, the better. I was ready to go hunting.

———

I drifted off into a dreamless sleep, waking with enough time to shower and eat before Zahariev and I headed to Hiram. We arrived half an hour before service was set to start, parking within view of First Temple.

When I was younger, I always thought the spires atop the church looked like teeth.

It's a monster, I'd said. *He wants to swallow the sky.*

My mother had not appreciated my imagination and told me that was an evil thing to say, so I thought it instead.

Now that I was older, I'd say my observation was pretty accurate. Lisk had turned First Temple into a state-of-the-art fortress of white marble and built a mansion to match.

Supposedly, it could withstand any disaster, which made Zahariev's theory that Lisk wanted to end the world more probable.

It made me think he'd had this plan for years—the temple was his ark; his chosen species, the rich.

All he needed now was the Deliverer to make his dreams come true.

"I thought archbishops were supposed to live modestly," I said, glaring at Lisk's matching pointy roof. It towered over the concrete wall he'd built around his home, which, like the temple, took up an entire block.

411

"I don't think Lisk liked the idea of living in a rectory while the families lived in lavish mansions," said Zahariev.

"So you're saying he was jealous?"

"I think he feared the people would listen to the families over the church."

"If he didn't have a nice house? That's ridiculous."

"Money's power, little love. You know that."

I knew it, but money didn't automatically grant anyone the skills it took to be a good leader, and neither did blood. Maybe the families would have been more effective if God had given them qualities like integrity, compassion, and the ability to admit when they were wrong.

"Do you think Lisk is at the church already?" I asked.

Zahariev glanced at his watch. "He usually arrives fifteen minutes before the service, but it's difficult to know exactly. When he remodeled everything, he added an underground tunnel so he could go between the church and his house unseen."

"Is it really about being seen, or do you think it's just another way he's preparing for the end of the world?"

Zahariev shrugged. "Maybe both."

Lisk would keep his chosen few in the temple while he slept comfortably in his own bed. I should have brought a bag of ground rose hip to sprinkle on his sheets. That would have him itching all night long, and the thought brought me more joy than I'd felt in a long time.

I needed a fucking hobby.

We waited.

At first, I was fine, but as the hour neared, I grew impatient.

"He has to be there by now," I said.

"Probably," Zahariev agreed. "But we need to wait for a lull in the electricity."

"Zahariev," I said, irritated. "That could take all night, and by then, that fucker will be home."

"Hiram is set to go dark around six," said Zahariev. "It's just thirty more minutes."

"If you knew, why did we get here so early?" I asked. "I could have slept a little longer."

I needed it too. I'd had a blissful, dreamless sleep and still woke up feeling worse than when I'd drifted off.

"Because we're not just here to search Lisk's house," he said. "We're here to see who comes and goes, and the most activity happens now."

"Then it all must be happening in that tunnel," I said. "Because I don't see anything."

Zahariev smirked, but he didn't say anything, and I grew restless waiting. The power had been flickering all day across Eden, especially in Nineveh, and now that we'd arrived in Hiram, it hadn't wavered once.

Where were those goddamn demons when you needed them?

I hated even thinking that since I actually wanted to eradicate their fucking gooey bits from the world.

"My ass hurts," I said. "Can't we just…I don't know, cut the electricity to the house?"

Zahariev gave me that amused half smile that I sometimes loved and sometimes hated. Right now, I couldn't decide.

"Sure," he said. "But then he'll have us on camera, cutting the electricity to his house."

At this point, I'd risk it.

I sighed and rolled my eyes, shifting in my seat.

"I could give you a massage," Zahariev suggested.

"You just want an excuse to touch my ass," I said.

Zahariev's brows rose and his smile grew, but his eyes

413

were trained on the house. "Touch is a rather tame word for what I want to do to you."

My whole body flushed. I wasn't used to those kinds of words coming out of his mouth, but I liked it.

"There's plenty of space in the back for a demonstration," I said.

"Space isn't really the issue," he said. "It's time."

"Well, we've been here for almost an hour. You could have given me at least two orgasms by now."

Zahariev's brows lowered. "I think that was an insult."

I shrugged. "I don't really have enough data to give a more accurate number, so you can just take it as a challenge."

"I'll accept your challenge, but I think I deserve to know the most you've ever had."

"In one session?"

"Yeah," he said. "I need to know what I should aim for."

I tried not to smile. "Five."

"Just five?"

"*Just*? You say that like you can have more than one!"

"Yeah, but I've given more than five in one go," he said.

I crossed my arms over my chest. "So you've been holding back?"

"It's not holding back. We've had sex once. I have to learn what you respond to."

"What's 'more than five'?" I asked.

"Nine," he said.

"You gave someone nine orgasms? Who?" I paused. "It wasn't Hassenaah, was it?"

His laugh sounded more like a scoff. "I don't know why you think I fucked Hassenaah."

"She acts like you have," I said.

"What does that even mean?"

414

"I don't know how to explain it. She just acts like she can go over your head."

"You act the same way, and that was before I fucked you."

"Whatever," I said, frustrated. Honestly, I didn't think I'd mind her obsession with Zahariev if she'd just acknowledge that I worked hard, but she wouldn't even give me that. *You got what you wanted the way you get everything: with your name.*

Sure, a name that had also made me a target for abuse and gotten my dad killed, but I guessed we all valued different things.

"I don't want to talk about Hassenaah." I looked out the window, glaring at the streetlights with an intensity that was making my head hurt. Maybe if I concentrated enough, I could make them go out with my mind.

"You brought her up," Zahariev pointed out.

"Yeah, well, that's the second regret I have about tonight."

"What's the first?"

"Thinking this would be fun," I said.

I wasn't even sure that was the right way to describe how I'd imagined this going, but I certainly expected to be in Lisk's house by now.

"Things like this are boring until they're not," he said.

The urge to say something sarcastic vanished when the lights dimmed and flickered. I sat up straighter in my seat and reached for the flashlight at my feet just as the street went dark.

Fucking finally, I thought.

"Let's go," Zahariev said.

We left the car and jogged down the sidewalk in the near dark. Unlike the night of the gala, the sky was clear and dense with stars. It was beautiful, but there was something unsettling about the world without power. Things just felt a little more dangerous and a little less certain.

Lisk's mansion sat away from the street behind a fence that was mostly concrete except for the front, which was barred by a set of iron gates.

"I'll help you," Zahariev said. He interlocked his fingers so I could use them as a step and hoisted me up. I held on to two of the spikes until I could rest my foot on the rail and jump. My landing was shit. My legs gave out as soon as I hit the ground, and I fell to my knees.

Zahariev followed, landing on his feet as I got to mine.

We headed for the side of the house, out of view of the main gate. Zahariev checked a couple of windows.

"There's one open on the second floor," I said.

He followed my gaze. "Let's check the back before I make any attempts at climbing."

Around the back, there was a set of locked double doors.

"Fuck," Zahariev said under his breath. "Wait here."

He left the porch, and I walked to the corner, watching as he scaled the side of the house like he'd been doing it since he was five, which was probably accurate. Once he vanished through the second-story window, I returned to the back door and waited.

It was a few minutes before I saw him approach through the glass, but he unlocked the door, and I entered Lisk's living room. There were two sofas, each covered in patterned velvet and trimmed in dark wood. A gilded *Book of Splendor* sat atop an ornate coffee table next to a small, wooden chest. I opened it, but the only thing inside was a remote for the television and another for the ceiling fan.

"It looks like Lisk raided your storage containers for

416

furniture," I said, glancing around the room, which felt too large for one man.

"Master's upstairs," Zahariev said. "I can check that room for a safe if you wanna start searching the study?"

"Can you crack a safe?" I asked, a little jealous. That was a skill I wanted, but Zahariev laughed, quiet.

"Depends on the safe," he said.

I wanted more details, but I'd ask them later. Right now, we had work to do.

"Where's the study?" I asked.

Zahariev led me down a hall, past a winding staircase and into the foyer, which branched off into two rooms. One was a formal dining room, and the other was Lisk's study. It reminded me of my father's, full of oversize, dark furniture. Without light, I knew this color scheme—dark wood, shades of brown, and gilded metals.

"You can use your flashlight, but be aware of the windows," said Zahariev.

There were five in total. The two on either side of the fireplace were concealed behind heavy drapes, while the three at the front of the house were stained glass.

I looked at Zahariev. "How long do we have?"

His attention turned to his watch. "I'd say an hour, tops."

"Got it," I said, already crossing the room to Lisk's desk.

It was unadorned except for a lamp that looked like it weighed a thousand pounds.

The desk had seven drawers, three on each side and one in the middle. I started on the left. The top had a worn copy of the *Book of Splendor*, the next was full of folders stuffed with what appeared to be old sermons, and the bottom was full of snacks, which actually impressed me. Who knew Lisk was human enough to be relatable?

The other side was much of the same, folders and folders of past sermons.

This man needs a filing cabinet, I muttered.

The middle drawer had personalized stationery and various fountain pens, but nothing blade shaped. Not even a letter opener.

I was a little disappointed. I'd hoped Lisk would make it easy on us and be just as careless with his three blades as I'd been with my one, but of course, we weren't getting that lucky.

I turned my attention to the bookshelves, which were lined with leather-bound editions. At first, I thought the archbishop had all his books rebound to match, green with gilded spines, but when I took one from the shelf, I discovered they were just bound, solid wood.

I hadn't actually expected Lisk to read much beyond the *Book of Splendor* or other supporting texts written by past archbishops. I had been a great reader when I was younger, but as I'd gotten older, books became less and less accessible. They weren't about great adventures or thrilling mysteries. They were about the glory of the church and the consequences of sin. Sometimes I wondered if the people of Eden would flock to Nineveh for entertainment if they were allowed a little more escapism in their daily lives.

Though the books were fake, I decided it was best to check them. Maybe there was a safe hidden behind the volumes, or maybe one of them was some kind of disguised lockbox, but as I neared the end, neither of those things turned out to be true.

I was starting to feel anxious, thinking I wasn't going to walk away with anything useful, when something caught my attention, or rather the absence of it did. There was an empty space at the end of Lisk's sixth shelf. I might have thought nothing of it if the other five hadn't fit so perfectly from one end to the other.

Something was missing.

I turned, scanning the study, but the only surface left in the room was a round table between two oversize chairs in front of the fireplace.

"Find anything useful?" Zahariev asked.

I jumped at the sound of his voice and whirled to face him.

"Fuck, Zahariev! Don't *do* that!"

"You should really be more aware," he said. "We are trespassing in someone else's house."

"I was just concentrating," I said, frustrated. I knew he was right. "There's a book missing from this shelf. Most of these are fake, but what if the one missing isn't?"

Zahariev's gaze darted to the fireplace. "It's not the one on the mantel, is it?"

I turned, finding the book sitting on its side.

"I hadn't looked there yet," I said, crossing the room.

"Let's not pretend you pay attention to anything above your line of sight."

"That's not true. I pay attention to you," I said as I retrieved the book from its place.

I knew it was real the moment I picked it up. It was heavier than the fake ones and floppy. When I opened it, I half expected to find the center carved out, but instead, I found the book was actually a journal.

The pages weren't full of any kind of daily narrative. They were notes. The handwriting was messy, almost like whoever had written them couldn't keep up. With just a glance at the page, I recognized some familiar things. The

Seventh Gate, the names Eryx and Ashur, and a drawing of a fiery sword. The Deliverer, if I had to guess.

"Well," Zahariev said. "Anything useful?"

"These are notes about the gods behind the gate…"

I turned the page and found a list of words I didn't recognize. Maybe they were names: *Iprus, Arcturus, Lamassu, Mahari, Irkalla, Syriac*. There was another word, *Ziru*, written at the bottom, but it was crossed out. The final word was *Seine*, which I recognized as the mountain range that housed the Seventh Gate.

"But also…shapes."

Zahariev looked over my shoulder. There was a drawing on the opposite page. It was a cluster of nine circles. The one in the middle was connected to the eight around it by lines. A few of the names from the other side were written there, but not all.

When I moved on to the next page, I found the handwriting had changed. It was far more legible, like someone else had taken over. I read the words quietly aloud.

She will ascend from the womb of her enemy,
A temptress cloaked in night, a nightmare bound in chains.
Her cries will rattle the earth.
Her blood will break the gates.

"That sounds like something from the *Book of Splendor*," said Zahariev.

"It does," I said, but it was what this book reminded me of that unsettled me. It was similar to Saira's notes, the ones she'd written in my notebook when I sat across from her in her store.

I met Zahariev's gaze. "Did you check the basement?"

He raised a brow. "For captives? No. Why?"

"This book has had several authors," I said. "And these

420

are all channeled messages. As far as I'm aware, no matriarch has the ability to speak to entities beyond the gates, which means Lisk is using witches."

"Maybe he forced them before their executions," he said.

I hadn't thought about that, but it was very possible. None of these entries were dated, so it was impossible to say how old they were, but this answered the question of how Lisk knew about the blades and the gods behind the Seventh Gate.

A chorus of laughs erupted. Lisk had returned with guests.

Zahariev took my arm and pulled me behind the curtain. The window was large and the sill substantial, so we stood on it to keep from moving the drapes while Zahariev fiddled with the latch.

"I hope you have better vodka, Lisk."

Zahariev and I exchanged a look. We knew that voice. It was Victor Viridian.

"Empty your flask already, Vic?"

That voice belonged to Serafin Sanctius.

"Fuck off, Sera," said Victor. "It's been a long week."

"It's Sunday." The final voice was quieter than the others but derisive. It belonged to Absalom Asahel.

"Drop the righteous act, Absalom," said Victor. "You're here, aren't you?"

Absalom did not reply. There was a lull in the conversation and the sound of glass clanking. I couldn't tell where the men were. I just knew they were close enough to hear clearly. Maybe the dining room?

"To Lucius," said Victor.

Hearing my father's name made my heart race. There was a pause, and then the quick, crisp sound of shot glasses tapping a table.

"Poor bastard," said Serafin. "Should have kept his daughter on a fucking leash."

I ground my teeth.

"Too bad she wasn't in that house," said Victor.

"If Lucius had done his job, she would have been," said Lisk. I wasn't sure when he'd joined the others. "He failed, even in his final hour. Now we're responsible for his trash."

"We could execute her," said Absalom. "Her behavior is a kind of witchcraft. It would send a message to other women who have been inspired to behave similarly."

"We'd have to pry her out of Zareth's hands," said Victor. "That fucker's in love with her even if he doesn't realize it."

"So he's fallen prey to her spell," said Absalom. "Perhaps when she is dead, he will realize the error of his ways."

"It's too risky," said Serafin. "Zareth knows too much. He'll ruin us all before we have a chance to hang her. It's better to wait until the fire and flood." There was silence, and then Serafin asked, "How close are we to the end?"

"Close," said Lisk.

I wondered if he was lying or if he'd learned something new.

"Until then, we will have to continue as though we are not starting anew," said Lisk. "Have you considered Macarius's request?"

"The commission cannot decide without Zahariev," said Absalom.

"Of course, but we know his choice," said Lisk.

"I am not eager to see the head of Hiram replaced so easily," said Victor. "This opportunity is rare. We could divide Lucius's territory and trades. Outwardly, we would share his public responsibilities. I think we are more than owed the opportunity, given what he put us through."

My hands fisted, my body vibrating with rage.

"We would have to offer a share to Zahariev," said Absalom.

There was a pause.

"Or we go to war with him," said Victor. "Three against one, I'd say those are pretty good odds."

There was a soft sliding sound, and I turned to find Zahariev lifting the window. He gestured for me to climb out and followed close behind. I clutched the journal tight as we retreated.

Once we were in the SUV, we sat in silence, too stunned to speak. I was having trouble comprehending what I'd just heard, because the betrayals went beyond anything I'd ever imagined.

I'd expected Lisk, but the other three families? They'd turned on my father, Zahariev, and their districts in their plot to end the world.

I also found it strange that none of them had mentioned my mother. It was like she didn't even exist, not as a target, a victim, or a survivor. Was it because they thought so little of the women who gave them true power? Or were they hoping to keep her hidden away and silent until they brought about the end of the world?

My shock quickly turned to anger.

"Please tell me we're going to fuck them up," I said.

Zahariev looked at me, and I was a little unsettled by how calm he appeared, but that was because I knew he'd been pushed to his limit. These men, they'd awakened a monster.

He answered with a soft half smile. "Yeah, little love. We're gonna fuck them up."

ZAHARIEV

This entire time, I'd questioned Lilith's self-control when I really should have been worried about mine. If she hadn't been with me, I'd have killed every man in that fucking house.

CHAPTER
TWENTY-ONE

W anna fuck?" I asked.

Zahariev had just parked. We hadn't left the SUV yet, but the ride home had put me more and more on edge.

"I always want to fuck," he said, shutting off the ignition. "You wanna go inside first?"

"I'm not picky," I said. "You can fuck me in the back seat like you promised and give me nine orgasms."

"Is that a fantasy of yours?" he asked.

I shrugged. My legs were bouncing. "It sounds hot."

He paused, staring at me, and then got out of the car. At first, I thought he was going inside, but then he opened the rear door and slid into the seat.

I grinned and climbed into the back, straddling him. Our mouths collided before I sat back and pulled off my shirt. Zahariev took that as an opportunity to squeeze my breasts.

"God, you are so fucking hot," he said, leaning forward to kiss my chest before closing his mouth over one breast. I gripped his head, then let my fingers graze through his hair. He moved to the other, tongue swirling over my skin.

"I need this," I whispered, pulling away to sit beside him.

"Then where are you going?"

"Undress," I said, shimmying out of my jeans.

Zahariev followed my lead, slipping off his shirt and pants. I reached for his cock as I straddled him again, pumping him up and down. He was smooth and warm, and as much as I wanted to taste him, I wanted him inside me more.

I positioned him between my legs and sank onto his cock. I loved the feel of the first thrust, when my body was still tight and aware of every movement he made.

Zahariev groaned, his hands smoothing down my back.

"God, it feels so good," I said, tilting my head back, hands on Zahariev's shoulders. "I should have made you fuck me sooner."

He looked at me with heavy-lidded eyes, hands spanning my ribs. I loved the lazy expression that came over him when he was inside me. He was rarely ever this relaxed. It was good for both of us.

"You'll never have to *make* me fuck you," he said.

"Yeah?" I asked, leaning closer, letting my arms slide around his neck. I liked the way my nipples grazed his body when I moved. I kissed him, tongue sweeping sweetly at his mouth. It was slow and sensual, but I could feel the heat building in the pit of my stomach.

"It's so hot," I whispered, pulling back to gather my hair, moving it to one side. "So fucking hot."

Zahariev slid down in the seat, moving his hands to my forearms.

"Lean back," he said. His voice was a quiet command.

It was that soft edge that made me stiffen. My desire for

him sharpened, cutting through me like a knife. I couldn't decide if I wanted to fight him or submit to him. Either way, I knew I was about to be fucked like never before.

I obeyed, more curious than anything, back resting against the driver's seat, my hands on his knees. We were still joined, and the change in position made me breathless.

"Like this?" I asked.

"Yeah," he said, smoothing one hand over my stomach to my breasts. "Just a fucking dream."

He took a few seconds to explore me, and it felt like worship. I liked the way he seemed to change while doing it, eyes opening a little more, darkened by an intensity that made me shiver.

God, this was going to be so fucking good.

It was almost like he'd heard my thoughts, because at that moment, his gaze lifted to mine.

"How do you want it, little love?" he asked. "Slow? Fast? Somewhere in between?"

His thumb was near my clit, and as he spoke, he took me through each option in real time. His touch felt good, but the demonstration made it all that much hotter. My body was already tensing.

"God," I panted. "I don't fucking care. Just don't stop."

He didn't, and I reached behind me, grabbing the headrest. I needed something to hold on to as he coaxed my body to release. At this angle, it was too much work to move up and down, so I rocked against him instead.

I whispered and whined as the pressure built inside me. It was hard to put into words how this felt. It was just so *fucking good*. He worked me until everything inside me clenched tight for a single moment and then released in waves of trembling warmth. Through it all, I didn't make a sound. I couldn't, consumed by each paralyzing wave of pleasure.

When I came down, it was like everything inside me had liquified. My eyes were so heavy. I wanted to sleep.

"Legs up," Zahariev said. Again, his tone was quiet and demanding.

It woke me up, and I rested my feet on his shoulders. His hands skimmed up my thighs, and he trailed kisses along the inside of my calves.

"You feeling good?" he asked.

"Yeah," I said. "You?"

"I'm having the time of my life," he said, gripping my hips. With the way we were positioned, he wasn't all the way inside, so when he pulled me toward him, it was just the slightest bit of movement hitting in just the right place.

I gasped and then held his forearms, pushing against the seat with my feet poised over his shoulders. I had never had sex like this before, but fuck, this was *exquisite*. It took me a moment to find a rhythm that worked, one that Zahariev encouraged with the slightest bit of movement.

"Oh my God," I gritted out, my expression morphed into something desperate and probably not the least bit attractive, but *holy hell*. I fucking sobbed. "It feels so good."

Zahariev licked his fingers and rubbed my clit until I came. This time, I screamed, curling into myself, my knees pressed together. I held on to Zahariev, nails digging into his skin. I couldn't do anything while my body processed this pleasure. It was like being electrocuted, but in the most erotic way possible.

I was so out of it. I didn't know how I got upright, but the next thing I knew, Zahariev's mouth was on mine. He kissed me hard before pulling away, gripping me tight. The ends of his hair were wet, falling in his face. His body glistened. I wanted to lick him, but he was in full control. One hand twisted into my hair, the other slipped between my legs as he brought me to release again.

And again.

And again.

And again.

I fell against him, breathless to the point of wheezing.

Holy fuck, I was tired. Zahariev's hands smoothed down my back to my ass, lifting me until I slid down his cock again.

"How the fuck have you not come?" I asked.

He laughed. It was a cute, amused sound I'd never heard him make before. I loved it, and I rewarded him by sucking on his neck.

He groaned and lifted his hips, grinding into me.

"You don't make it easy," he said, arms banding around my waist.

I brushed my nose against his, a slow smile curling over my lips.

"What?" he asked, grinning.

"Do you want to come?" I asked.

"So fucking bad," he said and kissed me. "Where do you want it?"

I pretended to consider the question as I adjusted my position a bit, moving more onto my knees, which also meant sliding up Zahariev's dick. I shuddered. I was so fucking sensitive right now, I'd probably orgasm if I sneezed.

"Come inside me," I said. Some primal part of me wanted to feel him dripping out of me. "How do you want me?"

His laugh was quiet and hoarse. He kissed my chest and held me tight before shifting me onto my back. "Exactly like this."

I giggled. I couldn't help it. He wanted to end our sex marathon with missionary after the way he'd taken command of my body, maneuvering me into positions I'd never experienced before.

"Are you sure? Seems pretty anticlimactic," I said.

"You're tired," he said. "And this won't take long."

I smiled even as he kissed me, slow and deep, bending my knees so they framed his body. I thought he would sink into me pretty quickly, but instead, he took his time exploring like I was all new to him again.

"I thought you said this would be over quickly," I said.

I wasn't complaining, only teasing. I was content where I was beneath him and under his appraising gaze.

I'd never been the center of anyone's world before, always more of an inconvenience. I used to think Zahariev believed the same, but now I knew the truth. He hadn't taken care of me out of obligation or as a favor to my father. He'd taken care of me because I was his entire universe.

The truth gave a deeper meaning to his actions over the last two years, and I felt stupid for not seeing it.

Zahariev paused after pressing a kiss to my stomach.

"What's wrong?" he asked.

My eyes were burning, and I tried to swallow the thickness gathering in my throat. I shook my head.

"I'm sorry I'm only now seeing you," I said.

His gaze was steady as he stretched over me. "Don't apologize, little love," he said. "I could have remained invisible to you, and my devotion to you would be unchanging."

I held his face between my hands and pulled him to me. We kissed, and then Zahariev sat back on his heels, shoving his damp hair out of his face before gripping my thighs and thrusting into me. My back arched at the blissful invasion.

430

He was zealous and focused, his mouth and brows pinched as he drove into me. He slipped out a time or two, and both times, he dragged his fingers through my heat and used that wetness to rub my clit.

I knew he was close when he started vocalizing his pleasure. It was a deep, satisfying groan that shivered through me. My stomach clenched and pushed me over the edge. As I came, Zahariev lowered to me, slipping one arm under me, pressing the other to the top of my head to keep me from hitting the door, which I suddenly realized I was up against.

He gave a few final thrusts, and when he came, he was breathless, growling with each exhale. I wrapped myself around him, shivering. It wasn't because I was cold. In fact, it was so fucking hot in this car I was sure I didn't have an ounce of water left in my body. Zahariev carried me through the aftershock, kissing and licking and teasing like we hadn't been having sex for an hour. It was languid and lovely, and while I didn't want it to end, I really needed something to drink and maybe a pizza.

Zahariev chuckled, kissing my forehead before he sat up and brought me with him. My head spun, and I had to close my eyes to make it stop.

"You okay?" he asked.

"Yeah," I said and then frowned.

"What's wrong?"

"Nothing. I just put my hand in something wet."

Zahariev chuckled. "Given how many times I made you come, it's probably yours."

I blushed, though I wasn't embarrassed. It was more from the memory of it, the deep, exquisite pleasure he'd given me.

"Well, you were short by one," I said. "But eight isn't bad."

He looked at me, unamused.

"You are such a fucking brat," he said.

"You like it," I said.

"I do," he agreed, grasping my jaw and pulling me close. "But next time, I'm going to fuck you like I don't."

I licked my lips. They were raw and rough and reminded me of my pilgrimage through the desert. I didn't know why my mind unearthed the memory, but it remained, even as I focused on Zahariev.

"Promise?" I asked.

Zahariev smirked and his grip lessened, thumb brushing lightly over my skin. I liked the way he tempered dominance with tenderness.

I needed both.

"Yeah, little love," he said. "Easiest yes I'll ever give."

We dressed and went inside, stopping in the kitchen to raid the refrigerator. Zahariev didn't have any pizza, even frozen, but he had cheese, which I happily devoured.

I downed two glasses of water and carried a third to the bedroom.

We showered together and washed each other. Zahariev paid special attention to my breasts, massaging my nipples until they were almost painfully peaked. By the time he was finished, his cock was erect, and I was fighting waves of prickling lust.

He might not orgasm more than once during sex, but he was quick to bounce back.

"Wanna fuck?" I asked.

Zahariev laughed, closing his eyes as he stepped back into the spray. I loved watching the water drip down his body. He was glorious.

"Given what I promised when we left the car, I think it's best to take a little break."

"I can handle it," I said.

He smoothed his hands over his head so his hair was slicked back. His gaze was searching and a little fierce.

"You aren't lying to me, are you?"

"Why would I lie?" I asked.

"To get what you want," he said.

My gaze dipped. His cock was literally pointing at me.

I raised a brow. "Are you sure it isn't what *you* want?"

"I told you," he said. "I always want to fuck, but we went hard, little love."

"Zahariev, if I'm asking you to fuck me again, we didn't go hard *enough*," I said.

His gaze darkened. I didn't think he liked the way I was critiquing his work.

"Dry off and wait for me in the bedroom," he said.

"Any particular requests?" I asked.

"I'll put you where I want you," he said. "Just fucking go."

I left the shower and toweled off, though my hair was still wet enough to drip coldly down my back. Zahariev entered the room shortly after, pausing just outside the door, eyes trailing my body hungrily. I suddenly recalled a time when I couldn't get him to look beyond my face.

"If it's too much, tell me," he said.

I appreciated that he always offered an out. I thought I could handle anything, but I could be wrong.

He only approached after I nodded and then gripped my jaw, his finger pressed against my lips.

"Suck," he said, and I took him into my mouth. He inched closer and spoke quietly. "I'm going to fuck your

433

mouth so hard, you'll forever think twice before you tell me I didn't give you *enough*."

All the blood in my body rushed right to my clit.

"On your knees," he said and released me.

I lowered to one and then the other, back straight and eyes level with the base of his cock. His balls were heavy, and I wondered what sound he would make if I took them into my mouth.

Zahariev's fingers sifted through my hair until he'd gathered it in his fist. With his free hand, he guided his cock to my open mouth. A thick bead of precum oozed from the tip, which he dragged over my lips. I made a noise in the back of my throat, relishing the eroticism of it all.

This was fucking hot.

"Suck me, little love," he said.

I was salivating as I reached for him. I was glad he let me play, because I truly loved the pleasure of making him moan. It thrilled me like nothing else. Each swirl of my tongue brought on a different, deeper noise, and it drove me wild.

I glanced up at him as I licked his balls and took one into my mouth, then the other. His hand was tight in my hair, and he watched, then tilted his head back, body tense and glistening. I thought he almost forgot his intention of fucking my mouth, but when I released him and started kissing up his dick again, he gripped my head in both hands, letting out a low growl.

"Fuck, you make this difficult," he said.

I grinned. "I told you I like going down on you."

"If this wasn't a sin, you'd be a fucking saint," he said.

It was probably blasphemous to even imply the possibility of sainthood for blow jobs, but I'd take the veneration.

After a brief pause, he let me start again, but this time

he actually held true to his word and thrust into my mouth. My eyes watered. Deep throating wasn't my expertise, but I tolerated it in the past. With Zahariev, it was different though. I liked how he looked while doing it, focused and yet completely out of his mind. Right now, I could be the vessel for his pleasure.

I gagged when he hit the back of my throat but breathed through it as he held me there. When he pulled out of my mouth, I was breathless but eager to take him again, except that he dragged me to my feet and pushed me onto the bed.

"Roll over," he said, and I moved to my stomach. He pulled my hips, guiding me to my knees.

Then his teeth grazed my ass as he sucked on my skin, and I gasped, back arching. I looked at him over my shoulder as he did the same to the other side and then squeezed both cheeks, murmuring a string of curses about how fucking great my ass was.

I appreciated that, considering I thought it was pretty flat.

Zahariev ran his hand between my legs, and I shivered. I was wet but also sensitive, still swollen from earlier, but I was going to try this even if we had to slow down.

He nudged my legs apart a little more, and then I felt the crown of his cock prodding. He leaned down and kissed the top of my spine.

"You good, little love?" he asked.

"Better than ever," I whispered.

He straightened, the palm of his hand smoothing down my back. Then he gripped me and slid inside. I'd prepared myself for a violent thrust, but Zahariev must have sensed the tension in my body, because he started slow, quickening his pace as I relaxed. Soon, I wasn't even aware of the ache, too turned on by his handling of me to even think.

He bore down until I was flat against the bed, alternating between hard, rhythmic thrusts and a slow, sensual grind. The lull was necessary because I found it hard to breathe when he slammed into me. I just held on and buried my face in the bed to muffle the sounds coming out of my mouth.

We couldn't do much about the bed though, which pounded against the wall. It wasn't long before a loud bang came from the next room.

"Stop fucking!" Cassius yelled.

We burst into laughter, and then Zahariev fell against me before rolling on his side. My back was against his chest, his cock wet but still hard against my ass.

"I thought he was going to move to the other side of the house," Zahariev said, breathless.

"Jerk," I said, elbowing him. "I thought you were asleep during that conversation. I could have used your help!"

"I would never willingly talk about my sex life with my brother," said Zahariev.

"But you'll fuck in the room next to his?" I asked.

"It's not my fault you're loud," he said.

"Are you serious?" I asked, craning my neck to look at him. "Not *your* fault?"

He chuckled, thoroughly amused. He placed a hand on the side of my face and kissed me.

"If you want, I'll take the credit," he said. "But I think you're also just really fucking sensitive. I've never had an easier time getting someone off."

I sighed. "And yet you still didn't manage to make me come nine times."

"Fucking brat," he muttered.

Our laughs were breathless as we kissed, and at some point, Zahariev was inside me again. He moved at an easy but deliberate pace, fingers circling my clit. My body was slower to respond, but the tide was rising, each wave taking me a little higher than the last.

When the feeling grew consistent, I knew I could come, and I rose onto my elbow and gripped the back of Zahariev's neck.

"Faster," I whispered.

Zahariev's eyes didn't leave mine, but his mouth tightened as his pace increased.

"Yes," I whined. "Yes, yes, yes."

My entire body flooded with a tingling warmth. Zahariev pulled out, pumping his hand up and down his cock until he came in a rush across my lower stomach.

I closed my eyes and worked to catch my breath.

"We should shower again," I said, though I wasn't sure I could convince my brain to actually move a single part of my body.

Zahariev's answer was to tighten his arm around my waist. I fit against him so snugly, and he was so warm, I drifted into a deadening sleep.

———————

I made my descent, spiraling down at a violent angle toward the thing that burned but was not fire. Though it was silent, its energy screamed. It was tangled inside me, straining and stretching but unable to change its clustered form.

The final turn brought me to it, a basin of entwined roots filled with a strange liquid. The substance was hard to describe, lead-like but iridescent. The glow was almost too faint to see. Some called it the heart of the earth, some the root of sin, but it was really an ancient kind of magic. It had been here for thousands of years, and in that time, it had become impure, no longer capable of serving its purpose.

This was my mission, to clear it.

I remembered my offering, the skin of the serpent. I took it from my wrist and laid it in the basin, watching as it slowly vanished beneath the surface.

Then I dipped my hands into the liquid and sipped.

I wasn't aware of the taste or how the substance settled in my stomach, because as soon as it touched my tongue, a blinding light filled my vision. As it cleared, I saw things, flashes of the past, present, and future. There were giants adorned in gold, wreathed in a brilliant aura. It was hypnotizing, and I felt like someone was prodding at my mind, trying to get in, but I resisted and felt the approach of something different, an entity I could only feel, but it spoke and gave knowledge of fire and forging.

Battle raged, and it was bloody.

I blinked, and the light dimmed a little more. The image before me was clearer.

I saw the doors of the Seventh Gate. There was an ancient script carved into the surface. I could not read the words because I did not know the language, but I knew it was a spell. The magic felt like the liquid in the basin and glowed with a violet light. The only exception was where the gate had cracked. That was where the spell was broken.

I trembled as I reached, tracing the rifts with my fingers, but the edges were rough and sliced into my finger. I drew my hand away quickly, but it was too late. I had left my blood behind.

The gate began to tremble, as if someone were pounding

on it from the other side. The cracks deepened, and from them, a thick pinkish substance oozed, dripping to the ground.

Somehow, I knew the name.

Melam, it was called.

It was the magic of the Elohim.

The magic of the gods.

Suddenly, I was far more aware of myself than any other time I'd made this journey. I was no longer just a woman on a pilgrimage. I was also Lilith, and I was angry.

My rage felt like magic as I screamed and fell to my knees, fingers burning as I dug into the melam, the demons who had torn my heart in two.

———

My fingers were throbbing when I opened my eyes, lashes wet with tears.

I lifted my hands and examined them front and back, but there were no signs I'd touched the demons, nothing stuck beneath my nails and no burns on my skin. For once, I wished my dream had been real. I'd give anything to tear those fucking demons apart.

I sat up and threw my legs over the edge of the bed. I gulped down the glass of water I'd put on the table last night and felt a little more awake, though my body was ridiculously sore.

Hopefully, I didn't have to fight anyone tonight, though I would not rule out the possibility, since Saira was going to take me to the Order of the Serpent. I dreaded meeting these women who had an affinity for a kind of magic I didn't really understand. Would I even be able to defend myself against their spells? Unless one of them was attracted to me, my power was worthless.

I rose and took a hot shower, dressed, and went in search of Zahariev.

I found him outside, leaning against the stone wall of his porch, smoking. He was alone and dressed in a pair of black sweats. He looked a little pale, but I thought that was because the bruises I'd left on his neck were so dark.

He blew out a stream of smoke just as I joined him.

"Morning, little love," he said.

I leaned against him, and he kissed the top of my head as he put one arm around me, hand resting on the curve of my ass.

"How did you sleep?" he asked.

"I had bad dreams," I said, shivering.

"About anything in particular?" he said.

"About demons," I said, pausing to look up at him. "I think I know where they are coming from."

Zahariev met my gaze, waiting for me to explain, but I suddenly felt ridiculous telling him something like it was fact when I'd only seen it in a dream.

"When I was at Sons of Adam, Abel mentioned to me that the gates had weakened. He said people think that's the reason the weather's harsher, why people are getting sicker and more violent. I didn't really think anything of it, but last night I dreamed there were cracks in the gate. They have interrupted some kind of spell carved into the stone. That's how the demons are getting in. And they aren't really demons."

The corner of his mouth lifted a little. "You don't say?"

I rolled my eyes. "It's a pretty accurate name," I said, pulling away. "I watched those fuckers possess a rat."

He drew from his cigarette then asked, "So what are they?"

440

"I think the Order of the Serpent's precious gods are sending their magic into our world," I said, pausing, brows lowering as I recalled more of my dream. "I saw them, the gods, but there were more than just two. They were basically a race of giants. They had this aura around them they could call up at will, and it would brighten until I felt hypnotized, like they were inside my mind. It's not so different from the demons."

Zahariev was quiet, considering. He took a final drag from his cigarette before putting it out against the stone.

"You know what this means," I said. "Their gods killed Esther. I'm not willing to free the murderers of my best friend."

Though I'd never been keen on the idea anyway.

"I'm not sure you should lead with a full dismissal of their goal," said Zahariev.

I glared at him. "You don't want the gates opened either."

"No, but the Order still has three blades," he said. "Or they claim to. We're going to need to know where they're keeping them if we want any chance of forging this fucking sword."

"Do you think we should risk it?" I asked, though without it, it was going to be a lot harder to kill off these demons. "Forging the sword will only make it easier for the families to get it."

"I'm not saying we'll keep it forever," he said. "But we have to be strategic. I can fuck with the families. They know it. That's why they're hoping to do me in with a flood."

I knew he was right, but I wondered if the families would forgo their plans if they knew we had the sword they wanted, but I guessed we would have to deal with things as they came. Right now, we were jumping ahead.

"The sword won't even matter if we can't seal the cracks in the gate," I said. "The demons will just keep coming."

Zahariev looked away, dragging his hand over his mouth.

"I wonder what weakened the gates in the first place," he said. "Did Abel have an answer for that?"

"No," I said. "Everything he told me was something he'd overheard. I think it's a question for the Order of the Serpent. Saira had the same markings carved in her door as the ones on the gate."

I assumed the runes were inscribed to seal the doors like the Book of Splendor said, except they had been disrupted.

"Have you read more of that book you got from Lisk's study?"

"Not yet," I said. "I've been a little distracted, but I'll read through today."

Between what I'd seen in my dreams and what I'd read so far in the journal, I was starting to believe Saira was truly speaking with entities behind the gate, but I hesitated to call them gods.

"Right," he said, though he seemed preoccupied as he nibbled on his bottom lip.

"When you say *we*, is it because you're planning to come with me?"

His gaze shifted to mine. "Well, you're not going alone. We don't know these people. What if the Order of the Serpent isn't even real? Saira could just be a plant working for the church, trying to get the blade back."

I understood his suspicion, but I wasn't so sure. I'd seen many zealous people in my life, and Saira seemed genuine.

"Or they are very real, and you'll just fuck up our chances of confirming it?" I said.

Hadn't he just said his goal was to locate all seven blades? If I lost the Order's trust right out of the gate, we were screwed.

"No matter how capable you are, I won't send you into the unknown alone," he said.

"I'm not saying I want to go alone," I said. "But if I walk up to Saira with you at my side, she'll likely not even try to lead me to the Order."

"I'll figure something out," he said. "I'll follow you or rig something up so I can listen in on your conversation."

I wasn't so sure the latter would work. Since the demons had overloaded the power grid, none of our technology had been the same. Not that it was great to begin with, at least in Nineveh.

We were quiet for a moment, and Zahariev lit another cigarette.

"Have you decided what you're going to do about the families?" I asked.

He expelled a stream of smoke, scratching his brow with his thumb.

"Right now, I'm going to act like they didn't stab me in the back."

"Can you do that if they decide to go to war over Hiram?" I asked.

"Yeah," he said. "I'll just offer an ultimatum. Unless you want me to fight for it."

"What's the ultimatum?"

He held my gaze as he took another drag. This man smoked like a fucking freight train.

"They can have it," he said. "So long as I can have you. Only if you agree, of course."

I licked my lips to keep from smiling as I stared at him,

though his proposal made my heart feel like it was about to explode.

"Do you really think that will work?" I asked.

"I think I can be pretty convincing," he said. "I imagine they will give me what I want for now, knowing they plan to kill me later."

He sounded so casual despite the morbid theme of our conversation. I wondered if his ease was confidence or rather that he did not fear dying. I hoped it was the former, because I couldn't handle losing him.

"What does it mean? To be yours?" I asked.

He smiled softly. "Whatever you want," he said. "I'll always be here, following in your shadow. I am not afraid of your freedom."

I held his gaze and closed the space between us.

"I'd take you over Hiram any day," I said. I let my hands smooth up his chest, wrapping my arms around his neck. He tossed his cigarette and pulled me close. "Just promise me you won't die."

He laughed quietly, eyes trained on my lips.

"Wasn't planning on it," he said.

Then he kissed me.

ZAHARIEV

When I opened the back door of my SUV,
all I could smell was stale sex. It was not
pleasant, which is why I'd decided it was
best to clean it before everyone piled in for
an evening of surveillance.

"What are you doing out here?" Cassius
asked.

I hit my head trying to back out of the
SUV and hissed.

"Fuck," I said, squinting against the
pain as I rubbed the spot before answering
between gritted teeth. "Cleaning."

"Cleaning?"

"It's better if you don't ask," I said.

It took him a moment before he realized
what I was saying.

"Oh no," he said. "Fuck that. I call

shotgun. I'm not sitting in your bodily fluids."

"You won't," I said, glaring. "That's why I'm cleaning."

"Still can't do it," he said. "It's just… ghost come then. If you can see it with a black light, it's not gone, Zahariev."

"I'll make a note," I said, returning to the task at hand when my brother interrupted me again.

"Hey, Z," he said.

I was careful this time and didn't hit my head when I met his gaze.

"I'm sorry for all that stuff I said before. I didn't mean it."

"I know," I said. "But you should tell Lilith. I think she needs to hear it."

CHAPTER
TWENTY-TWO

I had about five seconds before midnight, and I was book-
ing it to the top of Saira's Secret Overlook, as I had
dubbed it. She seemed like the kind of person who stuck
to her word, so I didn't expect her to be there if I was a
minute late.

As I neared the top, I slowed to catch my breath and
glanced back. Somewhere behind me, Zahariev watched
with Cassius and Gabriel. They were going to follow wherever Saira led. I just hoped that wasn't through another
tunnel. Going underground would complicate our plan,
but I trusted Zahariev to figure it out.

He had spent the day informing Cassius and Gabriel
about what we'd overheard at Lisk's. Their reactions were
what I expected: shock and anger.

Cassius was far more reactive, demanding to know what
Zahariev was going to do about the betrayal, while Gabriel
pointed out the advantage of knowing and quietly planning.

I understood both perspectives. At the end of the day, I
wanted whatever ensured Lisk and the patriarchs suffered

most, and I hoped this meeting with the Order of the Serpent got us a step closer.

I found Saira sitting beneath the tree, close to where we had left the tunnel. Or at least I saw her foot. She'd planted herself on the opposite side, facing the ocean. I didn't really blame her. The view was better, but fuck.

"You could have at least watched for me and met me halfway," I huffed as I approached.

I expected some catty reply, but when she didn't say a word, the hair on the back of my neck stood up.

Maybe she'd fallen asleep.

Still, I took out my phone and flashed it in Zahariev's direction to alert him before making a wide arc around the trunk, eyes darting into the dark.

"Saira?" I said, using the pale light from my phone to illuminate her.

She sat with her hands in her lap, her chin against her chest, too still to be breathing.

"Fuck."

I reached for my gun just as someone barreled into me from behind, their arms banding around my chest as they attempted to drag me away.

"Get off!" I yelled, dropping my weight and sliding out of my attacker's grip. From the ground, I pivoted and slammed my foot into his legs when someone else grabbed a fistful of my hair.

I cried out, reaching for his arms to ease the sting, but found his head was actually close to mine, so I dug my nails into his face.

"Fucking hell!" The man released my hair and tried to restrain my arms. "Grab her legs, goddammit."

I don't think I'd ever flailed so hard in my life as I tried to prevent these fuckers from pinning me to the ground.

448

"Zahariev!" I screamed.

Where the *fuck* was he?

A second later, the man at my feet gave a soft groan and then went limp, knocked unconscious by Cassius, who then pointed his gun at the one holding my arms.

Zahariev sounded cold and threatening as he spoke. His voice filtered in from behind me.

"Let her go, or I'll blow your fucking head off."

The man was off me instantly, and I scrambled to my feet, putting distance between myself and my attackers, though one lay unconscious on the ground.

"You all right, little love?" Zahariev asked.

I nodded, trying to catch my breath. I was a little shaken, crashing from the rush of adrenaline, but otherwise fine.

The man who'd grabbed my hair had his hands up and faced Zahariev.

He was young, probably in his early twenties. His hair was blond, short, but long enough to be parted on the side. He wore all black tactical gear, and so did his partner.

"I'm here on behalf of Archbishop Lisk," said the man.

"If you think that's going to keep me from shooting you in the fucking face, you're wrong," said Zahariev. "You have five seconds to explain what you're doing in my territory, and don't waste time telling me it's classified."

When the man didn't speak, Zahariev began counting down.

"Four…three…"

"We've been hunting this witch for a few days," he said in a rush, nodding to where Saira sat, dead beneath the tree.

My chest felt tight. I wondered if he had been present during the raid on her house.

"She has been plotting against the church. We were ordered to kill her on sight and bring her accomplice to the sanctuary at First Temple."

"Why kill one and take the other?" Zahariev asked.

"We were told she might have a lead on the dagger stolen from the church two weeks ago," the man said, eyes sliding to me. "Of course, I didn't expect *you* to be the one who showed up."

"I'm full of surprises," I said. "How did you know about the meeting?"

"I just took the orders," he said. "I don't know where they got the information. My guess is she had loose lips, probably blabbed to someone within earshot of an enforcer. Wouldn't be the first time."

Zahariev and I exchanged a look. We both knew this was an opportunity. Arriving at First Temple with the enforcers would give me access to Lisk and maybe his three blades.

"Interesting," Cassius said.

Everyone looked at him. He was holding up an old flip phone. I assumed he'd found it while searching the man who remained unconscious at his feet.

"It looks like your partner here has been updating someone about your mission in real time, and they are *very* impatient to know how it's going. Should I reply, boss?"

I answered instead. "Tell him target acquired."

"Lilith." Zahariev's tone was a reprimand.

I met his gaze. "*Think* about what we were just discussing."

His jaw tightened.

"Watch him," he told Cassius and Gabriel.

I rolled my eyes as he took me by the arm and led me away from the group.

"There are other ways to do this," Zahariev said, turning to face me fully. .

"This is an ideal situation," I said. "It's the easiest way to get into the temple without causing a stir."

"I'm not worried about you getting in," said Zahariev. "I'm worried about how you get out."

"Magic," I said, as if it were obvious.

"Lilith—"

"I know what you are going to say, but it is my choice." This was different than when I'd suggested using my magic before. I was different. "There will be no greater opportunity than this. Lisk doesn't know I am the accomplice."

The last time I'd come face-to-face with the archbishop, he had still felt lust for me. I hadn't been prepared for it then, but I would go into this aware and in power.

The element of surprise meant stronger emotions, making it easier to command him. I'd have him dismissing his enforcers and confessing to the location of the three daggers the instant his eyes connected with mine.

"He'll come after you," said Zahariev.

"Not if he's dead."

I didn't think I needed to justify taking this man's life after what he'd done to me as a child. His other wrongs only gave me more reason—my father's murder, his plan to destroy the world.

I could end it all tonight.

I inched closer to Zahariev, my fingers brushing his hand.

"Let me do this," I whispered.

I knew he'd relented when his fingers twined around mine. Warmth blossomed in my chest.

"I'll give you fifteen minutes before I come in after you," he said.

I grinned. "Deal."

———

The ride to Hiram was quiet. I sat in the back beside Gabriel, who kept a gun aimed at the enforcer. He said his name was Uriah, and his partner, who was still out, head resting against the window, was named Matthew.

My arms were bound behind my back.

"I really don't see why it's necessary for them to be so tight," I'd said, wriggling my hands back and forth before we left the overlook.

We were delayed in our departure while Zahariev returned to the compound to retrieve my knife. I hadn't brought it to the outlook for obvious reasons, but now that our plans had changed, I didn't want to go into the temple unarmed. It was a bit of a risk, taking the blade, but it was small enough to conceal and quiet when in use.

"They have to believe an enforcer actually restrained you," Cassius argued.

"Yeah, but I need to get out of them when I'm ready," I said.

"Can't you just seduce someone into freeing you?" Cassius asked.

"Cass," Zahariev snapped.

"You do it then," he said, throwing up his hands. "This is the *third* time!"

A second later, Zahariev approached to redo the bindings. I'd say on a scale of suspiciously loose to physically unyielding, they were somewhere in between.

When he was finished, I turned to face him.

"For future reference, I'm interested in this, but only if we're fucking."

The corner of his mouth tugged upward, and he tilted my head back.

"Noted," he said and kissed me.

Maybe my plan would go off without a hitch and I'd be back in Nineveh within an hour, fucking Zahariev's brains out.

I wasn't going to hold my breath though.

As confident as I was when I'd pitched this idea to Zahariev, I was also a realist. Uriah the enforcer was a wild card, and based on the number of potholes he'd hit on his way out of Nineveh, I was pretty sure he hated our guts.

Gabriel had to remind him he had a loaded gun pointed at his back, but I wasn't so sure he cared. I remained suspicious and glad I'd complained about the tight bindings.

My anxiety reached a new level as we turned, crossing the winding Es-Harra Bridge into Hiram.

At its highest point, I could see the fine points of First Temple's many spires before they vanished behind a wall of glimmering skyscrapers.

"I hate this place," I whispered, staring out the window, yet in the last few days, I'd been here more than I'd been in my own home.

"It's going to be all right, baby girl," Gabriel said.

I met his gaze. Usually, I believed him when he said things like that. Tonight, I wasn't as trusting.

Uriah made a final turn and suddenly, First Temple was before us. The light streaming in from the back window vanished, signaling Zahariev's departure from our procession. He planned to approach from another side, but I hated that he was no longer watching even with Gabriel at my side.

Uriah parked against the curb in front of First Temple.

When he exited the SUV, my heart started pounding. Gabriel turned to me. "I love you, baby girl. Don't let them win."

"I love you too," I said.

"Let's go," Uriah said impatiently, as he threw open my door.

"Did your balls grow two sizes on the drive over?" I asked, stepping out of the SUV.

He wrenched me by the arm onto the sidewalk.

"Hey, fucker," Gabriel warned. "I'm watching. I won't hesitate to paint all this shiny marble with your goddamn brains."

Uriah slammed the door but stopped jerking me around. His grip was still firm as he led me up three sets of steps, each separated by a short walkway. At the base of the third, the temple entrance became visible. It was surprisingly simple compared to what lay within, bearing the carved outline of a cross.

As we neared, I swore I could smell the pungent odor of anointing oil. I think the archbishop had probably used it so much, it seeped out of every porous surface. Lisk liked to say it was holy, made to bestow blessings upon those chosen by God, but it was really his way of awarding favor or withholding it. The congregation took notice, treating each other the way they were guided—either with respect and admiration or disdain and hostility.

I was never among the chosen, though by the time I actually understood what was happening, I didn't care to be one of them.

We entered the vestibule, where a statue of Raziel, the archangel of divine law, towered over us, his wings stretching from one corner of the room to the other. His features were severe, his eyes set to peer down at everyone who entered, not unlike those of Zerachiel.

On either side of the statue, beneath his feathered wings, was a set of doors leading into the sanctuary where I'd spent much of my childhood. Armed enforcers were posted at at each. I was overcome with a feeling of unease as Uriah pulled me through the ones on the right.

The sanctuary was large, with vaulted ceilings that sloped to a point at the very center of the room. The floor was clear. It wasn't uncommon to arrive at service without seating. It was Lisk's way of communicating to the congregation that they needed to repent.

Basically, it was punishment, one his following willingly accepted.

It wasn't the only way Lisk used the environment to control. The silence in this room was what usually got to me. It was the kind that wormed its way into your consciousness and made you feel guilty for existing. I'd found myself confessing to things I'd never done, just hoping to ease the burden, which never worked.

I expected to see Lisk waiting at the altar, but there were more enforcers, two each guarding the aisles. They nodded to Uriah as he passed, guiding me up the steps and to the right.

Suddenly, I knew where he was taking me, and my panic rose anew.

"I thought you said we were meeting in the sanctuary." I jerked in his grasp.

"Change of plans," said Uriah. His hold on me tightened as he pulled me through another door into a stairwell that twisted into the dark abyss of the baptistery.

"You know, lying is a sin," I said as we made our descent.

455

"Do not speak to me of sin," said Uriah. "Your existence is a stain upon our world."

I drew in a breath between my teeth. "Ouch," I said dryly.

The enforcer shoved me into the wall, the railing biting into my back. I was okay with it because it gave me time to slip my hands from the bindings.

"It is because of your arrogance that we suffer," he hissed.

"That's a lot to put on one person," I said.

I wondered if Lisk's men got a different sort of sermon, maybe one centered around me as the source of all their problems.

Uriah shoved his gun beneath my chin. "If I didn't know you were dying tonight, I'd kill you myself."

"You think that scares me?" I asked. "My mother's threatened to take me out for years."

"Too bad she didn't," he said.

"It really is," I said.

I'd freed my hands and slipped my dagger from its sheath. I'd only ever stabbed one thing in my life, and that was a glowing blob. I was surprised by how similar this felt, how easily the blade sank into Uriah's stomach. I reached for his gun, jerking it free from his hand as I stabbed him two more times. He didn't fight, but I think that was because he was too stunned.

He gave a wheezing groan as he stumbled back, tumbling down the steps.

I stood in the muted light, breathing hard and unable to move for a few terrifying seconds as I waited for the sound of approaching enforcers, but there was nothing, only the same stark silence as before.

I headed downstairs. Uriah lay face up, one arm trapped

beneath his body. I wiped my blade and hand on his clothes before sheathing it, then rose to my feet with Uriah's weapon.

I crept down the remaining steps, taking a deep breath before I pushed open the door.

The baptistery was a large room with a round pool at the center, though I thought it looked more like a raised fountain.

I was surprised to find there were no enforcers, only Lisk, who waited on the top step of the pool. By this point, I gathered he was expecting me, so there was no element of surprise, no surge of emotion.

In fact, I felt nothing from him at all, which I found strange, given that desire could take many forms, and I knew this man desired to see me dead.

He looked angrier than the last time I saw him. The lines between his eyes and mouth were deeper. Despite this, I think he tried to smile.

"Didn't I tell you there would be consequences for not returning to your family?" he said. His voice resonated differently in this room, echoing all around.

I cringed, grinding my teeth.

"Is that a confession to my father's murder?" I said.

He tilted his head to the side and the light gleamed off his glasses. It made him look menacing but also amused.

"You say murder. I say sacrifice," he said.

"Is that what you called it when you raped me?" I asked, voice trembling with anger. "A sacrifice?"

I suspected he had rationalized his actions over the years, convincing himself I was at fault.

Lisk's mouth tensed, then his lip rose into a snarl.

"I have a duty to condemn the condemners," he said.

"I was a *child*," I said.

Tears welled in my eyes.

"Even children know when to obey and be silent," he said. "But you couldn't do that. You never did learn."

"I hate you," I said.

"I know, Miss Leviathan," he said. "As always, you are too self-centered to see the truth. Your feelings are irrelevant."

They were only irrelevant in his world because they made him a sinner and a hypocrite. What filled me with rage was that he'd deluded himself into believing he'd truly done his duty. That he'd tried to exorcise my demons and failed. Not because he was lacking but because I was impossible to save.

"To the matter at hand," he continued. "Your mother has asked me to cleanse your soul before tonight's ritual, and I have generously agreed. So if you will enter the pool, Miss Leviathan."

He gestured to the baptismal font.

Lisk's confidence struck me. I had seen it before but never with a gun pointed at his face. Maybe he had a reason for his assuredness, but one glance around the room confirmed we were alone.

He was overconfident or knew something I didn't.

A thickness rose in my throat, and I lowered my weapon. Lisk's shoulders relaxed. The movement was so slight, I wouldn't have noticed if I wasn't looking, which told me everything I needed to know.

I dragged my tongue over the inside of my bottom lip as I stared at him.

"You will forgive my sins," I said. My voice was low and breathy. I was trying to keep it from trembling. "All of them?"

"Well, yes," he said in that gravelly tone I despised so

458

much. He inclined his head. "I have only ever tried to save you, Miss Leviathan."

A flash of light filled my vision. I didn't know where it came from, but it was like blacking out, and when I came to, I was in the middle of shooting Uriah's weapon.

I didn't know how many times I pulled the trigger, but it was enough to send Lisk staggering back into the water. I screamed as I unleashed on him, flinching with each shot. At some point, I remembered what I'd come here to do and I dropped the gun, racing to the pool.

Lisk was floating in the water, his white robes seeping dark red. I fisted the fabric of his clothes, shaking him.

"Where are the fucking blades?" I demanded. My voice was a panicked shriek. In the back of my mind, I knew it was too late, and still I screamed. "Tell me! Tell me where they are!"

"I think you've silenced him for good now," said a voice, one I recognized.

I froze and turned, coming face-to-face with my mother, Analisia Leviathan.

It was only then that I noticed magic quaking inside me. I could taste it on the back of my tongue.

Metallic. Familiar.

It was the magic from my dagger but multiplied and I could barely think beyond their strength. They had entered the room with my mother.

She paused halfway down the stone steps, having come from a balcony above. She held a wooden box, and I knew the power swelling my throat radiated from it.

She looked remarkably well for a woman who had been missing for three days. In fact, I was pretty sure she'd done her hair for this occasion. It was perfectly curled and softly styled. She wore a fitted, long-sleeved dress with a high neck.

I climbed out of the pool, cold all over.

"Mom?" I whispered, confused. The word slipped from my mouth before I could really think. It was too personal, too endearing for the relationship we shared. Still, I couldn't stop myself from reacting. The magic swirling around inside me didn't help. It felt volatile, sinking into every part of me, pulling me in all directions.

"Is this where you've been this entire time?"

Though I'd suspected, the confirmation still felt like a blow. I wondered how much of my exchange with Lisk she'd heard or if she even cared. Had he been so confident because she was watching? Was he expecting her to come to his rescue?

What did it mean that she hadn't?

"No," she said. "I only came here tonight, when it was time."

When it was time? It took me a second to process what she was saying, but everything was slower now that the blades had made an appearance. My eyes dropped to the box she held, clasped between perfectly manicured hands, rising to meet her gaze again. My throat felt tight as I spoke. "You were part of this...trap?"

"You could say that," she said, continuing down the steps. She waited to speak until she was at the bottom. "I suppose in some ways, we were motivated by the same thing, Lisk and I, though we each wanted a different outcome."

I stared, not understanding. "What are you talking about?"

Her delicate brows drew together. "You already know," she said. "Saira has told you."

"Saira?" I whispered. "You know Saira?"

"Yes," she replied. Her voice was so unhurried, so casual as she walked past.

I turned, watching.

"She was a faithful member of the Order of the Serpent. She will be pleased to know her sacrifice has led to this moment. Tonight, we forge the Deliverer and release the gods from behind the Seventh Gate."

Was she trying to tell me that *she* was part of the Order of the Serpent?

"There's no fucking way," I said.

Analisia turned to face me fully, eyes narrowing in a way that finally felt familiar. Maybe she didn't expect my reply to be so fierce, but I could think a little clearer now. My body was acclimating to the magic.

"You are Analisia Leviathan. You *rode* Alarich Lisk's dick for a living. You hate women and quote the *Book of Splendor* to prove it. You terrorized me my entire fucking life on behalf of a religion you're trying to tell me you don't follow?"

"I was trying to protect you," she said, taking a step closer. My stomach flipped, but I maintained my anger despite the sick feeling, fingers fisting as I seethed.

"Don't fucking go there."

"You were rebellious, always attracting the wrong attention. You constantly threatened my mission. That we are here now is a triumph given how many times *I* had to intervene to save your life."

"You? Save *my* life?" I asked, disbelieving. My voice rose. "You would not have mourned a day of my death."

"You're wrong," she said. "I would have mourned that I carried you for nothing."

461

I flinched at her words. My mother was cruel, but this was another level. She was inches from me, and I wanted to move, but I couldn't bring my body to comply. I think I'd made a mistake, letting her words shock me. The magic had taken root again. I didn't know what part of me it was battling, but it felt like being shredded from the inside out.

"I never set out to be a mother," she said. "But I was chosen by the Order of the Serpent to carry the sacrifice. They warned you would be a nightmare, a fault of your bloodline, but I confess, I wasn't prepared for you."

"Are you insulting my father? My *dead* father?" I made sure to ask in case she had forgotten that her husband was, in fact, deceased.

She gave a breathless laugh. "Lucius had no role in your conception. You were made from my blood and the blood of the Invader. You were made…to fulfill a prophecy."

She paused, and then she spoke familiar words. It took me a moment to recall where I'd heard them, but I soon realized I'd read them in the journal I'd taken from Lisk's study.

She will ascend from the womb of her enemy,
A temptress cloaked in night, a nightmare bound in
chains.
Her cries will rattle the earth.
Her blood will break the gates.
She held my gaze, unwavering.

"You see, Alarich thought he could forge the Deliverer and open the other six gates before the prophecy came to pass," she said. "But I never told him the truth, that I was responsible for fulfilling the prophecy he wanted to avoid." Her eyes darted to Lisk, floating in the pool.

She was so close now, I could smell her honeysuckle perfume. It burned my nose.

"You see now," she said, her voice muted by the sound of metal ringing against metal. She shifted the box, holding it with one hand as she slipped the gold chain of my necklace from beneath my shirt. "Your blood is the only important thing about you. You have never been nor will you ever be anything more than a sacrifice."

I stared at her, unable to think, but for a reason entirely different from the magic roiling in my blood. This time, I was just numb.

I always knew my mother was fanatical. I'd just been wrong about her loyalty. She believed she was the savior, chosen to free the true gods.

It was her only purpose, just like mine was to die.

Suddenly, there was a loud banging at the door to the baptistery, and I heard Zahariev roar my name from the other side. He couldn't get in the room. I suspected my mother's magic was pressed against the door, though I couldn't feel it over the power of the blades.

Her eyes didn't leave mine. "Perhaps I should let him bear witness to this," she said, studying me. "Then he will not want you."

Zahariev's voice broke through the storm of magic inside me. I ceased fighting and let go, easing into a blissful peace. For the first time since I'd stepped into the room, I remembered who I was.

I was not a victim.

I was not a sacrifice.

I was *Lilith*, a survivor.

My fingers flexed, and I saw the moment my mother realized her plan had failed. Her eyes widened slightly and then a little more as my knife sank home. She dropped the box. It hit the floor and broke open, scattering six golden blades across the floor.

I pulled mine free from her and she pressed her hand to her side. It was the only reason I saw any blood, because the color of her dress was too dark to show it.

The door to the baptistery flew open, and Zahariev entered the room. I assumed my mother had been unable to maintain a hold on her magic, though what happened next made me think she'd let go intentionally.

She released a breath that sounded almost like a disbelieving laugh and staggered into me. Then struck, clawing at me until her fingers slid beneath the chain of my necklace and tore it free.

The pain was a complete shock, freezing every muscle in my body as it ripped through me. It was like being split in two, severed on a molecular level.

My jaw opened, my head fell back, and I screamed.

I was being rearranged. I could feel my bones moving, tearing through the flesh of my back.

I don't know how long it lasted. Even as awareness crept in, the pain remained, an unpredictable rhythm, rising to blinding heights. It was during the fall I realized I was on my knees at the center of a crimson pool.

It was my blood, and my hands were in it, palms pressed firmly to the ground. Somewhere beneath were seven daggers.

I lifted my gaze, aware that I wasn't alone. Gabriel watched nearby, jaw tight. My mother sat propped against a wall at his feet. Her eyes were closed but she was still breathing. I knew because I could sense her heartbeat. It echoed in the space between us, and then all at once, others joined.

It overwhelmed my senses, and I had to close my eyes and push it away.

When I opened them again, I found Zahariev watching me.

He was watching me. I couldn't decide what he thought of me, but I knew it was not as my mother said, because he came to me and knelt in my blood, fingers touching my chin and then my cheek.

"You're something else, little love," he said in grim wonder.

It was only then that I became aware of the heaviness against my back.

I turned my head and reached, touching what felt like wet skin over bone.

"Lilith," Zahariev said. "You don't have to look now."

I ignored him and continued tugging at the strange mass. It hurt, and I became nauseous with pain, but I didn't stop until I had straightened what was pressed so firmly against me.

Then I realized what I was staring at.

Wings.

Bony, membranous *wings.*

I understood what I was seeing, but I couldn't comprehend it.

Wings. Attached to my body.

It was impossible.

The only creatures with wings were angels, and they were not like this.

I tried to tighten my grip and pulled harder, thinking that maybe I could remove them with enough force, but my fingers slipped.

"Don't, Lilith," Zahariev said, snatching my hands away.

I held his unwavering gaze, torn between relief and horror as he whispered, "I've got you."

My eyes filled with tears. Another second, and I would have collapsed in his arms, but I didn't get the chance. A loud boom kept us apart, focused on whatever was happening outside the temple. Then, the ground began to tremble, and I heard Cassius yell down the stairwell.

"I don't fucking believe it," he said, racing into the room. He was wide-eyed and breathless. "The statues. The watchers. They're fucking real. There are archangels in our city."

ZAHARIEV

They will call her a demon, but I watched
her transform, and I will call her *goddess*.

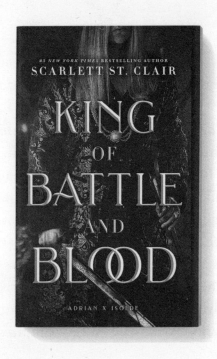

ONE

There was an army of vampires encamped on the outskirts of my father's kingdom. The black tops of their tents looked like an ocean of sharp waves and seemed to stretch for miles, melding with a red horizon that was the sky that extended over Revekka, the Empire of the Vampire. It had been that color since I was born. It was said to be cursed by Dis, the goddess of spirit, to warn of the evil that was birthed there—the evil that began with the Blood King. Unfortunately for Cordova, the red sky did not follow evil, so there was no warning when the vampires began their invasion.

They had manifested west of the border last night, as if they'd traveled with the shadows. Since then, every-thing had been quiet and still. It was like their presence had stolen life; not even the wind stirred. Unease crept through my chest like a cold frost, settling deep in my stomach as I stood between the trees, only a few feet from the first row of tents. I could not shake the feeling that this was the end. It loomed behind me, long fingers gripping my shoulders.

Rumors had preceded their arrival. Rumors of how their leader—I hated to even *think* his name—Adrian Aleksandr Vasiliev had leveled Jola, ravished Elin, conquered Siva, and burned Lita. One by one, the Nine Houses of Cordova were falling. Now the vampires were on my doorstep, and instead of calling arms, my father, King Henri, had asked for a meeting.

He wanted to reason with the Blood King.

My father's decision had been met with mixed emotions. Some wished to fight rather than succumb to this monster's reign. Others were uncertain—had my father traded death on the battlefield for another kind?

At least in battle, there were truths. You either survived the day or died.

Under the rule of a monster, there were no truths.

"I should not have allowed you to come so late or get this close."

Commander Alec Killian stood too near, just a hair behind me, shoulder brushing my back. If it were any other day, I would have excused his proximity, attributing it to his dedication as my escort, but I knew otherwise.

The commander was trying to make amends.

I took a step away, turning slightly, both to cast him a sullen look and to create distance. Alec—or Killian, as I preferred to call him—was commander of the Royal Guard, having inherited the position when his father, whose name he also shared, passed unexpectedly three years ago.

He returned my gaze, gray eyes both steely and somehow gentle. I think I'd have preferred only the steel, because the tenderness made me want to take two more steps back. It meant he had feelings for me, and any excitement I'd once had at catching his attention had now evaporated.

Outwardly, he was everything I thought I'd wanted in a man—ruggedly handsome with a body forged by hours of training. His uniform, a tailored navy tunic and trousers with gold embellishments and a ridiculously dramatic gold cape, served to accentuate his presence. He had a crown of thick, dark hair, and I'd spent a few too many nights with those strands wrapped around my fingers, body warmed, but not alight with the passion I'd really longed for. In the end, Commander Killian was a mediocre lover. It had not helped that I did not like his beard, which was long and covered the bottom half of his face. It made it impossible to detect the shape of his jaw, but I guessed he had a strong one that matched his presence—which was beginning to grate on my nerves.

"I outrank you, Commander. It is not within your power to tell me what to do."

"No, but it is within your father's."

Another flush of irritation blasted up my spine, and I ground my teeth. When Killian did not feel like he could *handle* me, he defaulted to using the threat of my father. And he wondered why I did not want to sleep with him anymore.

Instead of acknowledging my anger, Killian smirked, pleased that he'd hit a nerve.

He nodded toward the camp. "We should attack in the daylight while they sleep."

"Except you would be defying Father's orders for peace," I said.

Once, I would have agreed with him—why *not* slaughter the vampires while they slept? The sunlight, after all, was their weakness. Except that Theodoric, king of Jola, had ordered his soldiers to do the very same, and before they could even launch their attack, the entire army was vanquished by something the people were calling the blood plague. Those who had come down with the disease bled from every orifice of their body until death, including King Theodoric and his wife, who now left a two-year-old to inherit the throne under the rule of the Blood King.

As it turned out, sunlight did not stop magic.

"Will they have as much respect for us when night falls?" Killian countered. The commander had not been shy about expressing his opinion about the Blood King and his invasion of Cordova. I understood his hatred.

"Have faith in the soldiers you trained, Commander. Have you not prepared for this?"

I knew he did not like my reply. I could *feel* his frown at my back, because we both knew if the vampires decided to attack, we were dead. It took five of our own to bring down one of them. We simply had to trust that the Blood King's word to my father was worth our people's lives.

"No one can prepare for monsters, Princess," Killian said. I broke from his gaze and focused on the king's tent, distinct with its crimson and gold details, as he added, "I doubt even the goddess Dis knew what would become of her curse."

It was said Adrian angered Dis, goddess of spirit, and as a result, she cursed him to crave blood. Her curse spread— some humans survived the transformation to vampire while others did not. Since their incarnation, the world had not known peace. Their presence had bred other monsters—all kinds that fed on blood, on life. While I had never known anything different, our elders did. They remembered a world without high walls and gates around every village.

They remembered what it was like not to fear wandering beneath the stars as darkness fell.

I did not fear the dark.

I did not fear the monsters.

I did not even fear the Blood King.

But I did fear for my father, for my people, for my culture. Because Adrian Aleksandr Vasiliev was inevitable.

"You presume to know how a goddess thinks?" I asked.

"You keep challenging me. Did I do something wrong?"

"Did you expect complacency because we fucked?"

He flinched, and his brows slammed down over his eyes. *Finally*, I thought. *Anger.*

"So you're upset," he said.

I rolled my eyes. "Of course I'm upset. You convinced my father I needed an escort."

"You sneak out of your bedroom at night!"

I had no idea that sleeping with Killian would mean unannounced visits to my bedroom. Except, like always, he overstepped one night and found my room empty. He'd woken the whole castle, had an entire army searching the surrounding forest for me. All I'd wanted to do was watch the stars, and I'd done so for years atop the rolling hills of Lara. But all that ended a week ago. After I was found, my father had summoned me to his study. He'd lectured me on the state of the world and the importance of watchfulness and had given me guards and a curfew.

I'd protested. I was well trained, a warrior, just as competent as Killian. I could protect myself, at least within the borders of Lara.

Don't, my father had snapped. The word was so harsh and sudden, I jumped. After a quiet moment and a breath, he had added, *You are too important, Issi.*

473

And in that moment, he'd looked so broken, I hadn't been able to utter another word—not to him, not to Killian.

A week later, and I was feeling trapped.

"Since you are so keen to spill my secrets, Commander, did you admit to fucking me too?"

"*Stop using that word.*"

He spoke with clenched teeth.

At least he was passionate about something, I thought. Still, his order only served to provoke me.

"And what word should I use?" I hissed. "*Make love?* Hardly.*" I was being unkind, but when I was angry, I wanted the recipient of my wrath to *feel* it, and I knew Killian did. It was a trait I'd adopted from my mother, given that my father rarely expressed his frustration. "You seem to think what happened between us means something more."

It was like he thought he was suddenly entitled to me, and I hated it.

"Am I so terrible?" he asked, his voice quiet.

My fists clenched, and there was a moment when guilt clutched at my chest. I shook it off quickly. "Stop trying to manipulate my words."

"I'm not trying to manipulate you, but you cannot say you did not enjoy our time together."

"I enjoy sex, Alec," I said flatly. "But it doesn't mean anything."

They were sloppy words, but I meant them. I'd only chosen to sleep with Killian because he'd been there, and I'd wanted release. That had been my first mistake. Because it made me ignore other warnings, like his tendency to keep my father aware of my every move.

"You don't mean that," he said.

AUTHOR'S NOTE

First, I want to be clear that I think society is better off with religion. I also think the most devout people are willing to ask questions of their faith. Some of the kindest people I know are devoutly religious and embody what I consider to be the best parts of godly life. They are kind, compassionate, and honest.

I wish everyone who grew up or came to be part of a religious institution only had positive experiences. That's how it should be and yet, it isn't.

In October 2024, I saw an article in the *LA Times* about the Archdiocese of Los Angeles. It read "L.A. Catholic Church payouts for clergy abuse top $1.5 billion with new record settlement."

Attorneys for the case represented 1,353 people who had suffered abuse at the hands of Catholic priests. This settlement was for $880 million. The previous settlement was for $740 million.

Josh Johnson, a comedian, spoke about this topic in a comedy sketch.

"Anyone else would be closed," he said. "There's no other company I could think of that could do that much *harm* and still be in business…you'd have to be a gun manufacturer."

He went on to ask: Is it punishment if they can afford to pay the fines? This is when I learned, while around twenty-four Catholic dioceses have filed for bankruptcy, the LA Archdiocese will be paying this settlement via "archdiocese investments, accumulated reserves, bank financing, and other assets."

For a long time, leaders in the Catholic Church concealed abuse and there are receipts. Only recently have they begun to work toward transparency. Their efforts are paying off, as there has been a decline in abuse within the institution.

This isn't to say this harm happens solely in the Catholic Church. There is just far less research on abuse in Protestant Christian churches. Insurance claims estimate there are around 260 claims of abuse per year, but those are only reported cases.

The point is: Those who take on a leadership position in the church have power over their congregation. Anything, no matter intent, can become corrupt when the wrong people have those positions.

I have seen the people in these positions also be believed over the victims. It happened in my hometown.

A young woman at my school was very close to the pastor of her church and his family. People would talk about how close they were and how certain interactions (e.g., the young woman sitting on his lap) made them uncomfortable.

After the woman went to college, she confessed to counselors that she'd been sexually abused for years. When the pastor was arrested, despite all those previous feelings of unease and a VERY detailed affidavit, people came out in vocal support of the pastor—an adult male—and not the victim, a CHILD.

His hold over his congregation was hypnotizing, but of course it was—he was their pastor, the keeper of their private struggles and their greatest joys. Most of all, he was their spiritual leader, a reflection of their belief and impact on the community and if that were true, how could he be this other vile thing?

It took years for my friends to understand the young woman did not lie and that they had been betrayed.

Anything can become a weapon in the wrong hands.

ON COMMON RELIGIOUS MYTHS/THEMES

The religion in *Terror* is ambiguous but familiar and that's because, like all religions, the concepts and myths were borrowed from existing religions. Common stories include a garden or paradise, serpentlike creatures that represent temptation or terror, a flood story, and similar pantheons. I would say that Judaism was unique in its worship of one god, though some historians argue Judaism wasn't monotheistic at the start and more monolatry, so they didn't deny the existence of other gods but worshipped one.

The Epic of Gilgamesh is a Sumerian story and our first reference of "paradise" being a type of garden. The goddess Inanna moves her huluppu tree (believed to be a willow) to a garden where a serpent/dragon, a bird, and a Mesopotamian demon named Lilitu, come to live in the tree. Gilgamesh slays the serpent, and the bird and Lilith flee.

There is a similar garden in Greek mythology the Garden of the Hesperides (if you've read my Hades and Persephone series, you are familiar). The garden belongs to Hera. In some myths, the tree is guarded by an "immortal serpent" sometimes believed to be a dragon named Ladon who was eventually slain by Heracles.

We then have the Garden of Eden, the biblical paradise, where the first man and woman, Adam and Eve, resided until they were exiled by God. The garden is the location of the Tree of Knowledge (like the Tree of Life in previous mythologies including Judaism). In some scholarly journals, it is suggested that the myth of the Garden of Eden and similarly, the narrative of Gilgamesh, suggest that man cannot become Godlike. Essentially, they cannot have both knowledge and immortality.

Continuing, the creation and flood myths have their origins in the *Eridu Genesis*, an ancient Sumerian tablet. The story survives in fragments, but describes Enki, god of the underworld sea, warning a man named Ziusudra to build a boat. Similarly, in Greek mythology, Prometheus helps Deucalion build a chest with which he survives the deluge after Zeus floods the earth. Of course, we then have Noah who was instructed by God to build the arc and is present in Judaism, Christianity, and Islam.

Similarly, Judaism, Christianity, and Islam all acknowledge Adam and Eve to be the first man and woman. In Sumerian mythology, Namma, the primeval mother, placed clay in her womb and gave birth to the first humans who were made to serve the gods. You see a similar concept in *Terror* where the true gods created humankind to serve them.

NOTES ON LILITH'S ORIGINS
AND HER ROLE IN TERROR

As I referenced before, Lilith's introduction to history began in *The Epic of Gilgamesh*, where she is described as a shrieking demon who destroys Inanna's huluppu tree. Later depictions of Lilith seem to appear on tablets. One found in Syria was said to have probably hung in the house of a pregnant woman to protect against Lilith, a demon reponsible for killing children.

In ancient Babylon, there were many "lilu demons." They were said to be humans who died young. There was also a demon named "Lamashtu" who threatened babies.

Lilith is not mentioned in modern Bible translations, but she was mentioned in Isaiah 34:14 in the Hebrew Bible, also known as the Tanakh or Miqra in Hebrew. The King James Bible translated "Lilith" to screech owl. Lilith makes an appearance in the Dead Sea Scrolls with a similar reference to the one found in the Hebrew Bible.

In the Middle Ages, Lilith appeared in The Alphabet of Ben Sira, a satirical Hebrew text, and introduced her as Adam's first wife. She is all the things she was before, but more. Lilith refuses to lay beneath Adam during sex, which Adam believes is her rightful place. Lilith's argument is that they were created from the same earth and therefore equal. When Lilith pronounced God's name, she grows wings and flies away.

I'm sure I don't need to point out that Lilith only became a demon once she refused to submit to the will of her husband...right?

It isn't until the appearance of kabbalah that Lilith becomes the seductress, responsible for leading men astray (because obviously men cannot be responsible for their own temptation; they HAVE to be led there by a woman).

This leads us to Lilith today and her shift into a feminist icon. In 1976, the Jewish feminist magazine *Lilith* was founded. The editors, "inspired by Lilith's fight for equality with Adam," wrote an introductory article, "The Lilith Question." In the article, Aviva Cantor Zuckoff writes about the misogynist depiction of Lilith in The Alphabet of Ben Sira. She rightly points out that the less agreeable aspects of other figures in Jewish Folklore, like King David, are often overlooked and poses the question, why can't we do that for Lilith?

She states, "What is intrinsic to Lilith, what is the most central aspect of her character is her struggle for independence, her courage in taking risks, her commitment to the equality of woman and man based on their creation as equals by God."

Lilith's transformation over time is no different than the evolution of other mythology. She is like the creation and flood myth, the paradise and garden. It is this history and Lilith's trajectory that influenced my Lilith's journey in *Terror at the Gates*.

Lilith Leviathan is a woman who wants autonomy over her life and control of her future. She rejects social standards and the expectations placed upon her by the church and in doing so, becomes the other. She is a victim of her pastor and her congregation, turned upon because she refuses to fit the mold.

A FEW FINAL NOTES

If you have read *King of Battle and Blood*, you all know I was influenced heavily by a book called *When God Was a Woman*. I related to the author who reminded me when I was a child, my mother had told me giving birth would be painful because I was a girl and a descendant of Eve. I remember thinking that didn't seem fair, but I did not have the words to express why.

As an adult, I question why the sole responsibility of eating the forbidden fruit fell upon on Eve, as if Adam played no role—as if he did not choose to follow.

Of course, they will say Eve tempted Adam and again I will say—how many times will men blame women for their choices?

Honestly, these myths make men appear foolish and unable to think for themselves, but the same is true today when we say "boys will be boys."

REFERENCES

Cantor Zuckoff, A. (1976, Sept 2). The Lilith Question. *Lilith Magazine*. https://lilith.org/articles/fall-1976-29/.

Denney, Andrew S., and Loyola University New Orleans. "Child Sex Abusers in Protestant Christian Churches: An Offender Typology." *Journal of Qualitative Criminal Justice & Criminology*. 12, no. 1 (2023): https://doi.org/10.21428/88de04a1.000ff84d.

Ehrman, Bart D. *Misquoting Jesus: The Story Behind Who Changed the Bible and Why*. HarperSanFrancisco, 2007.

Gaines, Janet Howe. "Lilith." Biblical Archaeology Society, January 5, 2024. https://www.biblicalarchaeology.org/daily/people-cultures-in-the-bible/people-in-the-bible/lilith.

Lesses, Rebecca. "Lilith." *Shalvi/Hyman Encyclopedia of Jewish Women*, March 20, 2009. https://jwa.org/encyclopedia/article/lilith.

Spar, Ira. "Mesopotamian Creation Myths." In Heilbrunn Timeline of Art History. The Metropolitan Museum of Art, 2009. https://www.metmuseum.org/essays/epic-of-creation-mesopotamia.

Winton, Richard, and Hannah Fry. "L.A. Catholic Church Payouts for Clergy Abuse Top $1.5 Billion with New Record Settlement." *Los Angeles Times*, October 16, 2024. https://www.latimes.com/california/story/2024 -10-16/archdiocese-of-los-angeles-to-pay-880-million -in-the-largest-clergy-sexual-abuse-settlement.

ABOUT THE AUTHOR

#1 *New York Times* bestselling author Scarlett St. Clair is a citizen of the Muscogee Nation and the author of the Hades X Persephone series, the Hades Saga, the Adrian X Isolde series, the Blood of Lilith series, Fairy Tale Retellings, and *When Stars Come Out*.

She has a master's degree in library science and information studies and a bachelor's in English writing. She is obsessed with Greek mythology, murder mysteries, and the afterlife.

For information on books, tour dates, and content, please visit scarlettstclair.com.